THE BOYFRIEND BOYCOTT

THE HEARTWOOD SERIES

MEG RILEY

CONTENT WARNINGS

To check content warnings for this book, scan the QR code below or visit megrileyauthor.com/books

For B.
You are my safe place. You are my home.

CHAPTER 1
GRADY

"WHAT ARE YOU DOING IN THERE," Hudson shouts, "taking the shit of the century?"

"Jesus, Hudson," I answer. "No, I'm almost done." I've been in the bathroom for so long that my brother has resorted to pounding on the door.

Maybe it would be easier to tell him that I'm taking a shit. Then he wouldn't question why I've been meticulously grooming my short, chestnut beard, making sure there isn't a hair out of place. Usually, I spend a total of five minutes getting ready, not the half an hour I've already spent tonight, but something about this barbecue has me feeling antsy, jittery even.

I give myself a quick once over in the mirror, but something doesn't feel quite right. I cock my head to the side, undo the top button of my denim shirt, and assess the effect. It's the button-down, I decide. I hate button-downs. They're too stuffy, too put together. It's not *me*, and I'm not comfortable. Fuck it. I'll go with my usual T-shirt instead. Except the only ones I have are somewhat threadbare and worn.

"Hang on," I say, opening the bathroom door to Hudson's raised fist a few inches from my face, about to pound on the door again. He lowers it as I push past him. "I just need to change my shirt."

Hudson lets out a loud groan.

"Just throw on the same old ratty T-shirt you always do and let's go. What's gotten into you, anyways? Since when do you care about what you're wearing?" he asks, following me down the hall towards the master bedroom.

"It doesn't matter," I deflect, stalking through to the walk-in closet in my bedroom. The last thing I want is for Hudson, or anyone, to figure out why tonight feels so monumental in my mind.

"I don't understand what the big deal is," he says, leaning casually against the door frame and watching me frantically unbutton the suffocating shirt I have on. "We're just going over to Ally and Mason's for burgers and beers. You look *fine* dude. Look at me." He gestures towards the paint-stained T-shirt and jeans he's wearing.

"Everyone knows you've been working here all day." I pull out the only white T-shirt I own that doesn't have holes or grease stains from working at the bar, and a pair of khaki jogger-style chinos. "At least everyone from Heartwood is used to seeing you like that," I say.

Hudson is almost always covered in either paint splatters, sawdust, or a combination of both since he's been working in construction. The project I've enlisted his help with has been no exception. It somehow suits Hudson, giving his normally boyish features a rugged quality.

"It's just going to be Mason, Jett, Ally and—" Hudson cuts himself off, and his eyes go wide as if he's made some ground-breaking realization. "Ally's friend, what's-her-name."

"Spencer," I say, using every muscle in my face to keep my expression neutral.

"Dude. *Dude.* You want to hit that don't you?" Hudson jokes, landing a punch on my tattooed bicep.

"I don't even know her. We've met once. Briefly," I deflect, recalling the stormy night that Ally and Mason had gotten stuck at the hospital out in Calgary almost a year and a half ago. Spencer was waiting with them when I went to pick them up from the emergency department. I've never seen someone look so beautiful under fluorescent lights.

We spent the long drive back to Heartwood together in the front seat, with Ally and Mason still shaken from the storm that stranded them there, asleep in the back. Whenever I recall that night with anyone, I purposefully leave out the fact that she stayed over at my place. I still haven't told a soul about it.

"Yet you remember her name," Hudson jeers in a teasing, sing-song tone.

"It's a relatively uncommon name. That's the only reason I remember it," I lie. The truth is, Spencer has crossed my mind more than once since the first night I met her. More times than I care to admit. At first, she planned on staying at the motel, so as not to impose on Ally and Mason. But as soon as I went to drop her off, I took one look at the place and insisted she make use of my guest suite instead. She didn't protest. She needed a safe place to stay, and I provided that for her.

Since then, I haven't been able to get her out of my mind. She was fucking gorgeous. She was funny. Her eyes had this ... *fire* behind them. She felt dangerous in some ways, but she was also warm and inviting, like we had met in a past life. Now, she's back in town and I can't get control of myself. I'm excited and terrified all at once to see her again.

"Sure ..." Hudson drags out the word with a heavy dose of skepticism, and the corner of his mouth quirks up to the side. I pull my T-shirt on over my head and run my hand through my dark brown hair, smoothing the longer ends on top even though they'll still look dishevelled once my bike helmet comes off. "You finally ready?"

"Yeah, yeah," I say somewhat absentmindedly, as my phone

vibrating in my pocket draws my attention. It's Finn. I left him to look after the bar tonight and close up, which he's only ever done once, and I was there to oversee him.

FINN

Yo, where do we keep the rest of the float? I need to replenish the till.

It only makes me slightly nervous that Finn is already having to dip into the float for more cash. I realize I'm going to have to go over there myself since I keep it locked in my office, and it totally slipped my mind to give him the key.

"On second thought, I'm going to take my bike. You head over without me." I click off my screen and slip my phone back into my pocket. "I have to stop by the bar first."

"You couldn't have told me that before you made me wait this long to get ready?"

"Sorry, bud. Something came up and Finn needs a hand. I won't be long." I slap a hand on my little brother's shoulder. "I'll see ya over there, alright? Pop a beer in the fridge for me."

"I'll make sure to give it a thorough shake first." He points at me, finger-gun style, his lopsided grin making the dimple in his cheek visible like it has since we were kids. The sandy blond waves that he wears longer on the top flop over his forehead as he backs out of the door and pivots on the driveway to jog over to his truck.

I follow close on his heels, shutting the heavy wooden front door behind me before veering away from Hudson and heading over to my bike. I say bike, but it's got 120 horsepower engine and cost me a pretty penny, but it was worth every single one. I'll never get tired of the thrill that ripples through me when I turn it on. It practically roars to life beneath me, the rumble of the engine moving through me when I turn the key.

Spring has graced the mountains, and although the temperature has only just started warming up, it feels practically balmy after the deep freeze we've had for the last six months. This weather makes me giddy. It's motorcycle season, and any day that I get to ride is a good day. I feel like a kid who has just been let out for recess.

I glance over my shoulder at the drive that winds through the large expanse of property. I've lived here ever since Dad moved out of our childhood home and sold it to me three years ago. That was the year before he passed. He'd been living in the cabin to be close to the clinic, and the house became too difficult to manage with his Parkinson's. The bar took off after I bought it and started hosting trivia nights and other social events, and with Mason fresh out of residency and under a load of student debt, and Hudson and Jett still in their early twenties, I was the only one with the money to buy the place when Dad was ready to sell.

Since then, I've renovated almost every aspect to the point of it being hardly recognizable from the dated 1980s split-level we grew up in. It's much more *me* now, with moody, masculine paint colours, dark wood and stone, but still true to the era in a mid-century modern style. I also left some evidence of it once being our family home, like the tire swing about halfway down the drive that Dad hung up for us—or rather, hung up for Jett who begged and begged to the point that every single one of the Landrys was annoyed. We used it for one summer before we grew bored of it.

Leaning into the turn at the end of the long, winding driveway, I pull out onto the road and start the fifteen-minute drive into town. The house is close, but not close enough to feel suffocated by the goings-on of small-town life—the chitter-chatter and gossip that plagues every town with a population of just over 10,000. I like it that way. A bit of distance is healthy, safe. It means that I can avoid any drama, maintain my reputation as easy-going Grady. Unproblematic, well-liked, reliable when you need him but doesn't get in the way.

My bike slows as I down-shift, the rumble of the engine lowering to a soft purr as I pull up out front of the Whisky Jack. Normally, I would park out back, in the alley. But I'm not planning on staying long. I survey the front of the corner building. The worn wood siding is a little worse for wear, but it gives the bar a rustic, lived-in feel.

Something grabs my attention out of the corner of my eye—a bright red and white *For Lease* sign in the window of the store-front next door. My chest tightens when I register what it means. The storefront was occupied by the Parks for as long as I can remember. They ran a Korean restaurant that served the most mouthwatering bibimbap and bulgogi. The same recipe that they brought over in freezer-safe containers in quantities enough to feed a small army after Mom passed. That was over twenty years ago now, but what the Parks did for us will stay with me forever. My brothers and I survived off their food for weeks after her funeral. Yet, the traditional Korean dishes never bring back bad memories, they remind me of how the town came together and took care of us. They became the family we needed without even so much as a second of hesitation. Now, they're closing the restaurant. I rub my hand on my sternum, trying to soothe the ache I feel there, thinking about the last time I ate one of their delicious meals not knowing that it would be the last time. I didn't savour it enough, then.

I walk up to the dark windows and peer inside, cupping my hands around my eyes. The restaurant is empty. I wonder, with another pang of sadness, if the Parks have already left town without saying goodbye.

I pivot back towards my own establishment and see the patio full of customers enjoying the spring sunshine that is still warm in the early evening. People are chatting happily in the shade of the blue umbrellas, and a few of them offer me a wave as I pass them on the sidewalk and follow the path to the front doors. The doors creak, the heavy wood groaning as I pull it open by the wrought iron handle. It's even busier inside and most of the tables are full, including a big group of ladies who frequent the bar once a month for their book club.

Finn is scurrying around behind the bar, hurriedly pouring drinks for the large party, and I weave my way through the tables to go and help. I don't ask, I just pick up the order ticket from the counter and start pouring.

He looks up and gives me an appreciative grin before picking up the first tray of glasses and taking them over to the table. I finish pouring the last of the drinks and follow him over to the group of middle-aged women who are busy gushing over how hot the hero of their book is. If he's the guy that's featured on the cover, I would have to agree.

"Woah, ladies." I bend down in between two of them and set their drinks down on the table. "Is this the new book boyfriend?" I wink at one of the women and watch a flush spread over her cheeks. "Looks like I have some competition."

One of them smacks me playfully on the arm as I set her martini down in front of her.

"Oh Grady, you know there's no such thing as competing with you," she says with a flirtatious lilt.

"Don't say that too loud, Doris. I don't want to have to take on that hunk of a husband of yours." I pat her shoulder as I leave the table and make my way back to the bar. Finn is leaning against the counter, finally catching a moment to breathe. The bar is like this; sometimes it's dead for hours, and then all of a sudden a rush of people comes, making it tough to catch up.

"Are you sure you're okay to handle the bar tonight? I don't want you to drown here," I ask.

"It's all good. Enjoy your barbecue," he answers. Finn has been my right-hand man at the Whisky Jack for the last month or so since he moved back to Heartwood. We've been friends since high school, until he went away to play hockey. He's a good guy, reliable. You need reliable when you're a business owner. Having Finn around means that I get to take a step back from the bar now and spend more time with my family.

"I've got my phone on me, so just text me if you need

anything, alright?" Finn nods to confirm he knows I'm not throwing him to the wolves. Still, it's his first time closing on his own, and I worry that he'll be overwhelmed. "I mean it, anything you need, I'm here." He nods again and waves me off.

"I'll be fine, dude. But thanks, I'll text if anything goes sideways."

I turn to head out, but then I remember why I came here in the first place and dig the key to the float safe out of my pocket. Finn takes it from me with a nod of thanks.

"Hey, do you know anything about the Parks closing the restaurant?" I ask. In my peripheral vision I notice someone at the bar turn their attention to our conversation.

"They're leaving town. Guess they couldn't hack the pressure of being business owners," Carter Bouchard pipes up. As I recall, he was voted number one douchebag of Heartwood High's graduating class of '09. My graduating year. That is, I voted him number one douchebag in my heart. He's clearly been eavesdropping from where he's seated with his obnoxious, self-important buddies, sticking his nose where it doesn't belong.

"Yo, shut the fuck up, Carter," Finn snaps back. I make a mental note to give Finn a raise. I've been telling Carter to "shut the fuck up" since the tenth grade when he decided to start bullying Hudson. "They're leaving because Mr. Park can't look after the place anymore. They're moving to the city to go into an assisted living facility that's close to their kids. Have a little respect."

Carter lets out an indignant scoff. His almost black, gelled hair doesn't move an inch as he moves his head.

"I don't care why they're leaving if it means that building is up for grabs. It would look better as a brand spankin' new Urban Ember, don't you think? Class this place up a little," Carter says. It takes me a second, but I recognize the name as a popular chain of upscale restaurants. They have a few locations in Calgary and Vancouver, if I'm not mistaken.

"Good luck with that." I scoff. "There are laws in place against chains opening up shop in Heartwood." Laws that help keep the Whisky Jack afloat and have allowed so many other businesses to thrive in Heartwood. Those laws have preserved the charm of the town and prevented it from becoming the next big tourist destination.

"Not for long, if I can help it. That rule is so outdated. Some crusty old mayor probably put it in place because they hate change." My breathing becomes tighter as I consider the implications of Carter's words. There's a new mayor in office now, and Jodi Price's entire campaign was built on the notion of bringing Heartwood into the future. Though, she conveniently left out details about how she would accomplish it. I didn't think that sacrificing the local economy was going to be part of her plan when I voted for her. "I'm sure the council will be very interested to see how much money I can bring to the town at the next meeting," Carter says. He winks at me like he's explaining how politics works to a child. Fuck him. People come to Heartwood for a reprieve from the city, and that could be lost if Carter manages to convince the council to overturn the law.

"Do you realize what opening that door would do to other businesses in Heartwood? It wouldn't just be the Parks closing up shop," I argue, but I'm starting to realize there's probably no point in engaging with Carter.

"Not my problem," he says, standing up and smacking a fifty-dollar bill down on the bar. Far more than his one beer cost him. *Flashy*. It's gross. "And I have a feeling Mayor Price will agree. Especially when she sees the fat cheque I'm going to cut her as a donation to her next election campaign. Anyhoo, later fellas."

He gets up and stalks out through the large wooden double doors, the daylight illuminating dust motes floating in the air as it opens and then shuts behind him. I'm relieved he's gone, but it also irks me that he got the last word.

"Nice to know that some things never change," I say to Finn through gritted teeth.

"Don't worry about Carter, he's full of shit. Everyone knows it." Finn tries to reassure me, but there's still something that feels unsettled within me. I know how these things work, and the unfortunate truth of the matter is that Carter is right—money talks.

"Thanks, bud. Shout if you need anything," I say over my shoulder as I leave the bar after Carter. Thankfully he's made a full exit and isn't anywhere to be seen as I glance around the street. I climb on my bike again and look back at the *For Lease* sign hanging in the darkened window of the Parks' restaurant. Carter may have money to throw at this, but the town of Heartwood deserves to be protected.

A few minutes later, I pull up to the familiar A-frame cabin that now belongs to Ally and Mason, the gravel crunching under my wheels. They've spruced the place up since Dad lived here. Ally has planted swaths of brightly-coloured flowers in the garden, and a newly landscaped pathway curves around the cabin towards the backyard. They've also added onto the right side of the cabin to make room for their new arrival. My niece. Every time I think about her my heart just about explodes. Nothing has made me happier than seeing how excited Mason is to become a dad. Nothing has hurt more at times too, remembering the fact that Mom and Dad won't be here to meet their granddaughter.

Mason must have heard me pull up because he saunters out from around the side and greets me in the drive. His dark eyes have a sparkle in them, and his normally stubbled jaw is groomed. It's nice to see that he's started taking care of himself again since he's cut down on his hours working at the clinic. I worried about him constantly when he took over our dad's practice. The workload almost killed him. That is, before Ally came along and made him take a step back.

"Hey," he says, clapping a hand on my shoulder. "We're all out back, but feel free to head inside and grab yourself a beer. There are cold ones in the fridge."

"Thanks, I'll come around and say hi to everyone first." I survey the yard as we round the back of the cabin, and I spot Hud and Jett amongst the small group of five gathered in the yard. They're into what seems like their second or third game of Beersbee based on how loud they're getting. We've played the game ever since we were raucous teens, balancing an empty beer can on a wooden stake in the ground and trying to knock over your opponent's can with a frisbee. Jett lets out a holler as he sends Hudson's can flying with his frisbee, and Hudson drinks with a groan. It still baffles me why Hudson insists on playing any games with Jett, who is a professional skier, and a professional at anything that involves competition, even a silly game of Beersbee. He's *never* gracious about it winning, he's cocky as hell.

I find Winnie and Poppy seated at the patio table, engaged in a lively conversation over a glass of rosé, but there's still no sign of Ally—or Spencer.

I try, and fail, to shake off the nerves before wandering over to Winnie. I thought I had gotten a hold of my anxiety on the ride over, riding my bike normally settles me, but I'm jittery again. I feel like I just downed an entire pot of coffee. My heart is racing, I can't still my hands, and my T-shirt is sticking to the sweat on my back. I'm sure it had something to do with seeing the *For Lease* sign on the Parks' restaurant and the subsequent blood-boiling run-in with Carter. But a small part of me knows the truth—that it has less to do with that, and everything to do with the way my eyes have been constantly scanning the group for a stunning redhead.

"Hey, Mama," I say, calling Winnie by the playful nickname she inherited when she took us in to help Dad out after Mom passed. Winnie has always been insistent that she would never live up to the name of Mom—she and my mother had been best friends since they were little—but I started calling her Mama and it suited her just fine. I lean down to give her a one-armed hug and a kiss on the top of her cropped auburn hair. "Hey, Pops." Poppy lifts her glass to me in greeting. "Where's Ally? I want to say hello to my niece."

Poppy's dark, wavy bob swishes on her shoulders as she scans the yard for Ally.

"Inside, I think," she answers.

As if I spoke her into being, Ally comes around the side of the house, her hands full with a plate of burger patties. I run over to her, taking the plate out of her hands and giving her a peck on the cheek.

"Don't bother saying hello to *me* or anything," she jokes, running one hand down her belly and placing one on her lower back. "Spencer is coming out with the condiments soon, so once the burgers are ready, everyone can serve themselves."

I try not to focus on the mention of Spencer, or the way my hands become slick at the sound of her name. The fact that any moment now, she'll come around that corner and I will once again be face to face with the woman that has plagued my dreams. All from one night where I never even made a move on her.

Holy hell I need a beer.

CHAPTER 2
SPENCER

There's a six-and-a-half-foot wall of muscle and tattoos climbing off the motorcycle on the gravel drive outside the cabin, and I can't breathe. Whatever Ally has just said to me has gone in one ear and out the other. My eyes dart around the kitchen where we're sitting at the island, and I'm trying to look anywhere but towards *him*. Grady Landry.

Grady Landry, whose T-shirt is creeping up his waist, showing a sliver of his tanned skin as he lifts his helmet off. His dark brown hair is perfectly mussed in a way that makes me want to run my fingers through it. God, he's hot. I thought so the very moment I saw him, but who wouldn't? With his thick arms covered in matching inked sleeves, his short, groomed beard, and the almost child-like way he's smiling at Mason, he looks as if he came out of the same mould used to make all my other boyfriends. I give my head a shake. I'm strictly off men for now. Especially men who look like Grady.

It was stupid of me not to expect to see him here—my best friend is having his brother's baby, after all—I just didn't expect it to happen the night I arrived in Heartwood. Something Ally says sneaks its way past the all-consuming thoughts swirling around my mind, and I hear her repeat the question she just asked me.

"How's your mom?" Ally asks. It's a loaded question, and she knows enough not to even bother asking about my dad. Not that I would know how to answer anyway, given that we haven't spoken in over six months.

My mother is a different story. Marla Sinclair likes to make me aware of everything that is going on in her life. It has always been that way. She flits around, generally only caring about herself and whatever boyfriend or husband she has on the go, while I'm the stable one in our relationship.

"She's Marla," I offer. She is like no other. My eyes flick over to the large front windows of the A-frame cabin, out to where Grady is pulling Mason into a quick hug before moving out of sight around the side of the house. A muffled *whoop* from one of the Landry brothers, who has already arrived and is probably a couple of beers deep, drifts through the front door. "Living her best life in wine country, you know how she is."

"Still with Roy?" Ally asks. Marla moved to the Okanagan after her second marriage fell apart, found herself a house by the lake that she loved. I really thought she was getting her life together, finding herself, thriving in her own independence. Then she met Roy, and he gave her attention, and her pattern repeated.

"Yup. Still with Roy." I don't elaborate. Ally knows that Marla's relationship with Roy is her longest one yet at three years out from their nuptials. But the clock is ticking. Roy isn't a bad guy per se. He is just another replica of the other men my mother has dated—and married—in the past. Their love feels lukewarm, a by-product of the fact that Roy tells my mother she's pretty. All her past relationships have been the same. She is so easily swayed at first, but then the honeymoon period ends, and the butterflies fade, and the man she thought was so charming moves on to the next best thing.

The Sinclair women have whatever is the opposite of a green

thumb when it comes to dating. Any long-term relationship just withers and dies under our care, no matter how well we think we water it. I think we subconsciously pick men who are like orchids —pretty to look at, but a bitch to keep them that way. I seem to have inherited this trait from my mother.

That's why I stick to casual flings, 'situationships' if you will. Different city, different guy. It's a perk of being a travel influencer; I never stay anywhere long enough for anyone to catch feelings. Some of the men I've dated have been just memorable enough that I've kept them around for more than a night, but they all end the same way; a half-hearted "we'll keep in touch" as I head for the airport. None of the assholes I choose are around for the long haul anyhow, so it's better for everyone if no one gets attached.

"She's nothing if not consistent, at least," Ally says, rounding the small kitchen island with a plate of burger patties in one hand and placing her free one on my shoulder as she passes by. "I'm going to take these out so Mason can fire up the grill. Can you bring that tray of condiments?"

I nod. "Of course."

I set my wine down and turn to pick up the tray Ally has prepared on the counter. My eyes rake over the bottles. Something is missing. She's forgotten the ketchup. Ally has already disappeared around the side of the cabin with her plate of burgers, but it only takes me a second to locate the bottle on the door of the fridge. When I pick it up, the liquid inside is separated. *I'll just give it a good shake, we'll be good to go.*

Putting some necessary force into it, I lift the bottle and shake, but the lid must have been ajar, and it pops off almost instantly. Bright red ketchup *bloops* out, right onto the centre of my camisole. It's my favourite one, too. Jade green silk with cream-coloured lace trim around the bust.

"Fuck, fuck, fuck," I mutter, turning to the sink to grab whatever kind of cloth or towel I can find to clean the front of my shirt. Whatever I do, the blob of red only gets bigger as it smears around and soaks into the smooth fabric. "Fuckity fuck!" It comes out as a shout, but I get cut off from the rest of the string of curse words I want to scream when I hear heavy footsteps on the porch.

I swivel around to see Grady on the steps up to the cabin and I would love to just disappear into thin air. He's the type of attractive where I can't picture him doing anything embarrassing, so I'm not ready to face him with half a bottle of ketchup on my shirt. Scrambling, I look for anywhere to hide. Bathroom? No, maybe he's coming inside to use it. *Jesus, why is this cabin so small?*

With nowhere else to go in the tiny, open-concept cabin, I decide the pantry is my only option. It's a fair size with enough room for one, if not two, people. I slink inside quickly and slide the door shut behind me.

The slats in the bifold doors are parted just enough that I can see Grady stalk into the kitchen and crouch at the open fridge to find a beer. His broad shoulders curve around as he reaches down to grab a bottle, the muscles in his back rippling under his shirt.

I am such a creep, I think. *This is one secret that I will take with me to my grave.*

The beer bottle lets out a *pffth* sound as Grady pops the cap on the handle of one of the kitchen drawers. He takes a sip—okay, more than a sip—and rolls his shoulders. Something about him seems tense, and he cranes his neck to look around the corner. He's scanning the cabin almost like he's looking for someone.

As he turns around, I realize the gaps in the door might just be big enough for him to see me, or at least the outline of me. I slowly back away, into the shadow of the pantry, my breathing shallow and quick. My gut roils when I realize I'm going to have to explain my sudden appearance at the barbecue, and what the hell took me so long getting the condiments.

My elbow bumps something behind me that lets out a puff of dust on impact. I turn to find a bag of flour leaning precariously over the edge of the shelf. *Shit.* Moving as silently as I can, I push the bag back to a secure spot, but it's too late. The cloud of powder has made its way to my nostrils, which are now flaring as I wrinkle my nose in a desperate attempt to stifle my sneeze. No luck.

I sneeze, and I sneeze *loud*. Like the kind of sneeze that I would imagine only your middle-aged father is physically capable of—one that rattles the house. I cover my face with my elbow, hoping the sound was muffled enough that Grady will assume it came from outside. The heavy footsteps I hear cross the kitchen tell me that it didn't work, and I squint in the sudden bright light as Grady opens the closet door.

The way his hazel eyes rake over my body makes me very aware that I'm still covered in ketchup and now have a fine layer of flour adorning every inch of me. Grady's jaw flicks as the corner of his mouth quirks up into a playful, lopsided grin. His expression is amused but not mocking.

"This isn't—" I start, but he interrupts me.

"Nice place you've got here," Grady says with a casual nod, as if assessing the pantry the way he would if I was showing him around my home. "Ally said you had a ... unique living situation, but this isn't quite what I pictured."

And then, as if I've casually invited Grady in for coffee after a date, he squeezes himself in next to me and slides the door closed behind him. His broad chest takes up the vast majority of my field of vision and I crane my neck to look up at him. There's a playful smile on his lips as he waits for me to respond. He wants me to play along with the little scenario he's made up to ease the sting of my embarrassment. Colour rises to my cheeks as I realize what he's doing. I can't tell if this is more humiliating, or if I'm grateful for him making light of me spying on him from the pantry. I decide on the latter as I consider a quippy response.

"Yeah, the rent is killing me though," I answer. *Lame.* But Grady runs with it. He lifts his chin as he looks around the closet once more, exposing the column of his neck to me. I can just make out the outline of his Adam's apple in the dark, bobbing as he swallows.

"What does a stunning zero bed, zero bath studio like this go for nowadays?"

"Ally is charging me my first-born child. Didn't you know? She isn't pregnant with Mason's baby, it's mine."

"Wow, that's steep. But I guess there's a ton of storage in here." Even in the dark, I can tell that Grady's eyes are roaming over my face, and my mind stalls under the weight of his gaze. I'd be lying if I said I haven't thought about wanting to be this close to him, and my heart pounds as we stand here breathing each other's air. Grady is tempting in a way that wars with my resolve to not get involved with anyone.

I chew my bottom lip, considering my next remark, but I've run out of witty comebacks. Grady must register that the role-play has come to an end because he says, "Should we join the rest of the crew out back? Or would you prefer it if I closed the blinds and you can just spy from the window?"

I give him a playful shove and the solidness of the muscle under his T-shirt catches me off guard. Fuck, he's so *big*.

Emerging from the pantry, the light reveals the stain on the front of my shirt once again. Grady's warm, green-brown eyes flick down to my chest briefly in an obvious attempt to only take in the ketchup and nothing else.

"I look like I've been through the *Texas Chainsaw Massacre*. I don't know if I can go outside," I joke, but heat rises to my cheeks again, a flush spreading upward from my chest.

"It might be slightly alarming, especially for the medical professionals out there," Grady says, referring to Ally and Mason, both with years of experience looking at real blood. "But no one here is judging you, Spencer."

The way my name rolls off Grady's tongue it doesn't sound like a word that he's said for the first time.

Goodnight, Spencer. It was the last time he said my name—

when he lingered in the doorway to his guest bedroom the night I stayed over at his place. It had come out with a slight wobble then. But as he says it now, it sounds as though he's practiced it. The word is familiar in his mouth. As familiar as saying the word *hello.*

"That's easy for you to say, this is your family," I point out. "You forget that I'm meeting half of them for the first time."

"Tell you what," Grady says, crossing the kitchen and reaching for the bottle of ketchup on the counter. He picks it up, and before I can say anything, he flicks open the lid and squirts a blob down the front of his shirt, the crisp white cotton now marred with a streak of red. I clap my hand over my mouth, my eyes wide with shock at the mess he's just made of his otherwise pristine white T-shirt. Grady looks up at me and grins. That crooked, boyish grin. "There. Now we both look like *The Walking Dead.*" His eyes sparkle behind thick dark lashes as they linger on me, making my skin prickle.

I wonder how long we would have stood there, staring at each other, if Ally hadn't come back into the cabin at that exact moment.

"Spence, people are wondering where the condiments are," she says, then she stops in her tracks as she comes through the front door. "Oh. All over the two of you, by the looks of it."

"Yeah, we had a bit of an ... incident," Grady explains, tossing me a playful wink, an acknowledgement that we now share a secret, an inside joke. Something that's just ours.

"Well, I see you've beat me to the re-introduction. Grady, you remember Spencer, don't you?" Ally says, gesturing between us before picking up the tray of sauces I was supposed to take out ages ago. Grady's eyes are on me once again, and I feel hot, feverish.

"Of course, I remember Spencer," he admits. "She's not easy to forget."

I'VE BEEN COVERTLY WATCHING Grady from across the fire pit for the last hour. We didn't interact much during the rest of the barbecue—not during dinner or while playing lawn games—but that doesn't mean that I haven't caught Grady stealing glances. I've stolen a few of my own and, on occasion, our eyes have lingered long enough to make my neck flush.

Now, we're all seated on Adirondack chairs around the fire, and I'm having difficulty focusing again. I'm too busy watching the way the flames are casting shadows that accentuate the strong line of Grady's jaw. My thoughts are currently 80 percent on Grady's face in the dim light of the licking flames, and 20 percent on that line he used earlier. *She's not easy to forget.* Has he thought of me since the night I spent at his place? Or was it more like an "oh yeah, I remember her" as if seeing me again jogged a memory that he had all but forgotten?

As much as I hate to admit it, I've thought about that night an embarrassing amount. I've never been able to pinpoint why. It wasn't a night of crazy, wild sex. We didn't even touch each other. But that's what makes it stand out in my mind. Most guys would have jumped at the chance to hop into bed with me. That's all men want from me anyway, which normally suits me fine. Grady was different. He was respectful, reserved. It made me want him even more.

But that ship has sailed now. I'm closed for business, where relationships are concerned, until I can get back on my own two feet.

I realize now that zero percent of my attention is on Ally, who has been chattering away next to me about paint colours for the nursery. She says something about wanting to pick a powerful colour. Whatever that is.

Most of the group has retired for the night, leaving only Grady and Mason in conversation across from us. It's getting late now, and a chill settles on my back, making me wish I had brought a sweater to throw on over my camisole.

I snap out of my trance watching the crackling fire, as Ally says my name a second, maybe a third, time.

"Spence, are you okay tonight?" Ally has shifted in her chair so she's facing me. "You've been so distracted."

"Yeah, sorry. I don't know where my head is at. I'm just tired I think," I lie. "All the travel the last few months, and sleeping in the van has kind of done me in. I'm okay, I promise." In truth, this solo camping trip has been the most relaxed and rested I've ever been. It's just a shame that not all of my contracts are like this. Normally, I'd be hustling my ass off for very little pay beyond my travel expenses.

Ally squints her eyes, skeptical of my answer. I'm the energizer bunny of our friendship, down for anything—I never stop. So, my answer warrants some skepticism.

"Will you be able to come back for a visit once the baby is born?" My eyes snap back to hers, and I collect myself long enough to formulate a response.

"I will do everything in my power to make that happen, Ally. Really, I will," I say, twirling a stray lock of red hair that's fallen from my haphazard bun. Ally peers back at me from under raised eyebrows as she rubs her growing belly protectively.

She has a hard time believing that I can make any kind of concrete plans this far in advance, and I don't fault her for that. But with the baby due a whole two months from now, and my entire livelihood in the balance with my latest contract coming to an end, I don't even have an inkling as to where I'll be when my best friend's daughter is born. That thought is what sends a pang of guilt right through my gut.

It's not that I haven't enjoyed travelling around the world for my job; if you had asked little Spencer what she dreamt of doing when she grew up, it would be exactly this. To see as many different countries as possible, live by my own set of rules, never get tied down, only worry about me and my own needs. Granted, I would have been happy to do anything that got me the fuck out of

Vancouver and out from under the crumbled ruins of my home life.

"Once I can find a more stable job, I'll have a better answer for you."

"Any updates on that front?"

I let out the breath I'd been holding in through pursed lips. My agent, Sasha, has worked her magic with every contract I've landed, and now that those opportunities are dwindling, she agreed to do me a solid and send my resume to a few of her connections in the industry. Neither of us predicted that I would be a less-than-ideal candidate. So, my job situation already has me on edge, and Ally's questions aren't helping. Not to mention the fact that Grady is still within my line of sight.

"Nothing exciting." I shrug, taking a sip of my wine to keep myself from glancing over in Grady's direction. "Sasha has been sugarcoating it a bit, but I know I've been passed up for some of the marketing positions she's sent my resume to because I don't have a degree."

My free-spirited, go-against-the-grain attitude has always been one of my best qualities and has gotten me all the contracts I've landed as a travel influencer, including this last one. Now though, my reckless, teenage decision to skip out on university is biting me in the ass since I need a job with an actual title and a salary I don't have to hustle for.

Ally nods slowly, as if trying to hold back an, "*I told you so.*" But she doesn't say it; she's a better friend than that, even if she doesn't agree with my life choices.

"How long will you be in Heartwood?" It's a valid question, and one I don't have a clear answer to.

"Not sure. My contract with WanderLuxe is up in two weeks," I explain. I'm nearing the end of a three-month contract with the camper van company, where I've been using my social media page to promote the whimsical appeal of van life by driving it across Canada, stopping in all the most picturesque small towns. Heartwood was an intentional stop, the last one before I make the last leg of the journey down to the coast. "Then I have to give the van back. I'll need to figure something out before then."

"Maybe you can just stay until the baby comes. It'll only be a couple of months until she's here."

"A couple of months is a long time to go without a paycheck," I remind her. I'm on a tight enough timeline to find a decent job as it is. I've sublet my apartment in Vancouver until next month, and I need to be able to pay my own rent if I ever want to move back in.

"Right, well I'm sure you'll figure something out, Spence. You always do. We'll be here whenever you want to visit." Ally gives me a soft smile and places her hand on my arm. Her comforting touch is something I have never taken for granted. She is, and has always been, the most constant presence in my life. Even when things at home were falling apart, she never faltered. She just accepted me into her family and into her heart with open arms.

We sit around the campfire for a while longer, watching the flames consume the logs until the bark is nothing but glowing embers, and the chill of night is creeping over me from behind.

"I'm gonna need to head home, Ally," I say, implying that either she or Mason needs to give me a ride. It's not easy lugging all your belongings around in a van, and it's much less convenient to take it out once you've set up camp, so I've been relying on Ally for rides since I arrived.

Grady glances up from where he's sitting across from me, leaning forward, elbows resting on his knees. Ally yawns an exaggerated yawn and pats her belly, which I'm convinced she's pushing out a bit more for dramatic effect.

"Sorry, Spence. I'm beat too. Absolutely wiped," she says. "It's hard growing an entire human."

"That's okay, I'm sure Mason won't mind driving me," I suggest. But when I look around, Mason has conveniently gone into the cabin to start tidying up the remainder of the s'mores we've all consumed far too many of.

"I don't know. I don't like it when he's away from me for too long. In case the baby comes or something."

What the hell is she talking about? She's not due for another two months, I wonder, until I catch her eyes dart in Grady's direction. *Fuck me. I should have known.* Ally has been trying to play matchmaker for me since we met in grade nine, and she tried to set me up with Todd Pringle. *Puke.* I learned my lesson to *never* let her set me up again while I sat through an entire movie with Todd's clammy hands gripping mine.

"I don't mind taking you home," Grady chimes in because of course he does.

"Oh, no. I couldn't ask you to do that," I protest. "I'm staying all the way out at the provincial park. It would be out of your way."

"Nah. It's only a few minutes up the road from my place."

I plaster on a casual smile. It has become abundantly clear that I'm not going to weasel my way out of this. I can endure another fifteen minutes of pretending that I don't want to climb Grady like a tree. While straddling him on the back of his motorcycle. Sure. No problem.

"Great, thanks." My voice comes out an octave higher than I'd like, and I just hope Grady doesn't notice. The sparkle in his eye as his mouth forms that cheeky grin says otherwise.

CHAPTER 3
GRADY

CRICKETS CHIRP in the tall grass, audible now that everyone else has gone home for the night. Ally and Mason have retreated inside the cabin, leaving Spencer and I alone in the driveway. It's dark save for the glow of the moon and the porch light attracting some dizzy-looking moths. The air has chilled and Spencer is shivering in her camisole.

"I have an extra jacket on my bike if you want," I offer, opening the compartment on the back that houses my helmet and my leather bomber jacket. I feel less nervous around her now, having sat across the firepit from her all night. It was like exposure therapy if I had a phobia of beautiful, intimidating women. "And you'll need this." I hand over the jacket—which she accepts and throws over her shoulders—and my helmet. She loosens the messy bun that her hair has been falling out of all night, and the red waves are finally free to cascade over her shoulders in a way that makes my breath catch in my throat. Her hair is still wild, falling down her back as she clips the helmet on under her chin.

"What about you? Don't you need a helmet?" Spencer looks between me and the bike. I pull my baseball cap out of my back pocket and throw it on backwards, the way I like it, so it doesn't blow off in the wind.

"Sure, I normally wear one. But I've only got one, and we have to make sure that pretty little head of yours is protected." I place a hand on the top of her head and wobble the helmet around. "Besides, we're not going far."

I offer Spencer my hand, and she takes it to balance on one of her long, lean legs as she throws the other over the bike and scoots herself up onto the seat behind mine. I climb up after her and stick the key in the ignition.

"Ever been on a motorcycle before?" I ask.

"Uh, does a moped in Rome count?" Spencer lets out a nervous giggle. I cock my head, contemplating the similarities between a moped and the Harley beneath us. There aren't many, save for the fact that they both have two wheels.

"Sure," I lie. "Just be prepared for a few more horses underneath you." I kick up the kickstand, pull out the clutch, add some throttle, and we're off. "Hold on, tight," I shout over my shoulder. I feel the muscles in her thighs flex, squeezing me tighter. Her hands wrap around my waist sending a thrill through my chest that I don't think is from the roar of the bike this time.

Spencer lets out a shriek as I lean to one side to round the corner, and her fingers curl and grip my T-shirt. Goosebumps spread out from the concentrated spot where her fingertips graze my abdomen.

"You're alright," I reassure her, calling out over my shoulder. "Just lean with me next time." I catch her nod in my side mirror. She closes her eyes and takes a calming breath, and the corner of my mouth quirks up at the thought of how nervous she is behind me. Spencer doesn't seem like a woman who is ever nervous, and I wonder if it's the bike or me causing that reaction.

We round the next bend, the quiet street belonging only to us as I weave around the gentle curve. Her weight shifts with mine and we take the corner much smoother this time.

"Atta girl. You've got it." I can't help but flick my eyes down to my side mirror again, just in time to catch a smile spread across Spencer's face as she closes her eyes and lets the wind caress her skin. Her body is less tense, and I can tell that she gets it now, why I ride. That feeling of pure freedom.

The entrance to my driveway is a blur as we whizz by and continue along the road that leads past my house and to the provincial campground. I down shift as we approach, and the sudden drop in our speed makes Spencer's hips buck against my back. I'm suddenly acutely aware of how long it's been since I've had a woman so close to me. It's not that I'm against dating, I've just had other priorities. The dating pool in a town like Heart-wood is small, which means that, for the last few years, I've been in a strictly monogamous relationship with my right hand. I see no need to mess with a good thing.

My mind wanders for a moment, wondering how it would feel if she was straddling me like that from the front. But the fact that she's Ally's best friend makes her just a little off-limits. Not totally unacceptable, but unacceptable enough that I shouldn't be enter-taining thoughts like that. *Just drop her off and go home. It'll be better for everyone.*

"This is me," she says, pointing to a camper van parked on a gravel pad. It's nestled in the trees, the woods around it pitch dark except for the twinkling glow of the fairy lights Spencer has strung up on the canvas awning. The effect it gives is homey and warm, like she's made the best out of the fact that her house is on wheels.

I pull the bike into the campsite and come to a stop, neither of us making a move to get off just yet.

"I should let you off here," I start. "I was always taught never to go near a stranger's van."

"Am I a stranger?" Spencer's raspy voice hums in my ear. For all intents and purposes, Spencer is a stranger. This is only our second interaction, ever. I know nothing of significance about her, only that she doesn't stay in one place for long, so it may be in my best interest to keep it that way. That was the primary reason I didn't make a move on her when she stayed at my place. I knew that once I entertained the idea of Spencer, I'd fall hard and fast.

"Guess not anymore." She starts to lift her leg over the back of the bike, and I put my hand out to stop her, letting it land on her outer thigh. "Let me help you down." It takes everything in me not to let my hand linger there a little longer, but I climb off the bike and ensure that the kickstand is secure before extending my hand to her. She takes it and uses it to steady herself as she starts to lift one leg up and over the seat. The bike wobbles and a shriek escapes from her throat.

"It's going to tip over, I'm going to get stuck underneath it," she cries, her eyes pleading.

"I won't let that happen," I say, but I let go of her for a moment and move behind her, placing my hands on her hips and lifting her down in a swift motion. Spencer removes the helmet, her hair windblown, her cheeks pink from the breeze. She dusts off her ketchup-stained shirt as if any dirt is going to matter at this point.

"Thanks," she says, her arm outstretched handing me back my jacket. "And thanks for the ride."

"Sure," I say, but I hesitate before turning back towards my bike to leave. Something in me doesn't want this conversation to end. I want to stay in Spencer's presence as long as I can. For every day over the last year I thought about having the chance just to talk to her again. "Are you sure you're okay here, out in the woods all by yourself? You know, there are legends about these woods ... some pretty spooky stuff." I let my voice trail off, but I don't stifle my playful grin. I'm not trying to terrify her.

"Don't freak me out! I'm the one that has to sleep here tonight you know." She bounces on her heels and shakes her hands as if she can shake off the thought of anything in the woods around her camper.

"Maybe I should check the perimeter for you, just in case. You never know what might be lurking out there," I suggest. She can't possibly think I'm serious about there being monsters or whatever she's imagining out here. There are bears though, and cougars. Even I wouldn't be able to fight one of them off.

"Oh, fuck off, Grady!" Spencer whimpers.

"Better safe than sorry, right?" I joke as I stride past her and walk the edge of the gravel campsite pad, making an exaggerated show of peering into the woods, hunting for an imaginary threat. I round the back of the campsite, and a sound I was not expecting catches my attention. It's a scratching, scraping sound coming from behind the van.

"What the fuck is that?" Spencer says, suddenly right behind me, trying to peek out from around my shoulder.

"Jesus, don't sneak up on me like that!" I just about jump out of my skin. Okay, so I may have freaked myself out a little bit, too. Now that I know there's actually something over there, my shoulders tense.

"A little jumpy, are we?" She digs her index finger into my bicep. "You're supposed to be protecting me from monsters, remember? Go see what it is."

I nod. I can't really argue with her. I guess that makes me the first victim of whatever it is that could be lurking around back there. The Rockies are littered with grizzlies, and I might be about to come face to face with one. I lift a finger to my lips, indicating to Spencer to be quiet, and I creep along the back hatch of the van, stopping short of the corner and craning my neck to see around to the other side.

What I find, rummaging through some stacked-up boxes where Spencer keeps her trash, is worse than I was expecting. I back away slowly and turn to face Spencer.

"I'm going to need you to be very quiet, stay very calm, and back away from the camper, okay?" I instruct her, my voice no louder than a whisper, and her large green eyes go wider than dinner plates. *What is it?* She mouths, taking a tentative step back.

My heart is thudding in my ears. This could go very, very wrong. The last time I encountered this ... thing, it did. I position myself in between Spencer and the wild beast, which I can tell by the increasing volume of the scratching, is growing nearer.

It pokes its head out from around the back tire, and Spencer lets out a bark of laughter behind me.

"A skunk?!" she shouts and I whirl around, just about smacking a hand over her mouth. "That's what you were so afraid of?!" She cackles again. "I'm so sorry, Grady, but I cannot take you seriously right now. A skunk."

"Be quiet, you're going to startle it!" I say, remembering the absolute horror of the smell that made my eyes water and clung to my skin for weeks. Jett, Hudson, and I had been playing in the yard and the skunk that decided to wander through did not take kindly to Jett chasing after it. The spray aimed right for Hudson and I and, wanting to spare my little brother, I shoved him out of the way, taking the brunt of the gruesome stench. Jett never did apologize. Asshole.

"Look at it, it's cute. What's it going to do? Spray you?" Spencer admires the filthy animal that I despise so much for what one of its relatives did to me. I don't hold many grudges, except for Carter Bouchard, and skunks.

"Yes, that's exactly what it's going to do," I say, matter-of-factly. "Some people have never been sprayed by a skunk, and it shows. Do you know how many tomato juice baths it takes to get the smell out?" Spencer blinks back at me, a cheeky grin still toying with her supple lips. "No? Because I do. Approximately six. Even then, the smell still lingers."

Her grin widens.

"Well," she says, "it's a good thing we're both covered in ketchup."

"I don't think—" I start. "It's not like skunk repellent. Just be quiet until it leaves, okay?"

Spencer puts her hands up in defeat.

"Okay. But I don't know how to defend myself from a skunk. Are they the kind of animal where you have to pretend to be one big predator to get them to leave?" Spencer takes a step towards me, and I squint one eye, considering what she's suggested for a moment.

"Yeah, I think they are," I say, matching the step she took, closing the distance between us.

"Put your arms around me," she instructs, and I do. Spencer's head reaches just under my chin. "We have to get close. So, it thinks we're one person." I clasp my hands around her back to bring her tighter to my chest, and she rests her cheek on my peck. I just hope she can't feel the way my heart is hammering against my ribs.

"Like this?" I ask.

"Yes, exactly. Now we wait," she says.

"Aren't we supposed to pretend to be scary? Isn't that how this works?" I ask.

"No, dummy. That's how you get sprayed." Nothing about Spencer's tactic here makes logical sense, but it makes sense to me if it means I get to stand this close to her for a second longer.

We're both quiet for a minute or two. The only sounds are the skunk, happily sniffing around in the dirt, our breathing, and my pulse pounding in my ears. Eventually, the skunk moseys off into the woods.

"Is it gone?" Spencer asks, remaining perfectly still against me.

"Let's wait here until we know it's far away," I say, not wanting to pull away from her just yet. I give it another fifteen seconds or so, not long enough to be weird, and then I say, "I think we're safe."

Spencer glances around the campsite, confirming that the stinky pest is truly gone, and she leans back to peer up at me.

"You saved my life," she says, somehow maintaining a completely neutral expression. "How can I ever repay you?"

Her hands are still around my waist, and I fear that the

thoughts I'm having will soon make themselves known between us. A rogue erection is not how I want to make my declaration of my feelings for Spencer.

"I have a few ideas," I say, knowing that if I give myself any more time to overthink this, I won't let myself go near her again. I will slip into the ether of the friend zone as I have so many times before. Although I'm not one to regret the choices I've made, the one thing I can say with certainty is that I would regret not taking advantage of this second chance I've been given. The rational, responsible part of me didn't make a move last time because I wanted to be respectful. I never wanted Spencer to feel uncomfortable staying in my house. We didn't know each other then. But now ... even she admitted we're no longer strangers.

To my surprise, Spencer looks intrigued. One eyebrow quirks up as she perches up on her tip toes and twines her arms around the back of my neck, pulling my face down close to hers so our noses are almost touching.

"Then I would say great minds think alike, Landry." Her teeth sink into her bottom lip before she cranes her neck up and grazes them against mine. Those lips. Those pillowy soft lips that I haven't been able to stop staring at since the moment I caught her standing in the pantry cupboard looking like an absolute goofball. A really sexy goofball.

The first time she places them on my mouth it's soft and tentative, until she nips at my lip and lets out a soft moan that sounds more like a hum. It sparks something within me, and my hand grips the back of her head, my fingers twining through the back of her hair, tugging so her head is pulled back, face angled up towards me giving me better access to her mouth. I kiss her the way I should have done months ago.

I kiss her, and I wonder if the version of me all those months ago was more responsible, and whether that was for the best.

Because now that I'm kissing her, I don't want to stop.

CHAPTER 4
SPENCER

I'm kissing Grady Landry. I'm kissing Grady, and the flutter that ripples through me sucks the breath right out of my lungs. This is not what I had planned on doing tonight. In fact, I had actively tried to avoid it. I should be trying to avoid it. But the feeling of Grady's tongue as it sweeps across the back of my teeth has me coming unmoored, floating, untethered from the realities that I need to keep me grounded.

The night air is chilly, but the heat radiating from Grady's body keeps me from feeling cold. He backs me towards the van, never letting his mouth leave mine, until my back hits the turquoise metal, sending a different kind of shiver through me. The cold feels good on my feverish skin.

Grady bends down, running his hands from my rib cage to my hips, to the soft spot beneath the curve of my ass. In one swift motion, he lifts me off my feet, his large hands gripping my thighs in a way that feels secure, safe, even though I'm no longer on solid ground. I wrap my legs around his hips, steadying myself and taking some of my weight from his arms, and he responds by pushing his hard length against me.

Our tongues roll together in tandem, like they've always

known how to do this, together. The moment I saw Grady standing in that pediatric emergency room, all tattooed and just a little dishevelled in the sexiest way, I knew it would be like this. I knew that it would be explosive, like fireworks lighting up the sky for a brief moment, both of us watching in rapt attention knowing that in just a few seconds, it would be gone.

One night. This one night with Grady is intoxicating. *He* is intoxicating. His scent is intoxicating. Like vanilla and leather and tobacco, and I want more. My hands roam up his firm chest and find the sides of his face before I wrap them around his head and dig my fingertips into his scalp. Not hard, but with just enough pressure that a groan escapes his lips and vibrates through me down into my core.

Suddenly he's pulling me away from where my back was resting on the side of the van, and carrying me towards the door. I make use of the time he's walking me over by trailing kisses down the side of his face, along his jaw, his neck, feeling the burn of his beard on my cheeks. He's supporting me with one arm now as he reaches out and tries the handle.

He yanks on it a second time.

"Is there some kind of trick to this thing?" he asks, his voice deep and husky. It might have broken the mood if I wasn't so damn turned on already.

"Oh, sorry, it's locked." He sets me gently on the ground so I can find the keys in my pocket, and I unlock it as quickly as I can. "Welcome," I say, his hands finding the curve of my ass once again, as I climb up the steps ahead of him.

"This is where you're living, huh." Grady takes a moment to look around when I flick on the overhead light. The space isn't much to brag about. The revamped version of the vintage van boasts a tiny kitchen on one side that I can conveniently reach while I'm lying in bed, and a folding table big enough for two abnormally short people. "I think I liked the pantry better."

"Ass." I laugh, but the fact is, I've rather enjoyed the cozy van and I'll miss it when I have to return it to WanderLuxe. The sight of Grady having to crouch in the camper draws another laugh from my throat.

"At least I could stand upright in the pantry," he says, ducking slightly as he climbs up inside.

"Who says we'll be standing?" I quip back, flashing him my best sultry stare.

"I like to do all fucking entirely vertical. That's the only way I do it." His expression is neutral, waiting to gauge my response, but his eyes twinkle with a hint of mischief.

"Fucking? Oh no, sorry, I think you misunderstood me. I thought we were just going to watch a movie tonight. You know, paint each other's nails, braid each other's hair." The smirk on my face is enough to tell Grady that I'm joking, and he meets me over by the counter, once again hoisting me up so I'm seated on it. The ease with which he lifts me is slightly jarring and more than a little hot.

"You might be. But I've already decided how my night's going to go Spencer Sinclair," Grady growls, his eyes gripping me in his stare. He lowers himself to his knees in front of me and spreads my legs wide, so he's positioned between them. "Even if I have to beg."

Fuck me.

Kneeling in front of me, Grady's eyes just about meet mine. He sweeps his hands up from my thighs, taking the bottom hem of my tank top and sliding it up. His touch is light on my skin, and it sends a shiver through me. The air in the camper is cool, making my nipples harden in response.

Grady groans at the sight of me, his eyes roaming over my breasts, worshipping my body from where he's kneeling before me. He cranes his neck up while I lean down to meet him, and this time our kiss is softer, gentler. He lingers in it, taking his time before trailing his teeth gently down the column of my neck, across my collarbone. I throw my head back, giving him better access to places I want to feel his lips.

His mouth dips lower, hovering over my breast, making lazy circles around my nipple with his tongue.

"Oh god," I breathe as the sensation of his breath on my firm peak sends a needy warmth down between my thighs.

"You like that?" Grady looks up at me, his brown eyes searching my face for any indication that I want to take this further. I'm practically panting as I nod, and Grady takes that answer for what it is; I want more. I want it all.

His hands find the waistband of my jeans and make short work of taking them off, leaving me sitting on the counter in my thong.

"You are just as perfect as I imagined you'd be," Grady says, and the turn of phrase tugs at the back of my mind.

"You've imagined me?" I try to keep my tone light and flirtatious, but he returns nothing but complete sincerity.

"More than I'd like to admit," he answers, and now he's set off full-blown alarm bells, lights and sirens in my head. Just how deep have his thoughts about me gone? Because thinking about me in some vague way to get off when he's lying in bed at night is different than *thinking* about me, thinking about me.

I'm yanked back to the present moment, as Grady brings his hands up to stroke the inside of my now bare thighs. My eyes flutter closed at his calloused fingertips brushing gently over my skin, just for a moment, and then logic once again takes over. I need Grady to know what this is. Most importantly, that it's not going to be the type of relationship that he should continue *imagining*.

I pull away from him suddenly, and his eyes search my face for some indication as to why I put a halt to such a good thing. Because it is a very good thing.

"Are you okay?" he asks. My chest heaves as I try to hold myself back from kissing him again. I'm more than okay. I want this as much as I think he does, but we need some ground rules first if this is going to happen.

I nod to reassure him before I say, "We need to set some things straight."

He blinks at me, waiting for me to continue. The look in Grady's dark hazel eyes tells me that he will agree to whatever condition I set if it means he gets to be with me tonight.

"Rule one: this is just for tonight. We get whatever this is out of our systems, and then we're done." Repeats can only happen with strangers I know I'm never going to see again. A week in Amsterdam with a hot Dutch guy is one thing, but being with Grady, my best friend's brother-in-law is dangerous. I won't be able to avoid him forever.

He nods again. "Rule two: there are no strings attached, okay? I don't want flowers, I don't want dates, I don't want boyfriend material from you. Just sex."

So far, based on the openness in his expression, it seems like my first assumption was correct, and Grady is in fact, ready to go along with my rules. Good.

"Done." Grady leans in to kiss me, but I've thought of one more loose end that I need to tie up, so I put up a hand between us.

"Last rule: we don't tell Ally. In fact, let's never speak a word of this to anyone, just to be safe." My words are clipped, and I need to get them out as quickly as possible so we can resume what we were doing. "She catches one whiff of this and we can say goodbye to rules one and two. It won't be casual anymore. She's hardcore when it comes to relationships, monogamy. She's a penguin, and she thinks everyone else is a penguin too."

"A penguin?"

"Yeah, they mate for life. Ally and Mason are penguins. You and I are not."

"Got it," Grady says.

"Just like that?" I question. His willingness to accept whatever boundaries I set is slightly jolting. Part of me doesn't trust it. I've had one too many guys tell me the same thing, just to show up at my place unannounced, wanting me to get brunch with their mothers or some other giant overstep. I learned it the hard way, and I'm not going to deal with it again.

"Just like that. Let me be whatever you need me to be. This can be strictly casual if that's what you want."

"But is that what *you* want?" I push. The only way this works is if we're totally honest about being on the same page.

"Don't worry about me. I want what you want. But damn your pretty little mouth tasted so fucking good that I'm going to need you to shut up so we can keep this going," Grady murmurs, his voice sending a soothing warmth down my spine and low into my belly, making me forget what I was ever concerned about in the first place. He reaches his hand up to cradle my face, and when I open my mouth to utter my agreement, he swipes his thumb over my lips. "Not. Another. Word."

His eyes never leave mine, even as he brings the same thumb that brushed across my mouth downward to trace a feather-light line down my centre through the fabric of my thong. My breath hitches as my hips buck in response, an attempt at applying more pressure on my swollen clit. But Grady removes his hand and now I'm aching for his touch.

"Uh uh," Grady tsks. "I've thought about this for way too long. If we're doing the relationship rules on your terms, we're doing this on mine."

It's a good thing that Grady picks me up off the counter again because after that comment, I no longer have the use of my legs. He just about throws me onto the bed and I land on the soft duvet with a shriek. Grady lips slide into a smile I can only describe as *hungry* as he comes to lean over me.

My hips squirm beneath him and I wrap my legs around his waist, finding his hard length in his jeans and lining my pussy up against it. This time, he doesn't complain, and I feel the muscles in his shoulders slacken as I writhe against him.

He grazes his lips against mine before sweeping down and taking my nipple in his mouth, more forcefully this time, sucking and biting the hard peak.

His other hand finds the sensitive spot between my legs once again, pushing the fabric over to the side and sweeping down my slick core.

"You're so wet for me already," Grady moves back up, so his face is in line with mine as his fingers make a sweeping motion up and down my slit, stopping to circle my clit as he reaches the top. "I think you've been thinking about this for a while now, too."

I let out a guttural moan. I don't have the words to answer him. There is nothing in my head except the overwhelming sensation of his fingers rolling over that bundle of nerves.

Grady kisses me, and I can feel his grin against my mouth. "I'll take that as a yes."

I give a slight nod as our lips move together, and when Grady pulls away for a second, I manage to rasp the words, "take that as I need you to fuck me right now."

The word *need* is intentional. Having Grady fuck me is no longer a want. My body is yearning to feel him inside me the way my lungs yearn for air.

"Condom?" he asks.

"The drawer," I answer, looking over to the kitchen drawer that is also serving as my nightstand. Grady reaches in and pulls one out, before pulling down his jeans to reveal his already hard length. He makes quick work of the condom, rolling it down to the base of his shaft.

Sensing my urgency, Grady slips off my thong, gripping my knees and pushing them outward. Something flashes across his eyes as he stares at me, now completely bared to him. He sucks in a breath between his teeth.

"You're so fucking gorgeous," he whispers, using two fingers to find my opening. He looks me dead in the eyes as he stretches me open with them.

"Fuck me like it's your last time." I rasp. Grady removes his hand, and uses them to spread my legs wider, as he pushes his tip into me. My body stretches in response to his width, the pressure of him filling me sending intense waves of pleasure through my core. This is only the beginning, and I'm already wound so tight, so close to falling over the edge.

He only breaks eye contact with me to close his, as the sensation of me around him overtakes him. Grady pulls back slowly, and I savour the friction between us until he drives himself back in. I can only buck my hips as he pushes into me, our bodies making a slapping noise as we quicken our pace, each of us taking cues from the other.

In this moment, my body belongs to Grady, but he has not taken. He's not concerned about what he's getting out of this at all, like his pleasure is secondary. He gives and gives to me until the tight coil within me snaps. There's nothing I can do but allow the hot, tingling sensations surge through me in cascading waves.

Grady doesn't keep going as the waves of my pleasure settle into gentle ripples. He doesn't keep the pace to find his own release. He halts and removes himself from me with an inner restraint and strength that must be akin to the Hulk. Once again, he's kneeling before me, and he dips his head to plant butterfly soft kisses on my swollen, sore clit, as if to soothe it after the pounding he just delivered.

This time, his movements are gentle, and the change in speed and intensity has my pleasure building back up once again.

"Grady," I cry out. I am once again floating in a space between heaven and earth, and Grady's tongue flicking that sensitive spot is the only thing keeping me tethered to this realm.

Grady finds my edge with ease again, and though the waves aren't as intense, they roll in more slowly and linger, making all my muscles clench and tighten until they are too tired to hold on anymore. My breath heaves as I let my body relax into the bed. My eyelids are heavy, everything is heavy.

"Give me a minute," I rasp. "Now I owe you," I assure him, though how I'm ever going to pay him back for this escapes me at this point in time. I can no longer move, and every muscle in me is spent. As if understanding this, Grady lies on the bed beside me, resting his head on his outstretched arm.

"You don't owe me anything." His voice is low, gravelly, and slightly out of breath. He reaches towards me and brushes a lock of hair off my face.

"Good. Because thanks to you I have lost the use of my body."

Grady chuckles softly and leans over, placing a kiss on my forehead. I close my eyes and revel in the endorphin-induced bliss. I'm only half aware of Grady kneeling to reach over me and open the back hatch of the camper van. He unlatches it and the cool breeze from outside is a reprieve from the humid, sticky air inside.

Somehow, I manage to sit myself up and grab a blanket to wrap around my shoulders. Grady is sitting on the opposite edge of the bed now, my duvet wrapped around his waist, and he's looking out at the night sky, the moon high above. I meet him at the back door, dangling my legs off the bed out the back of the van.

"This has been my favourite thing to do since I've been on this contract. I'm going to miss this van," I say, gazing out at the shadow of the mountains, the last of the snow capping the tops illuminated by the light of the moon. "Sometimes I just lie in bed at night and look up at the stars. It's just so peaceful when the world is quiet like this."

"Has it been lonely? Driving across Canada all by yourself?" he asks, peeling his eyes away from the night sky to look at me.

"I don't really get lonely. I enjoy my own company," I say plainly. I've learned that my own company is the only thing I can truly depend on, and I've come to terms with the fact that I'd rather be single forever than spend even a day of my life relinquishing control to someone else.

"Do you ever think about settling down? I mean, not settling down, but giving up the constant travel? Making a life for yourself somewhere more permanent?" Grady points towards the wall at the foot of my bed, covered in a collage of photos. Some of them are of the places I've been, the friends I've made along the way. Others are magazine clippings, destinations I have yet to visit.

"Okay, I have a new rule," I say as a response. One open admission is enough for tonight. I don't need Grady caring about me or what I choose to do with my life. "No personal questions."

"Personal questions can just be friendly, no?"

"Not when you're hooking up with the asker of said questions. Personal questions lead to connection, and connection leads to feelings, and feelings are never good for either party involved."

"Noted. No more personal questions." Grady gives a curt nod, his mouth forming a tight line. "You can live in my mind as Spencer Sinclair, perfect stranger."

"Good." I look back at him, his eyes lingering on my mouth.

"Good." There's a pause between us that stretches on longer than is comfortable.

"Don't go falling in love with me, Landry." I point a warning finger at him. "This"—I gesture between us—"is just to get whatever attraction we have for one another out of our systems."

"Cross my heart." Grady makes an *X* across his impossibly firm peck.

"Promise that after tonight, we'll keep our distance from each other?" I ask. Tonight needs to stay limited to tonight. Feelings are easier to shut down when you don't keep revisiting them. I can't promise that I'll have any restraint if we're constantly around one another. Grady makes me feel like I want to throw caution to the wind, like I want to make bad decisions.

"Jeez. For someone so free-spirited, you sure have a lot of rules." Grady shoves my shoulder lightly.

"I do like to think of myself as a free spirit. But rules are good for me. They keep me in check." My mother could have used more rules when it came to men. I've witnessed first-hand what having a "free spirit" can do if you don't reign it in every now and again. Chaos. Utter chaos and avoidable pain.

I twirl the end of my hair around my finger, a nervous habit. Grady doesn't push it any further, thankfully.

Instead, he says, "I can respect that. But can I make one request?"

"Shoot."

"If tonight is our last night together"—Grady shifts so he's on his knees, crawling towards me, closing the distance between us—"I want to make you scream my name until the sun comes up."

CHAPTER 5
GRADY

THE SUN IS SHINING over the baseball diamond, and there's a very disruptive group of seven-year-old boys tittering away with each other in the dugout in anticipation of the game starting, but I can't stop thinking about my night with Spencer Sinclair. In fact, it's all I've thought about since it happened, and now I'm trying to beat my thoughts into submission to focus on this Little League game I agreed to coach.

I signed up for the year when a couple of dads in town approached me about it. The guy who used to do it moved to the city with his family for work, and none of the other parents know the difference between a foul ball and a strike, so I agreed. I may have missed my own opportunity to play for the major leagues, but these kids need someone who genuinely loves the game. And I do. I used to eat, sleep, and breathe it in high school.

I feel a gentle tug on my T-shirt, causing me to glance down to my right where I find Miles, looking down to where he's scuffing his feet in the dirt. He's timid and quiet, and when his Uncle Finn took guardianship of him he clammed up even more. I suggested that Finn enroll him in baseball, and here he is, looking out of his element and, frankly, terrified.

"What's going on, buddy?" I stoop a bit so I'm closer to eye level with him, but it takes a bit more encouragement to get him to speak. When he finally does, it comes out so soft I can barely hear it over the other kids whooping and hollering to start the game already.

"Why do I have to bat first?" Miles says, not wanting to look up at me.

"Because you can't face your fears unless you get out there and do it," I explain, crouching down low so he's forced to look at me. "You'll do great, Miles."

"You don't know that," he says, wringing his hands. "Did you see the first guy up to pitch? He's like twice my size. We're going to lose because of me."

"Listen, if we lose, so what?" I place a comforting hand on his shoulder, and I feel it relax slightly. "You want to know a trick from when I used to play?" I ask him and it earns me a curious look, so I continue. "Right when the pitcher gets up on the mound and is ready to throw, right when he winds up and his foot lifts off the ground ..." I bring my hand back to demonstrate the exact moment I'm describing. "Make a real loud fart noise with your mouth."

Miles's cheeks go red and he bursts out in a laugh, covering his mouth with his palm.

"You didn't really do that," he chides.

"No, you're right, I never had to use it," I admit. "But only because I practiced batting until I was so good, no pitcher intimidated me. I won't tell anyone if you want to, though."

I stand up from where I'm crouched and Miles smiles up at me now. If anything, the joke helped to ease some of his tension, so I've done my job. I give him a nudge to get out there, and he leaves the dugout, grabbing his bat along the way.

I watch the beginning of the game unfold, arms crossed over my chest, when the rattling of the chain link fence behind me catches my attention. A parent I recognize from pick-up and drop-off at practice is leaning against it, looking at me. He clicks his tongue once, twice.

"You want to say something, Mark?" I ask him, a bit of an edge to my voice.

"No," he says. But he does, and he keeps talking. "Just an interesting coaching tactic is all."

I don't turn to face him, I just talk sideways over my shoulder, eyes fixed on the game. Miles manages to hit the ball which goes rolling along the ground out into the field.

"You think you can do a better job? Have at it," I answer with a shrug.

"I'm just saying." Mark throws his hands up in the air, feigning innocence. "If that's your coaching style, then my son doesn't have a shot in hell at the MLB."

My gaze instantly finds the son he's talking about, standing in line to bat. The kid is leaning down with his forehead on the end of his bat, spinning around it. By the time he gets out there, he'll be so dizzy he'll think the pitcher threw four balls.

"I think that ship has sailed, Mark." I nod over to where his boy just about stumbles over into the dirt. It earns me a disdainful scoff. I've made him mad. "I think he's more of an inside kid."

"Only because he has a clown for a coach," he just about spits out. "Couldn't make anything out of his own baseball career so now he's going to let the kids ruin theirs too."

I try to shrug off the comment, but I can feel myself clenching my jaw, grinding my molars. It stings. To everyone else it looked like I quit baseball, gave up, didn't have what it took to go pro. But I know the truth, and there was more to the story than what most people assume.

When I don't respond to his snide remarks, Mark storms back to the bleachers across the field where he sits down next to his wife. He's fuming. I can see his beet-red face from here. I'm sure he's telling her all about our terse interaction, really highlighting what a chump he thinks I am. I'm turning my attention back to the game when my gaze catches on a shock of red hair in the stands.

Spencer. She's sitting beside Ally, coffee in hand. I briefly question why she's decided to come and watch a Little League game on a Saturday morning, but then I remember that this is Heartwood, and there's never a whole lot else going on.

My breath catches watching her as she throws her head back, laughing at something Ally said. I find myself itching to know what it was that Ally said to get that reaction. Whatever it was, I want to stash it away so I can make her laugh like that too.

A cheer from the crowd erupts as Miles runs across home base, and right over to me. He's beaming, and I give him a big high-five as he comes back into the dugout.

"I did it Coach Grady!" he exclaims, a bright smile lighting up his face.

"I knew you could, bud." I muss his hair as he passes by and takes a seat on the bench, the smile never leaving his face.

I wish I could say the rest of the game is as exciting, but once our inning is over, the other team is up to bat and they crush us. Four runs, although I'm not supposed to be keeping score. I know the parents do too, especially Mark. I meant what I said to Miles about it not mattering whether we win or lose. I've never approached the game that way. Even at my peak in high school, I just went out there to have fun. My only competition was myself, and I think that's why I excelled. Because I did it for the love of the game. No expectations.

The boys exchange disappointed groans as the game ends, and the other team runs off the field to where their proud parents are waiting.

"I am so proud of you boys," I say, but their eyes are downcast. "You guys played your hearts out and gave it your all. You should be so proud of that too."

Crickets.

"Hey, chins up. Look at me." Most of them do. "We are not sore losers. We celebrate the little wins, keep our spirits high. Miles got a run today, so I want you all to give him three cheers." I say the first *hip hip* and only get a measly *hooray* in response. But by the third cheer, most of them have perked up and joined in. "We'll try again next time, okay? Go say good game." The boys disperse, and form a line in the middle of the baseball diamond and shake hands which each of the boys from the other team. It used to be a tradition in any sport I played growing up, but it kind of fell by the wayside. I think it's important for the boys to learn good sportsmanship.

I shield my eyes from the sun with a hand across my forehead and search the bleachers for Spencer, hoping to see her one last time. As the crowd departs, I can't find her stand-out red hair. Something in my chest sags. I shouldn't be disappointed that she left already. I've been trying to respect her wishes and keep my distance anyways. Even though it's the last thing I want to do. Even though I've been fighting every instinct to call her or find a convenient reason to bump into her in town.

The bleachers are empty now, the field quiet, and I'm wandering around picking up the wooden bats that have been left on the ground. That's when I notice movement behind the stands. Two people are talking, just visible through the gaps in the steps. I squint my eyes and make out Mayor Jodi Price. Her son plays on my team, but I get the distinct impression that she wasn't paying attention to the game. She's been otherwise occupied, in a heated discussion with a man who has his back turned to me. They share an embrace, an intimate one, and when they both slink out from beneath the seats, it's not Jodi's husband following her.

It's Carter Bouchard.

Dread creeps up my back as I mull over the implications of this turn of events. The new challenge this poses for my campaign to stop Carter from taking over the town with his chain of restaurants. I refuse to resort to blackmail, although I certainly could. I don't think Heartwood would take too kindly to a mayor who is fooling around with business owners, so to speak. This means Jodi and Carter are even more entangled in each other's affairs than I assumed.

CHAPTER 6
SPENCER

"I WANT TO GO OUT TONIGHT," Ally declares over the phone. I was laying in the hammock I stretched between two towering spruce trees, enjoying my solitude and the sound of a raven off in the distance, when her call interrupted my peace and quiet.

"We were just out this morning." My voice is groggy, having almost fallen asleep in the warmth of the sun.

"No, I mean *out* out. That was just coffee and my usual daily walk," Ally says. I'm sure her usual daily walk does not include a quick stop by Grady's Little League game, so I question her motives for dragging me there.

"Okay, where do you want to go?"

"Anywhere. The Whisky Jack maybe?" she suggests.

I don't mind going out with Ally tonight, as long as we go anywhere but the Whisky Jack. I've expertly dodged Grady around town over the last few days. Good thing, too. Because just seeing him from a distance this morning had me replaying our night together in detail. I'm going to chalk it up to the fact that he was looking extra fine in his black athletic shorts, his grey T-shirt snug against his chest, showing off the black ink on his arms.

No, seeing him again would not be good for my boyfriend boycott.

"Hmm. How about Thistle + Thorne?" I offer. "You can't drink anyways, and that way Poppy can join us after she closes up." Poppy and Ally often sit in the cafe after hours, and that kind of secluded get-together sounds like just what I need tonight.

"Poppy already said she'll get Ethan to close, and I don't want to sit in the cafe alone. I want to go out, see other people," Ally counters. "Besides, just because I can't drink doesn't mean I don't want to get dressed up and go out to a bar. I have a limited amount of time to do it before my Friday nights look a lot different."

I imagine what Ally's nights will look like in a couple of short months. Poopy diapers, spit up, and so much screaming. I cringe for her. I'm not about to argue with my pregnant best friend, so I say, "Okay, the Whisky Jack it is." Maybe I'll get lucky and Grady won't even be working.

"Yay!" Ally squeals and I jerk my phone away from my face at her sudden outburst. "I'm excited, Spence. This will be fun. It's been so long since we've had a girls' night out. I'll pick you up at six."

"Isn't that a little early?" I say, checking the time on my phone screen quickly. It's almost five now.

"Not for me. My bedtime has been getting earlier and earlier these days," Ally explains.

"Fair enough. See you at six." I hang up the phone with Ally, and lay my head back in the hammock, letting the golden evening sun warm my face as I close my eyes. I've been trying to soak in every peaceful moment I have left out here in the woods, just me and Wilma. I gave the van a name because even though I denied it to Grady, there have been moments where I've been a little lonely. But now, I'm sad that my time with her is ending. One more week until my contract is over, and then I don't know what I'll do. All I know is that I'll leave Heartwood like I've left every other place I've visited.

My stomach sinks at the thought. This time won't be like every other time that I've left a place behind. I have nothing else on the horizon. I've typically secured my next gig by now, and while I had a few offers, none of them seemed that appealing. It's hard to motivate myself to hustle for contracts that I'll inevitably get passed over for a younger Instagram girlie with lip fillers and much, much smoother skin. Not to mention, the commission these companies are offering still won't be enough to pay my rent back in Vancouver.

I need to figure something out quickly. Sasha said she might have a lead the last time I talked to her, though I'm wary of getting my hopes up too soon. But if it doesn't come through ... I'll have no roof over my head once I return Wilma to Wanderluxe.

LATER THAT EVENING, Ally, Poppy, and I are seated around the table in the far corner of the bar. I caught a glimpse of Grady when I walked in, but I beelined for the booth that would offer me enough cover that I might escape having another interaction with him. As Ally and Poppy chatter away over something that I've lost the thread of, I try to sink low enough in my seat that I'm not visible from the bar.

"What can I get you ladies to drink tonight?" The familiar, husky voice that approaches our table makes me jump, and when I look up to see Grady standing over me, my stomach flip flops.

"Spencer," Grady says with a grin, "lovely to see you again." It's an innocent comment at face value, but I know that he's playing at something else. It's not that I dislike Grady, quite the opposite. The physical chemistry we have is downright addictive. Men like him are my vice, and I am trying to stay sober.

"Likewise." I nod, trying not to take in the way his apron is tied low around his waist, low enough that if his shirt lifted slightly, I would bet anything that you could see the two lines that form a V above his waistband.

"I'll have a gin and tonic." Poppy, oblivious to the tension between Grady and I, orders, and I hope that Ally is just as blind to it. I don't need her asking questions.

"I'll have ... Gosh I don't know what to order if I can't get my usual rosé." Ally taps her chin with her index finger. "Surprise me, Grady. Make me some kind of fancy mocktail."

"Okay, and for you?" Grady's eyes are boring right through me. Coming here tonight was a terrible idea.

"Uh," I hesitate. "I haven't even looked at the menu yet." My mind has been so preoccupied that I never decided what to order. Now I feel like an idiot.

"Tell you what, I'll surprise both of you. If I don't get it right, it's on the house." Grady backs away from our table, but not without shooting a wink in my direction that makes my insides turn to goo.

"What was that about?" Ally turns back to me, eyeing me up.

"What was what?" I force my face into the most neutral expression I can muster.

"That. You and Grady." Her voice raises an octave. She would love nothing more than for Grady and me to get together, and she should know better than anyone why that can't happen.

"Me and Grady, nothing. He said hello, I said hi back. That was it." I give her a casual shrug.

"That was not nothing. There's no chance that you haven't thought about him. You have a type, and that type is Grady Landry. Looks-wise, at least."

It's nothing I don't already know. But my type also involves them being emotionally unavailable, and I can already tell that Grady is fundamentally different, even if he looks the part. Even if he agreed to keep things casual.

"Yes, and there's a good reason I have sworn men off. I need to practice some self-discipline, so Grady is firmly off the table." I snap, a little too defensively and I know Ally caught it. Whatever she thought she saw, I need to shut it down quick. "I'm going to go use the restroom."

Ally squints her eyes at me as I make my escape. Hopefully by the time I'm back, her and Poppy will have moved on to something else. Ally won't let this go if she even has an inkling that there might be something between Grady and me.

I weave my way through the tables, and find the short, narrow hallway that leads to two restrooms. The bathroom is small, a little cramped, but I check myself in the mirror, smoothing out my long red waves, and rub any remnants of lip gloss off my teeth. I didn't need to go to the washroom, so I just wait long enough that Ally thinks my trip wasn't just a ruse to get away from her for a moment.

After a couple of minutes, I start to open the door into the hall, but now I'm met with someone standing just outside, blocking my exit. There's some sort of heated discussion, and I crack the door open slightly to see who it is. I make out a recognizable sleeve of tattoos through the small gap, but the other person I can't place.

"The minute we start letting big corporations like this in, you can say goodbye to the Heartwood you know and love," Grady says. "As soon as that happens, you'll have assholes like Carter Bouchard all over the place, it'll be lousy with assholes."

"Carter is ..." The other voice starts but then trails off. It's a woman, and her tone is nothing but professional, diplomatic. She's weighing her words. Her tone is firm when she says, "Carter owns and operates a respectable chain of restaurants. He has the numbers to prove that opening a location in Heartwood would be financially beneficial to the town. It would be a welcome addition for tourism."

"Have you consulted with Eleanor about this? I think she might have something to say about tourism."

I put a few pieces together and realize he's talking about the same Eleanor that I've been communicating with about the Wanderluxe promotion. She's the chair of the tourism board, and she's a sweet lady. I can see why Grady is skeptical that she would be on board with a restaurant chain opening here.

"People come to Heartwood for its charm, not to go to the same restaurant they go to every Friday night in whatever city they came from. No one wants an Urban Ember here, I can assure you that," Grady points out. Having visited several small towns like Heartwood over the last few months, I've seen this before, and Grady is only partially right. The truth is most people don't know what they want. A new restaurant or business is exciting initially, but it isn't until after the landscape of the town has changed that people think twice. By then it's usually too late to undo.

I shouldn't be listening in on this conversation, but I have no choice. I'm trapped in this tiny washroom and there's no way that I'm going to reveal myself now. I make a mental note to stop spying on Grady for the rest of my time here. Although, in my defence, this time was entirely accidental.

"When is the council meeting?" he asks.

"The council meeting is in three weeks, feel free to make your case then. Although it'll be tough to beat Carter, I'm warning you right now," the woman answers.

"I'll be there," Grady says, his voice flat but firm.

"With all due respect, Grady," the woman says, "Carter has a lot of connections, especially with the council. We'll hear you out, as we would for anyone. But an argument against a change that would financially benefit the town, coming from someone who would be in direct competition ... it's not a good look. Besides, we all know you. You're the polar opposite of Carter. He gets shit done and puts up a fight when he needs to. This is going to be a fight. One that isn't even in your arena. You own a dive bar. You don't care what people think about you, you never have. Don't think I don't remember you from high school. Class clown, doing whatever it took to get people to like you. Forgive me if I don't think you'll take it that seriously."

"I guess we'll see at the council meeting, Mayor," Grady says, and the woman turns to leave, but he reaches out for her, causing her to turn back towards him. "Jodi, we've known each other a long time, and I care about you. Just ... be careful if you're going to get involved with Carter."

I don't have time to contemplate what Grady means by this because, suddenly, my phone rings. I scramble around to find it and shut it off, but whoever was talking to Grady on the other side of the door stopped what they were about to say, their train of thought interrupted. *Fuck. Well, now is as good a time as any.* I push open the door, Grady's eyes going wide as he sees me.

"Sorry, excuse me," I say, pushing past them and refusing to make eye contact. When I reach the safety of our table, I check my phone to see who called and find Sasha's name on my screen. I'll call her back later. She's probably calling with some new contract opportunity, but I highly doubt that it's going to be the lucky break that I need.

Ally's eyes dart from me, who took an inexplicably long time in the bathroom, to Grady, who is just coming out from the hallway and heading to the bar. Her eyes narrow, gaze fixed on me.

I slide across the leather bench and sit back down in the booth.

"What did I miss?" I plaster on a fake, unruffled smile as I try to take control of the conversation and steer it away from the fact that it looked like Grady and I were just in the bathroom ... together. A change of subject is the only way to handle it. The more excuses I come up with, the more damning it will be.

"We were just talking baby names," Ally says. "And I wanted to get your opinion ..."

My phone chimes again. Sasha is calling back. Two calls in a row? What could be so urgent at this time on a Friday night? I stand from the table again and hold up my phone. "Sorry, Ally. I have to take this. I'll be right back, and you can tell me all about your baby names."

Ally goes back to her conversation with Poppy, but I can feel her eyes on my back as I wander outside.

I click on my phone once the front doors shut behind me, and the sound from inside the bar dies down.

"Hey, Sasha," I say.

"Spencer. I've been trying to get a hold of you all day." My heart picks up its pace as I weigh whether she's calling with good news or bad news. Her voice is always so monotone, I can never tell. Just when I think I'm getting a read on Sasha, she'll send me the dreaded we-need-to-talk text, only to tell me I've landed a career-changing contract.

"Sorry, the reception is bad in the campground I'm staying at. What's up?"

"I have an opportunity for you," Sasha starts. "Now, it's not your typical travel blogger contract, in fact, it's not really anything like that at all."

"That might be a good thing." Clearly, the travel influencer contracts are not quite cutting it anymore.

"It's a job in public relations."

"Like PR?" I ask. I've never done anything like that. Influencing, that's marketing in its most basic form. It's selling a product or a service that I already believe in. And, if you're attractive enough, people will buy whatever you tell them to. PR is different, it's more involved. It's making a product, a service, or a person look appealing even though they might not be. That takes just the right eye and ability to make people see what you want them to see. It's something that people go to school for, get four-year degrees in. All I have is a carefully curated Instagram page.

"Yeah, that's what PR stands for." Sasha's tone can only be described as an audible eye roll. "The position is salary, $80k a year with benefits. Everything you're looking for. There's still some travel involved." My mind stalled on 80,000 a year. Some people wouldn't bat an eye at that figure. In fact, a lot of people would try to negotiate higher. But that's more than I would need to be able to afford my life in Vancouver. It's a number that would mean I wouldn't have to rely on anyone but me.

"I don't have any PR experience. What do they want me for?" I ask. Maybe they have the wrong Spencer Sinclair. There's no way I would be the first person they would choose.

"It's a tour company, Mile High Tours. They do group trips all over the world. Apparently, the consensus is that it's just an opportunity for singles to hook-up. They're worried that they're sending the wrong message and attracting a very niche crowd of only young singles, ostracizing other potential clients and sullying their reputation. Now some woman is blasting them on socials, saying that they're responsible for her getting chlamydia. It's a whole thing," Sasha explains. "They love what you've done for Wander-Luxe, how you've turned living in a van into 'hashtag van life,' and suddenly camping is cool. They want you to do the same thing for them. Make chlamydia cool again, or something like that." The job Sasha describes sounds involved, and frankly, more intense than taking photos for social media.

My mind wanders to the possibility that I won't cut it, and I'll be back at square one, jobless and homeless. My insides drop, leaving me breathless at the thought of it. But I can't let myself go there. This is an opportunity that likely won't come around again, not with the number of rejections I've received in the last few months.

"Okay, but that still doesn't solve the problem of me having zero experience doing PR," I say again.

"Well, you don't have the job yet. They want a portfolio of any PR-related experience you do have, so I suggest getting to work. Spin some of your marketing jobs to sound more public relations-y and you're a shoo-in."

"The first thing they need to do is change their name." I scoff.

"Wait, why?" Sasha sounds genuinely confused.

"Mile High Tours? Like the mile-high club? If they don't want to cater to singles, then they shouldn't be advertising that the hook-ups are starting before you even arrive at the destination."

Sasha barks a laugh on the other end of the line. "See? This is why you'll be great in PR, Spencer. You catch things like this. They'll love you. Get the portfolio to me *asap*." She pronounces the word ASAP phonetically, not as an acronym.

I turn around and peer into the window of the bar. The sun has set, and dusk is blanketing the town, just enough that the inside of the Whisky Jack is illuminated. I catch a glimpse of Grady, serving drinks to a table by the window. I watch his movements, fluid and sure, as he passes out the glasses from the tray he is balancing on one arm. He makes one of the women at the table chuckle with something he's said. I'm sure it was some cheeky one-liner. The kind that would also make me giggle and blush.

The way that woman had been talking to him by the restrooms, made him sound like a total schmuck. I've known Grady for all of two days, and I can already tell that's not who he is.

"Give me three weeks?" A nebulous idea is forming, the shape of it I can't quite make out, but it's there. "I think I have just the project in mind. Three weeks, and I'll have a portfolio ready for you."

"I can hold them off for now, but there's no guarantee that they won't find someone else by then."

"Please, just make up some excuse, buy me some time. Promise me. I need this, Sasha." I don't tell her that I've exhausted all of my other options, and if I don't land a job that pays well enough soon, I will officially be a twenty-nine-year-old burnout with no job, no prospects, no home of my own. That's the part that makes my palms clammy, the very real possibility of losing my apartment.

It wouldn't be the first time in my life that I've been homeless, but everything, *everything* I've done with my life up until now has been to make sure it never happens again.

"I'll do what I can, Spencer."

I click off my phone and swing the door open before beelining towards the bar. All I have to do now is convince the one person I should be staying far away from that we are the perfect team. Grady Landry has gone from a one-night stand to my only shot at a job that will secure my livelihood in a matter of minutes.

CHAPTER 7
GRADY

My blood is still boiling from my conversation with Jodi when Spencer sidles up to the bar and plops herself on the last open bar stool. The heat burning my face from anger and the heat from Spencer's eyes on me are almost impossible to differentiate. She observes me for a moment, not saying a word as I tilt a chilled glass against the beer tap and pull the long handle back. A perfect half inch of foam forms on the top, and I set it down on the tray that Finn is waiting to take out to some customers.

"Your drink is at your table," I inform her, in case that's the reason she's sitting here. She wasn't there when I dropped them off, and it caused an unexpected pang of disappointment, thinking maybe she had left. But here she is, blinking her green eyes at me in the dim light of the bar, chewing on her bottom lip as if contemplating her next words.

"What did you make me?" she asks.

"Something spicy. You strike me as someone who enjoys a little heat," I answer, nodding towards the spicy margarita sitting on the table in front of her empty seat. Something spicy, and a little sweet. Just like her.

"Accurate assessment. But that's not why I came over," she says as I pick up the next bill to start working on the order. "I have a proposition for you."

Her words are enough to make me halt what I'm doing and raise my eyebrows at her across the counter while I lift another glass to the beer tap.

"Breaking our rules already," I tease. "Rebel. I like it."

"No, not that kind of proposition, perv. Those rules are very much still in effect." She waves her hand in front of her face, dismissing the notion of us ever hooking up again. It wasn't that ridiculous to assume, and I feel a twinge in my chest that sucks my breath out for a moment, not unlike a mild punch to the gut. "It's a business opportunity. Well, business for me. I'm still unclear as to what's in it for you, but based on the conversation I overheard in the restroom, I'm assuming that this will benefit both of us. A symbiotic relationship if you will."

I flash her a quizzical expression. Recognizing my confusion, she elaborates.

"You know, symbiosis. I'll be the little barnacle that eats up all the gross bacteria off your back, and you'll be the whale that takes me where I want to go."

"I'm not sure that's entirely accurate." I cock my head at her. "And do I have to be a bacteria-ridden whale in this scenario? Is there no other option I can choose from?"

"Yes. And no. That's how the symbiotic relationship works, I'm positive. Didn't you ever learn that in elementary school?" She smacks her hands down on the bar, before announcing what it is she came to propose. "I know for a fact that you need help improving your reputation so you can take down the 'corporate elite' or whatever." She says the last part of that sentence with finger quotes. "I think we can help each other. Let me be your personal PR guru."

"I don't know, Spence," I hesitate. I want nothing more than to spend all my time with Spencer, but working together sounds an awful lot like not keeping our distance from one another. The fact of the matter is, I no longer trust myself to be around her. Spending more time with her is dangerous territory where my heart is concerned. "I don't think it's a good idea for us to work together. I mean, you said it yourself. The only way for our one-night stand to work is for us to stay away from each other."

"We have the rules for a reason. They'll keep us in line," she counters. "As long as we follow them, we'll be in the safe zone. No feelings, no attachment. Just two friends helping each other out. You scratch my back, I'll scratch yours." That's what I'm afraid of. The 'just friends' aspect of our agreement. I don't know if I can be just friends with Spencer, not without getting hurt.

"Let me think on it, okay?" I've been wading through my feelings about our hook-up the other night, and I haven't come to any solid conclusion about what having Spencer in my life will mean for me being able to keep this relationship casual. My gut is telling me it's not going to help.

"Fine. Okay. You can think on it," she agrees. "Just don't take too long. I don't have all day, you know. I'm hungry for your bacteria, Grady." The reference causes a few people to give her odd stares from down the bar.

Before Spencer has the chance to hop off the barstool and make her way back to her friends, Carter Bouchard has blocked her in and is leaning casually against the counter.

"You must be new in town because I swear if I had seen you before, I'd remember," he says, a slimy smile creeping across his face. To an outsider, Carter might seem charming, but I know better.

"Just in town for a couple more weeks," Spencer says, her voice clipped. She's getting a read on him, and I see her wall go up. The same one she erected with me that has all of her rules carved into it.

"Carter Bouchard." He shoves his hand towards her, his Rolex watch glinting as it catches the light.

Spencer takes his hand and shakes it, and my face is heating with rage all over again. I haven't had the chance to warn her about Carter, and here he is, trying to make a move on her. Her eyes flick briefly over to me, where I'm pretending to focus on the order I'm working on. If Carter makes one wrong move ...

"Nice to meet you, Carter." Her tone is friendly, cordial, and it's too nice for him. I know I don't have a right to be jealous of Spencer talking to other guys. I have no claim on her, as much as it might pain me to say so. But I can't help the sticky, burning feeling that is bubbling up the back of my throat. I could kick Carter out of the bar if I wanted, right? I'm the fucking owner, I can do whatever I want. Ban him. Plaster his photo all over the windows outside so everyone in town knows he's no longer welcome here.

"What are you drinking? Let me get the next one." I glance up long enough to see how Carter's eyes have landed on Spencer's breasts, and I swear I see a glint of drool pooling in the corner of his mouth. *Fucking pig.*

"I should get back to my friends." Spencer gestures over to where Ally and Poppy are sitting, sipping their drinks and watching the situation unfold. I feel half tempted to go and make them some popcorn the way they're looking over here.

"Just one drink. Your friends can wait." Man, Carter is insistent when he wants to be. I see Spencer weigh over her options in her head. "I'll let you in on a secret."

Spencer's eyebrow quirks up with curiosity.

"My friends over there"—he points to the table of equally arrogant guys sitting around one of the larger booths—"bet me that I couldn't convince you to have a drink with me. And I *never* lose," he says, a pointed phrase that earns me a glance in my direction. Prick. "So, what's it going to take?"

"Uh, how about a rain check?" she finally offers. A rain check. Meaning, no drink with Carter tonight, but she's essentially agreed to go out with him, and he won't forget that. Bile rises in the back of my throat, and I fight the red-hot rage burning behind my eyes. I think if I stare at Carter for too long, he might combust. "Technically I haven't said no." Spencer reaches across the bar and plucks the pen out of my shirt pocket before picking up Carter's hand and scrawling what I can only assume is her phone number on his palm.

"I'm gonna hold you to that, Red." *Red.* Like he couldn't think of anything better to call her. Red. It's so obvious it's infuriating. He winks at her before finally retreating back to his friends and leaving her alone.

I disliked Carter before, but now I realize that I *hate* him, *loathe* the very existence of him on this earth. For the sole fact that he has the guts to make a move on Spencer, and the audacity to present himself like someone who is charming and worth her time of day. The arrogance that allows him to just go after what he wants and get it.

"Well, nice chatting with you, Grady. I'm going to go back to Ally and Pops. Let me know if you change your mind about my proposal," Spencer says, as if the interaction meant absolutely nothing to her. It meant everything to me. It just ruined my fucking day.

She turns on her heel to walk away from the bar and throws a little backward wave towards me over her shoulder. Suddenly, the rage that was bubbling up within me turns into something palpable—motivation.

"I changed my mind," I blurt, and Spencer stops in her tracks.

"Don't you need more time to think about it?" she says, whirling around on her heel, her brows pinched together in question.

"I've thought about it. I want your help. Let's work together. Let's do this." She's still squinting at me skeptically, as if she's trying to make sense of my sudden change of heart. She must decide that she doesn't particularly care why I've changed my mind, because she strides back over to me, reaching her hand over the bar to shake mine.

I extend my arm out towards her, but I pull back the moment before we make contact.

"Just promise me one thing," I start, hesitating before making my request. Spencer blinks back at me, her green eyes wide. She's clearly not used to me making demands. "Don't go out with Carter. He's ..." I struggle to find a way to warn her about Carter without coming across like a jealous asshole. "He's not a good guy." I hope that Spencer doesn't read too much into what I've just asked of her. It's the truth. I would tell anyone to stay away from Carter.

Spencer's mouth works as she mulls over my request before she shrugs and grips my outstretched hand. I release a long exhale through my nose.

"I wasn't actually thinking of going out with him, Grady," she says dropping her hand at her side. Something in her tone is sincere, reassuring. "Boyfriend ban, remember?" Right. That. The double-edged sword. One side keeps her away from the likes of Carter Bouchard, but the other keeps her away from me. "Besides, he's too clean-cut for my taste. I like my dates to have a bit of an edge." I don't miss the fact that when she says the word *edge*, her eyes momentarily dance over the sleeves of tattoos covering my arms.

"So, what are you going to tell him when he calls to cash in that rain check?" I cock my head, a satisfied grin forming on my lips at the thought of Spencer turning Carter down.

"He won't call. Or maybe he will, but I won't get it." Spencer shrugs. "Women learn at a young age to never give a stranger their real phone number."

"Oh, so you're a ruthless little rebel." My smirk twists even more. She just stares back at me, those green eyes aglow.

"It's not ruthless, Landry. It's survival." Spencer glances back over her shoulder and nods towards Ally and Poppy. "I better get back. It'll be a pleasure doing business with you."

I flex my neck in either direction, coming to grips with what

I've decided to do. The deal I'm about to strike up with the little devil sitting on my shoulder. The muscles in my jaw twitch as I grind my molars together.

Somehow, I doubt it will feel like a pleasure for me. Only a straining, ripping pain at the fact that she's right there within reach, and I can't have her.

CHAPTER 8
SPENCER

"Explain to me again what you're trying to do?" I ask Grady. He's sitting across from me at the wooden picnic bench that is currently serving as my dining table. I didn't waste any time nailing down some concrete plans after we shook on our agreement the other night at the bar. Grady suggested coming to the campsite to hash things over out of the prying eyes of the town. He talks about the place as if it's Wisteria Lane, but then again, I've never truly experienced small-town life, so I didn't push back.

"The town council is three weeks away, and from what I understand, Carter is going to introduce a motion to get rid of a law that has been in place for decades. It prevents chain companies from coming in and taking over the town. Right now, the only businesses allowed are independently owned, local businesses, and I intend to keep it that way."

"What's in it for him?" I ask. Something shady, is my guess. I don't trust Carter as far as I can throw him, not after his pick-up stunt from last night, however much that played in my favour.

"He's an investor in the chain. Ever since the Parks left town, he's been eyeing up the vacant building next to mine. Right now, Jodi—Mayor Price—is on his side. Probably because she has her hand so far down his pocket she's practically jerking him off." Grady explains with an eye roll. "I think she actually might be jerking him off. I saw them together behind the stands at the baseball game the other day. I don't want to make any assumptions, but it was pretty obvious they have more than a professional relationship."

I try to hide my shock and fail, my jaw dropping open.

"You mean, you think Jodi and Carter are ..."

"Having an affair? Yeah," Grady confirms.

"That could ruin her career," I add, and he nods grimly.

"I wouldn't do that to her. Not for my own gain, anyway. I grew up with Jodi and she was never a bad person. She's just clearly lost all her better judgement," Grady explains. "I want to win this the honest way, for myself."

"So, you're going to attempt to convince her not to take a very large sum of money and boost her lover's business. Seems doable," I tease.

"It's not about the money, at least not for me." Grady scrubs a hand over his short, groomed beard. "I'm trying to get them to see how getting rid of this law will only hurt the town in the end. People come to Heartwood because they want to get away from the hustle and bustle of big cities. They want to experience the small-town charm that we offer. Part of what makes Heartwood great is our local economy. If big companies come in and start competing with the little guys, well, there won't be any more locals. All it takes is one, and this town will be overrun with tourists. The money might be flowing, but at what cost? It's not just the people, it's everything. The environment, too. Banff has started having to restrict people from going to Lake Louise because of how crammed it is with tourists. So now no one gets to enjoy it," Grady explains, his words full of passion. I can see it so clearly, how motivated he is to stop this from going through, so why can't everyone else see it, too?

"What about the rest of the council? You seem to have a decent argument, I'm sure they would agree with you if you phrased it just like that," I say.

"That's the problem. I'm not sure they would. The last few years have not been kind to small towns, or small businesses." I take a sharp inhale as I nod. I know Grady's right, I've seen it first-hand. It seems every town I visited over the last month is changing, growing. "The thing is, I know this motion isn't the way to fix the problem."

"Mmhmm," I hum in agreement. "And you're worried that they won't hear you out."

"I know they won't. You heard the conversation I had with Jodi." As embarrassing as it was to be caught eavesdropping, I'm now very glad I did. "She essentially told me not to bother trying because no one takes me seriously enough to listen. They don't think I take anything seriously. Or they think that all I care about is the bar and getting rid of any competition. It has nothing to do with me, or the Whisky Jack." The way his voice wobbles makes me wonder what this is really about for him, what is lacing his words with so much raw emotion.

"Well, do you?" I ask. "Take things seriously, I mean."

"Of course." Grady pins me with his stare, his expression genuine. "I just don't always show it. I like to make people happy. Besides, life is serious enough as it is without me being a downer all the time."

I inhale through my teeth and contemplate what Grady has just told me.

"Which is where I come in," I conclude. "In order to change their perception of you, I have to know what I'm working with here, what makes you tick."

"What about no personal questions?" Grady asks, as if he can see my thoughts. His question is laced with flirtation, a reminder of the night we shared. I give him a blank stare, hoping that my non-reaction is enough to tell him that it's never going to happen again. "You said personal questions lead to connections, and connections lead to feelings."

"I know what I said." I ruminate on his point for a moment, tapping my index finger on my lips. "We can get rid of that rule for now," I decide. "It will work against us. I have to know what aspects of you I can sell to people. PR is just marketing the things you want people to see, what you want them to focus on. You're well known around town, so in order to work, our plan needs to be authentic. What makes this so important to you, Grady? Why is Heartwood worth all the trouble?"

Grady purses his lips a moment and gazes off toward the mountains that loom over the campground. "I think it would just be better if I show you." I stay where I'm seated and watch as he gets up and strides over to his bike.

No, no, no. The last time I got on his bike with him did not end well. I mean, it ended *amazing*, but it can't happen again. I don't know how much resolve I'll have once that bike is vibrating beneath my crotch, my hands gripping Grady's firm torso ...

Get a grip, Spencer. I make a mental note to research chastity belts. I may need one if I'm going to be around Grady for any length of time.

Grady already has his own helmet on, and he's opening the back hatch to pull out a jade-green one. He holds it out to me, and I take it from him hesitantly, eyeing him through a squint.

"You got me a helmet?" I ask, and Grady climbs on the bike. He flicks his head, motioning for me to climb on behind him. I pull the helmet on over my wild hair and climb on as he steadies the bike with his feet.

"I realized I should probably have a spare anyway," he says over his shoulder. I nod, but I don't say anything. One, because the engine starting would drown out my voice anyway, and two, because I don't want to point out the fact that it's the same colour as the camisole I was wearing the other night. I sure as hell don't want to mention that this particular shade is my favourite. It means he thought about me when he was buying it, and I won't entertain the idea of Grady thinking about me when I'm not around.

Grady rounds the corner and speeds up as we turn onto the main road, heading away from town. The end of the road past the campground that I have yet to explore. I allow my body to lean in sync with his, and I realize there's a level of comfort sitting behind him on the bike now that I didn't have the first time. It's a sense of ease ... and trust.

As we make our way down the winding road, houses become fewer and farther between until there is nothing at all except the never-ending expanse of trees. The bike's engine roars underneath me as Grady shifts gears to start climbing up a hill that curves around the side of the mountain, looking as if it will just disappear from beneath us. As we reach the corner, the road continues on in gentle switchbacks hugging the side of the rock.

Eventually, we round a corner and the road becomes wider, creating a space off to the side of the cliff's edge to stop and enjoy the view. My breath catches as I take in the mountains sprawling out before us as Grady pulls the bike over to the side of the road and comes to a stop. I hop off the bike with more ease this time, and before Grady has said anything about why we're here, I've wandered over to the lookout, the view of the sprawling grey mountains pulling me towards it like a magnet.

We're high enough now that Heartwood looks like a tiny model in a museum display. The Rockies rise up all around it, leaving the sleepy little town nestled right down in the bottom of the valley.

I close my eyes and take a deep inhale of the crisp, fresh air that's laced with the sweet smell of wildflowers, blanketing the hillsides as the warmth of spring draws out every sign of life in the cold, grey mountains. I've seen many incredible places, big bustling cities in international locales, but one thing I've come to know since making my way across Canada—there is nothing quite like this.

"It's beautiful, right?" Grady asks, wandering over to meet me. He sits on a low fence that provides a barricade to the jagged hill below, and I take the spot next to him, just close enough that my arm brushes up against his.

"I've never seen anything like it," I admit.

"Never? Not in all your travels to all the wonders of the world?"

"Nope. I've seen some stunning places, sure. There's something about the grandeur of these mountains. It just makes me feel small and insignificant, in a good way. They're kind of comforting. They've been here for eons, and they will continue to be here for eons, long after we're gone. It makes me feel like my problems don't seem as scary, as all-consuming." Like no matter how tumultuous my life is, it's still just a blip in time compared to these mountains.

"I get that." Grady follows my gaze out to the mountain range beyond the valley. Something in the sincerity of his voice makes me believe him, although I get the sense that we have very different sets of worries. "This is my favourite view of Heartwood. When people ask me what's important to me, this is what I think about. This town. The natural beauty that we are so lucky to have around us. This is the version of Heartwood that my parents fell in love with when they came here. This viewpoint is where my father proposed to my mom, with this as the backdrop."

"You're afraid that if this motion passes, this will change," I say, finally realizing the gravity of what's at stake, why Grady is so passionate about fighting this.

"I know that this will change. See, look." Grady leans in closer so he's almost touching me, my shoulder grazing his chest. He points down into the valley. "There's Thistle + Thorne. Poppy took that building over from her aunt and, since then, has worked so hard to make that café the place where people meet on a Saturday morning, or where they go on their way to work. It's a part of our everyday routine now. Or there." Grady leans in a little closer still, and I can smell the warm vanilla and tobacco scent on him. "The grocery store that Mack has owned since it was passed down to them from generations before. It's not just me that has history here, everyone in this town does."

The emotion in Grady's voice is palpable, especially at this proximity, and it's causing a flurry of butterflies low in my belly.

"All of this, the café, the town square, will all be blotted out by big box stores if they open the door for them even just a crack. Jodi doesn't see that this is wealth, too. This is what makes Heartwood rich."

I peer up at Grady's face, just inches from mine, his eyes lined with silver. It hits me at this moment how connected he is to this place. How badly I wish I could have had something like this myself. Somewhere to call home. A family with real roots.

I reach around in the bag slung across my chest for my phone, wanting to capture this moment, this flawless place, to remind me when I need it that this is here. Wherever I go next, wherever this job takes me, I never want to forget.

My camera clicks as I snap a few, and I look back through them, letting out a sigh.

"Why is it that a phone camera never seems to capture the mountains the same as they look in real life?" I mumble, half to myself as I start to put my phone away. It rings before I drop it back in my purse, my mother's name lighting up the screen

I hit the green button, lift the phone to my ear and mouth, *One sec*, to Grady. She starts speaking before I can even get a word out. I wander away from where we were sitting, leaving him to admire the view without me so I can have this conversation in private. I know that whenever my mother calls, there's going to be some sort of drama I'd rather not discuss in front of anyone else.

"Spencer. Have you heard from your father?" she starts, her

voice is crackly on the other end, the altitude of where we are interfering with the connection.

"Hi, Mom. Nice to hear from you, too," I say, although I sometimes wish there was more time in between our conversations. "No, I haven't heard from Dad. I haven't heard from Dad for like, five years." That might be a bit of an exaggeration, but that's how it feels. He still calls once a year on my birthday, but I don't count it since we only exchange surface-level pleasantries.

"I thought he might have told you. You remember that woman he was seeing," she continues, and though the reception is breaking up her words, I can tell that she's slurring her words just slightly.

"Yeah, was it Sherry?" I ask. "Which one was she again? The flight attendant? She seemed nice." She did seem nice, based on photos that I saw of her online.

"Yes. Well now he's engaged to the *tart*." My heart drops, but not at the fact that he's engaged. My father and I have been so far removed from each other for so long, partly my doing, that I try not to even think about him. But for some reason this news has caused my mother to spiral once again, and I'll be left to pick up the pieces. "She posted it on Instagram this morning."

"What does Roy think of all this?" I phrase the question delicately. I'm not asking it because I want to know, I want to remind her of the fact that she has moved on—twice now—and remarried since my dad. She, on the other hand, doesn't see it that way. She allows how men treat her to dictate how she feels about herself, and I am bound and determined not to repeat the same pattern. It's part of the reason why I just don't get into relationships.

"Oh, you know Roy," she answers without answering my question at all, and it's clear she isn't going to say anything more.

"I can't really talk about this right now, Mom. I'm sorry, I'm just ... out," I say, glancing back at Grady seated on the fence. The line on the other end is quiet. "I'll call you later, okay?"

"Okay," she says. Then adding, "Oh, Spencer darling. Do

remember to call my injector and book yourself in for the next time you visit. Your crow's feet were looking quite ... severe in the last photo you posted. If you want to keep getting these influencer contracts, you can't let people think you're getting *old*. Just looking out for you, sweetheart." I reach up and brush my fingertips along the outer corner of my eye and scrunch my face. I certainly have more wrinkles than I did before, but I wouldn't call them severe.

"Sure, Mom. Love you," I say before hanging up the phone and rejoining Grady at the lookout.

"Who was that?" he asks, and I'm sure he can see the shift in my expression. A two-minute conversation with my mother has taken the wind right out of my sails, and I'm suddenly very tired.

"No personal questions," I remind him, although he catches me in my double standard.

"Hey, if you get to ask me personal questions, I'm allowed to ask them back. One for one," he argues, and I guess it's only fair.

"It was my mother. The one and only Marla Sinclair," I say, trying to mask the bitterness in my voice. "She's drowning her sorrows in wine because my father announced his engagement to his new girlfriend."

"How do *you* feel about that? Do you need to go drown your sorrows in wine, too? Because you know, I own a place," Grady says, his eyes searching my face, making me very aware that this is information I share with *no one*. Treading into this territory feels like free falling, and yet, just like when I felt the surge of fear as his motorcycle accelerated the first time, Grady is something solid to hold onto.

"I don't really get to have an opinion," I say. "I've never had an opinion where my parents' relationship is concerned. They divorced when I was young."

"You get to have an opinion now. What is your opinion now?"

I chew the inside of my cheek as I consider Grady's question, and the fact that he's cared to ask. No one has ever asked me how I feel where my parents' dysfunctional relationship is concerned. I let out a long sigh through pursed lips.

"That my mother needs to take a good long look at herself. Otherwise, her relationship with Roy is going to end up the same way as all the others before him. We're tornados, her and I. We leave a path of destruction everywhere we go. The difference is, I'm aware of it," I say with a self-deprecating laugh. Grady nods, trying to understand, though I can tell by the line that forms between his brows that he doesn't. Not really. And I don't feel like explaining more than I already have. "Okay. That was your personal question. Let's get back to the drawing board, shall we?"

"What do you have in mind?" Grady shifts gears at the sudden change of topic.

"Jodi made some hard-hitting arguments about your reputation in town." I begin laying out my plan of attack.

"You really were eavesdropping." He laughs.

"Yeah, and you can thank me for it later. Pay attention." I snap my fingers in front of his face.

"Have you ever thought about working for the CIA? You're really good at spying, Spencer. I bet they'd love to have you." He's still laughing, so I smack him on the arm.

"We need to take this seriously if we're going to get this done in three weeks," I say, with the straightest face I can manage.

"I'm sorry, I'm sorry!" he says, raising both hands in surrender and I flash him a withering stare. "I'll focus."

"As I was saying," I continue, "she said you were the class clown. Which, as it turns out, is something I happen to like about you." I don't miss the way his eyebrow quirks at my admission, but I continue, counting out the list of things we need to tackle on my fingers. "She said you own the local dive bar, so she clearly has an issue with that, even though people love the Whisky Jack. And she pointed out that you're in direct competition with the new restaurant, which implied that you have an ulterior motive and are just afraid to lose customers, right?"

"When you put it that way, it seems pretty bleak, doesn't it?"

"I mean, I'm not going to lie to you, Grady. We have our work cut out for us," I say. "But we're going to attack this from all angles, step by step. I think we can make this work."

"What's in it for you? You never told me why you're even helping me with this."

And for good reason, I think. I don't want to jinx this one shot I've been given. Anytime I've ever allowed myself to think something is a sure thing, it gets ripped out from underneath me. Not this time.

"It may be hard to believe, because I'm so well-adjusted and normal," I start, but Grady cuts me off.

"No one is well-adjusted and normal, Spencer. We're all a little fucked up in our own way." I nod in agreement, and I can't help but think that Grady and I might make a good team after all.

"Well, I've never had anything like this," I say, and I hold my hands up, gesturing to the town below. "I understand why you want to protect it so badly. I do. Because I would give anything for it. Somewhere to call home, to feel grounded. If this is successful, I might finally have a shot at some stability." I leave out the part where if I don't get this job, I will lose all the ground I've gained to create an established life for myself. It would technically make me homeless, and the thought makes me feel panicky in a way that he could never understand. You can't understand it when you've grown up with two stable parents for a good part of your childhood. Not to mention, in a beautiful home on a sprawling property.

"Fair enough." Grady accepts my half-answer, but I can still hear some wariness in his tone.

"Do you trust me?" I ask. For this to work, he has to put his faith in me and follow my suggestions, even though I have no idea what I'm doing. But Grady doesn't have to know that.

"I don't have a choice, do I?" Not a convincing answer, but I'll take it.

"First things first," I say, "you need to lose the bike."

"Absolutely the fuck not." Grady just about shouts, his expression looks like I've just told him I enjoy kicking puppies.

"I'm kidding! Jeez, I never thought I'd have to tell you to lighten up." I bark out a laugh. "I would never make you get rid of your bike." His shoulders visibly relax. "You are getting a makeover though."

"Spencer, what the fuck," he groans, and I can't help but smile.

"It'll be fun bossing you around, don't you think?" I joke, but inside I'm dead serious. This is my comfort zone. Calling the shots. Making the decisions. Maybe I will be good at PR. I've always seemed to figure out how to get my way.

CHAPTER 9
GRADY

I SHUT the front door behind me and follow the sound of classic rock that's blasting through the house down the hall to the spare bedroom. Hudson didn't hear me when I came in, but he turns around now, as I shout his name over the music.

He sets down his paint roller and clicks off the old silver boombox he still uses on the job.

"It looks great in here," I say, assessing the progress that he's made today. He's been working on this room over the last week, a special project I enlisted him for. I can tell he's been working hard by the way his damp T-shirt is clinging to him, his sandy blond hair is damp as well, mussed and sticking up as if he's just scrubbed his hand through it. Yesterday he finished putting up the trim that makes up the board and batten along the lower half of the wall, and today he's finishing painting it a soft dusty blue. The same dusty blue paint dots the fabric of his T-shirt.

It's not just this project he's had a hand in; he's put a lot of work into the house for me since I bought it from Dad. We've just about renovated the place top to bottom, which involved a lot of tearing down wood panelling and ripping up green shag carpet.

This was the last room left, and I've been saving it for a special purpose.

"The final coat of paint just went on. Then I just have to hang up the light fixture. You can start bringing in furniture and finishing touches whenever you like," Hudson says.

"Thanks for doing this, Hud." I give him a smack on his shoulder. "I know it doesn't need to be done for a couple of months yet, but I appreciate you fitting this in." Business has been booming at the construction company, but the paycheck I offered him to work on this side project was enough motivation for him to reschedule his upcoming projects.

"You're just lucky you asked me early. The next few months are going to be insane," he answers, turning back to the paint roller on the drop cloth covering my hardwood. "Where have you been today anyways?"

"Out," I say, dodging his question. "Care for a beer once you're done cleaning up?" Hudson was one of the few people who saw how Spencer's first visit to Heartwood threw me for a loop, and he'd be the first to call me out on spending time with her now.

"Sure. Let me finish cleaning up, and I'll meet you out there." Hudson retreats down the hall, and when he finds me again a few moments later, I'm already seated out on the patio, a cold beer in my hand, and one cracked for him on the table next to me. He picks it up and takes a swig, and I notice some sweat beading on his forehead.

"You never answered my question from before," he says.

"Which one?" I deflect, but I know that Hudson is just curious about how I spent my day. He's always been like that, interested in other people's lives just for the sake of knowing them a little bit better.

"Where you were all day," Hudson clarifies. "You weren't at the bar, because you don't smell like fry oil." Hudson is the only one of the Landrys that inherited our mother's blue eyes, and now they are piercing right through me.

"I took my bike out," I half lie, and only by omission. "It's such a beautiful day, wanted to take advantage since I haven't been able to ride through the winter." I don't return Hudson's eye contact. Instead, I let my gaze drift off towards the woods surrounding the back of the property where the four of us used to spend our days from sunup to sundown.

"Sure." He takes a casual swig of his beer, a smug look on his face that I can't quite place.

My phone buzzes on the table in between us, vibrating repeatedly. My eyes dart down to see Spencer's contact on my screen, and her name comes up as *Rebel*. The moment she admitted to giving a fake number to Carter the other night at the bar is a moment I wanted to memorialize. There was something about the fire behind her eyes that I couldn't get enough of. Hudson is also looking at my phone screen, and I click it off, ignoring the call. I'll call her back once he leaves.

"It's her, isn't it?" he says, more a statement than a question. "Spencer. You've been talking to her."

I say nothing. Instead, I scrub a hand over my face.

"Just be careful, dude. That's all I'm gonna say," Hudson warns. Might be a little late for careful.

"There's nothing going on between us," I deflect, although I don't sound convincing, and I know that I'm trying to convince myself more than Hudson at this point.

"Listen, I did the math. The last time she was in town was right before you went into that weird mopey phase of yours last year. Don't think I don't know what's going on."

"I did not *mope*." I emphasize the *p*, popping my lips. Did I creep through every single one of her Instagram posts after she left? Sure. But I did not mope.

"You sure as shit did. I know what moping looks like because I'm an expert at it myself," Hudson says, referring to the rough patch he went through after he graduated and his high school sweetheart left town. It took him years to get over Wren, if he ever did. The jury is still out on that one. I would bet anything that if she showed up in town tomorrow, Hudson would be just as fucked as I am when it comes to Spencer. "It was written all over your face. Now I'm convinced it was because you couldn't stop thinking about her. I've never seen you so hung up on someone."

"And there's a good reason for that," I answer. The fact is, Hudson has never seen me hung up on a woman because I don't let myself get hung up on women. I made a point not to date again after my high school prom when shit went sideways, and I realized that I was going to have to be there for my brothers. When I did finally start seeing someone a few years ago, it ended with me heartbroken over a woman who was never meant for me in the first place. She got bored, said I was too predictable, too nice, and left. I didn't know it was possible to be *too nice*, but apparently it is, and I was.

"We don't need you to be looking out for us anymore, Grady. Jett and I are adults now. We can take care of ourselves." Something in Hudson's words causes a sharp pang in my ribs. Realistically, I can tell myself that they don't need me anymore. In reality, the thought of not being there for them makes me feel like I no longer have a purpose.

With Mom no longer around, Dad as good as absent with his workload at the clinic, and Mason already gone away to med school in Ontario, that left me as the man of the house. I didn't know how to be the man of the house, so I was the next best thing. I was a big brother. I swore to myself that I would take care of them up until the day they didn't need me anymore. I guess I never realized that day had already come and gone.

"It wouldn't matter anyway, Hud. There's nothing between Spencer and me. She's sworn off men anyhow." I let out an imperceptible sigh and close my eyes to feel the afternoon sun on my face.

"Is she thinking of becoming a nun or something?" Hudson

asks. "Because that's the only reason I can think of why she would be so opposed to anything happening between you."

"No, no. Not a nun." I chuckle to myself at the thought of Spencer in a nun's habit. Spencer would be the worst nun alive, I'm pretty sure. The obedience to God part of the job would be her downfall. Spencer clearly doesn't obey anything or anyone other than her own internal compass. "It's something to do with family drama, I think. Her dad is getting remarried, and her mother sounds like a bit of a hot mess. So, I highly doubt she's in the headspace to jump into a relationship."

"She could still jump into bed with you, though." When I don't respond, Hudson's expression changes, it flattens. "Don't tell me you've already hooked up with her," he says, finally putting it all together.

"It was just sex," I say, taking a swig of my beer, the bottle making a pop sound as I pull it away from my lips. "And like I said, never to be repeated."

"Jesus, Grady. I know you, and if there's one thing you can't do, it's casual flings."

"Hey, I'm easygoing, laid back. I can do casual if I want to do casual."

"She might *do casual,* but you don't. You're just going to bend over backwards for her. Spencer is a different kind of woman. I've seen her type before. She'll rip your heart out if you let her," Hudson warns.

"It's not that simple," I say, remembering the rules we've already broken. I don't even know how many there were to begin with, but I know we've broken two. I felt a rush both times it happened. The night she asked me to work with her, shirking the promise we made to keep our distance, and today when I shared a part of myself that I rarely share with anyone. But it's the things she shares with me that have me completely captivated by her, the glimpses of her that she lets me see through the cracks. Those beautifully imperfect parts of her make me that much more attracted to her. If Spencer is a tornado, then I want to be that one cow you always see get swept up in the wind in movies.

"What, did you already manage to knock her up?" Hudson asks, and I just about choke on my beer. I collect myself enough to shake my head no.

"She's helping me out for this town council meeting coming up," I explain. "I want to oppose Carter's motion to get rid of the local business law, and I haven't exactly built myself a reputation in town that people respect, unfortunately. She's going to help me change that."

"Suit yourself, Grady. It's a noble cause, and I agree that you'll need all the help you can get on that front," Hudson gives in. He pauses for a beat before adding, "I'll be here for you when you get your heart trampled on."

"I know how to control myself. We're keeping things strictly platonic. It was a one-time thing. Just sex," I repeat, but even saying that feels robotic, like the words are just syllables that I've strung together with no real meaning. It's the same feeling I get when I'm telling a bold-faced lie.

As if on cue, my phone vibrates on the table again. Then a second time. And a third. And when I look down at the screen, I have three texts from the beautiful rebel herself.

> **SPENCER**
>
> Call me back when you can.
>
> Actually, don't. I'm at Ally's and she just came out of the bathroom.
>
> Can you take the day off tomorrow?

I consider Hudson's warning before responding. He's right about me. I don't do casual. I'm not generous with my affection for just anybody, but once I've given you a part of me, you're getting all of me, take it or leave it.

And nothing about my night with Spencer felt casual.

Nothing about it felt like I could turn off my emotions. Nothing about it felt like I could compartmentalize. Just the opposite. I let Spencer into a corner of my heart, and now she's bled over into the rest of it.

> Sure. It's Finn's day to work the bar anyways.

I may as well accept my fate.

SPENCER

Good. We're going shopping.

> Is it going to take all day?

Maybe. We'll have to drive into Calgary.

> Can't we go shopping in Heartwood? We have clothing stores here.

The Shirt Shack isn't going to cut it.

> The Shirt Shack has some great finds.

I think we need to go to the Big and Tall.
Heartwood doesn't have a Big and Tall.

> I may be big, and I may be tall. But not so big and tall that I need to shop at Big and Tall.

Take a shot every time you say Big or Tall.

> Brat.

Pick me up at 9?

> Sounds like a plan.

Great. Don't bring the bike.

> Is this part of your plan to slowly make me get rid of it?

The three little dots that indicate she's typing appear and then disappear, as if she's thinking of something snarky to say back.

SPENCER

I wouldn't tell you if it was. But no, we'll have stuff to bring back.

An uncontrollable grin tugs at my lips, though I feel a strange sense of disappointment that the conversation seems to be over. I could talk to Spencer for hours, even if only over text messages.

"Dude." Hudson's voice snaps me back to the reality outside of my phone screen. "You're smiling like an idiot. What the fuck were we just talking about? She's going to leave again. That's what Spencer does. It's her job, her way of life. It's going to wreck you just like it did last time."

"I know, I know. Don't worry about me, Hudson. I'm fine," I reassure him.

I am not fine. I am not fine in the slightest, and this conversation has made that glaringly obvious. There's this small shred of hope that's been tugging on my heart, telling me that maybe if I can be what Spencer needs, she'll see that I'm worth sticking around for.

I PULL into the campsite bright and early. Spencer is already outside, perched on the step of the camper waiting for me. She gets up as soon as she sees me, and saunters over to the passenger side of my hatchback. I strictly don't drive this thing once the weather is above ten degrees Celsius, but Spencer insisted. Apparently, we'll have a whole carload of clothing to bring home, which is strange because I am not planning on buying anything. Spencer will see once we get there, a makeover is not what I need. It certainly isn't what's going to help me win at the council meeting. Anyone who judges me by the clothes I'm wearing can go kick rocks. But if it makes her happy, and if it means I get to spend the day with her, I'll suck it up and try on some clothes.

"Morning, sunshine!" Spencer says, climbing in beside me. She's got her hair back in a clip which she takes out so she can rest her head on the seat, and her hair falls down around her shoulders. It doesn't matter how many times she does that, the sight of her letting her hair down is always going to make my heart ache. Though, this morning I feel something else, and my cock is suddenly uncomfortable, pressing against my jeans. I thought jerking off in the shower would have helped me to keep my mind on the task at hand today, but clearly that was a pipe dream.

"Morning," I respond, trying not to look at her, and busying myself by handing her the coffee I brought her in a travel mug. "I figured you could use some coffee that wasn't boiled over a fire pit or something."

"I do have a coffee maker in there," she fires back, waving towards the camper van. "It doesn't look like much, they wanted to keep the vans kind of retro, like the old Volkswagen ones. The inside is more like 'glamping' than it is like camping. That's why it's called Wander*Luxe*. I guess you know that already, you did see it when you, uh, dropped me off. I appreciate the coffee, though, thank you. Hey, this is a Volkswagen, isn't it?"

The corner of my mouth lifts as I glance over at her. She's rambling. Almost as if she's nervous to be spending the day together.

"Yes, it is," I admit. Not a very macho car, but I picked the most sports car model I could find, and I like how it handles.

"It's cute," she says, twisting around to put on her seatbelt. I don't know if I'd go as far as to call it *cute*, but I can imagine Spencer putting one of those solar hula girls on the dash, and the thought of it makes me smile even more. I might even get one to see if she notices.

We have to drive through town to get to the highway that will take us into Calgary, and the streets are quiet at this time of day, except for the odd go-getter up for a morning walk or a jog.

"Tell me why we had to leave so early?" I ask as I slow my speed down along Main Street. It will only be a few more weeks until the street is closed off to vehicles, only allowing bicycles and pedestrians down the strip through the summer months.

"We need to get there when the mall opens. It'll already be busy by eleven," Spencer replies, as if everyone should know this. But I don't. I can't remember the last time I went into the city, let alone into a mall.

"Tricks of living in the city, I guess..." My voice trails off as my gaze catches on the window of the Parks' restaurant, or what used to be their restaurant. There's a new sign next to the one that reads *For Lease*. I pull the car over to the curb to get a better look.

"Yeah, I'd imagine you don't exactly have to fight for a parking spot when you go to the Shirt Shack." Spencer is giggling to herself when she notices that I'm no longer paying attention, and she follows my line of sight. "'Urban Ember,'" she reads aloud from the advertisement.

The picture depicts a man and a woman laughing together on the patio of an upscale lounge type restaurant, with modern fire tables on the patio. It looks like the type of place that serves overpriced cocktails and 'tapas' for people who want to go to a restaurant but don't actually want to eat any food.

I can feel my blood pressure rising, my pulse thrumming in my ears as my fingers grip the steering wheel until my knuckles turn white. The building isn't even his yet and Carter is laying claim to it. And since when did Heartwood become 'urban?'

"I don't know, Grady ... people might like to have a restaurant like this here," Spencer says, her eyes still fixed on the sign. "The bar is great, but sometimes people enjoy getting dressed up for a nice date night."

"Then they can come to the Whisky Jack," I counter. "It's not even about the restaurant, Spence. It's the foothold it will give to other chains, just looking to make a buck at the expense of the locals."

Spencer nods, her eyes narrowing as she thinks.

"I don't like that look. I have a feeling it's going to involve another makeover or some shit," I say, flicking my eyes over to her momentarily before fixing them back on the road ahead of me as I pull away from the curb.

"Not quite," Spencer says. "But we need to respond. PR is all about being one step ahead, Grady. When people see that sign and think about having somewhere more upscale to go to, we're going to lose the advantage."

"How do we get the advantage back?"

"We need to remind Heartwood what their values are. Remind them what's at stake. I think I know how to do it." A secretive smile plays on her lips. It gives me the distinct impression that she's already formulated a plan and that I don't really have a say anymore. The cogs in her brain are turning, and she hardly speaks for the rest of the drive.

CHAPTER 10
SPENCER

"This place looks kind of douchey," Grady points out as I lead him into a trendy men's clothing store. The mannequins in the window are silver chrome and wearing slim-fit trousers and button-downs. Not exactly what I would consider douchey, but they've styled them with the first three buttons undone, so I guess I can see where he's coming from. "Slacks and a button-down aren't really my style."

"Are you from the 1970s? No one calls them slacks anymore," I say, flicking through shirts on the rack by the front of the store. The music in here is loud and the lighting is almost too dark, but I can see Grady bouncing on the balls of his feet in my periphery. "Keep an open mind, okay? And stop doing that, you're making me feel rushed."

Grady immediately stops bouncing, but he's started fidgeting with his hands. He catches himself before I can say anything and shoves them into his pockets.

"Let's just get this over with sooner rather than later."

"This is not a process you can rush," I say, whirling around to face him. "This is phase one of the plan. We want you to look like you give a shit, Grady. That includes giving a shit about yourself.

People will take you seriously when you take yourself seriously. No more of this"—I point a finger and wave it up and down at the outfit he's currently wearing; faded jeans, a black T-shirt that is so threadbare I can just about see right through it, and that god-awful baseball hat—"scruffy bar owner look. And no more backwards ball cap."

"First the motorcycle, now my ball cap?" Grady protests. "You are a cruel, cruel woman."

"Sometimes you have to be cruel to be kind," I retort, turning my attention back to the rack of clothing.

"Be careful, Rebel, it's kind of turning me on." The nickname he just used causes an interesting warmth to melt down my spine, but I ignore it and flash him a glare over my shoulder. I rummage around in the rack a little longer, choosing not to respond to his comment.

"Here. Hold onto these," I say, pulling out a few shirts I like and shoving them towards him.

"These are not my style. Can't we go somewhere else?"

"Stop being a baby about this. You're just trying them on," I scold. "And I'm not saying you need to wear a button-down and trousers every day, but you need something nice to wear to the party."

"The party? What party?" Grady follows me like a puppy as I make my way to the back of the store and start sorting through the folded pants on a table.

"Phase two. The party," I say, realizing that I'm only just filling Grady in on this part of the plan now. I spent the entire drive planning it out in my mind. A cocktail contest at the bar. Kind of like the Christmas trees in the mall, where businesses can decorate their own and have them on display. The winner of the cocktail contest would be featured on the Whisky Jack menu for a whole year, and proceeds will be funnelled back to the community. It's genius, really. It gets people involved and shows them how tight knit the community is. But mostly, it proves that Grady is forward-think-ing, that he prioritizes the town.

"How many phases are there?" Grady's tone is aghast.

"You told me you'd trust me, right?" I hand him a stack of pants that complement the shirts, and his arms adjust to the weight of the clothing, his thick forearms tensing. "Also, I haven't decided how many phases there will be yet. Phase two only came to me about two hours ago on the drive here."

"Do you care to fill me in?" A muscle in his jaw twitches beneath his groomed beard.

"Later. Right now, you need to go and try those on." I turn Grady around with a hand on his shoulder and direct him toward the changing rooms. "Come out and show me everything."

"Okay, Mom," Grady grumbles. But as much as Grady complains about it, he does as he's told, and then steps out from behind the thick black velvet curtain in the first outfit. He's wearing a pair of navy blue trousers, a button-down shirt with a faint blue pattern, and a brown belt that accentuates his trim waist.

"Give me a turn," I instruct, and he does so with hands on his hips in what I can only assume is the only pose Grady knows. He doesn't give off model energy, and I hope to God the man is never in a situation where he has to walk a runway for his life. Though the shirt fits like it was made for him, the fabric hugging his broad shoulders. I quickly pick my jaw up off the floor before he turns around, schooling my face into casual indifference. "It looks great. Why do you look like you're wearing a shirt made of poison ivy?"

"It's kind of ... stuffy." He shifts around as if he's allergic to looking good. I uncross my legs and stand up from the bench where I was seated. I approach him to assess the outfit.

"It's the way you've styled it. Or rather, haven't styled it," I say. "You've got the top button done up. Here, let me help." I get close enough to him to adjust the buttons on his shirt, and as I do, I feel my movements slow down, like somehow Grady's gravitational pull fucks with time. He's looking down at me, and his breath is a soft puff of warmth on my fingers.

"You don't have to undo too many. Otherwise, you'll look like the mannequins in the window, and yeah, I admit they're a little douchey." I undo the first button and clear my throat, backing away from him. "There, take a look now," I say.

Grady turns to the mirror. He's standing a little taller now and the way his body language has transformed in front of me sends a zing of electricity down my spine. This is the side of him that he showed me in bed the other night. The confident, take charge, and take no shit version of Grady that he needs to embody if he's going to walk into that council meeting and get what he wants. The way he's turning in the mirror a few times, admiring what he sees in himself tells me he realizes why it's important, too.

We finish up at the store and wander back out into the mall, bags in hand. Grady bought more than he initially thought he would, and I credit myself and my impeccable sense of style for that.

"Spencer!"

I turn on my heel at the sound of my name to find Eleanor walking toward me, arm extended in a wave. She's the chair of the Heartwood tourism board, and the last person I expected to see today.

"Hey, Eleanor." I greet her with a warm smile and a one-armed hug. She's been nothing but gracious and welcoming since I arrived. The brand deal with WanderLuxe played in Heartwood's favour too, and she's gushed about it non-stop.

"What a coincidence seeing you here. Oh, hi Grady," she says, and Grady gives her a curt nod in greeting. Eleanor turns back to me, eyes wide with excitement. "I was just telling my husband this morning how much I'm looking forward to having you for dinner this week."

The dinner. Right. I totally forgot that I agreed to have dinner with her and her husband later this week. Eleanor wanted to thank me for what I've done to promote Heartwood.

"Yes, absolutely, me too," I fake, my voice rising to that octave I use when I'm feigning excitement. Eleanor's eyes flick towards Grady, and then back to me.

"Feel free to bring a date if you'd like," she says behind a hand that is meant to conceal what she's saying. I catch Grady looking down at his feet awkwardly, a smile playing on his lips.

"Uh, Grady and I aren't—" I start, but Eleanor interrupts me.

"Well, he's more than welcome if you change your mind." She checks her watch quickly before adding, "I've gotta run, but we'll see you soon. Hopefully both of you." She saunters off with a wink in my direction.

"She doesn't have anything to do with the event you're planning, does she?" Grady asks once she's out of earshot.

"No, I totally forgot that I agreed to have dinner with her," I say, contemplating how I need to rearrange my schedule to fit everything in.

"Can I propose another phase?"

"Oh no," I protest. "I am the decider of the phases of Grady. We can't just go running amok here throwing in phases willy-nilly." I've earned myself a glare, and the eye contact makes my face heat.

"You said yourself that you're making it up as you go."

Fuck.

"Fine," I huff. "What is your idea?"

"Bring me to dinner with Eleanor." I'm already shaking my head before he can get the words out.

It's a good idea, maybe even a great idea, and I can see why Grady would suggest it. But it means going to dinner with him, and that is strictly against the rules.

"No way. No. Absolutely not."

"She already said I was welcome to come," he counters.

"Yes, and she meant as a plus one. We are not in a relationship, so I cannot bring you as my date. We'll find another way to win her over."

"You can go out with someone and not be *dating* them, Spencer," Grady argues. My mouth twists to one side as I consider the potential ramifications and the ripple effect this might have. Sure, would it be helpful to get the chair of the tourism board to back Grady at the council meeting? Absolutely. Would it look great in my portfolio to show that my plan is garnering support for Grady already? Yes, in a way that I don't think I can reasonably say no to. Am I willing to make exceptions to my rules in order to achieve it?

"Okay," I say and Grady's expression lifts. "On one condition."

"Cool. More rules." His voice is monotone and unimpressed.

"No boyfriendy stuff. It's not a real date, so don't act like it is."

"Nope. You already agreed to the date," he says, and he takes a step forward so we're close enough to be sharing breath. "And if I'm taking you out, even if it is just to Eleanor's house, I'm not going to half-ass it."

"We agreed on those rules, Grady. *You* agreed to them." I'm getting angry now, my hands forming fists at my sides.

"I'm just about ready to say fuck the rules, Rebel. After all, aren't rules meant to be broken?" His lip lifts into a smirk and I hate it. Whatever that perfectly fitting button-down awoke within Grady, I hate it. I hate that it makes me want to kiss him, right here, right in the middle of a goddamn shopping mall.

Grady and I hit a few more stores after our encounter with Eleanor, and I struggle to keep my thoughts under control as he tries on outfit after outfit that makes me want to rip them right off his chiseled body. My mind has been like a runaway train, careening into territory that I actively want to avoid.

We're going on a date. A fake date, mind you. At least to me. Grady seems to think otherwise, despite my best efforts. I'm mentally contemplating the ugliest possible outfit I could wear to deter him when he interrupts my thoughts as if he could read them.

"I think I'm sufficiently outfitted. You Queer Eye'd the shit out of me today. I need to repay you," he says. *He can repay me by staying the hell away before I completely cave,* I think, but I refrain from saying. "Let's find you something nice to wear."

"Oh, I don't need anything. This trip was for you." I wave him off.

"You'll need something to wear on our date." Before I can protest, Grady has me by the hand and is leading me towards a far too fancy, and far too expensive, store. "Pick something out for yourself." I glance around nervously.

"You don't have to do this. You don't have to spend money on me, really. This place is way too expensive," I point out, noting the way the saleswoman is looking me up and down, assessing my financial status by the distressed jeans and Birkenstock sandals I'm wearing over bunched-up wool socks.

"I can spend whatever I want on you. Besides, this is the only way I really enjoy shopping. I hate looking for things for myself. But for other people ..."

I scrunch up my face as I weigh Grady's suggestion. He's gone along with my prodding today, despite his initial pushback. If all he wants is to buy me a dress, the least I can do is try one on. Besides, it might be fun to play dress up. Even if I'm not going to let him buy anything.

I peruse the racks, looking for something that might catch my eye. My gaze stops on this stunning boatneck ruched midi dress. The pattern is a faint tie-dye of pastel pinks, purples, and rusty orange. It's gorgeous.

"Try it on," Grady says, following my line of sight to the dress. He picks it up and hands it to me, and I reluctantly accept.

"Just this one, but you're not getting it for me." Grady shrugs like it's not my decision anyways, and I glare at him as I make my way to ask Judgy McGee for a fitting room.

I pull the dress on and zip up the back with ease, the fabric conforming to the shape of my body. I turn around, twisting to look at how the back accentuates my curves, and I decide not to leave the fitting room and show Grady. Sure, the dress lifts my ass in a way that defies gravity, but I actively stay away from anything figure-hugging. To other people, I have a great body; I'm tall and relatively lean. But when I look in the mirror, all I can see are the flaws.

"Come out and show me," Grady says through the curtain.

"No," I say.

"Look, I had to show you all the clothes I tried on." I can tell by his voice that he's standing directly on the other side of the thick curtain, waiting for me to open it. Which I won't.

"I'm going to take it off now," I say, reaching my hand over to grab the zipper when Grady swings the curtain to one side. "Hey!" I squeal. "What if I had been naked in here?"

"Well, you're not. And it's nothing I haven't seen anyway," Grady says teasingly, but his face falls when he stops to take me in, standing in the dress he practically forced me to try on.

"It's a little too snug, don't you think?" I start. "I would need some military-grade Spanx if I'm going to pull this dress off."

"Spencer, you look ..." Grady's voice trails off, and I know it's because he can't find words that won't hurt my feelings.

"It doesn't matter how I look, you're not buying it for me anyway." I check the price tag once again and see a couple too many digits before the decimal point. "There's no way."

Grady stands up and comes over to meet me by the mirror where I'm twisted around staring at the price tag on the side of the dress. His impossibly large hand pushes mine away from the tag and covers it as he rests his hand on my hip.

"Spencer, there is nothing too expensive when it comes to you. Look at all you're doing for me." Grady is standing close behind me now, looking at me in the mirror over my shoulder. His eyes roam over my reflection as he takes in the curves of my body. "I know I've been resistant to change, but the feeling I had today when I was trying on the clothes you picked out for me... I see it now, how much of a difference it can make to your confidence when you put in a little effort. I have more hope today than I did yesterday that we might be able to make a difference for Heartwood. That's all thanks to you."

I don't speak the words that I have on the tip of my tongue because Grady has dipped his mouth down to my ear, and I can no longer think about anything else but his breath on my neck as he whispers, "So you'll let me buy this dress for you. Not just as a thank you. But because you look so fucking stunning in it that I'm fairly certain it was made for you and only you."

CHAPTER 11
GRADY

Spencer has fallen asleep next to me in the passenger seat. It must be true about what they say, that if you want kids to fall asleep on a car ride, get them McDonald's fries. Spencer finished hers about five minutes into the trip back to Heartwood and it was only another five before her head was lolled to one side, mouth open. That pretty little mouth. What I would do to that exquisite mouth.

She rouses as we turn off the highway and the vehicle slows through the exit.

"Have a nice nap?" I ask as she lifts her hand to her mouth to check for any drool.

"What time is it?" she croaks, her voice groggy.

"Ah, almost five," I answer. Spencer looks around, a little disoriented.

"I'm fucking starving," she says, and I bark out a laugh.

"Starving? You just ate." I remind her of the ten-piece chicken nuggets and fries she slammed back as we left the mall earlier.

"That was almost two hours ago. And now I'm hungry," she says.

"Okay, okay. Fair enough." I do a quick shoulder check and

flick on my signal, turning onto the road that leads through Heartwood and toward the campground. We drive through town once again, and the sight of the Urban Ember sign makes me bristle as we pass by.

When we reach the familiar long winding road, I keep driving until we come to my driveway, and I hang a left. I could make that turn with my eyes closed.

"What are we doing here? Aren't you taking me home?" Spencer asks. She knows where we are. She's been to my place before. I admit that I have ulterior motives for bringing her back here. If she gets to have her multi-phase plan, I get to have my own —my multi-phase plan to win over Spencer Sinclair.

"I'm going to make you dinner." My statement is firm, no room for debate. I don't know exactly when I decided that I wanted to win her affection beyond just a casual hook-up. It was sometime between the moment I flung open the curtain and saw her standing there in that gorgeous dress, and the moment she let out a soft snore in the passenger seat. Spencer is both an unattainable goddess and so very human that I have an insatiable need to protect her.

"I have food back at the camper," she protests.

"Cup O'Noodles isn't a proper dinner." I put the car in park on the drive and get out before Spencer can say anything else. She doesn't put up more of a fight. Instead, she gets out after me and follows me up to the front door.

I hesitate a moment as I open it and step back to let her inside. The moment is reminiscent of the first night that Spencer stayed here. The one that has lingered with me, making me wish it had gone differently. Wish I hadn't waited to kiss her then. The ghost of missed sexual opportunities past, still haunting me. Maybe had I not hesitated, things between Spencer and I could be different, and I wonder if I missed a crucial window to evade the friend zone.

Minutes later, Spencer is seated at my kitchen island, sipping on a glass of red wine as I prepare one of my all-time favourite dishes for her—a chicken sausage orzo with spinach and sundried tomatoes. The room fills with the warm fragrance of garlic as I add it to the sausage cooking in the pan.

"You're such a natural in the kitchen," Spencer says. I wipe my hands off on the towel I've thrown over my shoulder, place a lid on the pan, and turn back towards her. I shrug.

"I do own a restaurant and bar," I say with a chuckle. "And I grew up cooking for my brothers. Had to learn at a young age. There isn't much in town in the way of take-out, so I made do with what I could find at the grocery store," I explain. Her shoulders slump slightly.

"All I had growing up was instant noodles," she admits. "Not just instant noodles, but easy stuff. Things I could throw in the oven on my own when my mom wasn't home, which was often."

Her words grab at my heart, thinking about her alone, making herself a sad frozen meal. The fact that she had to fend for herself so young.

"Do you want to help me? I'll show you some things," I offer, though I say it somewhat selfishly, wanting to give her a reason to come around to the other side of the island, wanting to be close to her. To not have this barrier between us.

"Okay. But I have to tell you, I really have no idea what I'm doing." She rounds the kitchen counter, sweeping her crimson waves up into a ponytail as she nears me. I gesture to the onion I have set out on the cutting board.

"We can start here. Ever diced an onion?"

Spencer shakes her head, her brows knitting together. I hand her the end of the knife, but as she takes it from me, I hold my hand over hers, guiding it over the onion that I've already roughly chopped in half. "It's easiest if you cut it in half first, and then just make small slices."

She nods, and I remove my hand from hers, watching her follow my instructions.

"I feel like such an idiot that I don't know how to do this," she says with a self-deprecating laugh.

"You're not an idiot, Spencer. Far from it."

"I mean, I don't have a university degree or anything. Isn't this what they teach you in university?"

"No, you have to go back for a master's degree in chopping onions," I deadpan, earning myself a laugh from Spencer that warms the kitchen more than my cooking ever could. She throws her head back when she does it, and it rests on the soft spot between my shoulder and my peck where I'm standing behind her. My heart quickens, thundering against my ribs.

"Careful, watch." I turn her attention back to the knife she's holding. "Don't cut yourself."

She goes quiet again and continues cutting it like I showed her. The only sound she makes is a sniffle, though the fragrance isn't particularly strong.

"Are you okay?" I ask.

"Someone's cutting onions in here." She gives me a wry smile that doesn't quite reach her watery eyes.

"Boo. Bad joke," I say with a playful nudge of her arm. I move towards the stove again, adding it to the pan with the fragrant garlic, and drizzling some more oil over it.

"I like how you do that."

"What?"

"Make me feel like I'm not stupid for not knowing something." My lungs hollow out at her statement. At the fact that having someone be patient with her, not make her feel less than, is somehow a foreign concept to her.

"It's not hard. You're not stupid, Spencer," I say, regarding her across the kitchen. She's quieter than usual as she considers my words. No quippy remark at that. "So, you never filled me in on phase two of the plan," I say, shifting the topic. I lean on the edge of the counter with both hands. Spencer's eyes dart towards my forearms as they flex. I love when I catch her looking at me like that. It gives me a shred of hope that I still have a chance with her.

"I don't think you're going to like it based on how you reacted to the suggestion earlier." Spencer returns to her barstool and gulps the last of her wine down. I instinctively reach across the counter and grab the bottle to top off her glass.

"Try me," I say. "I'm feeling more open-minded now."

"Okay." Spencer hesitates, searching for just the right words to position her suggestion. "I really think it would benefit you to revamp the bar, just a bit. Not an overhaul, but elevate it a little."

I take it back. I'm not that open-minded. The thought of changing the Whisky Jack makes me grind my molars together. I made the bar the way it is for a reason. The whole point is that it's not elevated. It's accessible, it's for everyone. It's how I honour my dad in the only way I can.

"The Whisky Jack has always done well here," I explain. "My customers like it just the way it is."

"That's because they've never had anything else," Spencer says, and I hate to admit that she has a point. Sure, there are other places to eat in Heartwood, but they aren't quite the same as the bar. "I hate to even go here, but if you don't win against Carter and he manages to push through the motion to open Urban Ember, you will need to rebrand it anyway just to compete."

"I need time to think about it," I say, but I know time is something that we're running out of, and fast. If we want to do this, it needs to happen quickly. I pivot over to the stove, turning my back to Spencer as I dish out her food.

"Just don't take too long," she adds, like I need reminding. I hand her the bowl of steaming orzo and sausage and bring my own over to sit on the barstool next to hers. She takes the first bite, blowing on it carefully before putting it in her mouth. Her eyes roll back as she savours the flavours of the herbs.

"See," she says, pausing to finish her bite. "This is the kind of thing you should include on the menu. This is incredible. Instead, you just keep slinging burgers."

"Well, *I* don't sling the burgers. Doug does that. And everyone loves a burger and a beer."

"I'm not saying you have to get rid of your burgers. Just add a few more options to the mix. We could redecorate inside so that it feels a bit fresher. Keep the homey, cozy vibes, but bring in some nicer decor. More whisky bar, less dive bar."

I mull it over as I work on my bite of food.

"I want to show you something, and you can't get mad," she says, reaching down to her purse to pull out her phone. She opens her social media page and clicks on a picture I didn't know she had snapped. It's a great shot of the hand-carved wooden sign that hangs above the door of the bar. But it's not the picture she wants to show me. She clicks on the first comment, and when she does, a whole lot more open up with it. "Just read through some of those."

My eyes skim through the comment section and my heart drops. Remarks like '*Heartwood is such a cute spot, wish there were more places to eat,*' and worse, '*I liked the Whisky Jack, just seemed kinda dingy.*'

They go on and on, listing reasons why the Whisky Jack didn't satisfy them the way they thought it would have. It feels like a kick in the balls. All the work I put in to try and make people feel comfortable at the bar, and this is what they really think.

"Fuck. Reading them all laid out like that, it's kind of brutal," I admit.

"Sorry." Spencer apologizes even though it's not necessary. It wasn't her who wrote those things. "I thought you should see it for yourself." I release a breath through tight lips.

"Let me hear your big plan," I say, but Spencer looks distracted suddenly, her eyes glazed over and zoned out on her phone screen. "What is it?"

"Nothing." She clicks the screen off and sets it down on the counter in front of her. "Just my mom. She wanted to inform me that she's booked herself in for a boob job."

"A boob job? I can't imagine that anyone related to you should ever need to get work done. Not that anyone *needs* to get work done ..." I backtrack.

"I know what you meant," Spencer reassures me. "She doesn't need to get work done. She never has. This is the thing with my mother. She picks all the wrong guys who treat her like trash, and then she assumes that it's something wrong with her. Now with my father about to marry someone twenty years her junior ..."

"She's feeling a little insecure." I finish Spencer's thought right as her phone starts to ring on the counter in front of us. The name Marla pops up, along with a photo of her that is the spitting image of Spencer. The same red hair, the same green eyes and gorgeous smile, just thirty years older and a little more botoxed.

"Hey, Marla," she answers, and I can just make out her mom's voice on the other end asking if the service is better now. "Yeah, I can hear you. What's up?"

They sound almost identical, raspy in the way that makes my toes curl when Spencer says my name.

"Don't ever get married, Spencer. I swear to God. It will only make you miserable. And that's before you get divorced. It's even worse once he runs off with some hussy and trades you in for a younger model. That's all men care about, I swear." Her voice is a faint buzz against Spencer's cheek, but I make out most of what she's said and cringe. Spencer doesn't miss my visible wince at her words.

"Don't worry about me, Mom. I'm not planning on getting married any time soon. It's hard to get married when I'm not even dating." I wince again, and this time she doesn't seem to catch it, thankfully.

"Good. Did you get those pictures I sent? Dr. Bloomfield wanted some inspo pics for my new boobs."

I can't be certain, but I could swear I heard her say she sent

Spencer pictures of boobs. I'm praying she said *boots*, and that Dr. Bloomfield is a doctor in the same way that Dr. Scholl's is a doctor.

"No, I haven't looked yet," Spencer says, her voice flat, tired. "I'll let you know what I think of them later."

"Okay, just text me back with your favourite."

"Will do. Bye." Spencer puts the phone down and stares at me. "Want to look at pictures of boobs with me?"

I choke on my beer.

"For your mom? No thanks. Just leave me out of this one."

"I may not have a degree, but at least I'm not overhauling my boobs for a mediocre husband. I can get by with my looks for now. Although, my thirties are approaching rather quickly." She says it as if getting older is a bad thing, like aging is something to be avoided. I don't know how to tell her that aging is a gift. That, as someone who lost their mom young, I wish I could tell her how precious every passing year is. "These wrinkles are getting deeper by the day."

Spencer goes back to eating, and it's silent between us for a moment before I decide that I can't let that statement go. My fork clanks on my plate as I set it down.

"You are beautiful, Spencer. I would be willing to bet anything that even at a hundred years old you'll still be turning heads. You would certainly turn mine."

"You aren't the first to tell me that, Grady. Most of the guys that want to get in my pants tell me I'm beautiful at one point or another. They don't mean it. Even if they do, my looks will fade. It happens to everyone. Then what will I have going for me?" Spencer dips her chin, dabbing her mouth with her napkin like that's the reason why she's refusing to look at me. It's crushing. How could this gorgeous, incredible woman not see in herself what everyone else does—what I do? She's stunning, but she's so much more than that. I turn on my stool to face her.

"You have more to offer than your looks, Spencer. University degree or not," I say.

Her gaze is still fixed on her dish, but I need her to look at me. I need her to know how much I mean it. Half a second after Spencer sets her napkin down on the counter, I grip the seat of her stool and swivel it, pulling her in so that her legs are positioned in between mine. I try not to think of her thighs grazing mine as I stare into her eyes which are wide with surprise.

"I'm not talking about your looks," I say, my voice lowering an octave. My eyes flick down in time to see goosebumps forming on Spencer's arms, and it's so fucking satisfying to see her have a physical response to me. "I mean, of course you're stunning. There's a reason that I'm so fucking attracted to you that I can barely hold myself back from you even now." I clear my throat, past the lump that's forming there. "You're beautiful because you're strong, you're witty, and smart. You grab life by the balls and make every fucking day count. You are not a tornado, Spencer. You are a whirlwind. You're passionate and fierce, but you don't leave destruction in your wake. You leave people better than they were before, their lives turned upside down in the best way possible."

I speak the words that Spencer needs to hear, the ones I can no longer contain in my heart. Suddenly, she's leaning forward, her hands on either one of my thighs, and she's kissing me. Her lips are salty as a tear escapes and trickles down her cheek, but I don't wipe it away. Her tongue finds the crease of my lips and parts them. She tastes sweet and tangy from the wine. I let myself get drunk on her.

Soon, we're both standing; Spencer on her tiptoes and me bending down to meet her. Our lips are more desperate now, and our hands roam each other's bodies with urgency. I'm tempted to lift her into my arms and cart her off down the hall to my bedroom but ...

"What about the rule? One night. Your boyfriend ban." I pull away, breathless. I'm hoping for an answer I know I'm not going to get. All I want is for her to say, 'Screw the boyfriend ban.' I want her to say that she doesn't care about it. I'm hoping it's one of those flexible rules, like the other two boundaries we've already crossed.

"The boyfriend ban is only a problem if you want to be my boyfriend," Spencer rasps.

It's as though the air gets sucked out of my lungs, the feeling of disappointment crushing. I can't say anything more, because now she's lowering herself to the floor and unbuckling my belt. My mind slows, words refusing to form. By the time I have an inkling of a response, Spencer has pushed my pants down around my ankles and she's parting her lips around the head of my already hard cock.

And now the only word I can think of is *fuck*.

Spencer takes more of my length, her lips wrapping around me while her tongue flicks the sensitive underside of my shaft. I brace one hand on the counter to steady myself, and one hand wraps around Spencer's ponytail, pulling it firmly.

"God, you have no idea how many times I've imagined fucking your mouth."

Spencer lifts her eyes to meet mine while she sucks deeper, longer, my head touching the back of her throat. She watches me, my hips bucking in response, her eye contact intensifying the sensation of her tongue on my cock.

I thought I had seen the extent of Spencer's beauty today in that store, but here, on her knees, she is a beauty not of this world. I would do anything to be worthy of it, of her.

She keeps her mouth around me, and *hums*. She fucking hums. The vibration at the back of her throat makes my knees buckle, just about careening over my edge. Before I find my release, I'm hauling her up off the floor, kicking my pants off, and lifting her off the ground.

"I wasn't finished with you!" she cries as I carry her down the hall to my bedroom.

"I'm far from finished," I say, tossing her on the bed. "But all I could think about back there is how I missed the taste of your perfect little cunt."

I remove Spencer's bottoms as she swiftly removes her top, baring her breasts to me. She wastes no time climbing over me as I lie back on the bed. She straddles my hips while she rolls her nipples between her fingers. Spencer throws her head back and lets out a moan as she rocks her hips on my hard length.

"I told you, Spencer, I want to taste you," I remind her, my voice lowering as I rasp. "So come here and sit on my face like a good girl."

Spencer does as she's told, maybe for the first time in her life, and positions herself over me, hovering over my mouth.

"Sit," I growl, pushing her hips down, my tongue finding her slit. Spencer jolts forward, the sudden sensation causing her to lose her balance until her hands find the edge of the wooden headboard. She steadies herself, and her body slackens, using the leverage to rock her weight between me and the bed. I let her find her rhythm, and then I match it, using my tongue to provide counter pressure on her clit.

Spencer moans as the repetitive motion brings her closer to the orgasm I can feel building. Her eyelids become heavy with ecstasy, fluttering as the rest of her face slackens.

"I'm going to ..." she cries, and the sudden release wracks her body, her core tightening, her body shaking. I catch her in my arms before she falls, and lower her onto the bed next to me. She comes to rest next to me, the tension leaving her muscles, and I bring myself on top of her.

I kiss her once, twice. My mouth is tender on hers as she catches her breath, and I slide myself into her tight opening, still pulsing.

I gave her what she wanted from me, an orgasm and nothing more. But that's not what I want. I want Spencer to feel how badly I need her, how being with her is the single most important thing to me. I'm going to show her how it feels when I look her in the eyes and make love to her.

CHAPTER 12
SPENCER

GRADY and I are lying next to each other under his duvet, while the last rays of sunlight cast a golden haze over the room. His eyes are closed, dark lashes resting softly on his cheek. I search his face for an answer to the question that popped into my mind after I came down off my last orgasmic high. The question that hasn't left me alone. Why did that last time feel so different? Why am I lying here, staring at his face, the pink flush in his cheeks, the strong line of his jaw? Why does my chest feel like it's been pried open, and the only way to soothe the raw vulnerability is to curl myself into Grady's body?

Sex, for me, has always been fun, but this was different. This was layered. Grady looked me in the eyes, his strong hand cupping my jaw so that despite all of my instincts to look away, I had to peer back. To let him see me. He fucked me slowly, gently, letting each thrust go deeper until he had reached my inner sanctum. The part of me that I keep under lock and key. He fucked me until all of my pent-up feelings about my mother, about myself, disintegrated into nothing. All that was left was me and Grady. It was terrifying, yet I didn't balk at it.

Until now.

Now the heat of the moment has dissipated, and I'm feeling exposed.

Grady's eyelashes flutter as he opens them, catching me staring at him.

"What are you thinking about?" Grady says, his tone open and soft, still holding space for me and all of my fucked up, tangled mess of emotions. Ready to confront the swirling thoughts before I am.

"I'm thinking that I need to pee," I say, getting up and grabbing the first piece of clothing I can find off the floor. When I slip it on, I realize it's Grady's T-shirt. The hem comes down to the tops of my thighs, so I don't take it off to pad down the hallway to find the bathroom.

I open the door directly across the hall from Grady's room and stand there, suddenly frozen in place, until I hear him approach me from behind.

His arm wraps around my waist and he buries his face in my hair.

"You know my room has an ensuite," he mumbles. I don't answer, because I'm stunned. What I'm standing in front of looks like a little girl's nursery.

The walls are wallpapered with delicate florals in pinks and blues, and cornflower blue board and batten wrap the bottom portion all the way around the room. There's a crib in one corner, a rocking chair in another, and on the far wall, a bookshelf already filled with books.

I pull away from Grady slightly. I can't tell if he has a secret family, a child he's never told me about, or an entire secret identity.

"If you're thinking that this room is for a child of mine, then it's not what you think," he starts, and I turn to face him, his arms still wrapped around me.

"I don't know what to think ..." I frantically search his face for an answer as my mind races with every other possible explanation for this. I come up short.

See? My brain screams at me. *This is why you shouldn't trust people. You never know when they're going to tell you they have a secret family.*

"Well, if you're thinking that I'm crazy because I turned a spare room in my house into a bedroom for my niece-to-be, then you'd be right on the money."

I back away at what he's just told me, not out of hurt or betrayal, just surprise. I wander around the room and take in the folded linens in the crib.

"Are you planning on kidnapping her?" I ask, and Grady laughs with a smile that crinkles the corners of his eyes.

"No, but I'm sure it will be difficult to resist." His expression falls as he brings his hand up to rub the back of his neck, and colour blooms across his cheeks. "Ally and Mason are always so busy with the clinic. I don't know if they'll be able to take much time off. I offered to babysit for them regularly. It's why I hired Finn. I'll be able to leave the bar a bit more and help them out. I just want her to feel at home here."

I swallow past the lump that has formed in my throat. Ally is the one person in this world that I love more than anything, and now, by proxy, that extends to her daughter. The fact that Grady has done this ... I can't fathom it. He says that he doesn't know how to show people how much he cares, but this. This right here is Grady's heart exploded all over this beautiful, delicate, soft room. No one in my life has ever gone out of their way to make me feel welcome, or like I have a space to call my own. The best I got was a curtain around a couch in some middle-aged guy's basement, and only if my mom remembered to ask.

I'm walking the perimeter of the room, taking in every word of what he's saying and trying not to let my emotions get the better of me. I stop at the bookshelves in the corner that he's stocked with every book a kid could ask for, and sit down on the rug.

"You know, I always dreamt of having something like this," I say, running my finger along the colourful spines, and taking out an old classic, *Where the Wild Things Are*. I thumb through the pages, thinking about how much I related to Max as a kid. A wild imagination, a heart for adventure, but an insatiable need to return home.

"What, a library?" Grady asks, cocking his head to one side.

"No," I answer simply. "A room."

Grady is quiet for a moment, unsure of what to say. I've just opened up about a very tumultuous time in my childhood, a part of me that is so far from his own reality, and I'm sure it will be too much for him.

"Spencer ..." His voice has dropped in pitch. "You never had a room?" His tone reveals the realization like a heavy weight has been placed across his shoulders.

"Nope. Well, occasionally. When we had enough money for a place. But I never decorated or anything because it was almost always a temporary space." I try to say it with as much neutrality and nonchalance as I can muster. Even after almost three decades of living in my reality, the wound still feels fresh, raw. I'm still flipping through the pages, examining the illustrations. Anything so I don't have to look Grady in the eye. "Mostly we slept at my mom's boyfriends' houses. It wouldn't have been so bad if any of them ever cared about me or remotely wanted me sleeping on their couch."

"Well, how would you have decorated your bedroom, if you could have?" he asks, and he comes to sit beside me on the rug.

"I've thought about it a lot," I admit. "That's how I used to fall asleep at night, lying on whatever lumpy couch I could find. I'd try to build a mental map of a room and imagine myself there, cozy in my bed." It feels odd telling Grady about this. I said no personal questions, yet here we are, and I'm offering it to him without prompting. Friends can share things like this with each other, right?

"The walls are a dark, cozy green," I start. I haven't let myself think about that bedroom for years now. I told myself that I had made it on my own, so I no longer needed it as a coping mechanism. I close my eyes and let my mind find that room again, trying to recall all the details. A feeling of warmth washes over me like it always did. "It's moody, but offset by the fact that everything else, all the decor and accents, would be baby pink. And there would be so many florals, like walking through a rose garden. I always imagined fairy lights across the ceiling, and I'd pretend that I was lying in bed staring up at them. I'd save those fairy lights for the worst nights." I pause, because the memory of that loneliness is still painful. I like to think that I am who I am in spite of those nights.

"I always pictured myself in a white bed, with a proper headboard and footboard, and there were always more blankets than I could use. I'd have one of those canopies over it. But more than that, I used to—" My voice cracks. The last detail of the room that I can't get out. When I glance up at Grady's face, his expression is soft and open. A safe space. So, I continue.

"I used to imagine my mom's room being right next to mine. You remember when you were a kid, and you would go to bed before the adults and you could still hear everyone moving around the house? I used to love listening to my mom and dad up late talking or doing whatever. So, after my dad left and we had to couch surf, I would imagine falling asleep in that room listening to her in there, getting ready for bed. I used to imagine the light from her room casting a glow into the hall. Just enough that I knew she was there. Maybe that sounds pathetic," I say, shrugging off the uncomfortable vulnerability.

"It's not pathetic," he says, though he's looking down into his lap now. "I used to do the same thing after my mom died. The house was always so quiet, even with the four of us boys. I'd hold onto that feeling of listening to my mom around the house. She would hum softly, and it felt like being wrapped in a warm blanket, comforting and cozy. That's why I did this. I want my niece to know the feeling of having her family around her. No matter where she is, if her mom and dad are busy working at the clinic, she can always come here and feel the warmth of people she loves around her."

"She is so lucky to have you for an uncle, Grady." He shrugs off my comment, so I rise from where I'm seated on the floor, and Grady follows. I stretch up, wrapping my arms around his neck. The hem of the T-shirt I'm wearing rises over my thighs. "I mean that. You don't know what I would have given to have one of the men in my life care about me the way you care about her. She's not even been born yet, and here you are, making sure she feels loved. I'm literally jealous of a fetus."

Grady's hands cover the curve of my ass, scooping upwards and lifting me onto my tiptoes as he leans down to kiss me.

"Any man who hasn't realized how special you are is either blind or stupid, Spence," he mutters with a smile against my lips. "All I want to do is show you how special you are." Grady interrupts himself, planting soft kisses on my mouth.

"I want to spoil you."

Another kiss.

"I want to give you all the love you never had."

Another kiss.

"I want to make you come over and over again."

Those few words have my pulse quickening, the pressure growing between my thighs. I take Grady's hand in mine as I pull away from our kiss. Tugging him back towards the bedroom, I flash him a grin over my shoulder. I shove back the thought of the rule that we're breaking now. One night has turned into two, and *willpower* is no longer in my vocabulary.

I turn and sit on the edge of the bed, spreading my legs towards Grady, bared to him as his T-shirt rides up around my waist.

"So eager." Grady's voice dips as he admires my pussy, his gaze motivated. I am eager. So eager, and so, *so* horny. More so than I have ever felt before for a hook-up. The thought is brief, and I don't pause to pay it any attention because Grady has removed his blue-striped boxers, and his cock is rock hard in front of me. My teeth sink into my bottom lip to stop myself from whimpering at the pressure building behind my swollen clit.

The T-shirt lifts over my head, Grady's hands coming to cup my breasts as he pushes me back on the bed. His movements are more hurried now, desperate, and I match his need as he pulls my hips to the edge of the bed. He finds my opening with his tip but doesn't give me what I want. Instead, he drags it in languid movements up and down my slit.

"Don't tease me," I rasp, my back arching with every movement of his tip on my clit.

"I'm not teasing you, Spencer. I'm just getting started," Grady says, the end of his sentence trailing off with a moan as he finally gives me what I want, filling me inch by sweet fucking inch.

Grady leans down toward me, wrapping his hand around the back of my neck as he drives further into me. His eyes never leave mine as our foreheads come together. I thought that it was sex with Grady that I was addicted to, the pure carnal pleasure, yet staring into Grady's eyes, I realize I was wrong. It's him.

"Fuck me like it's your last time," I whisper to Grady, repeating the words I spoke our first night together. I'm free falling. And I need to pull the rip cord.

Something flashes across his hazel eyes for less than a second, almost imperceptible. For the moment it was there, it looked like disappointment. He schools his features, and brushes his lips against mine, bringing his mouth down to my ear. His breath as he whispers sends a shiver through me, and his words make me melt more than they should.

"You and I both know that this isn't the last time, Rebel," he murmurs. "You and I are inevitable, and if you can't see that yet, let me see it for the both of us."

The only noise I'm capable of making in response is a muffled moan as I bury my face into his neck, and he buries himself deeper in me.

Grady slows his movements, but he doesn't stop, and I match his rhythm. Our hips rock against each other creating a delicious friction that warms me through to my very core, my very soul.

We find our release together, our bodies melting into each other. The feeling overtakes me and I want to be closer. I want to feel him in all my cracks, my broken spaces, in between each of my cells.

When Grady and I finally pull ourselves apart, unravelling our limbs and untangling the less tangible parts of ourselves from one another, we lie back in bed. There are no sounds except the occasional creak of the old house settling on its foundation as the temperature outside drops. Moonlight casts shadows on our faces through the window, lighting up the high points of our contented smiles.

Contentedness. That's the soft, supple emotion that has settled within me. It's probably just the endorphins, the oxytocin coursing through my veins. A physical response to a physical feeling. A human body having a human experience.

Not because of the way my eyes stung with held-back tears as Grady gazed down at me, seeing me as I've never been seen before. Not because of the way Grady claimed me, or because of how confident he was that what we shared is not over. No, those feelings are not the cause of my contentment. Those feelings are terrifying. Allowing those feelings would be naïve, ignorant to the path of destruction all the Sinclair women leave in the wake of their love lives, the way I leave a path of destruction, whether Grady chooses to see that or not.

My emotional capacity is for sex and sex only. I have proven that to myself time and time again. It's better to be upfront about that right from the start.

"I should go home," I whisper in the dark.

"What? You want to go home?" Grady brings a hand up to

brush a piece of hair away that had fallen over my face. The sensation of his calloused fingertips on my cheek warms my skin, but the tenderness with which he did it makes my heart drop. I made a promise to myself; no relationships. Sleeping over is the first step into relationship territory. "Are you okay? Did I do something to make you feel—"

"No, nothing like that," I interrupt him, my voice still hushed. "I think we need to re-establish some rules," I say, the only way I know how to protect myself in these situations. "You know, before things get out of hand."

"Out of hand? All I want is to get out of hand with you."

Fuck. This has already gone too far, and as I suspected, I'm the only one now who can see it for what it is.

"No strings, remember? That's the only rule we have left. We can do this, but there's no expectations. Let's call it a friends-with-benefits situation." Deep down, I know friends-with-benefits is still risky. I don't trust Grady to keep his feelings in check, but I don't want this to end yet.

"Whatever you need, Spencer," Grady says. "You don't have to worry about me." He makes an *X* over his heart like he did that first night, a promise to keep it guarded. Okay. Maybe this will work.

CHAPTER 13
GRADY

STEAM HISSES as I throw a handful of prawns into the sizzling frying pan. I give it a shake and set it back down on the stove, before I turn around and jot down the last few ingredients I added. The aroma of garlic permeates the air making my mouth water.

It's just me in the industrial kitchen at the back of the Whisky Jack this morning. The gas range heats the space, and a bead of sweat forms on my temple despite the fresh, dewy air wafting in through the back door.

Spencer was right the other night. Perhaps it's time to uplevel, to give people a reason to come to the Whisky Jack that isn't because we're the only sit-down restaurant in town. So, I'm here before opening, testing out some ideas I had after I took Spencer home.

Developing recipes has always been a hobby of mine, one that I haven't indulged in for a long while. Between running the bar and coaching Little League, I haven't found the time. I forgot how satisfying it is when a recipe comes together. Not only that, when you can serve it to someone else and see how they savour that very first bite. That look of pure ecstasy as they experience a new combination of flavours is what I live for. That was the look on Spencer's face when I cooked for her, and it reignited something in me.

My head is elsewhere though, because I have a different image seared into my brain. The look on Spencer's face when I was buried to the hilt inside her sparked something in me, too. It felt almost forbidden, to indulge in a feeling so sweet, so delicious.

Then, she told me she wanted to go home, and the spark snuffed out. Extinguished, but not forgotten. Whatever this is between us, it's real. I feel it in my bones, in every fibre of my being. The connection we have is like a living, breathing thing. It's only a matter of time before she sees it, too.

The corner of my eye catches a familiar flash of red hair before I hear the knock on the door. I glance up from the fresh herbs I'm chopping to find Spencer, peeking around the corner from the alley out back.

"Knock knock," she says, as if actually knocking wasn't enough. "I swung by the house this morning but obviously you weren't home, so I figured I'd try here. Can I come in, or is this entrance for staff only?"

"No, come in. It's for you, too." I gesture for her to enter, and wipe my hands on my apron. My gaze flicks down to Spencer's arms as she waltzes in through the door. She's carrying a heavy-looking binder under one arm and a large tote slung over her shoulder. A welcome cool breeze wafts in behind her. She smells like springtime, sweet sunshine and wildflowers. She looks like springtime too, eyes deep green like the first signs of life after winter or fresh cut grass.

I realize I've been gawking at her longer than any sane person would when I smell something burning.

"Shit," I say, hurrying back to the pan and shaking the almost-charred prawns around before setting them on a different element and turning off the stove.

"You're here early today," Spencer points out, surveying my workspace, and I try to ignore the fact that she has familiarized herself with my work schedule. "Something smells incredible. Other than whatever is burning."

"Yeah? Hopefully it tastes just as good," I say, stirring the pot of sauce I've been toying with. I think I finally nailed down the right combination of spices. "Do you want to try it?"

I scoop up a small amount of red sauce into a spoon and blow on it gently before holding it out for her. She doesn't take it from me, she just approaches and allows me to feed it to her.

"Fuck me," she mumbles past a full mouth. "That's incredible. What is this for?"

"You got me thinking about what I could do to improve the bar, and this is what I've come up with. I thought about rolling some of these out as specials, see how they land," I explain.

"How would you feel about saving them for our special event?" Spencer flashes me a *pretty please* look, and I'm still trying to figure out what special event she's talking about. I always feel about ten steps behind with Spencer.

"Is this phase three?"

"Still part of phase two," she says, as if it's common knowledge. "The party, remember?"

Ah yes. The party she's told me nothing about.

"Will there be a phase three?" There could be fifty phases for all I know.

"Why yes there is, thanks for asking." She plops the binder down on the prep table and opens it to the tab labelled *Phase Two*. Of course she has a tabbed binder.

"Okay, tell me about this event."

"Here's what I'm thinking. We redecorate a bit, revamp the menu, and host an exclusive re-opening event for the other business owners and the city councillors."

"It's kind of genius," I admit.

"I'm glad you agree." Spencer lifts her chin and flashes me a smile. "But there's a twist. They'll all bring a cocktail and submit it for a contest." I regard her for a moment, and it dawns on me that I still don't know what Spencer's motivation is for working so hard to help me. Part of me hopes that it's just for me, just because she wants to, but the realistic side of me knows there has to be more to it.

"Why are you doing all of this?" I ask, searching her face to try and understand the enigma that she is. She lets out a sigh.

"I wasn't going to say anything because I thought I might jinx it if I said anything too soon," she starts. "I have a job opportunity. A travel company looking for someone to do PR for them. I don't have official PR experience, but they like my marketing style and asked if I could submit a portfolio."

"Ah." My mouth tightens into a line. So, not because of me then.

"I need this job, Grady. I have no contracts lined up, and I'll be in a real bind if I don't figure it out quickly."

"Where is it?" All I can focus on is the fact that it might take Spencer away from me, and when she answers, my worst fear comes true.

"All over the world. The office is based in Vancouver, but they want me to travel on their tours to make sure they're projecting the right image. The salary will be consistent, and it's a permanent gig. No more hustling for short-term contracts, wondering where my next paycheck is coming from."

I suck a breath in through my teeth, stuffing down my feelings about what she's just told me. I have no claim over her, no right to keep her here. There's no denying that this job sounds like an incredible opportunity, and I like Spencer enough to want what's best for her. Yet, I feel like if I can help her with this, if I can just connect with her, be the person she needs me to be, she might just choose me.

"Well, now I need to see what you have on the laptop," I say, nodding towards it.

"Oh, yeah, this," she says as if she's just remembered why she came here in the first place. She doesn't seem like herself this morning; her shoulders appear tense, and her normally raspy, buttery soft voice is tighter. She's guarded, and now I understand with a bit more clarity as to why. She's preparing to leave. "It's the plans I've been working on for the bar. How we'll redecorate."

Spencer pulls out the laptop and sets it down on the small patch of the expansive metal table that doesn't have ingredients and cooking utensils strewn about.

When she opens it, the screen is already on a mood board with inspiration for what looks like a sophisticated, yet laid-back and cozy, whiskey bar. The colours she's chosen are dark and moody, the decor unpretentious yet elevated.

"This is ..." I was nervous about what Spencer was going to come up with when she said she wanted to revamp the bar. I've always been protective over the Whisky Jack, and the experience of my guests. I never want anyone in the town to think that they can't come if they aren't dressed a certain way, or that it's a place for special occasions only. The Whisky Jack is for everyone, and Spencer managed to preserve that feeling perfectly in her version. "You crushed it. Absolutely nailed it. I can't believe you came up with this design."

"I can't take all the credit. Ally and I have a friend from high school who went into interior design, and I may have called in a teensy favour." Any previous apprehension I had about Spencer's plan for the bar dissipates, the knot in my stomach loosening a smidge when I see her vision. It somehow makes the bar feel elevated but still approachable, cool but still cozy. It's exactly how I would have redesigned it if I had the clever thought to do so.

"It doesn't matter. You are incredible." Neither of us says anything for a moment, and Spencer gazes back at me, our eyes locked on one another. I know these are things she doesn't want to hear from me, but I'm done holding back. She clears her throat, a blush spreading from her neck up to her cheeks, before she turns back to look at her computer screen.

"The best part is that we don't have to change everything. The wooden bar stools are perfect the way they are, we'll just get some cozy leather chairs to create more of a conversation space by the fireplace at the back. We'll close for a couple days to get a fresh coat of paint and put up some bookshelves." Spencer turns towards me, adding, "With your new menu, and the new look, the bar just needs a new name."

"A new name?" I sputter in shock at her suggestion. "No. Sorry, Spence. That's where I put my foot down. We're not changing the name."

"The Whisky Jack is a little ... rustic, don't you think?"

"No. I'm not changing it," I protest. It's the one thing I will stand firm on. I won't budge. Not even with Spencer staring up at me with those sparkling green eyes that normally make me melt into a puddle on the ground.

"You said you'd trust me. You need to trust me." She crosses her arms and something inside me is pleading to give in, to let her have this if it will make her happy, like I give in to everyone else. But I just ... can't. It means too much to me.

"I do. I've trusted you on everything we've done together so far," I say. She squints at me again in skepticism. "Just give me this one thing. Please."

"Why is this so important to you?" Her tone shifts into a softer, more inquisitive one. As stubborn as Spencer may be, she genuinely cares about what this means to me. She knows me by now, that although I may present a lighthearted exterior to the world, it doesn't mean that I don't give a shit. I sigh, my shoulders slumping from their defensive position.

"I named it after my father Jack. The bar represents everything he stood for, as strange as that may sound. He was so warm and inviting, non-judgemental, a safe space for anyone no matter their social status. It made him a great doctor. Mason got to keep his legacy alive by taking over his clinic, this is the one thing I can do to honour him, too," I explain, and I realize it's the first time I've told anyone about it. It's always felt heavy to talk about my dad and his death, what it means to me. I've never wanted to burden anyone with it, but sharing it with Spencer feels like I can finally lighten the load.

"Oh, Grady." She breathes, and her eyes are glassy when I finally look up at her. "I'm sorry I pushed, I didn't know. Of course, we'll keep the Whisky Jack," she concedes. I clear my throat to get rid of the lump forming there and turn to put the prawns back on the burner, shaking the pan to swirl them in the garlic butter.

"So, when is this event happening? Who do we need to invite?" I ask once I've refocused on the task at hand.

"No need to worry about that, I already sent out the invitations."

"God, I—this is amazing, Spence." I shake my head in awe of what this woman is capable of. Even if she is doing this for her own reasons, her own end goal, I can't get over the way she just goes out there and does it. I put the pan back down on the stove and turn to face her where she's still standing with her arms crossed over her chest, pushing her breasts up to her neckline. Her hip is now leaning against the shiny metal prep counter. I marvel at her. I'm captivated by her. Her drive and her motivation are contagious. There's something about Spencer that satisfies the part of me that wishes I was more of a go-getter, the way she is.

I take two strides and close the distance between us, bringing my hands up to cup her cheeks. My eyes roam her face, taking in her plump, bow-shaped lips, the freckles smattering her nose. And then I kiss her deeply, inhaling her scent, her very essence. I don't care if Spencer has laid down the law, if she's deemed that we're just casual. If she can go out and get what she wants, so can I.

Finn walks into the kitchen as I'm kissing Spencer and whistles.

"Hey, lovebirds. I don't know if making out in the kitchen is very food-safe."

Spencer yanks herself away from me and straightens her top as if Finn hasn't already caught us red-handed. A flush spreads up her neck and even though she's really fucking adorable when she's embarrassed, I could punch Finn for interrupting. He's a great guy and all, but he has terrible timing.

"I should go." Spencer starts to turn away from me, but I grab her hand, turning her back to face me and plant one last kiss on her perfect mouth.

"I'll see you tomorrow," she says as she pulls away again. "Don't forget about dinner."

"Right," I say, trying to appear casual about the whole thing, but the reality is I haven't forgotten. It's all I've been able to think about since she agreed to let me take her to dinner at Eleanor's. "I'll pick you up at four."

"Dinner isn't until six." Spencer cocks her head at me, her eyebrows twitching together in question.

"I told you I was taking you on a date. I'm going to take you on a date," I tell her. Phase one of my plan to win over Spencer involves an evening of showing her more of my favourite places. The way she visibly fell in love with the sight of Heartwood when I took her to the lookout, the way she talks about wanting somewhere to call home … It makes me wonder if there might be a chance that if I show Spencer all the reasons to love with this place, she might just fall in love with me. Heartwood is such an integral part of who I am, after all. "Be ready at four."

"Got it," she says over her shoulder as she disappears through the back door of the kitchen into the alley.

When I turn around, Finn is leaning against the wall, arms crossed, a grin on his face.

"I don't want to hear a word out of you," I warn. "And keep

this to yourself, okay? We're just friends, and I don't need this getting out all over town."

He throws his hands up in the air and gives me a *keep me out of it* look as he turns and heads out into the front of the bar to start opening in time for lunch.

CHAPTER 14
SPENCER

I CAN'T STOP STARING at their smiling faces. I can't stop staring and feeling like I want to punch them right in the veneered mouths. The picture on my phone screen becomes blurry as tears collect on my lashes. The burning behind my eyes catches me off guard. I strictly don't cry. That is, I don't cry over other people. I bite the inside of my cheek to try and quell the sob that is threatening to burst forth like a tidal wave from the back of my throat. But no matter what I do, a tear escapes and rolls down my cheek.

My dad never looked that happy when he was standing next to my mother and me, but in this picture, he's absolutely beaming. Standing next to his new wife, Sherry, a stunning brunette wearing a cream-coloured silk wedding dress, and her daughter. I guess, his new daughter. The twenty-something that shares nearly all of the same features with her mother. I study her face, wondering what she has that I don't. What makes my father want to put his arm around her protectively like he's doing in the photo, and not me.

They got married so quickly, as if it wasn't even a difficult decision to make. I wonder if my dad spent as long contemplating marrying this woman as he did about leaving my mother and me. Had he even considered the consequences of leaving at all? Did he know that my mother and I would become homeless for so many years without him? An unfamiliar ache radiates behind my sternum, and I rub it with my hand to try and relieve it. I hate this feeling, the sting of betrayal, of rejection.

It's not even about the fact that my father remarried. I might have been able to find some shred of happiness for him. My hatred and blame towards him has certainly dissipated over the years. But it happened so suddenly and without so much as a 'Hey, just wanted to let you know I'm eloping in Italy next week.' An invitation at this point is not something I would ever expect, but it would have been nice to have a heads up, so I wasn't learning about it on social media from my father's new daughter's page. That Marla sent to me without even a warning.

I clicked open her text message and saw a link to Instagram. It's not unusual for her to send me funny videos here and there, but it is unusual for her to send me a picture of my father, grinning next to his new bride, with no explanation except for an eye roll emoji.

What's more unusual for me is the flood of emotions that has consumed me ever since I saw it. I've been so careful, so deliberate, in avoiding this kind of betrayal. I always kind of expected this behaviour from my father. So, my solution was to not reach out, not even attempt to have a relationship with him. But that's an unfortunate fact about life. You don't get to choose your family, as much as you might try. You can build all the walls in your relationships that you want, pretend that what they do doesn't bother you. The cruel fact of the matter is that when it comes to family, some part of you will always care about earning their approval. Whether you want to admit it or not.

I throw my phone down on the bed and pull my fluffy duvet up over my shoulders, cocooning myself in it. I close my eyes as more tears threaten to fall, and I breathe in the warm pine air through the back hatch of the camper that I've left open. Say what you will about living in a van, this has truly become my peace. It's where I've learned to be alone and sit with my feelings. Lying in bed listening to the birds, the trees swaying in the wind, the gravel crunching.

A car engine pulls to a stop. Footsteps through the campsite. Someone is here.

"I'm back here," I call, not leaving the comfort of my bed but quickly wiping the sticky tears from my face. I'm assuming it's Ally. I'd be willing to bet anything that Marla sent her the photo too, and she's come to make sure I'm okay. However, the voice that speaks is deeper than Ally's, and it rumbles through me as they say my name, soothing the remnants of the rage burning in my gut.

"Spencer?" Grady calls once more before finding me around the back of the camper. The moment he lays his soft green-brown eyes on me a line forms between his brows. Concern. I don't need Grady to be concerned about me. I don't need anyone to be concerned about me. I'm fine.

Grady quickly closes the distance between us with two swift steps, and holds my face in his hands, eyes frantically searching for answers. I'm suddenly very aware that I'm still in my pajamas, late into the afternoon.

"What the hell happened? Who do I need to kill?" he asks when I don't say anything, clearly picking up on the fact that if Spencer Sinclair is crying, it's A) for good reason, and B) likely the cause of someone else. A someone else that Grady Landry looks 150 percent ready to murder just to avenge me.

"No one. It's nothing," I stammer.

"It's not nothing, Spence. Anyone or anything who makes you feel this way is not nothing." His voice softens, and he swipes a thumb across my cheek to dry the tear that has collected anew on my lower lashes.

"Just my fucked-up family. That's all. It's nothing that I won't get over. I'll move on, like every other time before."

"Do you want to talk about it? Would that help?" Grady hoists himself up, so he's seated next to me on the edge of my bed again, and the image of him from my first night in Heartwood flashes across my mind. The way he crawled to me, promising that I would scream his name. The way he held true to that promise. A flutter ripples through me and replaces the last of the ache in my chest.

"I don't want to think about it, honestly. I just want a distraction." I drop my gaze, undressing Grady with my eyes.

"Spence, I don't know if now is—"

Before Grady can protest anymore, before he can change the subject so that we're discussing my emotions and treading dangerously close to the line between fuck buddies and something more, I lean towards him and brush my lips gingerly against his.

"Let's not talk anymore," I whisper next to his mouth, and I notice the way his eyelids droop, the part in his lips that is beckoning me to kiss them.

Grady's hand sweeps around to the back of my shoulder blade and he lowers me back down onto the bed, leaning over me on one elbow. His other hand comes up to cup my face.

"Whatever you need, Spencer, I'm here." His voice is soft and low, and I push back the alarm bells that his words have fired off in my head. I focus instead on the fact that Grady is willing to give me whatever I need at this moment, and right now, that's sex. "But I'm not letting you use sex to numb yourself. Let yourself feel, and then let me take care of you."

He presses his warm mouth on mine, sweeping his tongue along my bottom lip. I open myself to him, let him in, the way he's asking. I imagine my ribs cracking open, showing him the parts of me that I keep so heavily guarded. Grady sees it, and the way he kisses me is tender and soft, taking my sensitive parts and holding them gently. Just like the last time, I don't let myself shy away from him. I do what he asks, and I let him take care of me.

I guide him over so I can position myself on top of him, let him see that I'm ready to give myself to him. I sit upright, our hips connecting as I straddle him, and slowly work the buttons of my cotton pajama top until my breasts are exposed, and Grady groans in admiration.

We make short work of the rest of our clothing, and I sink myself onto him, his length already hard between us. This time it's my turn to give to Grady, and I lift my hips, guiding him inside of me.

"You take me so well," he rasps as I lower myself onto him, taking his full length.

"Shh," I shush him, bringing a finger to his lips. "No more talking." Grady's hazel eyes meet mine, his gaze pinning me as he grabs my hand and takes my finger into his mouth, sucking on it as he slowly drags it back out between his lips.

My walls clench around him as the warmth of his mouth on my finger travels up through my arm and into my core. I rock my hips, feeling the friction building between us and I increase my pace. I fuck him until I feel all my pain, rejection, and heartache dissipate, replaced by the softness with which Grady is looking at me now. The pleasure that breaks through my pain is something I've never felt before, it heats my whole body, every fibre of my being humming as I lose control, lose myself to the waves that crash over me.

"God, you're so beautiful when you come." Grady moans as I feel his release pump into me. I fall forward, our bodies still connected, curling up on him as he wraps his arms around me and buries his face in my hair.

I close my eyes, my cheek resting on his chest, and release a breath, my body relaxing into him.

"My father found a new family." I whisper. Saying the words out loud, they have less bite to them than when I kept them in. I unravel myself from Grady, and lower myself onto the bed next to him, but he keeps an arm around my shoulders, so I'm nestled into the crook of his arm. He doesn't respond, his silence creating space for me to share more. "I don't care that he's remarried. Hell, my mother has done it three times now. I'm happy if he's happy. But he didn't even have the decency to tell me. I shouldn't expect it, because we don't really talk all that much. I just thought maybe he would ... I saw it online, a post from his new and improved daughter."

Grady sucks in a breath through his nose as he kisses the top of my head.

"I think he's forgotten about me," I say, my voice cracking.

"Anyone who doesn't want you in their life doesn't deserve to have you anyway. You have done nothing but make my life more spectacular, more enjoyable, more exciting since you've been in it. Maybe it's cliché to say, but it's his loss. It really is."

"You hardly know me. That's how it's supposed to be, no strings attached, right?"

"Spencer, I don't think either of us can deny that there are strings here. My heart has been so tangled up in you since the moment you walked into my life. Strings are not bad, it means that you're connected to someone. I know you've tried so hard to avoid connection, but it doesn't always have to mean that you're going to end up hurt. I would never do anything to hurt you." Grady's words tug at some deep part of me, a part of me I didn't know I needed to pay attention to. He's offering me *safety*. He's promising to be harmless, and the fucked up part of me has no idea what to do with it.

"No one can promise that. No one can promise that they'll never hurt someone else. You're a human being, and human beings hurt others. We're flawed, imperfect. You can't always give me what I want, and I wouldn't ever expect that of you. It wouldn't be fair."

"Let me try, Spencer. Give me one chance. Let me take you on our date tonight and let me try."

"Our date! Oh my god, I totally forgot about our date." The flash of hurt in Grady's eyes causes a feeling in me that I can't make sense of. I recognize the hollow feeling as guilt. I'm getting a little tired of new emotions and figuring out how to handle them. I've stood up many dates, but it never mattered because they were always the kind of guys that I assumed would have done the same thing to me in a heartbeat. Not Grady. "I'm sorry. I'm so sorry."

"It's okay, you don't have to apologize, really." Grady's face softens, and his calloused hand strokes my shoulder as I sit up in bed. "You have a lot on your mind."

"No, Grady. It's not okay. You made plans before dinner and now..."

"I made plans before I showed up and found you hurt and upset. Then my priorities changed. We can skip out on dinner if you want." Grady's eyes are earnest, and I'm trying to rearrange my fucked-up mind to parse how someone would make *me* a *priority*.

But I don't have time to try and make sense of it right now. I dig around in the sheets and locate my phone. I have a notification from Eleanor.

ELEANOR

Looking forward to seeing you later!

Ugh. I not only forgot about the fact that I had agreed on a date—a fake date—with Grady, but I also forgot about the fact that we were supposed to go to dinner with Eleanor and her husband. Standing up a date is one thing, even though standing up Grady feels different somehow, but missing a work commitment is something I never do. I check the time again. Thirty minutes until I told Eleanor that I would be at her house.

"No, I can't stand up Eleanor. She's been so kind to me, and so excited about my work here. I have a presentation prepared for her and everything." I rapidly type out a response, letting her know we'll be there soon. "And I owe you that date."

I lean down and give Grady a peck on the cheek, before climbing over him and out of bed to get myself cleaned up and ready to go out. I'm running a brush through my scarlet hair, letting it fall around my shoulders instead of in my usual messy bun, when Grady gets up and goes to wait for me outside.

The dress he bought me is hanging in the small cupboard behind the driver's seat of the van, and I hesitate before pulling it out. He bought me this dress to wear specifically for this occasion, and although I was adamant that this isn't a real date, I find myself wanting to wear the dress anyway. Actually, I find myself liking the idea of going on a date with Grady. I almost feel … giddy.

I slip the dress on, and the look on his face when I climb down out of the van is the same as the one when he first saw me in that change room. A mix of awe and desire claims his features before he clears his throat and schools them back into submission. He's leaning against the passenger side of the car and crossing his arms over his chest, tattooed biceps flexing.

"I don't have big red splotches all over my face from crying, do I?" I ask, approaching him where he waits for me.

"No. Not at all. You are breathtaking." I lean my body against his and he unravels his arms to bring them to the sides of my waist. He leans down and plants a kiss on my mouth. "Hi," he whispers, resting his forehead softly against mine.

"Hi," I whisper back. Butterflies careen around inside my gut. I'm going on a date with Grady. "You didn't bring the bike," I point out.

"I didn't think you'd want to show up to Eleanor's with wind-blown hair."

"Smart man." The corner of my mouth tilts up, thinking about Grady considering me, considering my wants and needs, and making accommodations for them. *Prioritizing* me.

He pulls away from me, only to open the passenger side of the car, and stands back to let me climb in.

I'm going on a date with Grady.

CHAPTER 15
GRADY

"No overt displays of affection, please," Spencer says out the side of her mouth as I knock on the front door that belongs to Eleanor and Marko. I have to watch where I knock to avoid the large, brightly-coloured wreath that's adorning the door of the craftsman-style home. The flowers strategically match the ones in the planter on the stoop. "This is a work dinner for me."

"Whatever you say, *dear*," I tease. At this point, I'm used to Spencer telling me what to do, and it's not lost on me that we sound like an old married couple. "I'll be on my best behaviour, I promise."

The door opens and reveals Eleanor standing on the other side, a wide smile on her face. She's a petite woman and fit for her age. Tonight, she's wearing a classy navy shift dress, and a string of pearls around her neck to match the ones dangling from her ears.

"Spencer and Grady, what a treat it is to see you here together." She holds her arms out towards us and Spencer leans in for a hug. Eleanor's husband, Marko, appears from around the corner, followed by a large, loping black-and-white Great Dane. He nuzzles up to Spencer, leaving a streak of drool along the side of her hip.

"Wallace, *no*. Not everybody wants to be greeted with your slobber," Eleanor scolds, sending him back into the living room.

"It's okay, really," Spencer says, wiping her hand down her dress to smooth it out. "I love dogs. Wallace is cute."

Marko approaches me with an outstretched hand, and I extend mine back. Of course, I already know Marko and Eleanor. They were long-time friends of my parents, and Eleanor is still close with Winnie. Though having dinner in their home, with Spencer, is like meeting them in a whole new capacity. One I know they aren't used to seeing me in, either.

We get the mandatory greetings out of the way and follow them through the entryway and into their large open-concept kitchen and living space. The home is cozy, with warm dim lighting and candles already lit on the dining table. It's a different sort of feel from my place, more farmhouse than mid-century modern, but the effect is lived in, in a way that I like.

"Can I get anyone anything to drink?" Eleanor inquires. Spencer doesn't hesitate to ask for a glass of red wine, and I ask Marko if he has a cold beer. He gets one out of the fridge and proceeds to pour it into an already-chilled glass.

"You have beautiful taste, Eleanor," I say, looking around the room as I take the glass from Marko. "I can't believe that I've never actually seen the inside of your place before tonight."

"You never were one to stop in for a visit, which you could have done anytime you know. You don't have to stay hidden away in that old house of yours." Her tone isn't accusing, just the opposite. Eleanor doesn't have it in her.

"I like it over there, if I'm honest. Keeps me out of any gossip or town drama. You know I hate drama."

"Well, I guess you still managed to snag yourself a date, even hiding way out in the boonies." My shoulders tense, my body going into defense mode, ready for Spencer to deny that we're together, but she doesn't. Instead, she casually sips her wine as if unaffected, but I notice the pink flush that's spreading up her neck.

"I sure did."

Eleanor turns her attention to Spencer now.

"How are you liking Heartwood?" she asks, gesturing for us to take a seat around the table, as Marko starts plating our food. I pull Spencer's chair out for her, and she sits, offering me a shy smile. I take the seat to the right of her, opposite Eleanor and Marko.

"I absolutely love it here. Some of my very favourite people are here in Heartwood." I know that Spencer is talking about Ally when she says this, but when her eyes dart over to me I can't help but wonder—*hope*—that I might be included in that group of people now as well.

"Right, you're Ally's friend. I forgot that you had some connections here," Eleanor says as Marko places a steaming plate of pasta in front of her before returning to the kitchen to get his own. "Now that you have another one, will you stay here a while longer?"

Spencer hesitates with her answer, and the hope I felt earlier dwindles.

"Maybe," she offers, giving a half-hearted answer to placate Eleanor. "I have a job opportunity that I'm hoping comes through. It's based in Vancouver and would require more travel." I lean my elbows on the table and rest my mouth against my fist, hoping it disguises any evidence of the disappointment I'm feeling. I've been actively trying to avoid thinking about Spencer leaving. Just focus on the positive, focus on the plan.

"Too bad, we could really use someone like you here. The tourism board has absolutely adored what you've done so far, the posts you've shared of Heartwood are incredible. We've already seen an uptick in people wanting to visit. Rosie said that her inn has more guests calling about booking and she hasn't even opened the place yet."

"Well, it's not me, Eleanor. Heartwood really has a lot to offer.

I'm just showing people that." Spencer deflects the compliment, and it pisses me off how humble she is when she is always the most incredible woman in the room.

"Don't sell yourself short, Spencer," I cut in. My tone comes out more gruff than I anticipated, but I've made a point up until now not to let those kinds of comments from her slide. "I've seen the photos that you've taken around town and the way you captured the essence of it, it's amazing. You have a talent for it, for seeing the things that make a place special and allowing other people to see it, too."

"Thanks, Grady," Spencer says, her eyes lingering on me for a beat before looking down at her plate of half-eaten pasta. For the last few minutes, all she's done is push the noodles around without taking a bite.

Eleanor covers her mouth and swallows her bite of food before speaking.

"I would love to see what you've prepared for the tourism board. You did bring your presentation with you, right?" Spencer nods in response.

"It's not quite ready yet though ..." Her voice trails off. I don't know where this side of Spencer has come from, and I hate it. The woman who exudes confidence in every other area of her life, has suddenly shrunk herself at the mention of something she has every right to be proud of—her knowledge, her expertise.

"I'm sure it's wonderful," Eleanor decides. When Spencer only replies with a shrug, Eleanor says, "That's settled. After dinner, we'll clear the plates, and you can show us all what you've done."

Spencer has suddenly gone a cute shade of green, but she nods silently and finishes her food without another word. I use the lull to shift the conversation to the reason that I really came, although now I'm not so sure of my motivations. I'm more than happy to just have an opportunity to be out with Spencer in a capacity that is more than friends-with-benefits.

"Spencer really has highlighted all the best parts of Heartwood," I say, twirling some noodles around my fork and trying to make the segue sound natural. Three pairs of eyes land on me and my palms sweat, my fork becoming slippery in my grasp. They're all waiting for me to elaborate, so I come out with it. "It would be such a shame if the town were to change."

"Why would it change?" Eleanor shoots me a quizzical stare.

"You know, with the law that Carter Bouchard is trying to overturn. The one that prevents big chain stores from setting up shop here."

"Oh, that." Eleanor takes a long sip of her wine, a gulp more like. "That seems like a done deal, as much as I hate it, too," she admits.

"It's not a done deal though, not until the council meeting," I remind her.

"If Jodi is offering the other council members 'incentives' to vote in favour of overturning it like she did for the tourism board, then I'd say the decision has been made. I don't think the other councillors have as much integrity as I do, but who knows? I can smell a bribe from a mile away." Eleanor shoves a forkful of pasta in her mouth as if she didn't just drop a bomb. *Bribing* the council? How the fuck am I supposed to make anything happen in this town when she's got them all eating out of the palm of her hand?

"You're not planning on fighting it, are you?" Marko pipes up. I almost forgot he was here. I shake myself out of my thoughts, as all-consuming as they are right now.

"Sure am," I answer, though my resolve is waning now.

"Good for you, son. Someone needs to. It would be a damned shame if they let this happen. Heartwood would never be the same." Validation settles over me, calming me a little. If Marko feels this way, surely other people do, too.

"Thank you, sir. Spencer is going to make sure I have the best shot possible at the council meeting." I lean back in my chair and place a hand between her shoulder blades. She doesn't recoil the way I expect her to, given the fact that I just broke my promise to limit the PDA.

"Just don't give yourself false hope, Grady. I know how the council members are, and once they see dollar signs, which Carter has a lot of, they don't tend to budge no matter how hard someone tries." Eleanor casually picks up her napkin and dabs her mouth, even though there was nothing on her face.

"At this point, I don't care. Someone has to try. And the only person I see willing to do it is me," I say.

"It is nice to see you so passionate about this. It's been a very long time since you've been this fired up about anything," she says. I give a slight nod in agreement, but I keep the thought to myself that my newfound passion is thanks to the gorgeous redhead sitting next to me. "Regardless of how it all turns out, Grady, you have my support at the council meeting." A feeling buzzes within me, from my solar plexus all the way down to my fingertips. *Hope.* I stifle it just a little, for now. Eleanor is just *one* of the council members, and although it will help immensely to have her on my side, the battle is far from won.

"I appreciate it, Eleanor. More than you know." I hold my glass up towards her, and she clinks hers against it, toasting our newly formed alliance.

We finish up dinner, and I stand to help Marko clear the plates, taking mine and Spencer's over to the sink. The plates clatter together when I drop them in the soapy water, but I still hear Eleanor say something to Spencer in time to turn around and catch a flush blooming behind the freckles on her cheeks. Marko thanks me for clearing the plates, but I barely hear him, my ears trained on the conversation happening at the table. I just make out Eleanor's hushed words, something about how natural Spencer and I look together, how she can tell that we're made for one another. I could tell her that all day, how I think she was made for me. It's just Spencer that needs convincing now.

Spencer changes the subject, diverting the conversation away from me, us, and she gets up to fetch her laptop from her bag at the front door.

Once we're all seated again, she opens it up and turns it so her presentation is facing Eleanor across the table from her. She starts flicking through photos of Heartwood. They're all familiar places, but the way Spencer has photographed them shows them from a new perspective.

"This is the version of Heartwood that the tourism board should sell. Highlight the locals, the lesser-known places, the corners of the community that make you feel like you're home, like everyone here is family." As Spencer speaks the words, she's taking them right out of my mouth, right out of my heart.

Eleanor reaches a hand across the table and places it on Spencer's arm.

"Spencer, this is beautiful. You truly did capture the essence of our little town, and I speak for the whole tourism board when I say that we are so grateful. I will present this to the board at our next meeting. I think they'll be very pleased with the new direction for marketing." Eleanor's face suddenly brightens, and she clasps her hands together. "On that note, we should have dessert."

As she says it, everyone at the table jumps at the sound of a clatter in the kitchen, followed by loud, wet, slurping noises behind the kitchen island.

"Wallace, *no!*" Marko jumps up and runs to the kitchen, shooing the Great Dane out. He sulks off towards the living room and makes himself comfortable on his cushion in the corner, licking his jowls with loud smacking sounds. The three of us round the counter hesitantly, and collectively cringe as we take in the pile of pastry on the floor.

"My pie! My pie is ruined!" Eleanor shrieks when she sees the dessert lying crumbled on the floor, the blueberry filling oozing out of the crust onto the tile. A good portion of it is missing now thanks to Wallace. Eleanor covers her face with her hands. "It's ruined. It's done."

"It's not that bad, honey. I'm sure we can salvage some of it," Marko offers, clearly trying to help. *Sorry, Marko. You're on your own.* There's no way I'm eating that, not even to console Eleanor.

"We can't serve this," she says. Spencer lets out an audible sigh of relief at the decision, and I mirror the sentiment. I'm not about to sit here pretending to enjoy floor pie. "I'm so sorry." She turns, apologizing to Spencer and me.

"It's okay, Eleanor. I'm already stuffed from the delicious dinner," I say, trying to come up with something to make her feel better.

"I'm just so embarrassed. I really had this evening all planned out. It was going to be perfect."

"It was perfect," Spencer chimes in. "I think Grady and I should go, we don't want to get in the way of the clean-up." We both watch with no small amount of horror as Marko tries to scoop the pie off the floor with his hands, the filling spilling out of his fingers across the floor, making the whole situation worse.

"Okay," she replies, her voice a bit dejected.

"Thank you for a lovely dinner." I lean in to give her a peck on the cheek. "I'll come and visit more often, I promise."

The corners of her downturned mouth lift slightly at that.

"I'll hold you to that, Grady. Don't make me hear about your engagement or something through Winnie."

Spencer and I exchange a brief glance, before saying goodbye and seeing ourselves out. She is the first to mention the comment as we get back into the car.

"Our *engagement*? What did you say to her when I wasn't listening?" Spencer turns in the passenger seat to face me, the light from the streetlight outside casting shadows across her face.

"Nothing, I swear." I throw my hands up in a show of innocence, but I can't hold back my grin. "Just that I'm in love with you, and I'm fairly certain that I've been in love with you since the moment I saw you."

Spencer throws her head back and laughs, and the sound is

almost melodic. I could die a happy man if that was a sound I heard every day for the rest of my life. She laughs, and I don't care that what I said was not a joke, because I just love hearing it.

"I ACTUALLY FEEL REALLY bad for her," I say, making the turn off Eleanor and Marko's street, onto the one that leads into town.

"Me too. But you have to admit, it was pretty fucking hilarious. Wallace had his *fill* of that pie." Spencer chuckles, and I can't help but laugh, thinking about the manic slurping sounds coming from the kitchen as if Wallace was trying to eat as much as he could as fast as physically possible before someone found him.

"Yeah, dude won the fucking jackpot," I answer, a comfortable silence falling between us as Spencer's laughter trails off. "Thank you for coming up with an excuse to get out of there. I thought for sure that Marko was going to make us all sit down and eat it off the floor."

"I mean, that pie looked so good, I was almost tempted. I was eyeing it on the counter all through dinner."

I flick on my turn signal and veer off the main road.

"Where are you going?" Spencer asks, but I've already turned down the alley behind the bar. It'll be packed tonight, and I don't exactly want to socialize with anyone.

"You wanted dessert, so I'm getting you dessert." I throw the car into park and hop out of the car, making my way around and opening the passenger side door. Spencer is looking at me as if she's trying to decide whether or not it's safe, like I'm a serial killer leading her into a dark alley. "Come on. It's just dessert."

"Fine. Just dessert. And only because I'm still fantasizing about that pie."

"Well, I have something better than floor pie." I take her hand, helping her out, and lead her through the back door into the bustling kitchen of the Whisky Jack.

I was right, the place is jammed, and the din of the crowd floats through to the kitchen every time the door swings open. Rather than taking Spencer out into the fray, in front of prying eyes, I lead her through the kitchen in the opposite direction and into the quiet of my office. The office I set up but hardly use, other than to do the bookkeeping once a week or so.

It's small, only room for a desk and a couple chairs. She sits and I lift a hand in a *stay right there* motion before going out to get my latest creation from the big industrial fridge. Thankfully, the cheesecake is still intact, and Finn and Doug haven't dug into it for themselves.

When I get back, I set down the plate of cheesecake and offer Spencer one of the two forks I'm carrying. She's looking around the office, taking it in, before she looks back at me and says, "Wow, nice place you got here. How much does something like this go for, anyway?"

My mouth quirks up to one side.

"An arm and a leg," I answer. "It's great for folks who work from home. The whole space doubles as an office."

"Wow. Incredible deal."

"How long were you waiting to make that joke?"

"Pretty much since you left to get the"—She looks at the plate I've set down in front of her—"cheesecake."

I laugh, a full belly laugh, and Spencer joins me. My favourite sound in the whole world. I shut the door behind me, and the clattering noises and chatter from the kitchen are muffled, so it's just her and I in my office that is the size of a pantry. I take the seat next to her as she takes a bite of the cheesecake and stares back at me wide-eyed.

"Holy shit, this is like, better than sex," Spencer says, her words garbled by the cake in her mouth.

"Is it better than sex though?" I ask. "Clearly, you haven't been having the right kind of sex."

"I've been having sex with you, haven't I?"

"Fair point. Well then, I'm obviously not doing enough to satisfy you."

"You do plenty to satisfy me." Her eyes meet mine and hold onto my gaze for a beat before she adds, "This cake is just really fucking good." I glance up at her as I pick a piece up onto my fork. I would cook for Spencer every day, so I can get the satisfaction I feel right now. Making her happy is addicting.

"It's a brown sugar bourbon cheesecake. I thought it would be a good addition to the new menu. Like a play on the Whisky thing."

"It's amazing." She shoves another bite into her mouth, and the room is quiet again except for the sound of her chewing.

"Hey, so you really went along with the whole date ruse tonight," I say, pointing my fork at her and closing one eye to focus on her at the end of it.

"I didn't want it to seem like I didn't want to be there with you. I know you need to make a good impression and whatnot," Spencer says, swallowing hard. Is she nervous? Sometimes it's hard to tell with Spencer. She keeps her emotions under tight control. "And I kind of enjoyed being on a date with you. Even if it wasn't technically real, it felt like you had my back. I don't know if you could tell, but I was super anxious about that presentation."

"Yeah, I could. But only because I know you. I don't think Eleanor would have noticed," I reassure her. "I didn't know that you were supposed to give a presentation."

"I wasn't when she initially invited me. It was a last-minute thing she asked me to do. I threw it together. I'm not the best at formal presentations or sounding smart or eloquent. I've never had to do anything like that."

"Well, you knocked it out of the park. Really. I think Eleanor loved it. *I* loved it."

"See, that's what I mean," she says, setting down her fork and placing her hands in her lap. Her green eyes are piercing right through me. "That's what you do."

"What?"

"You believe in me. You cheer me on, root for me. Why do you do that?"

"Why wouldn't I do that, Spencer?" The answer to her question is so simple. There's nothing that Spencer can't do, I firmly believe that.

"Because I don't always believe in myself. I've always been told that as long as I'm pretty, I don't have to be smart."

"Who the fuck told you that?" I snap in a way that doesn't sound like me, but I don't care. It's the stupidest fucking advice I've ever heard. Not because Spencer isn't pretty, not because she isn't smart, but because she is both of those things and so much more.

"My mother. She's like Jennifer Coolidge in *A Cinderella Story*."

"I'm not following."

"*A Cinderella Story*?" She pauses and waits as if repeating the name of a movie I've never even heard of will jog my memory. "I guess you probably haven't seen it. Jennifer Coolidge is the evil stepmother, and she tells Hilary Duff that she's not very pretty and not very bright while she's baking in the sun with tanning goggles on. That's my mother."

"Ah. Well, that's simply not true. You are bright, Spencer. In so many ways."

"I never went to university. Now that's costing me job opportunities, as you are aware." Spencer's beautiful green eyes roll as she takes another bite of cheesecake.

"So? When have you ever let that stop you? You have single-handedly gone out there and gotten everything you ever wanted. You dreamt of travelling as a little girl, look at you. You did that. You got paid to do it. You hit an obstacle, not having PR experience, and you found a way around that. Not very many people can do what you do."

Spencer doesn't answer me, because her phone has started ringing, and she's fishing it out of her purse.

"Hey," she answers, and mouths *it's Ally* to me. "What the fuck? Why?"

Spencer pales as a look of pure shock and panic washes over her face. She finishes the conversation with a frantic "I'll be right there" and hangs up.

"Speaking of Jennifer Coolidge. My mother is here."

CHAPTER 16
SPENCER

My mother is already into Ally's wine when we arrive. She looks exactly how I'm used to seeing her, curled up on the couch under a blanket, cradling a glass in her hand, looking forlorn and mopey.

"How long has she been here?" I ask Ally as she swings open the front door. Her eyes shift between Grady and me. Ally is apparently so distracted by our appearance that she's rendered speechless, so I decide to clear things up for her. "Yes, Grady and I were out. *Together.*" I watch as her face changes from confusion to complete and utter elation. Great.

"Took you idiots long enough," she quips, her face beaming. "I thought I was going to have to force you into a room alone together, but you figured it out."

Ally is still blocking our entry into the cabin, looking a little too pleased with herself. My eyes flick back towards Grady, standing behind my shoulder, and I can tell by the smug way his lip just twitched that he's just as satisfied. He'll be able to rub it in my face later that *I* was the one who broke the 'don't tell Ally' rule.

Remembering why we came over in the first place, Ally opens

the front door wider and steps aside, allowing us in. She gestures towards my mother on the couch.

"She's been here for about a half hour. I haven't been able to get anything out of her, just that she wanted to know where you were and that she needed wine. I supplied both," Ally explains.

"Thanks," I say, flashing her an apologetic smile. I round the large wooden coffee table and sink down onto the couch next to my mom. Ally, Mason, and Grady retreat to the kitchen to create an illusion of privacy, but in this tiny cabin, I know they can still hear every word. I trust Ally will provide enough detailed commentary to bring everyone up to speed on the chaos that is the Sinclairs.

"Hey, Mom," I say, keeping my tone gentle and light, as if I might spook her. "What's going on?"

"You saw that your father got married," she says, and I suddenly feel very stupid for not anticipating that she might show up in town. All the feelings I had earlier in the day threaten to bubble up to the surface. My dinner with Grady had been a nice distraction for a few hours, but the pain is still lurking there, waiting until just the right opportunity to rear its ugly head. I know I haven't fully dealt with it, but I shove it down, ignoring it for the moment. My mother is clearly handling this situation worse than I am, numbing herself with wine. She needs me to be her support in this moment, the way I always have been. It's why she came here in the first place; she knows she can rely on me to console her. And I will. Just like I always have.

"I did see that, yeah." Anger and betrayal nip at my words despite any attempt to hide it. "How are you feeling about it?" It's no use telling my mom that she's being unreasonable. Even though she is. She's remarried three whole times to my father's one. Marla will feel the way she needs to feel, and she'll let everyone around her know it.

"Awful. Just awful. How dare he do this, and right now of all times?" She says it as if my father intentionally did this *to her*. What she doesn't realize is that my father doesn't think about us at all, not even enough to do anything vindictive. Her words spark another question within me.

"What do you mean *right now*?"

She takes a long pull of her wine and tips her head back, struggling to find the words to answer me. I'm momentarily distracted by the rom-com playing on the TV, and I notice that Marla's gaze has drifted there too, so I pick the remote up off the coffee table and click the screen off. Marla looks up at me finally, the sudden silence jarring her.

"Roy wants a divorce," she spits out, and I'm taken aback. Whatever I thought might have brought her here, it wasn't this.

"What? Why? Did he find someone else?" I hate to assume that's the reason, but it's the one that occurs the most frequently in my mother's relationships, so statistically speaking, it's the most likely scenario.

"No. Not even," she says, forlorn. "I'm just not enough for him anymore."

"Mom, that's not even remotely the conclusion you should draw from this."

"It's the only conclusion to draw, Spencer. I don't have what Roy is looking for in a wife, to spend his golden years with. He didn't even trade me in for a younger model. He traded me in because he'd rather be alone than with me. I think it's my boobs. Never have children, Spencer, keep your boobs as perky as they are now, and you'll be able to hang onto a man."

Suddenly a few pieces clink together from the last few days, like chips falling into a game of Connect Four and lining up just right.

"Ah. So, this is the reason for the boob job."

Marla nods.

"He told me he wanted a divorce a few weeks ago. I didn't think he was serious. I thought he was saying it in the heat of an argument. So, I told him I was getting a boob job, thinking maybe it would convince him to stay. You know, that's all men care about. But it didn't work, and he said it was so *me* to think that it would. I don't even know what he means by that."

"Have you ever thought, Mom, that you might have more to offer men than just your appearance?" I say tentatively, repeating the words that Grady had spoken to me. Something within them rang true, helped me see myself in a different light. The only light I had seen myself in prior to that was my mother's.

"Don't be naive, Spencer." She scoffs. "Men only care about one thing. They're all the same." I glance over to the kitchen where Grady is bent down, his hand pressed gently against Ally's belly, talking to his niece. A warm sensation ripples through me, and in that moment, I know that what my mother has told me my entire life is wrong.

"They aren't. We just haven't been choosing ones that care about more. I think that's been intentional. It's easier to let go when it ends. Pick a guy who is enough of an asshole and the breakup will never be your fault."

"I just don't have the energy to be dissecting this tonight." She sighs. "I am exhausted from the drive, from all of it."

"How long are you planning to stay in Heartwood?" I ask her. If she truly is here because of her divorce with Roy, this could be a long and very bumpy road.

"I don't know yet. Long enough to feel okay going back to an empty house. Long enough for Roy to pack his shit and leave." That's not really an answer. That could be just the weekend, or it could be months.

"Where are you planning on staying?" I ask. She can't stay with me, there isn't enough room in the van, and I am sure as hell not allowing her to stay with Ally. She doesn't have enough room here either, and with the baby coming so soon, Marla Sinclair invading her space is the last thing she needs.

"I guess I'll just get a room at the motel. It looked decent. Have you stayed there? How many stars does it have?" she asks, and I'm not sure how to answer. The last time I planned on staying there, Grady took one look at the place and deemed it unfit even for me, and I'm used to sleeping in hostels.

"Uh ... well it has five stars if you consider the fact that it's currently the only place to stay in Heartwood," I offer, trying to make it sound even slightly more appealing.

Grady, the eavesdropping little snoop, wanders over from the kitchen at this exact moment, and chimes in.

"She can stay in my guest suite," he offers.

"No," I snap a little too quickly, jumping to my feet. This is a slippery slope if I've ever seen one. A favour like this is ... well it's not exactly aligned with our rules. "I can't have you put up my mom."

"It's no big deal, really. The suite has already been made up anyway," he answers. Then adding, "And besides, it's not the first time I've spared a beautiful Sinclair woman from the bed-bug-infested motel." Grady winks at me, and my pulse zings. I quickly run through all the available options for my mother and come up short. She'll complain about anything else to the point of being insufferable, so having her stay with Grady is the only way that I can hack having her here.

"Okay. Fine," I give in. "But on one condition."

Grady flashes me a playful grin and I think I can hear his thoughts. *So many rules.*

"I'll park my van in your driveway and stay there, too. That way you don't need to worry about hosting. I'll take care of it all."

"Deal," Grady says. Out of my periphery, I can see Marla looking up at Grady and me, practically squaring off. She glances between us, realizing the decision has been made.

"Great. It's settled." She claps a hand on her knee and gets up from the couch to refill her wine glass.

Grady cocks an eyebrow towards me.

"I guess it's settled," he repeats, and I realize that this is the only condition left between us. Any of the rules we previously agreed upon have been broken. Just one night, no relationship-y things, don't tell Ally. They've all been completely shattered. There is nothing left keeping me in check, and now I'll be staying on Grady's property, mere feet away from him.

"I THINK your mom is all set up in there," Grady says, approaching me across the driveway. "She seems to have made herself right at home."

I look up at him standing over me, slightly out of breath from trying to crank down the jacks at the back of the van. I've parked it a safe fifty feet away from the house.

"Here, let me," Grady offers, and I let him take over, wiping the back of my hand across my damp brow.

"Thanks." The muscles in Grady's thick arm flex as he cranks the jack down with ease, barely breaking a sweat. He stands and wipes his hands off on his jeans, regarding me for a moment.

"Are you sure you're going to be okay staying out here?" he asks. I see no alternative with all the rules broken now, I have to hold myself together. The council meeting is looming, and so is my upcoming departure from Heartwood. Now, with my mother showing up, I'm reminded of my commitment to my relationship ban and why it was important in the first place.

"Yeah, I'll be fine. I'm used to sleeping in the van on my own by now. Tonight is no different." A brisk breeze blows between us, sending a chill through me.

Grady looks up at the dark night sky, the stars obscured by clouds, exposing the stubbled underside of his jaw to me.

"Okay. If you need anything, I'll leave the front door unlocked for you. You can come in anytime," Grady says, angling himself away from me as he heads back towards the house.

"Thanks," I say again. I watch as Grady leaves me in the driveway and closes the front door behind him. It's better this way,

I remind myself before climbing into the van through the driver's-side door.

I make my way around and pull the shades down over each of the windows. This is where I prefer to be anyway, in my own bed, my safe space.

Quickly going through my bedtime routine, I wash my makeup off in the kitchen sink, brush my teeth, and throw on my flannel PJs before crawling under my thick duvet.

The soft sound of rain on the metal roof lulls me, the steady *plink* of the drops getting louder, almost blurring together. The wind outside is picking up speed, howling around me, shaking the van slightly.

Just as I'm drifting off to sleep a sudden *crack* of thunder jolts me awake. I fucking hate thunder. Something about never knowing when it's going to happen sets me on edge. A flash of lightning illuminates the inside of the van through the clear hatch in the ceiling.

It'll pass, I tell myself, tucking my duvet up under my chin and squeezing my eyes shut. *It has to pass.*

Another loud boom overhead makes me cringe. Goddammit.

I yank the duvet up so I'm fully covered by it now. Maybe if I can't see the light flash, it won't be as startling.

Crack!

My heart just about stops dead. Well, that clearly didn't work.

One ... two ... three ... I count the seconds between the lightning, and with the next boom, I can tell that it's getting closer. The storm isn't going to pass as quickly as I'd hoped.

I consider my options. You can't get struck by lightning in a vehicle, right? The rubber tires act as an insulator. I think. I can't be sure, and when the next flash of lightning comes, I decide I don't want to take any chances.

The only other option I have is to go inside, into Grady's house. Nope. Not gonna happen.

Crack! A little shriek escapes from my throat.

I could sleep on the couch ... if I wake up before sunrise, I can sneak back out to the camper van and Grady will never know the difference. Still ... not my first choice.

Crack! I flinch again. Fuck. I have to go inside.

Once I've made my plan, I climb out of bed, and root around for my light puffer jacket, the only jacket I packed, and my rain boots. I tuck the pant legs of my flannel bottoms into the boots and assess the look, praying to a god that I don't believe in that Grady doesn't discover me in this ensemble.

My light, down jacket does nothing to protect me from the rain as I hunch over and pull the hood around my face. I can already feel the dampness seeping through to my clothes underneath, sending a shiver all the way through me, chilling me to my bones.

I'm looking down at the ground, doing my best not to trip as my eyes adjust to the darkness, and swiftly make my way to the house, when I smack right into a solid wall of ... someone.

Only a psychopath would be out here in this weather. I squint my eyes trying to make out the large shadowy figure in the dark. The shadowy figure then grabs my shoulders and now I'm positive I'm going to die.

Crack! I let out a scream.

Lightning flashes and lights up the person standing over me.

"Woah ... calm down, Rebel. It's just me," Grady says, catching me by the shoulders and crouching slightly so his face meets my eye level. I push the useless hood off—it's not doing anything—but the heavy raindrops have already started making my hair stick to my face.

"What are you doing creeping around out here?" I ask, my back stiffening as I realize that the worst has happened. I've been discovered sneaking into the house. Grady's gaze roves over me, taking in my purple plaid pajama bottoms tucked into hot pink polka dot boots. And I've been discovered in this god-awful outfit.

"I could ask you the same question," he retorts. "Cute look, by the way."

"I asked you first." I cross my arms over and straighten my posture, letting the rain run down my face until my hair is plastered on my forehead.

"I was coming to make sure you were okay," he answers, his voice laced with genuine concern. My defensiveness gives way a tiny bit. "Now you."

I blink twice, raindrops collecting on my eyelashes. I consider how to tell Grady that I was planning on sneaking inside, leaving before he ever knew I was there. Looking into his face now, the way his dark eyebrows are knitted together with concern, I don't have the heart. I also realize with disturbing clarity that I don't want to keep avoiding him. Avoiding this.

"I wanted to come inside. I was originally planning on just sleeping on the couch to not wake you." The excuse is weak. I hear the bristle of his hand against his stubbled beard as he scrubs his palm over his jaw.

"That's not why you were going to sleep on the couch. You were going to pretend like you didn't want to crawl into bed next to me, even though that's not the truth, is it," Grady says, as if knowing that the moment I stepped foot in the house I wouldn't have had the willpower to stay in the living room anyway. Not with him sleeping mere feet away down the hall. "I think the truth is ... you wanted to get caught. I think you wanted me to find you and drag you to my bedroom so that you wouldn't have to be the one to admit that you were thinking about it all along." I swallow hard, my mouth suddenly very dry. I don't have a rebuttal. On some level, I know he's right. He dips his face close to mine, his breath forming a cloud of warm air between us. "Well good news. You're coming inside, but you're going to sleep with me. I won't have it any other way." His voice rumbles through me, and I know that the shiver snaking down my spine is no longer because of the cold rain seeping through my coat.

Grady takes my face in his hands and wipes the hair off my forehead. His lips meet mine in a wet kiss, warming me against the chill.

The last boundary within me snaps, like an elastic stretched too tight. The feeling is a relief. I don't have to keep pretending that I don't want Grady anymore. When he pulls away from our kiss he reaches down and tugs my hand, and I follow him inside. Into the warm comfort of his home.

I follow him up the split stairs, away from my mother sleeping soundly in the ground-floor guest suite, my feet quietly padding on the hardwood. I follow him into his bedroom, and without a word between us, Grady turns to me and unzips my soaking wet jacket, peels off the damp shirt I have underneath. I step out of my flannel bottoms, now completely soaked as well. Grady doesn't make a move on me the way he has in the past when I've been standing in front of him, naked except for my underwear. I thought him seeing me in my PJs and rain boots was embarrassing, but I'm suddenly very self-conscious of the dainty floral print granny panties I chose to wear to bed. Grady doesn't seem to care. He plucks a folded T-shirt off the end of the bed as if it was set out for me. As if he knew he would be bringing me back inside with him. As if he knew me well enough to be sure that I would come.

He slips the T-shirt on over my head, the soft fabric on my skin warming me from the outside in. It smells like him, the spicy vanilla and tobacco cologne he wears warming me from the inside out.

Grady walks over to the side of the bed, and pulls back the covers for me to climb in. He crawls in next to me, pulling me close, his body matching the curve of my spine from behind. He puts one arm behind my head, one arm draped over my waist, and buries his face in my still-damp hair.

Thunder cracks again outside, and though my shoulders still tense slightly, I don't jump the same way I did before.

"Distract me," I whisper into the dark.

He reaches his hand down, finding the edge of my panties and pushing them down. His fingers find my slit, while his breath warms the spot on my neck just below my ear. I moan softly as his fingers make contact with my clit, forming soft slow circles around it. He finds my opening and uses my wetness as he returns to the sensitive bundle of nerves. The circles become tighter, faster, and I find my release quickly.

My body slackens and sinks deeper in beside Grady, his arms wrapping me tighter into him. I close my eyes, savouring this feeling of comfort and safety, and it isn't long before I drift off to sleep.

CHAPTER 17
GRADY

I'VE HAD to remind myself several times this morning that the woman sitting at my kitchen counter is the senior Sinclair, and not Spencer. When I have my back turned, focusing on the omelet I'm preparing for Marla, their voices are nearly identical. Their mannerisms are, too. Especially this morning. Marla seems lighter than she did last night, and something about having her as a guest in my home is nice, familiar even.

It's just the two of us in the kitchen, and Spencer is still in bed. I crawled out of bed as quietly as I could, letting her sleep after the harrowing night she had before I brought her inside. She looked so peaceful lying there, her shock of red hair splayed across my charcoal grey sheets. It felt like she was always meant to be there. Like my bed was missing something fundamental before her.

Even without Spencer here to bridge the gap between Marla and me, our conversation this morning hasn't been forced or uncomfortable.

"I keep having a bit of a jump scare every time I turn around. You and Spencer are so much alike. You could be sisters," I say, earning a hearty laugh from Marla that fills the kitchen in the same way that Spencer's laugh fills a room with her presence.

"You flatter me, Grady." She waves off the compliment, just like Spencer would, too, I note.

"No, really. You two are like twins."

"I have had a lot of Botox to keep my youthful appearance, so I'll pass the compliment along to my injector. Who, by the way, Spencer still needs to call about those horrid crow's feet she's getting." Marla sips her coffee with raised eyebrows, like we're co-conspirators. She's read the situation all wrong. I wouldn't change one thing about Spencer.

"I quite like Spencer's face just the way it is," I say, squeezing out a line of whipped cream cheese onto the egg before rolling it gently into a perfect omelet. "Aren't crow's feet just from laughing too much? I think it's nice that she's had so many reasons to smile, that her face shows it."

Marla makes a punctuated *hm* sound, so I steer the conversation back to something more neutral. Something that won't get me in trouble.

"So, what's the plan for today?" I ask as she sips her coffee.

"Not a clue. Whatever Spencer is up to, I'll probably just tag along," she answers, and I grin to myself, imagining Spencer rolling her eyes at that statement.

"That sounds like a great day. Spencer will be busy running errands and setting up for the event later tonight."

"What event? Spencer never said anything about an event." *Shit.* I flinch and try to recall if Spencer ever said anything about not mentioning the party to Marla, and I come up short.

"I'm sure she just didn't anticipate you being here for it is all. It's a fundraiser that we're hosting at the Whisky Jack. She'll fill you in, I'm sure. She's done most of the leg work for it."

"I would love to help her with it," she says, as I slide the plate across the kitchen island to her. She takes the first bite, and I watch for her reaction. She doesn't compliment the food, I note, but she squints at me for a moment, assessing me before saying, "I'm glad my daughter has found you, you know." And that sentence is better than any compliment I could ever receive on my cooking. Hands down.

I nod to her in thanks, unable to speak past the overwhelming squeezing behind my ribs.

"I've worried about her for a long time. Always the lone wolf. I know my life certainly hasn't been perfect, God knows it hasn't. But I've had a lot of love in my life. I've had passionate love, soft love. While it was hard when those relationships ended, I always had this sense that I wouldn't have changed a thing about them. Better to have loved and lost and all that." Marla sets her coffee cup down on the granite countertop with a clink and wraps her hands around the warm ceramic.

"You're a romantic, Marla. A rare breed these days, it seems," I say, and though I know her assessment of Spencer is accurate, all I can think about at this moment is that I want to give that to her. I want us to have a passionate, soft love. One that she cherishes, even if it doesn't last. God, I want it to last.

"That's not the word my husband would use, I'm sure." Her tone is somewhat exasperated as she says it. "Ex-husband now, I guess. I don't know how I'll go back to living without Roy. The house will seem so empty now." I'm listening, but I have my back turned while I crack two more eggs into a bowl and whisk them briskly.

"Spencer told me you live in wine country. The Okanagan?" I ask, still occupied with breakfast preparations.

"Yes, Peachland."

"It's beautiful there. I went once on vacation as a teen, and I've always wanted to go back."

"It is. Every day I wake up and think about how lucky I am." I can hear a wistfulness in her voice.

"What's your favourite thing about living there?" I crack two more eggs into a bowl and grind some pepper into it.

"What don't I love about it?" She chuckles in a way that sounds almost relaxed, an unfiltered version of her. "I love having my coffee on the porch and looking out over the lake. I love getting up on summer mornings and going for a swim."

"That sounds like a dream, really. When did you move there?" I inquire, pouring the eggs into the pan with a sizzle.

"Oh, several years ago now. After my second divorce. Wow, that makes me sound like such a mess. It was about a year before I met Roy. Now I can't imagine being there without him," Marla says, and although she and Spencer look alike, and behave alike, this is what makes them fundamentally different. Spencer has a hard time imagining her life with a man in it, while Marla can't live without one.

"I think you can. You bought that house for *you*. You built your life for *you*. Sure, it will be an adjustment. But you'll adapt, with or without Roy. I think you'll land on your feet because you created the life you love before Roy even came into it."

Marla regards me, her face pensive.

"See, this is why I like you, Grady."

"Why do we like Grady?" Spencer's groggy voice interrupts us as she comes around the corner to join us in the kitchen. She's still in my T-shirt, I notice, which does something funny to my chest. She's bleary-eyed, and her hair is mussed, just the way I like it.

"A multitude of reasons. I'm just a likeable guy," I answer. Spencer beelines to the coffee pot, and I slide a mug in front of her, which she takes as if it came out of nowhere and she isn't going to question it. Not a morning person, noted. "Your omelet is almost ready," I add, planting a soft kiss on her temple. She responds with a soft, sleepy smile.

"Thank you. I'm sure it is a perfect omelet, but right now I just need caffeine in an IV drip, please." She shuffles over and takes the bar stool next to her mom.

"You'll have to go to Ally's for that, I'm afraid. Here we just serve coffee in a mug." Spencer flashes me a *ha-ha* look.

"What have you two been yammering on about out here? If you think you're quiet by the way, neither of you are." Spencer's comment makes me wonder if she heard our conversation, and if so, how much. Not that it matters. Whatever I said to Marla I would say in front of Spencer in a heartbeat. Though, I can't help but worry that I'm coming on too strong with her, that today might be the day I push her away.

"We were just talking about the cocktail party tonight. Your mom is excited about helping you with your errands today," I answer.

"Oh, is she?" Spencer says through a smile, though her teeth are gritted.

"I am. I am so excited. Just tell me what to do and I'll do it. Put me to work." Marla sounds giddy. Whether it's because she needs to take her mind off Roy, or because she gets to spend time with daughter, I'm unsure.

"Great," Spencer says, and her tone is less sarcastic than I anticipated. "We have a lot of ground to cover today."

"You can take the car," I offer, knowing that Spencer doesn't have wheels other than the ones attached to her home. "Oh—" I run down to the entryway, grab my spare set of keys off the hook, and come back to join them in the kitchen, taking the stairs two at a time. "Take a house key. It's yours if you're going to be staying here now."

I hand it to Spencer, who takes it from my hand gingerly. She doesn't put it in her purse, she holds it tight in her palm while she finishes her breakfast, like she's afraid she might lose it. Like it's precious to her.

"I guess we'll meet you at the bar later?" Marla clarifies.

"Yeah, I've got a few things to sort out today and then I'll head over. The boys will be over soon to see if I can make servers out of them."

"Good luck with that." Spencer scoffs, and I'll need it, knowing my brothers.

Spencer gobbles up her omelet, plants a kiss on my cheek, and heads off to take a shower in my ensuite. It takes everything in me not to go and get in with her.

"I'm up here!" I call from upstairs as I hear Hudson and Jett come through the front door. They're anything but quiet when they're together, and their footsteps on the few stairs leading to the open-concept living space sound reminiscent of the thunder from last night.

"What's Spencer's van doing in your driveway?" Hudson asks. As he and Jett come lumbering into the kitchen, I see him pause and assess the mess I've left from breakfast, the three plates still on the counter. "Were you cooking her *breakfast?* Like, as in, she stayed the night last night?"

"It's not what it looks like," I try to explain. But it's exactly what it looks like. "Her mom showed up in town, so I offered to host. Spencer just insisted that she stay in the van so that she could be here."

"Did she stay in the van? That's the real question," Jett prods.

"She didn't, did she? I thought we talked about this." Hudson sounds disappointed in me, and it kind of irks me that he feels the need to worry about me. It's never been this way in our relationship. I've always been the older brother, the one to worry about him, to make sure that he's okay. Not the other way around. It's not going to start now. "Jett, back me up here. This is a bad idea. Spencer's got one foot out the door. You know Grady's not the friends-with-benefits type."

Jett shrugs.

"Don't look at me for relationship advice. I am not the one to talk to when it comes to feelings and shit. It sounds like the perfect scenario to me. Two words: *fuck* and *chuck.*"

"God, Jett, why are you such a dick?" Hudson says. "It's going to catch up to you one day."

"Yeah? Tell me how it's worked out for you pining over your high school sweetheart," Jett chides.

"Don't bring Wren into this. You don't even know the half of it."

"It's not like that with Spencer. I don't know, something is different between us. There's a connection, I can't really describe it," I explain.

"Whatever, dude." Hudson dismisses what I've said. "I just know what she did to you last time she left. You try to be what everyone else needs, hoping that someone will see *you* and do the same. Just don't assume she can read your mind. If you really want her, you gotta go after it, okay?"

"Like you've gone after Wren?" Jett sneers, and from the colour blooming on Hudson's cheeks, I think he might actually explode.

"Okay, okay. Enough. I didn't bring you two bozos here so you could argue," I say, shoving two serving trays I borrowed from the bar towards each of them. "You're here so I can whip you into shape for tonight."

"Why doesn't Mason have to be here?" Jett whines.

"You know why Mason doesn't have to be here. He's got important shit to do, unlike you clowns."

"Hey," Hudson protests.

"Sorry Hud, you're right. Jett is the clown here." I walk around the living room where I've set up various surfaces to mimic the layout of the bar. I shouldn't really be making fun of Jett. After all, he did volunteer to help with the cocktail party tonight. I needed extra hands behind the bar to help Finn make all the drinks, which left me short a few servers, and they stepped up. I'm not calling it a success just yet. Neither of them has ever served a day in their life, so my expectations are low. "Each of these tables represents a table in the bar. I'm going to hand you drinks on your tray and you deliver them to the right table number, got it?" The pair of them nod. "Let's get to work."

I take my place behind the kitchen island, my makeshift bar, and load up a tray with two glasses. We'll start off easy. Jett takes his tray, one hand underneath, and whips it around as he turns towards the tables. A glass goes flying, spilling the water and shattering on my hardwood floor.

Fuck me, this is going to be a long day.

CHAPTER 18
SPENCER

"THIS PLACE IS SO … QUAINT," my mother says as we wander down the main street, and I ignore the subtle hint in her tone that what she really wanted to say was *rustic* or *ramshackle*. But the day is perfect, so I'm not going to let Marla's judgment sour my mood.

The sun is out and more people have started to emerge post the winter deep freeze in the mountains, so Main Street is bustling with people out enjoying their weekend. After having Marla show up unannounced, my mood perked up when I overheard Grady giving her the life advice she needs. I've always been the one having to dole it out, but she's a little like a petulant teenager. I'm hoping if she hears how messed up she is from someone else, it might finally sink in.

We pass by a few storefronts. Some shop owners are setting up their displays on the sidewalk. I spot Poppy doing the same, arranging some wrought iron bistro sets on the makeshift patio in front of the cafe.

"Hey, Poppy!" I say as we approach. Her face brightens when she sees me, her dark doe eyes alighting. I turn to introduce Poppy to my mother, but she's no longer beside me. Marla is like a crow when it comes to new and shiny things, and right now that new, shiny thing is the rack of dresses outside the Dragonfly Boutique, across the street from Thistle + Thorne.

"Hey, Spence! I have all your plants ready to go for the cocktail contest tonight. I had Jaime put together some arrangements with dark greenery, ferns and stuff, to fit the bar."

"That sounds perfect, Pops. Did you submit a cocktail?"

"Of course I did! I absolutely love the idea. We've never done anything like this here." Poppy finishes setting down a couple of chairs and wipes some dust off her hands onto her apron. "Don't tell anyone, but mine is the Earl Grey Martini."

"My lips are sealed," I say, making a zipping motion across my mouth. Though, I'm sure everyone will be able to guess which one is Poppy's. "I'll be back to get the arrangements, as soon as I can pry my mother away to help me."

I wander across the street and find Marla flipping through the hangers. She's stopped on a vibrant pink shift dress.

"Pretty," I say, approaching her from behind. She glances over her shoulder at me, holding the dress outstretched, head cocked to one side, considering. "That colour would look really good on you."

"Not too bright?"

"Nothing is too bright or too bold for the Sinclairs. Isn't that what you always say?"

"Roy prefers me in more earthy tones. I have to agree they suit me better," she answers, and her comment takes me aback for a moment. If there's one thing I know about my mother, it's the brighter, the better when it comes to her wardrobe. I know it's been a while since I've seen her, but I wonder when, in the last three years, that changed. "The bright colours draw too much attention, I think."

Does she think that? Since when does she not like attention?

"That magenta colour has always been your favourite. I think you should try it on."

"Oh, I don't know..." Her voice trails off, but she's still

holding the dress out in front of her, admiring it. "It looks a little fitted, don't you think? I didn't bring my Spanx with me."

"Just try it on. There's no harm in seeing how it looks," I encourage her.

"Okay ... But I won't buy it. I'd never wear it again."

I drag my mother by her elbow into the boutique and ask for a fitting room, which she begrudgingly goes into and closes the curtain behind her.

The dress fits her like a glove, and I manage to convince her that it no longer matters what Roy thinks anyway. She's getting the dress. I had been just as stubborn when Grady forced me to try on that stunning midi number, and now I'm grateful he did. That outfit, and the look on Grady's face seeing me in it, altered something in my perception of myself. I want that for Marla, too.

The look on her face reminds me of a child on Christmas morning as the store clerk carefully folds it and wraps it in tissue before placing it in a matching pink bag. Ten minutes later, and fifty dollars poorer, Marla and I leave the boutique, dress in hand.

With my mother having now satiated her need to shop, we head back over to Thistle + Thorne, and Poppy helps us load the arrangements for the cocktail party in the back of the car. One task down, only one more to go, and everything will be in order for tonight. A ripple of excitement flutters through my chest. Poppy did an incredible job designing the arrangements, the bar is going to look so much more chic with the changes I suggested, and everything is going to plan.

"We just have to pop into the grocery store now, and then we can take all of this over to the bar," I explain to my mother, who is now distracted by her phone and has clearly lost all interest in what we're doing. She seemed so keen to help this morning, but I should have known that she'd grow bored of it quickly. "Why don't you wait in the car while I go in?" I offer. Marla nods, still looking down at her phone screen, and absentmindedly opens the passenger side door to climb inside. I don't hide my eye roll.

I pivot on my heel and march over to the grocery store on the opposite corner to Thistle + Thorne, the bell overhead chiming as I enter. A tall, burly hulk of a man looks up from where he's bagging the last of his customer's groceries and wipes his hands on his apron before waving hello.

"Spencer!" he calls, his bushy white eyebrows rising as his expression lifts when he sees me. There's something about Mack that I've liked since the first day I met him. His energy feels like a warm hug, and I don't know what it means that I feel the urge to ask him to adopt me whenever I see him. All he's done is remember my name and make me feel welcome, and I don't care to analyze why that feels so monumental to me.

"Hey, Mack!" I call back, smiling broadly. "Do you have that order Grady called you about?"

He raises his hand in a *just a minute* gesture as he remembers what I'm there to pick up before he scurries away to the back room. When he returns, he's accompanied by a cart with a few crates, full to the brim with all the ingredients Grady had listed.

"Odd assortment of stuff you got here, kiddo," Mack points out. I nod, but I'm too busy examining the crates, going over the list once more to ensure that everything is there.

"Are you coming tonight?" I ask him. I hope he is.

"You betcha." He winks at me. "Mine's the Everything but the Kitchen Sink."

"Clever." I chuckle at the name, fitting for the owner of the grocery store. Though I'm a little skeptical about how a cocktail like that will taste. "See you later."

I pull the car up to the back of the bar a few moments later. Marla hasn't said a word beside me. Whatever was occupying her attention on her phone seems to have shifted her demeanour. I'm trying my best to ignore the black hole of a sour mood next to me, when I see Grady practically skip out to meet me. I feel my face lift into another broad smile, and I realize that no matter what feelings

I'm trying to avoid, seeing Grady makes it so much easier. I can't help but be *happy* around him.

Grady comes around the car, opening my door for me, and I get out to greet him. He's been here all morning, making sure everything is set up, and there's a sheen of sweat on his brow.

"I hope Mack didn't give you a hard time about some of those specialty items," he says, planting a kiss on my temple as he approaches the car. He's started doing that. Casual kisses. This is the first one in a somewhat public place, and I realize that I didn't pull away like I thought I would. Like I maybe should have.

I scoff. "He wouldn't dare. Then he'd have to contend with you." I let my gaze roam over Grady's face, a playful grin twisting my lips.

"You're damn right, he would," he says, picking up all three crates stacked together without so much as a grunt or a groan. I could barely lift one. My eyes catch on the way his forearms tense, the muscles like thick ropes under his tattooed skin.

"How does the bar look?" I ask when Grady comes back from dropping the crates just inside the backdoor to the kitchen. He's been hard at work with Hudson over the last few days making the changes I outlined in the design brief I showed him, but he still hasn't let me inside.

"You'll just have to wait and see." He winks at me. "You head back to the house and get ready for tonight. I've got things handled here," he says, and I know he's not going to give me any real details, so I turn back toward the car. Marla is still preoccupied with her phone.

"Okay," I say, standing behind the open car door. "See you later, I guess." I smile at him as our eyes linger on each other for a moment over the roof of the sedan.

"See you later, Rebel."

I TURN the key in the front door with a click. Letting myself into Grady's house feels as if I'm trespassing for a moment. This isn't my home. Yet, when I open the door and take in the smell of his house, the unique scent that only Grady's space would have, it feels more like home than I've ever felt. It's the same warm vanilla and tobacco smell, with something else. The smell of *him*. Without his cologne. The smell of his skin when he's clean out of the shower.

My chest squeezes. The pang feels momentarily like jealousy, like longing, for something I've never had before. A home that I've lived in long enough for someone to walk in the front door and instantly recognize the smell as mine and mine alone.

My mother goes one way down the stairs towards the basement guest suite, and I head up to the master bedroom as if that's where I live now. Though I know I don't.

I pad down the hallway to Grady's room, and something catches my eye on the charcoal-coloured bedding.

Flowers. Orange lilies. I pick them up off the bed and take in the sweet scent of them, a juxtaposition to the modern, masculine space. It's then that I notice an envelope balancing on top of a carefully wrapped box labelled *Rebel* in loopy writing. My heart flutters, swelling to a size I didn't know it was capable of. I've warmed up to the nickname, and the way he says it as if my wild side doesn't need to be tamed.

I open the envelope, being mindful not to tear the paper.

To capture all the places you have yet to explore. All the moments you want to savour.

My heart clenches as I reach for the box. The paper is sparkly. Jade green.

When I unwrap it, I find exactly what I expected I would. Even though I know what the box contains, I'm still shocked by the burning behind my eyes. The thought that Grady put into this is ... I don't know why I'm so surprised. This is just how Grady is.

I pull out the camera, the kind that professionals use, complete with different lenses. A wide angle for those panoramic shots, like the one I couldn't quite capture with my phone from up on the lookout. It's one that I never would have been able to afford on my own.

I hear light footsteps behind me, and realize that my mom is ready to go, and I've just been standing here, slack-jawed and haven't even moved to change yet. She stands hesitantly in the doorway, watching me where I sit on the edge of the bed, turning the camera over in my hands.

When I look up at her, I see that she's wearing the dress. The deep magenta somehow compliments the red of her hair, the hair that I inherited. I lift the camera, pointing it at her. She opens her mouth to protest and before she speaks, I know what she's about to say. She's never loved having her picture taken, and it's only today that I realize it's because she's always allowed other people to shape her opinion of herself.

"You look beautiful, Mom," I say, snapping a picture of her leaning against the door frame. She does. This is the version of my mother that I love, that deserves to be documented. The version of her that wears what she wants because she loves it.

"Roy didn't seem to think so," she says with an eye roll.

"What?" I don't bother to hide the disdain in my voice. "When did Roy see the dress?"

"Earlier. I sent him a photo of me in the change room, trying it on. I thought maybe ..." Her voice trails off, and when I don't say anything more it prompts her to finish her thought. "I thought maybe he would be a little jealous or something. That I'm going out and about, and looking great, too. At least I thought I looked pretty good ..."

"You look amazing in that dress, Mom. You look amazing in everything you put on. He didn't think so?"

"He never responded. I just sat there like an idiot, staring at my phone, hoping he would. He never did." Ah. That explains the foul mood after we left the store, the fixation on her phone screen. I nod solemnly, my mouth forming a tight line.

"Well. Fuck Roy, then," I say, and she reels at the comment.

"Spencer, that is my husband. That is the man I am committed to and am trying to salvage a marriage with." Why she feels so much loyalty to Roy is beyond me. Why Roy deserves her loyalty is another glaring question I don't currently have an answer to. But that's my mother. Giving all of her power away to whoever will look in her direction.

"Nah, fuck him, Mom," I say, more resolute in my decision to throw Roy under the bus. Her face is stunned for a moment, but I think that means she's finally fucking listening. "If he doesn't treat you like absolute gold, then fuck him." I don't fully understand where these words are coming from. I haven't exactly had a good track record of choosing men who treat me right either. My thoughts drift to Grady, and the way he's shown me how valuable I am to him more than anyone in my life ever has. Maybe, just maybe, Marla and I both deserve that.

I finish getting ready, and by the time Marla and I park on Main Street and start walking toward the bar, nearly all the parking spots have been taken, and others are already filing through the double doors.

"Are you coming?" Marla turns and asks me because I've stopped, and am standing stock still, taking in the sight of a brand-new sign above the wooden doors of the Whisky Jack. Or, rather, Jack's, as it's apparently now called. The sign is brand new, the wood fresh and unweathered, making it stand out against the worn siding of the building. *Jack's* is written in bold block letters, with smaller writing beneath it that reads *whiskey bar*. The corner of the sign has the silhouette of a whisky jack, perched on a branch. A smile claims my features.

He did it. He not only changed the name to fit with the new

branding, but he also kept the tribute to his dad front and centre, just like he always wanted. Pride blooms in my chest thinking of the way Grady has come into his own, the way he's taken charge. Pride, and a little bit of something else. Something my heart isn't ready to acknowledge just yet.

"Yeah, I'm coming," I say as I catch up to Marla on the sidewalk, and we enter the bar arm in arm.

CHAPTER 19
GRADY

"You double-checked all the ingredients, right?"
I ask Finn, who is busy behind the bar preparing a jug of chilled
Earl Grey tea. I'm fidgeting, organizing and reorganizing the recipe
cards I printed out for him. They had been arranged in alphabet-
ical order, and now I've got them sorted by the alcohol base, with a
separate category for mocktails.

"Quadruple-checked. We're good to go. Relax." Finn places a
hand on my shoulder. The number of cocktail submissions was
staggering, and I'm not going to lie, I'm nervous. The reassuring
smile on Finn's open expression eases some of the tension within
me. "People are here to have fun, raise a little money. It'll be
great."

"Yeah, I know. I just want this to go well." I give him a sheepish
look.

"It will. You've got this."

"I just wish I knew what we were raising money for. Spencer
still hasn't filled me in on that part," I admit.

"Damn. That's one ambitious woman," Finn says, placing the
jug of iced tea in the mini fridge below the counter.

"She is," I say, and she's found some way of rubbing off on me, giving me a voice I never had. Over the last few weeks, she's shown me a side of myself that I never even knew I possessed. She's brought out the part of me that is passionate, driven, and wants to get shit done. Maybe I have known that part of me is in there somewhere, but I had let myself neglect it. I'd forgotten that I could go after something and make it happen. I was always making things happen for other people, for my brothers, my family. Doing this now, it's allowed me to have both. I can be of service to others and still honour the things that matter to me. What matters to me right now is Heartwood. The town where my parents met, where I grew up, where I want my own family to thrive one day.

"You've got guests," Finn says, nodding towards the door. I turn to see Eleanor and Marko arriving first, Winnie close behind them.

Rounding the bar, I weave through the tables to meet them, giving Eleanor and Winnie both a quick kiss on the cheek.

"Ladies," I say. "Good to see you, Marko." I shake his hand.

"Where's Spencer?" Eleanor asks. "I thought for sure she'd be here by now, sneaking in some one-on-one time with you before it starts." Eleanor winks at me, and I catch the smile playing on Winnie's face. Eleanor obviously filled her in on Spencer and I's dynamic at dinner the other night, and Winnie looks like a proud mother hen.

"She's coming. Her mom is in town, so they're getting ready together at home." I catch the way I've said home, as if it's implied that it's Spencer's home, too. I clear my throat, trying to stifle the colour that's flushing my cheeks now. "Go and get yourselves a drink." I reach into my jeans pocket and pull out six red tickets, handing them each two. "Everyone gets two drink tickets, and then the rest is on you."

They move towards the bar, making room for the next guests. Mason opens the heavy wooden door for Ally, a protective hand placed on her lower back as she enters, and her face lights up when she sees me.

"Grady! You've outdone yourself," she says. "This place looks incredible!" She gestures around her at the new paint job, the new tables and chairs I brought in, and the bookshelves lining one wall, housing some vintage books and bottles of whiskey. Exactly like Spencer's design.

"It was Spencer's idea," I admit. I know this whole evening is supposed to be about fixing my image, but whatever recognition, compliments, or attention this event and the bar gets tonight, I want it to go to her.

"It's really ..." Mason starts, but as he looks around, I can tell he's at a loss for words. All he's able to say is, "Dad would have loved this place." It hits me in the chest, sending a pang right through me. I've never told Mason that the bar is my outlet for my grief, but his assessment skills are astute, and he's always had a special way of knowing what I need to hear.

I hand him two drink tickets, and as he takes them from me, I clasp my hand around his in a meaningful handshake.

"Ally, your drinks are on me tonight. There's a decent mocktail menu, too. Elsie made a non-alcoholic cotton candy drink that looks incredible," I explain.

Ally and Mason head towards the bar as another group of people file in. I recognize one as another city councillor. Suzanne, the chair of the board of education, came with her wife, and a few others that I welcome with handshakes and one-armed hugs.

My line of sight is briefly drawn to the door, and I do a double-take. Spencer and Marla managed to sneak in behind them all, and for a moment, Spencer the only person I see. Standing there in a red dress with white polka dots, the short hemline showing off her beautiful long legs, made even longer by the strappy white heels she's wearing.

God, she's stunning. When I glance over at the woman next to her, it's obvious to everyone in the room where she inherited her looks from.

Spencer's gaze meets mine, and her mouth widens into an open-mouthed smile when she spots me. She flashes me a wink and lifts the camera from where it's hanging around her neck, mouthing the words *thank you* as I'm pulled into another hug by the petite elderly woman who owns the antique shop.

I mouth the words *of course* back to her, over the woman's shoulder. Before I'm able to get to Spencer, another group of people have filed in, all wanting my attention, all wanting to say how much they love the idea of the cocktail contest. By the time I'm able to look for Spencer again, she's gone.

I scan the dimly-lit bar, my gaze catching on that burgundy dress. She's deep in conversation with Suzanne in the back booth, her hands waving around. By the intent way that Suzanne is listening to her, I get the distinct impression that Spencer is sharing one of her wild, genius plans with her. It piques my curiosity. What business does Spencer have with the board of education? And why are they talking as if they already know each other?

"She's a lovely girl." A familiar voice approaches me from behind, catching me in the act of staring at Spencer. Winnie.

"Hey, Mama," I greet her, having to lean down as I always do to pull her in for a hug. I didn't get a chance to give her one in the throng of people when she first arrived.

"Eleanor told me you and Spencer were quite the pair," Winnie says, and my cheeks heat. I adore talking about Spencer like we're a real couple, but the conversation feels off limits.

"You know how she likes to get ahead of herself." I dismiss the comment, hoping that it's enough for Winnie to want to change the subject.

"I don't know ... you wear your feelings pretty close to your chest. If Eleanor picked up on something between you two, I'd be willing to bet there was a reason for it." Winnie is right, the good-natured exterior I put on is often a mask to hide my true feelings. Spencer is the first person who has seen *me* through it. My heart flutters. If I believe that what we have is real, and so many others are starting to recognize it, maybe Spencer will start to see it, too.

"It doesn't matter what I feel, Winnie. She's just passing through. I doubt there's anything I could do or say at this point to convince her otherwise. Spencer goes wherever the wind takes her."

"Sometimes if you want something, you have to go after it. You can't just sit there and hope that the wind changes direction." Winnie looks me in the eyes when she says this, and it rings true somewhere deep within me, a new part of myself opening up to the concept. A part of me that's never truly considered what I want, let alone how to get it. When I was young, people asked me what I wanted to be when I grew up and I never had an answer. Not an astronaut or a professional baseball player. I never dared to let myself dream. When we lost Mom, my life shifted to make sure that my brothers were okay. Now that I have something in my grasp, something I want more than anything, I know it's worth chasing. I know it's worth the discomfort of going after it. Even if it means getting my heart broken.

I can't say all this to Winnie. How could I put into words that I've let myself go with the flow my entire life because I never knew anything different, and that I'm only now finding my way back to the shore?

So instead, I shrug, and as I do, I feel a small soft hand wrap around the inside of my bicep.

"What are we talking about?" Spencer says, leaning her weight into me. Winnie excuses herself with a knowing glance, and I turn to face Spencer once she's walked away.

"Just how incredible you are," I say, Winnie's words offering me a bit of courage to say what's on my mind. I'm even more moti-vated now to be candid and truthful, and to say how I feel about Spencer in plain language so that there is no more questioning what she means to me. To start saying the things I've been feeling for Spencer since she arrived. Longer. Since I saw her for the very first time. "And how well you fit in here, how quickly you've made yourself at home here."

"You've made it easy to fall in love with Heartwood." She smiles as she looks up at me, and I wonder if she could be falling in love with me, too. The way I've fallen for her. Looking into her eyes now, an endless sea of green, I realize that I have. Whatever happens, I have to figure out how to keep her. Her eyes roam over my face, and I pray for time to slow down, wanting to bask in her gaze forever. "You changed the name of the bar."

"I thought about it a lot, what you said." I consider my next words. "You made a good point."

"I did what now?" Spencer brings her hand up to her ear and cups it, a cheeky smirk lifting her lips.

"I said you had a point. Several, actually."

"It sounds like you're admitting I was right, Landry," she says, crossing her arms over her puffed-out chest in a show of vindication.

"Fine. Yes. You were right. You've been right about all of it," I say, letting my eyes roll playfully.

"Okay, so keep that in mind for this next part ..." Spencer grabs me by the shoulders, her small hands unable to wrap around my biceps, and she turns me toward a microphone set up in the corner. It's beckoning me in a way that makes my palms sweat. "It's time to make your speech."

I whirl back around to her, a *please forgive me* look on her gorgeous, freckled face.

"Speech?" I stammer. "Spencer, I am not a public speaker."

"Sure you are. You talk to people at the bar all day. You're a charmer. Just go be a charmer up there." She's dragging me across the bar now, and I feel bile rising in my throat.

"I can talk to people, sure. One on one. Small groups."

"What about trivia night?"

"That's different. I have questions prepared. I have nothing prepared."

"Then it's a good thing I do." She shoves a folded piece of paper towards me, and I unfold it, realizing that she has, in fact, written me an entire speech. I just have to say it. Now I don't have an excuse.

I approach the microphone and give it a couple of taps to make sure it's on. It is, and I feel about a hundred pairs of eyes on me, waiting for what I have to say. This is it, my moment. The moment that is meant to garner support for me and my cause, to change people's perception of me. My palms are sweating. The paper in my hand crinkles, the sound amplifies across the bar.

"Good evening, everyone," I start, scanning the page. The microphone screeches slightly before I start speaking again. "Thank you all for coming and participating in the First Annual Cocktail Contest."

First annual? I shake my head slightly. I guess this will be a yearly occasion. My eyes find Spencer in the crowd, she's beaming from ear to ear, her hands clasped in front of her. Since I have no willpower where Spencer is concerned, I keep going.

"The turnout is incredible, and you all put so much time and effort into the cocktails. As you all know, the purpose of this event is two-fold. First and foremost, to highlight all the amazing small businesses that make Heartwood what it is. You are the beating heart of this town. Second, as you are all aware, the winner of the cocktail contest, that is, whoever sells the most cocktails tonight will have their drink featured on the regular menu at the Whi—at Jack's," I correct. "Proceeds of tonight, and drink sales for the rest of the year, will go towards supporting up-and-coming entre-preneurs."

A few people clap at this announcement, and I continue, still unsure of how Spencer has planned on achieving this.

"This support will come in the form of a bursary available to graduating students of Heartwood High, to support them through business school or as a start-up fund for their business idea. Later this week—" I pause as I quickly scan the page ahead and realization dawns on me of what Spencer has planned, the commitment she's made on my behalf. I can only keep reading now, so I continue, "I will be at the Heartwood High career fair, where the first student to be awarded this bursary will be announced based on nominations from their teachers."

The bar erupts into applause and hollers, and I look up from the paper, an incontrollable smile taking over my face. I'm starting to get a glimpse of Spencer's master plan now, and hope blooms inside my chest. This might just work. A flash blinds me momentarily, and I realize it came from Spencer's camera. She's beaming with pride, in herself, in me.

I thank everyone one last time and click off the microphone before weaving back through the crowd to find Spencer. I'm about to scoop her up into my arms, twirl her around, and give her a kiss, because I no longer give a fuck about showing my affection for her publicly, but she's launched into an excited rant before I get the chance.

"Oh my God, Grady, that was amazing!" she cries when I reach her. "I can't believe that worked! I mean, I can. I put a lot of thought into that speech, and your delivery killed it." She's talking about a mile a minute and all I can do is just listen to her with a big, dumb smile plastered on my face. "Wait until I send Mile High the footage of that. I might just be the best damn publicist they will ever see."

Whatever this newfound wave of confidence is in Spencer, I'm eating up every bit of it. Finally, she recognizes how talented she is, how amazing she is. Though, something she's said also causes me to pause. This is still about her end goal, not about me or Heartwood, but about how it's going to get her to where she needs to be.

Spencer has managed to get her way again. She does what needs to be done in order to come out on top. Her entire life, she's fought for everything she has. Despite the encouragement Winnie gave me earlier, I suddenly feel inadequate for Spencer. A feeling of dread washes over me at the thought that if leaving is what she really wants, then it isn't going to matter what I say or do. I can be as candid and as transparent as I want, and still, this relationship has been and always will be on Spencer's terms.

CHAPTER 20
SPENCER

GRADY HAS BEEN STUCK to my side ever since he made his speech. I decided to keep the scholarship a secret. Mainly because I wanted Grady to be surprised, but also because I already promised the board of education five thousand dollars for a student this year, and if we didn't make that tonight, the rest would be coming out of Grady's pocket. I figured it was a small price to pay to show the town just how much Grady values them. Not only the town, but the future generations in Heartwood.

The fundraiser was a good time, and brought everyone together, but the scholarship was the show-stealer. It was the proof we needed that Grady isn't just trying to weed out the competition, but that he actually cares about the future entrepreneurs of Heartwood.

That's what really matters for Grady's cause at the end of the day, isn't it? The way we leave something behind for our children and our children's children.

The kind of life we set up for them.

I glance over at Marla seated at a table with Winnie. I wonder what kind of future she envisioned for me. If she even thought about it at all. The kind of life she led is not the kind of life that sets a person up for success. Somehow, here I am, Grady's arm around my waist, and I feel successful.

I feel like I've won just by having him near me, having him claim me in front of everyone here. I haven't won yet, though. Not even close. My job, my livelihood, the only home I've been able to call mine, hangs in the balance. It's the only home I've had that can't be taken away from me, and I will fight for it with everything in me, like I've fought for everything else I've achieved.

I turn my attention back to the conversation Grady is having with Mack. He's yet another person expressing how much it means to him that Grady has decided to fight for this cause.

"You know," Mack says, "I remember when I took over the grocery store from my father. It was dire times for businesses here. The economy took a huge hit, but I made a promise to myself that I would keep my prices low. People needed food, people needed jobs, and I gave that to them." He gives Grady a comforting smack on the shoulder. "We've always taken care of our own here. So, I think it's commendable what you're doing for the town. You can count on me to be at the council meeting."

Grady's mouth forms a tight line as he nods. I peer up at him from where I'm tucked under his arm, and I can tell he's forcing a lump down his throat. This is how it's been all night since he gave his speech. People have been approaching him to tell him how much this means to them, how it would impact their businesses if a massive corporation moved in as direct competition.

Progress. We're making progress. People are starting to believe in Grady, to see what I see in him. Grady may crack jokes when he should be assertive, may choose to look on the bright side instead of demanding more, but it doesn't mean he's not passionate or that he doesn't care. Grady cares for the people he loves by trying to lift them up through actions, not words. Unfortunately, actions are often what go overlooked. He's not flashy about it, but he would be there for you in a heartbeat if he felt like there was some way he could help.

The only people left to convince, the opinions that truly matter, are the town council. They have the final say, and although Suzanne and Eleanor both seem to be on board, I didn't see any of the others in the crowd. Nor did I see Jodi Price. She ignored my invitation.

We say goodbye to Mack, and most of the other guests have also started filing out of the bar, heading home for the night. The few left standing are the ones I have come to know as Grady's inner circle, his family. Eleanor and Marko are still here, chatting to Winnie and my mother at one table. My mother, to her credit, actually looks interested and engaged.

Ally, Mason, and Poppy are gathered around another booth in the back corner celebrating Poppy's win tonight. Everyone adored her Earl Grey Martini, and more than a few people drank a few too many. Hudson and Jett are helping Finn close up behind the bar, making some sort of game out of a very menial task. Between the two of them they only spilled one drink, so I'd call the night a success even if the entirety of it did end up all over Elsie.

"You've gone quiet." Grady releases his arm from around my waist but still keeps his hand on my hip as he turns to look at me. "What's going on in that beautiful head of yours?"

"I'm just taking it all in. It's kind of amazing to see how you have all these people in your life that come out to support you, without so much as batting an eye," I say, and I wonder if that's something I will ever be able to create for myself. All the blood, sweat, and tears I've put into being able to afford an apartment on my own, to create an online business from nothing, and I'm not sure if I've really made it. This kind of love is not something you can pull out of thin air. It's not something that exists for me back in Vancouver. The thought of going back now sucks the air right out of my lungs. The idea of leaving Grady makes me feel sick.

As if Grady can see the storm swirling around within me, he pulls me into a hug, his thick arms almost wrapping around me twice. I breathe in the warm scent of him. The raging storm in my heart settles into a calm breeze. This feels like home. Grady feels like home. Nevertheless, this feeling wars with the definition of home that I've always known. Home has never felt safe, and safety is what I need, what I'm working for.

"I have an idea," he says, leaning down to whisper it into my ear. He pulls away from me and the cold air where Grady's body once was is a shock to my system. I don't have to wait long before Grady has plugged his phone into the speaker by the microphone, and he's extended his hand to me, inviting me toward him.

A dance. Grady wants to dance with me. In front of all these people. I hesitate a moment, chewing on my lip, as I consider what this would mean for us. But my head is soon empty of all thought, because the way Grady's hazel eyes are pleading with me across the bar is making my heart race, a deafening, thunderous beat drowning out all sense of reason.

Screw it. I want to dance with Grady, too. I may not be in Heartwood for much longer, but I'm going to enjoy the rest of my time here while I have it. So, I take his hand, and I let him lead me to a small opening between the tables, only big enough for the two of us.

Grady wraps his arm around my waist, his fingertips curling low on my spine, and takes my other hand in his. The warmth from his hand on the small of my back radiates through me, right down to my core. Someone whistles, and I have a feeling it's Ally. A couple of short weeks ago this would have been against the rules of my boycott. It would have been against a few of them, actually.

"So much for the rules, I guess, huh?" I say, twisting to look at Grady, my face only a few inches from his. He gazes back at me, his eyes twinkling in the dim light as his smile makes the corners crease. I love it when he smiles like that.

"I told you, Rebel," he says, and then leans down so the next thing he whispers is warm against my ear, "fuck the rules." Goose-bumps skitter across my skin, and I get an irresistible urge to be alone with him. Grady has confirmed my suspicions that he was never on board with the rules in the first place, that he's been trying to convince me to forget about them since the beginning. Whatever hesitations I have been feeling up until this point, the determination in Grady's eyes makes me want to let go of them. Even if it's just for tonight.

"So, you've just been going along with them, what, to entertain me and my crazy ideas?"

"Yeah, that sounds about right." He chuckles, the sound reverberating through me, but then his expression falls as he says, "I just wanted you. Whatever that looked like. Whatever you needed, I wanted to be that for you." Grady says it like him wanting me is the only singular truth. The only thing that he's absolutely sure of. If only I could be so confident. If only I was as prepared as he is to take the risk of getting into a relationship.

The boyfriend boycott isn't something I decided on because I was tired of dating. It's there to protect me from uncertainty, to keep me safe. No matter how good or reliable someone may seem at the outset, the fact is that human beings are flawed. Putting your life in someone else's hands is always going to be a risk.

Grady's firm body is solid against me. He's solid and steady and reliable. In this moment, I allow myself to fall, just a little bit, even if this thing between us is only temporary. Even if the expiration date is looming closer. I lean my head against his chest, listening to the rhythmic beat of his heart, the steady sound of his breath as his head dips close to mine.

It's a sound that I'm fairly certain is there just for me.

"Your mom seemed to really hit it off with Winnie and Eleanor," Grady points out as we walk into the master bedroom we've now been sharing and clicks the door shut behind us. Marla had been tipsy when we got home, so Grady made sure she made it down the stairs to her bedroom. She said goodnight to him with an over-the-top statement of unconditional love and a dramatic kiss on his cheek. It was heartwarming in a way. She seemed freer with her feelings, at ease.

"Yeah, because Winnie made sure her drinks were flowing all night." I chuckle with a shake of my head.

"Well, I'd say the evening was a hit," Grady says, unclasping his watch from around his wrist and loosening his tie.

"It was a blast," I agree. "I just wish more of the councillors had come." Only two out of the eight I invited had been there, Suzanne and Eleanor, and only because they've been directly involved in our cause. Suzanne had jumped at the chance to offer a student a scholarship when I approached her about it.

"We've still got time," Grady reassures me, but I'm not so sure. The clock is ticking, and I only have one more trick up my sleeve. The career fair is in a few days and after that ... the council meeting.

I wander into the bathroom and start taking off my jewelry. It feels oddly natural coming home with Grady tonight, and even more so getting unready with him. This is something I've never had, someone to debrief the events of the night with.

"Has it been weird for you to sleep here with your mom in the basement?" Grady asks me as I remove the thin gold hoops from my ears and set them down on the counter in his ensuite.

"I mean, I did live with the woman for the better part of my life," I answer. Although there were only a few years where it was just the two of us. I tried not to be home as much as I could, which resulted in a lot of sleepovers at Ally's house. Her parents never minded that I was over all the time; I think they knew how fucked up my own life was. They initially said no sleepovers on school nights, but that changed the night that they found out I had snuck into Ally's room because my mom had passed out drunk and her boyfriend was making me uncomfortable. Nothing ever happened with my mom's boyfriends, but I think if I hadn't been spending the majority of my nights sleeping on an air mattress on Ally's floor, it might have been a different story.

"Yeah, but never with your ..." Grady hesitates, choosing his next words. I'm not a mind reader, but I had a feeling he was about to use the word boyfriend. Instead, he goes with, "The guy you're sleeping with."

"My mom sent me pictures of boobs she wanted. We don't exactly have normal mother-daughter boundaries," I counter.

I push past where he's standing in the door to the ensuite and start to unzip the back of the dress I'm wearing. Grady instinctively comes to me, taking the zipper and working it slowly down my back.

"I really, *really* don't want to be talking about your mother's boob job right now." Grady dips his head to nuzzle into my neck from behind. His fingertips lightly brush over my shoulder, pushing the strap down and letting my dress fall to the floor.

He kisses my shoulder now, trailing a line with his lips up my neck to the spot beneath my ear. His hands roam around my body where my dress once covered, the fabric now piled around my feet.

"What do you want to do instead?" I purr. I've gotten the distinct impression that Grady is used to serving everyone but himself, thinking about everyone's needs above his own. Including mine. *Especially* mine. Tonight is going to be different. I want Grady to have everything he has ever dreamed of.

"I want to bend you over"—Grady's breath on my ear sends a shiver down the length of my spine—"and watch your perfect pussy take me until you're coming all over my cock."

I squeeze my thighs together at the sudden gush between my legs, and I'm swollen almost to the point of pain, needing the release of him inside me.

Grady splays his hand between my shoulder blades, pushing me gently forward onto the bed, onto my knees. His hand wraps around my hip and pulls my ass back towards him, and then he moves to undo his belt. I hear the snap of the leather as he whips it out of the belt loops, and then, before I can even process, he has his hard length out of his jeans, and he's stroking it between my ass cheeks.

He pushes my head down further, and I grip a pillow as he lowers himself and licks a long line from my clit all the way to my ass, stopping only to make a languid circle around my pert hole. My hips buck in response to the sensation, but his hand is once again on my hip, pulling me back, his tongue circling my opening.

"Is this okay?" he asks, now forming tight circles with his thumb. I look back at him over my shoulder and nod. I want it *all*.

My vision goes blurry, and all I'm aware of is Grady sliding a slick finger into my asshole. *Holy Fuck.*

He rises up and pushes into me, stretching my pussy with his thick cock. I have the satisfying sensation of complete fullness, Grady occupying every part of me. Body, mind, and soul.

He fills me, thrusting until the sensation morphs and takes over my entire being, muscles clenching and releasing in waves. I pulse around him, helping him inch closer to his own edge. He removes himself and his cum releases, warm and wet, on my spine.

My body finally relaxes, flopping down onto the bed, my energy fully spent even though Grady did most of the work. He retreats into the bathroom and I let my eyes close. When he comes back, he's holding a warm washcloth and starts gently cleaning me.

"You don't have to do that," I say, lifting my head to look at him, although my limbs feel leaden.

"Of course I do," he says as he continues to wipe between my legs. "I meant it when I said I wanted to take care of you," he murmurs, his voice low and gravelly.

My face flops back on the pillow, and I do, I let him take care of me all he wants. All I can manage in response is a muffled *mmhmm* into the pillow.

It's not long until Grady climbs back into bed with me, and we lay together, me nestled under his arm. His breath evens out next to me, into a rhythmic soft snore that tells me he's asleep.

I am not even close to sleep. I've been staring up at the ceiling for the last hour. My body is relaxed, but my mind is not.

Grady turns over, facing away from me now, so I lift the covers back gently and climb out of bed. I sneak out of the bedroom as silently as I can, closing the door with a soft click, and I head out to the kitchen.

I flick on the oven light, just enough to see by, not enough to wake the whole house, and I pick up my laptop from the counter. It dings to life when I open it, and the first thing I see is a red circle over my mailbox. When I open it, I find an e-mail waiting for me from my landlord.

DEAR TENANT,

I HOPE this message finds you well. I am writing to formally notify you that the apartment located at 302-1250 Nicola Street will see a rent increase in accordance with local regulations. Below, you will find a new rent amount with a detailed breakdown of other associated fees such as parking, etc.

In addition, the building strata has decided that units are no longer allowed to be sublet, and as you are currently subletting your unit, your tenant will be obligated to vacate the premises within thirty days.

Thank you for your understanding.

SINCERELY,
People-First Property Management

. . .

I skim the new rental agreement and my pulse thrums in my ears. The new number at the bottom of the page is staggering. A vice grips my throat as I consider how I could ever pay the amount with the sporadic contracts I've been getting. It isn't even that nice. The place is just an outdated one-bedroom with parquet floors and a tiny galley kitchen on the third floor of an ancient walk-up. But it's mine. It's the first home that I felt certain wasn't going to be taken away from me. Until now.

People-First Property Management. What people? More like *profit-first.* My blood simmers in my veins.

Anger. It's a more productive feeling than the hopelessness that this turn of events could send me into. Anger sends me into problem-solving mode. I open my browser and scour the classified sites for rentals in the same area. I like that area. It's familiar to me.

As I filter my search results from least expensive to most expensive, a pit forms in my stomach. The least expensive apartment in the West End is still six hundred more a month than what I've be paying. There's no way I can manage that. Not unless I get this job at Mile High.

Once I have a signed contract, the cost of housing won't seem as dire, I'm sure of it. I can negotiate a good salary. Sasha promised me that they would compensate me well. It would be a steady income at least, and I could stop fighting tooth and nail just to make ends meet. Once I sign that contract, I will have made it. All by myself, and no one will be able to take that away from me.

I pick my camera up off the counter and plug the memory card into the side of the laptop, clicking through the pop-ups. Maybe looking through photos from the night will help settle my mind. Despite the evening not garnering as much attention from the council as I'd hoped, I did manage to get some great photos that I can include in my portfolio.

The first picture I open is the first one I took of the evening. It's of Grady. He didn't know I was taking it and that's part of what gives it the intimate quality I can see in it now. He's standing behind the bar, lit from behind, the sleeves of one of the new shirts I picked out for him rolled up around his thick forearms. He's smiling, the kind that reaches up to his sparkling hazel eyes and it makes my insides feel warm. Grady was happy, in his element, with everyone he loved in one room. Including me. From the very start of the cocktail party that smile never left his face.

All the photos show him this way. The pictures are dark and moody in the dim light of the bar, but Grady's smile lights them all up. I copy a few to a folder that I'll send him, that he can use for branding or his social media page.

As I continue sifting through the images, I stumble across a photo I don't remember taking. In fact, I couldn't have taken it. The picture is of me. It's towards the bottom of the folder, so it must have been taken once most people left. When I had left my camera on the table in front of Winnie.

There I am, pulled in close to Grady's chest, my cheek resting on his peck. I feel like I'm looking at someone else, a person that I don't even recognize, because the look on my face is ... *peaceful.* Maybe even, dare I say it, *in love.*

I click the window closed and slam my laptop shut. It doesn't matter how peaceful, how *in love* I look in that moment. I'm not in love. I can't be. Love is what tears people's lives apart, and I've only just started to build mine into something that feels stable. I told myself I wouldn't go there, I wouldn't tread anywhere near that territory. Love has never worked out for me in the past. I think my lineage is cursed when it comes to love.

Now I'm certain that sleep will be impossible. My mind is racing through a list of possible scenarios, envisioning how this thing with Grady is going to end.

Because it will end ... eventually. I'm the one who has to do it. Grady is in too deep. I know that for sure now. The way we interacted at the party was far beyond a hook-up relationship. This is no longer just sex. There's something more, and I know what it is, but I won't admit it. Not even to myself.

CHAPTER 21
GRADY

THE SMELL HITS me the moment I walk through the door. Everyone knows the smell of a high school gymnasium. The smell of rubber and teenage hormones sent me right back to my own high school years. This was the place where I walked across the small stage when I graduated, and watched Hudson and Jett walk across the stage after me. It's where I shared my first dance with a girl. It was our prom night. We went outside as the dance was winding down and sat on the bench around the side of the school. I was going to kiss her. I was so close to getting my first real kiss when my phone rang. Dad had gotten a call from the police department saying Jett had been out at a party in the woods and got caught drinking underage and doing God knows what else. He was too busy at the clinic to go and pick Jett up, and no one else was available but me.

I thought I had won the lottery that night. I thought I had won the lottery, and it was ripped out of my hands. I spent weeks ignoring Jett. It was the first and only time I was angry enough to let him know it. He had stolen an opportunity from me that I could never get back. Now I'm back at Heartwood High, in the same spot with Spencer, and I realize that I had no idea back then how good life could get.

The gym looks very different now; they've painted a new mural on one side, the image depicting a very predatory-looking bird for the Heartwood Hawks. Although I'm fairly certain whoever did it painted a falcon and not a hawk but that's what you get in a small town on a budget. The rest of the gym is filled with tables and booths from all the businesses in Heartwood with job openings for new graduates. Some colleges from neighbouring towns are here also, along with a couple of big universities in Calgary. Those booths are popular, judging by the size of the crowd gathering around them. I guess most students recognize that a post-secondary degree is their best ticket out of Heartwood.

There's a small crowd forming around my booth, too. Though they're not at all interested in working at Jack's. They're more interested in Spencer Sinclair, travel influencer and social media personality. Spencer is chatting with them as if she's known the group of girls gathered around her for years. There's something so easy and natural about the way that she talks to her fans. I hear her compliment one of them and the girl blushes, like she just received a compliment from a celebrity. Spencer is a celebrity in a way. With her social media following, most people who use the app either already follow her or they know of her.

Though, the way Spencer carries herself is not what I would expect of someone who has so many people always fawning over her. I spent enough time poring over her social media page last year to know that she doesn't subscribe to the usual influencer trends, doesn't take brand deals she doesn't like, doesn't post photos for clout. Most of the photos she's posted are of the places she's visited, and if she's in them at all, her back is turned to the camera. Like she would rather hide her face.

"What is your all-time favourite place you've ever been?" One of the girls asks her, her expression open and expectant. The others are hanging on every word that Spencer has said. I do that, too.

I drop my eyes down to my lap so it doesn't seem like I'm eavesdropping on their conversation, but I just can't help it. I want to hear every syllable that comes out of Spencer's mouth.

"Hmm. That's a tough question. I think I'd have to say Cappadocia."

"Cappa-what-ia?" a brace-faced girl asks, and I stifle a laugh because, same.

"It's in Turkey," Spencer explains. "They fly hot air balloons there, and I just loved waking up every morning and sitting on my balcony watching them. They dot the sky like stars. Especially when they're all lit up at night." At that moment, my stomach drops. It plummets through the floor. Hearing Spencer talk about all the amazing places she's been and things she's seen, she's in a league of her own. And *way* out of mine. I can't offer her a wild and adventurous life in Heartwood. I've barely done any travelling myself. What could I give her here that could ever compare?

In my peripheral vision, one of the girls takes out her phone and starts typing, as if she's already planning her own trip there.

"The travel is great, it's the best part of my job. If you decide that you want to do what I do one day, just don't forget that what you have here in Heartwood is beautiful, too. Don't forget where you come from. It's important to have a connection to your roots. You might not see it now, but it is."

I can't help the smile that creeps across my face at this. She sounds as if she longs to have a place like Heartwood to call home. Hope blooms in my chest that maybe she's open to staying. Maybe I can show her that she can have this, too, if she allows it. If she accepts it.

The girls wander off, giddy and shrieking that they just met Spencer Sinclair.

"Come on." I get up and place a hand on Spencer's arm. "Let's wander around. I'm tired of sitting here."

"Someone needs to man the booth." She points toward my pathetic-looking booth. The table is bare, no cool freebies or swag to attract the teens. Now that the girls have left, there's no one interested in our booth at all.

"Ah, kids don't care about working at the bar. I'm here for the scholarship presentation and that's about it," I say. "Which, by the way, I'm shitting my pants about, so thank you so much for signing me up for this."

"You'll do great. You killed it at the party the other night, and now you'll have even more practice for the council meeting." Right. The council meeting, and the speech that I absolutely cannot fuck up. Spencer gives me a reassuring pat on my shoulder and her touch sends a zing of electricity down my spine.

"Are there any surprises in this one that I should be aware of?"

"It wouldn't be a surprise if I told you, would it?" She winks at me, and I roll my eyes back at her.

Spencer follows me to take a lap around the gym, saying hello to everyone who came out today. I want to show her what the community of Heartwood is like: friendly, welcoming. Although I think she already knows. A few people wave from their booths as we walk past. Spencer is close beside me. Close enough that I could reach down and grab her hand, but I don't. The comfort of her arm brushing against mine as we walk is enough right now.

Eleanor waves us over to the Town of Heartwood booth and greets me with a warm smile before pulling Spencer into a hug.

"I didn't know the town was hiring," I say, noting the stack of application forms on the table in front of her.

"We weren't. But after Spencer's presentation the other night, I figured we could use some young blood at the tourism board. Fresh eyes."

"There was a group of girls over there that might be interested. They wanted to know all about what I do," Spencer offers.

"Oh, honey, I think they were just interested in you," Eleanor says, pointing out the obvious.

"I'm really not that interesting."

"I think they would beg to differ." Eleanor cocks her head to the side. Her expression changes when she sees someone approaching us from behind. "I think *he* would also disagree."

I don't even have to look to know who is walking up from behind us. His cologne gives him away from a mile off.

"Nobody at your booth, I see." Carter sneers. "I guess they like the idea of working somewhere a little more upscale." He gestures towards the table he's set up a few down from Eleanor's. There are a handful of teens surrounding it, and I wonder if he's slipped them some money just to stand there looking interested.

"It's not exactly fair to offer jobs that don't exist yet," I retort. "If they ever do."

"My chances are better than they were a few weeks ago. Better read over that law again if you want to be up to speed at the council meeting. All it says is that the business owner needs to be local to Heartwood."

"It also says it can't be part of a chain. Besides, you haven't lived here in years."

"I grew up here. I have a permanent address here. Gotta go after what you want, right?" He makes a point of glancing at Spencer. "Any more thoughts on when we can schedule that date you promised me?"

"I never promised anything." Her tone is flat but not assertive. Not enough to close that door and lock it, throw away the key. It makes my vision blur with rage. She still hasn't agreed to an official date with him, but all I want is for her to shut him down in a monumental display. A very public one. I want him to walk away with his tail between his legs. Actually, doing it in Heartwood High, the place where Carter reigned as King Asshole for so long, would be kind of poetic.

"A rain check is as good as a promise, Red."

"A rain check is a rain check," Spencer answers. Carter inches closer to her, and I can't fucking stand here any longer and watch this. I just want to get Spencer far away from him. Maybe I didn't have any right to be jealous about Carter asking Spencer out the first time, but I sure as hell have a right to be pissed now. There's only one thing I know for certain now: Spencer is mine. She's been mine since she set foot in this town a year and a half ago. She might not realize it yet, but she and I are only a matter of time.

I grab Spencer's hand and turn on my heel, dragging her away from Carter, away from the career fair. I don't know where I'm going but it doesn't matter. I just need her all to myself.

The noise spilling out of the gymnasium becomes fuzzy and distant as the doors close behind us. The lobby is empty save for a couple of kids making out against some lockers down the adjacent hall. They scurry away when we burst through the doors.

Spencer yanks her hand out of mine the moment we're alone. I suddenly don't know what to do with my hands anymore. They had just found their one purpose in life, holding Spencer's. So, I shove them in my pockets to keep myself from reaching for her.

"What was that?" Spencer almost shouts, shocked. Her arms cross over her chest as she waits for my reply. I reach a hand up to rub the back of my neck, trying to formulate an answer that doesn't come across as possessive.

"I don't know, Spencer," I say, my chest heaving. "I had to get out of there." Spencer's shoulders loosen, accepting my answer, and she wanders over to the display case against the wall, perusing the photos and trophies inside. My breathing is still ragged, my anger reducing to a low simmer.

"Is this you?" she asks, pointing at the team photo from my championship year. She's trying to change the subject, to distract me, to settle my lingering rage, and it's working.

"Yes."

"And this is Carter?" Well, it was working.

"Yes." One-word answers are all I can manage right now. I'm out of breath. I feel like I ran a marathon in the fifty steps it took to get out here.

"I didn't know you actually played baseball. Though I did

wonder why you seemed so natural coaching." Spencer runs her finger over the glass of the display case, leaving a little smudge.

"Yup. All through high school," I grit out.

"Were you any good?" Her eyes stay fixed on the photo of me holding the trophy that now sits beside the framed picture.

"I guess. We won the championship because of my hit. A homer. I got offered a scholarship. A few of us did. I didn't take it," I answer in short, clipped sentences.

"Why not?" Now her eyes flick to me, fire behind her green irises, making them glow.

"Jett was really starting to get into skiing. He was good. Like, really good. Everyone knew that Jett was going to be amazing right from day one. But I was the only one who could get him to the mountain."

"You gave up on your dream so Jett could have his?"

I pause when she asks me this question and ponder what she's perceiving in me. Spencer has this way of seeing right through me, through my light-hearted façade, and right to the version of me who grew up watching everyone around him struggle. She sees me for who I am, the little boy who lost his mom and just desperately wanted everything to be okay again. I did it through jokes, and lifting people up, making them laugh, but I also did it through sacrifice.

"I didn't really think about it like that. But yeah, I guess. Taking the scholarship would have meant being away from my family, not being there for my brothers. So, I turned it down."

"Did Carter take it?"

"Yeah. He sure did. He ran the bases off my hit and got to take credit for something I did." Her mouth opens to form a silent *ah* as if she's realizing that my grudge against Carter doesn't just stem from this squabble over the Parks' restaurant, or her. It's over a decade old. "Why are we still talking about Carter?"

"You're cute when you're jealous, by the way," Spencer says as a way of answering me. "You don't need to be jealous of Carter.

He may have the life you envisioned on the surface, but he's a dirt-bag. You, Grady, are not a dirtbag."

"No," I agree.

She's right, but it doesn't staunch the sticky, murky feeling in my gut. The fact that he had the balls to hit on Spencer in *my* bar was just the tip of the iceberg. He's gotten to live the life I wanted, off my back and at my expense. He took the scholarship, got his business degree, opened a successful restaurant, and now he has his sights set on Spencer. The most frustrating part of all of it is that it's not his fault. Carter is a dick, but the only person I can be angry with is myself for not fighting back.

"That's why we came out here, isn't it?" Spencer asks, inching closer. "Because you were jealous." She's close enough now that her sweet floral scent is awakening something carnal within me.

I regard her, cupping her cheek in my hand, and her breath hitches under the firmness of it.

"I just couldn't bear one more second of you sharing the same space as Carter." I slide my hand around to the nape of her neck, and twine my fingers in her hair, gripping it in a fistful so I can tilt her head back to look at me. "So yes, Spencer. I am fucking jealous. I hate it when he even so much as looks in your direction. Fuck Carter Bouchard and fuck not getting what I want."

I bring my lips to hers and kiss her firmly. Without hesitation. Confident. Certain. This is what I want. She is what I want. Every-thing she touches becomes better just for being in her presence. Including me.

Her lips return my fervour, and she inhales deeply through her nose, as if she's taking in every aspect of me as she parts my lips with her tongue.

I'm suddenly aware that this is what redemption feels like. I'm finally taking back the kiss that I sacrificed after my prom because I was so used to sacrificing myself for others. Now, I'm getting what I want.

The screech of a microphone interrupts us, causing us to pull our mouths apart, but I don't take my eyes off Spencer, and she doesn't take her gorgeous emerald eyes off of me. We stay in this moment as long as possible before we hear Heartwood High's principal introduce himself, and then start his announcement about the scholarship.

"I think you're up," Spencer whispers between us. I don't want to pull myself away, but the testosterone coursing through my veins makes me more motivated than ever. So, I plant a quick kiss on Spencer's forehead, and she follows me back to the door of the gymnasium, watching me stride up the steps to the makeshift stage with more confidence than I've had in decades.

CHAPTER 22
SPENCER

I AM SO FUCKED. Like, royally screwed. One minute you think that you have your shit firmly together, resolute in never dating again. Then suddenly you're making out with your situationship that is feeling less and less like the casual fling you intended it to be.

It's like I'm a teenager again, but this time without the constant anxiety and pit in my stomach knowing I have to go home to my mom's boyfriend's house after school. Or that I'll go home to find all of our shit thrown out on the front lawn, or find my mom heartbroken and crying.

Whatever this feeling is that Grady gives me is the opposite of anxiety. I don't get butterflies when he kisses me; I get quiet, peaceful, calm. Less fluttering and more like the steady whooshing of a river.

Some people might find that feeling boring, and I might have too at one point in my dating history. Now though, I recognize his solid, steady presence as a grounding force. A gravitational pull keeping me rooted to the earth.

I lean against the frame of the double doors to the gymnasium and watch as he climbs the few steps and meets the principal on stage. He's smiling wide as the principal shakes his hand, and it takes me a second to register that I'm smiling, too. It's subconscious, my body physically reacting in time with his.

The principal pulls out one of those big cardboard cheques and thanks Grady for his commitment to Heartwood, to the Heartwood High students, and to ensuring their future here in their hometown. It's heartwarming, and I can tell by the expression on Grady's face that this means more to him than just beating Carter. He really does believe in this, that supporting locals is the way forward for Heartwood.

Grady takes the microphone, and he calls a student by the name of Alice Montgomery to the stage to accept her award.

"How does it feel, Alice? To be the first recipient of the Landry Young Entrepreneurs Scholarship?" he asks and extends the microphone towards her so she can answer. Her eyes are misty, and she clears her throat before she speaks.

"It feels incredible. Thank you. Really, I have no words."

"What do you hope to do with the money?"

"I want to open my own pet store. Offer grooming services and maybe even boarding. This money will help me with the deposit on the vacant storefront on Main," she explains.

The Parks. She's going to apply for the Park's restaurant. Good for her. Yet another reason why we need to make sure Grady wins at the council meeting. My eyes flick over to where Carter is standing. His face is beet-red, the muscle in his jaw flicking as he grinds his teeth. It's almost comical that he feels the need to compete with this sweet girl who just wants to look after other people's dogs. You have to be a special kind of prick to look at Alice up on that stage and hope for her downfall.

Grady poses for a photo with Alice, taken by the news reporter I ensured would be there myself. The camera flashes a few times, Alice and Grady both beaming. My phone vibrates in the back pocket of my jeans, stealing my attention, and I fish it out.

Sasha.

I answer as Grady makes eye contact with me from onstage, and I throw him a thumbs up before slipping out through the lobby of the school again.

"Give me an update, Spencer. What's the sitch?" Sasha says, half distracted. I can hear her typing on the other end of the phone.

"I'm almost at the finish line. One more week, and I'll have a completed portfolio for you," I explain in rapidly-uttered words. "What I can tell you is that things are going to plan. So far."

"Good to hear." More typing. The smacking sound of her chewing gum. "The recruiter from Mile High is getting impatient. Can you send me what you have?"

"Now? I haven't—" I stammer. I know that what I have so far isn't exactly a compelling application. All I have are outlines of plans, how they may impact people's perceptions of Grady. Nothing concrete. Nothing to say that my strategy was successful in any way. I won't have that until we've won over the council, and even then ... I wonder if I could collect some interviews from people in town. Maybe Eleanor would be willing to attest to how Grady has changed over the last few weeks ...

"Just something, Spencer. Anything." She's more focused on our conversation now. The typing has stopped, and her tone lowers to a more serious cadence. "Listen, they called me today and told me that they have another candidate that's come forward for the position. They're getting antsy. I guess chlamydia girl is threatening real legal action. They want to find someone, and soon. There's only so much I can say about how great a fit you'd be without some concrete proof."

My heart drops with a solid thud inside me as I take in this new piece of information. It's the fear I was trying to shove down, the insecurities that tell me I'm not good enough. What if this candidate is way more qualified than I am? Who am I kidding? Of course, they're more qualified than me. Panic licks at my throat, my breathing becomes shallow. I took too long, and now the only opportunity I've had is going to be taken away from me.

That right there is the sobering thought that reminds me of the mantra I have lived by my entire adult life. *I am the only person I can safely rely on.* And I'm not going to let myself down.

I have watched my mother have everything taken away from her, the rug completely ripped out from beneath her feet because of other people, because of her over-reliance on other people to give her what she needs.

This job was mine. It *is* mine. I worked for it so that I could secure the life that I need, the one I never had growing up. Where the roof over my head isn't going anywhere, where I know that I'm coming home to sleep in the same bed. It's the only reason that I've hustled for every contract, every opportunity to make that dream a reality.

"Don't worry, Sasha. Stay close to your inbox. I'll send some stuff over to you soon," I promise, trying to force my racing mind to form a logical thought, one that might actually help me. *Eyes on the prize, Sinclair.* The final hustle. The last push.

I hang up with Sasha as I hear a roar of applause from the gymnasium. I can see from where I'm standing that Grady is coming down off the podium, his smile still just as bright as before. Now though, mine has faded as he beelines towards me.

He embraces me the second he reaches me. His warmth is comforting, and all I want is to sink into him.

But where I usually feel comfort against Grady, a sticky, sick feeling bubbles up my throat. My conversation with Sasha was yet another reminder clock ticking on this project, and on my relation-ship with Grady. I'm more determined than ever to prove that I can do this. I don't need anyone else to take care of me, I can take care of myself. I will get this job, and I will live the life I've always imagined. One where I am independent, self-reliant—alone.

CHAPTER 23
GRADY

It's been a few days since the career fair, and the deadline for the council meeting is looming. So is my deadline to convince Spencer to stay in Heartwood. She spent the last few days furiously working on her computer at my dining table, putting together her portfolio for this job that she's determined to get. Little does she know, I'm just as determined to show her that she can have everything she wants right here in Heartwood, too. Something she said at the fair gave me all the inspiration I needed, and now I have a laser-like focus on my end goal.

"Where are we going that you had to get me up at the ass-crack of dawn?" Spencer groans, her voice still sleepy. The sun hasn't even risen over the mountains, and that's the point, but knowing how much she hates mornings, it was a risky move on my part. Waking her up today was like poking a sleeping bear.

"You'll see. Just drink your coffee," I say, handing her the thermos I brought with me for this very reason, to keep her from getting too grizzly.

We round the corner, and I pull the car into the lot next to the baseball diamond. It was the largest open space in town, and the only place that Carl agreed to meet. The moment I park the car and turn towards Spencer is the moment I realize that the risk of waking the sleeping bear was worth it. The look on her face when she realizes what we're out here to do …

"A hot air balloon?" She beams at me, jaw nearly in her lap. "You got me a hot air balloon? Are we going up in it?"

"No, we're just here to watch it from the ground," I deadpan. "Of course we're going up in it."

Spencer just about spills the carafe of coffee as she flings the door open, squealing with delight at the surprise. I realized yesterday that if Spencer is going to be convinced to stay in Heartwood, it's going to take something *big*. It's going to take something that can compete with all the exciting adventures she's been on around the world. If she loved looking at the hot air balloons in Turkey, then I'm willing to bet that going up in one over the Rocky Mountains at sunrise would be a close competition.

Spencer is halfway across the field, approaching the bright rainbow balloon. By the time I've reached her, she's craning her neck to look up at it in awe.

"Howdy," Carl says, climbing out of the basket and landing on the ground in front of us. "Ready for your flight?" He makes it sound like we're getting ready to board an airplane, but the reality of it makes my stomach feel watery. This is no airplane. Up close this thing is … terrifying. The basket looks as though it could barely hold two of us let alone three, and the sides seem … a lot lower than I would have thought for something that is supposed to keep us thousands of feet above the ground.

I'm second-guessing my decision to do this when Spencer pipes up.

"Yes!" she squeals "I have dreamt about doing this for years!" She claps her hands like a kid waiting to open presents on Christmas, and it almost makes it worth the fact that I'm about to shit my pants. I thought public speaking was terrifying, but this …

Carl waves us over and starts to go through a brief explanation of the basket, the balloon, and what we can expect throughout the ride.

"What kind of safety equipment is there?" I ask. My voice comes out shakier than I expect it to. Carl looks back at me and blinks slowly. Once, twice. It's not the first time he's been asked this question, right? Was that a stupid question?

"I've got three parachutes on board, and a fire extinguisher."

"Parachutes?" I say, aghast.

"Yup. Not much you can do once this thing decides to go down but jump ship. I've never had to use them though. The chance of a ballooning accident is rare."

"But not impossible," I add, the words squeaking out of my throat that is getting tighter by the second.

"No. Hence, the parachutes." He winks, but I'm not amused.

"Come on, Grady. You like a little danger, right?"

"A *little* danger." I emphasize the word *little*. Like not wearing a helmet on my bike when I ride it a block or two home. Not like plummeting to my death. Suddenly, Carl and his Costco jeans and New Balance sneakers don't seem like someone I should be entrusting my life to in a virtual picnic basket three thousand feet in the air.

Yet here we are, and Spencer is taking his hand as he helps her up the step into the death trap. I follow close behind, but I don't take Carl's hand even though he's extended it to me.

Why did I think this was a good idea again?

Spencer is practically buzzing with excitement as I climb into the basket after her. Right. That's why. If this is what it takes to get Spencer to see what she can have here, I would do it ten times over. Hell, I would bungee jump off this thing if that's what I had to do.

Carl is the last to join us, and he closes the gate, latching it behind him.

No turning back now. I decide that my only option now is to

trust Carl. After all, he came highly recommended by Eleanor when I called her last night. Though now I wonder if that had more to do with him being the only hot air balloon tour offered in Heartwood. The fact that he just happened to have an opening the very next morning could also be interpreted as a red flag, but it's no longer a helpful thought as he releases the ropes around the outside of the basket holding us down. My stomach lurches as the basket lifts off the ground.

Spencer twines her hand through mine. It's soft and warm and it settles my nerves. Heat radiates from the flame keeping the balloon aloft overhead, heating us against the cool spring morning. If this is my last day on earth, I decide, this is how I want to go.

We rise higher and higher into the clear sky, coming to meet the height of the mountains around us. As we do, the sun comes into view over the horizon, casting a warm glow on our faces. I glance down towards Spencer. She's closing her eyes, leaning her face against my arm. A tear trickles down her cheek.

"Talk to me, Rebel. Are you okay?" I ask her, my heart dropping at the sight. Maybe this wasn't the right thing to do. Maybe this hot air balloon has made her realize that she misses the wide-open world. Maybe this has worked against me.

"This is perfect, Grady. Absolutely perfect." My panic eases as she stretches up onto her tip toes to place a soft kiss on my cheek. "Thank you for doing this."

We float up here, weightless, for another hour or so before Carl brings us back down to earth. As magical as the whole experience was, I can't help but let out an audible sigh when I get out of the basket and feel solid ground beneath my feet. I can feel the colour returning to my face.

"That bad, huh?" Spencer asks with a smirk, noticing the way my shoulders visibly relaxed when my feet hit the grass.

"I don't love heights," I admit.

"Grady!" she shrieks, playfully shoving my shoulder. "You didn't tell me you were petrified the whole time!"

"Okay, well I wouldn't say *petrified*. I think I held it together."

"Yeah, if you call closing your eyes the whole time holding it together."

"The sun was bright," I lie. In fact, the sunrise was just a convenient cover.

"Sure." Her eyes crease at the corners as she squints at me, forming those little crow's feet that I wouldn't change for the world.

She flops down on the seat next to me when we get back to the car. I open my mouth to ask her if she wants breakfast, but she's distracted by something on her phone.

"Everything okay?" It's the same look she gets when her mom texts, but I happen to know that Marla will still be asleep when we get back.

"Yeah. It's just my agent." Right. The portfolio she was working on. "She said she loves what I've put together so far." A half-smile forms on her mouth.

"That's good, right?" I ask. Every fibre of my being hopes that Spencer will say no. That my plan is working, my grand gesture enough to convince her that she doesn't need that job. She doesn't need to leave. There's something in her expression that seems like she's deflated a bit. She shakes her head, a crease forming between her brows.

"Yeah. No. It's great," she says. "It's just still not enough for the rep at Mile High. They want a guarantee that I'll be able to deliver. They want to know that what we've done here has worked. That we've won at the council meeting."

"We will win at the council meeting," I reassure her, though every part of me wants to tell her that she should turn the job down regardless of what happens. That I would do anything to take care of her, give her a home here. I know that won't work. I've also come to accept the fact that when it comes to Spencer, this has to be on her terms. All I can do is continue to show her that what we have is worth more than any job, apartment, or trip could ever give her. The feeling I get from this thought isn't all that different from the feeling I had going up in the balloon, my gut tightens, bracing myself. I just hope that when Spencer decides what she wants, it doesn't send me crashing down to earth at terminal velocity.

CHAPTER 24
SPENCER

"I STILL DON'T UNDERSTAND why no one wanted to watch *House on the Bloodstained Hill*," Poppy groans. "This is cheesy."

"Horror movies don't exactly scream girls' night, Pops," Ally calls from the kitchen.

"Whatever." Poppy playfully rolls her big doe eyes. "It's okay if you can't hack it, Ally. Just admit it." In an interesting turn of events, Poppy is an avid lover of horror and gore.

It's not my cup of tea, either, but to be fair, though neither is the Hallmark rom-com Ally has decided on. Naturally, the opening shot is of a well-dressed woman, stumbling her way onto a train platform in what I can only assume is a small town where she will be stranded for the next hour and a half.

Ally joins us in the living room, handing each of us a bowl of popcorn and a glass of wine. She flops down onto the worn sofa with a sigh that makes me think her belly might completely deflate.

"Just so you know, I officially hate you all for drinking around me right now."

"When are you due, Ally?" my mother asks. I brought her

along to our girls' night because it felt wrong to leave her out when she doesn't have anything else to do. Truth be told, I'm enjoying having her around now. She's settled in here and even started making friends when Winnie invited her to weekly bridge at her house.

I've been trying not to get my hopes up, but I can't help but think that this breakup might be different for her. She's wearing the clothes she likes to wear again. She's making her own friends here. She seems to be listening when people tell her that she can have a fulfilling life on her own.

Tonight is reminiscent of my favourite times growing up, rare as they were. We'd have girls' nights like this occasionally, once she was able to get her life back in order post-breakup. Even then, I knew that girls' nights were to be enjoyed in the moment, and that they would inevitably end when the next guy came around. I decided early on that I wouldn't be like my mother, and that the women in my life would always come before any guy I was seeing. I stayed true to that. Despite my affinity for one-night stands and casual hook-ups, I never *ever* let a guy take me home from the bar if Ally was going to be left alone.

Things with my mom are different now, I can feel it in my bones. She's changing.

"I'll be thirty-four weeks tomorrow," Ally answers. "But I feel like I'm going on sixty. Pregnancy feels so much longer when you find out about it right away."

"It'll be over in no time," my mother consoles her. "Motherhood is like that. Everything goes by so fast. Don't spend all your days just wishing for the next phase. You'll look back and wish you had soaked it in more."

I cock my head, listening to Marla talk about motherhood as if she's Mother Mary herself feels like having an out-of-body experience. Ally flashes me a glare, recognizing that the look on my face is one that I make when I'm trying to stifle a scoff.

"What was your pregnancy like with Spencer?" Ally asks and I can't hold it in any longer. This should be rich. I'm going through all the possible complaints, no booze … no Botox …

"It was magical," she says wistfully. Well, that's not what I was expecting. "The moment I found out about Spencer I was so excited. I felt like a mother the second I saw that positive result. I wasn't working at the time. Spencer's father made a good living, so I stayed at home. I spent my days in her nursery, decorating here and there, folding her tiny clothes so they were ready for her. Some days I would just sit on the floor and imagine how my life would change once she came."

My eyes start burning, my mother's admission reaching a deep part of me that I had long forgotten about, the little girl that desperately wanted to hear this. I swallow past the lump in my throat, staring into my wine glass as I swirl the liquid around.

"What was it like? When she arrived?" Ally asked again, glancing over at me knowingly. Ally knows what hearing this is doing to me, how it's healing me.

"The first moment I looked at her, she felt like my best friend in the whole world. I felt like I had already known her for a lifetime. The first few days were hard. She cried and cried, didn't want to be held. Didn't want a soother. Nothing. I should have known then that she would grow up to be so stubborn and fiercely independent. But we figured it out, together. We had to. When Spencer's father left a few months later, it was just her and I against the world. I had no idea what I was doing half the time. I was so young, barely an adult at that point. I didn't have a good reference point. My parents weren't around and were never healthy even when they were. I know I've made mistakes, but Spencer was the only thing that got me through. Her spark, her fire, that's what inspired me to keep going when I felt like it was impossible."

I'm still staring down into my glass, my heart cracking in two. She's never told me about this time in her life, in my life, and now

I'm realizing that I also never asked. I finally brave looking up at her from where I'm seated cross-legged on the floor. Her face has more lines in it than I remember, and in the dim light cast from the fireplace, she looks ... human.

She's peering back at me with watery eyes, and our gazes meet, a silent understanding passing between us. So many years of hurt and anger dissipating all at once.

"I'm sorry. I didn't mean to get emotional," she says. "All I mean to say, Ally, is that your life is going to change in ways you could never even imagine right now. For better and for worse. Remember, you are just one human, doing your very best with what you have, with what you were given. You just wake up each day and try again. You'll make mistakes. But you're already miles ahead of where I was at your age. So, the mistakes won't be as big, and you'll get through it."

Ally doesn't say anything, she just regards my mother, a contemplative smile on her lips, a gentle hand on her belly. Ally's questions weren't for her, anyway. Ally is going to be an amazing mother. All the things Marla wasn't, and so much more. She knows babies, she's trained for this. And Mason will be here to support her.

A few seconds of silence stretch out between the four of us, and then we turn our attention back to the movie. A scene is playing out where the woman bumps into a man that she had had a fling with the last time she was in town. He's tall, dark and handsome as all Hallmark men are. Rough around the edges, the opposite of her in her Louboutin's.

"What's Grady up to tonight, Spence?" Ally asks, and I cock my head at her. What's with all her questions?

"How should I know? I don't keep tabs on what Grady does." The words come out faster than I intended, my mouth suddenly going dry. I refuse to admit that I do know where he is. He's started texting me when he's out, keeping me updated on where he is and when he'll be home. And I like it. It's grounding, consistent. He's working the bar tonight and gave Finn the night off. Something about a rec hockey game he has every week.

"Well, you're basically living with him now, aren't you?"

I am living with him for all intents and purposes. It's been two weeks since I stayed out in the van. It's not even a conscious decision anymore. I just go and get myself ready for bed in Grady's ensuite like I've always lived there, and tuck myself into his bed as if I've always slept in it.

"I am not living with him. I'm staying with him while my mom is in town and has nowhere else to go. Very different things."

Marla raises her eyebrows like she's the only one aware of the lies. I flash her a withering glare, a warning to keep her mouth shut about anything that has transpired at Grady's house.

"Grady would have no problem if you moved all your stuff in and declared that you were living there from then on. He'd probably sign over the deed to the house," Poppy adds with a giggle. I forget that she grew up in Heartwood too, only a few years younger than Ally and me. She went to school with Jett, so she would know the Landrys better than I do at this point.

"That's not how it is between us. We established rules very early on that we were just going to keep this strictly a sex thing," I state.

"You gave him rules? Did you like, write them out and have him sign a contract or something?" Ally says it like it's ridiculous, but maybe I should have, fuck. Maybe a legally binding document would have made sure we stuck to it.

"No, Ally. I'm not a sociopath. But yeah, I gave him rules. No relationships over here, remember? My heart is closed for the season. Possibly forever."

"But your vagina isn't." Oh, so *now* my mother chimes in.

"Mom! What the fuck." I shriek, covering my face with my hands.

"I'm just saying. I know what I hear through the floorboards."

Poppy giggles even harder at that, and Ally's jaw just about hits the floor. I feel my cheeks burn.

"I have needs, okay?" I defend. Needs that Grady satisfies a little too well. "I just don't want to be tangled up in feelings for anyone. That's when things get messy. That's when you start making sacrifices, and I can't do that."

"Okay, let's just put a pin in the rest of that for later. What are your rules?" Ally presses.

"We agreed on three, to start with. I added a few more because he started to cross some lines, and I had to nip it in the bud. Number one was one night only." I start counting off the rules on my fingers. "Two was no strings attached. And three was ..." My voice trails off, realizing that number three will be devastating to Ally. My mind spins trying to think of something to tell her. I could say we didn't want to tell anyone. Yeah, I'll say that.

"What was it?" she asks again. I glance around at Marla and Poppy, both waiting expectantly for my response.

"We don't tell you," I blurt. God, I'm a horrible liar. "What is in this wine?" I deflect, fanning my face to cool my hot cheeks.

"What the hell, Spencer!"

"I mean, you found out anyway ... We clearly didn't try very hard to keep it from you."

"Yeah, but come on, we tell each other everything. Why did you think you couldn't tell me?"

"God, Ally, look at you. You have this perfect life with this amazing man, you're pregnant with his baby. This is what you've always wanted for yourself, and that's amazing, I'm so happy for you. But you don't think that maybe other people don't want this. You've always been trying to set me up, and it always goes horribly wrong."

"I do not!"

"Remember Todd Pringle?" I cringe.

"Oh. Yeah," Ally concedes. "That was one time."

"And Jeremy?" I say, referencing a date that Ally set me up on a couple years after high school. Some guy that she met in her biology class. That was a special one because it is simultaneously one of the worst dates I've ever experienced and one of my best anecdotes to tell at parties. "The guy sat facing *away* from me the entire dinner. He didn't ask me one question and answered all of mine with one word. It was like he was terrified of women."

"Okay fair enough. But Spencer, isn't this what everyone wants?" She gestures at the cozy cabin around us. "I mean, not *this exactly*. Don't get married and don't have kids if you don't want to, but wouldn't you want a life where you aren't running anymore? Where you aren't fighting for your life to have something stable?"

"Yes. I do. That's what I have been working towards. That's why I need this job. Relationships are risky, Ally. You're putting your life in someone else's hands. I've worked too hard for far too long to throw it all away for some guy." I catch the words as they come out of my mouth. *Some guy.* It's how I would have described all the other guys I've been with, but it is not how I would describe Grady. In all honesty, that's what makes the risk even scarier. I wouldn't just be betting my livelihood now, I'd also be betting my heart.

"That's where trust comes in. Do you trust Grady? I can tell you with absolute certainty that man would do anything for you," Ally says. The word 'trust' snags on a memory I've tucked away. The day I asked Grady to trust me implicitly with his project. He extended his trust to me so easily, so why can't I do the same?

Poppy nods in agreement with Ally, and I catch my mother doing the same. Great. They're all ganging up on me now.

"This is girls' night, not an intervention," I remind them, excusing myself to refill my wine glass and hide the flush still staining my cheeks. If this is how tonight is going to go, I may as well just start drinking out of the bottle.

"It's true though, Spencer. Just the other day, Grady came into the café and there was something ... different about him. Like he was taller, if that's physically possible. He wanted a bag of coffee beans, specifically ones with the most caffeine. He said if he couldn't give you coffee in an IV drip, he could at least make sure the house was stocked with the best beans. So, I gave him my favourite blond roast."

Fuck. Grady has broken the rules more times than I can even count.

"I also see the things he does for you around the house," Marla chimes in again. "Yesterday I came upstairs and found him staring at your underwear, a puzzled look on his face because he had done laundry for you and was trying desperately to figure out how to fold them."

Jesus. Doing my laundry and folding my underwear? That's not even boyfriend shit, that's like, husband-level shit at this point. I bite the inside of my bottom lip, contemplating how I might still be able to make a clean break without shattering Grady—or myself—to smithereens in the process. We've somehow become intertwined, connected in a way that I never intended on happening. Now the idea of leaving feels daunting. No, impossible. The thought of being away from Grady, being away from here, makes my heart ache.

My mind drifts back to this morning, being up in the hot air balloon with him. The exquisiteness of that moment, the warmth of the sun dawning on me. It found its way through the cracks and lit up the dark corners of my heart. That golden, healing light caressed my face as if to say, *Today is a new day. You are a new you.* As if I have the choice to wake up and choose the path for my life. It didn't feel like a coincidence that the person standing next to me in that moment was Grady.

Then we landed, and the reality of my life snapped me out of whatever delusion I had let myself live in for that moment. I am choosing my path. I'm choosing the path that feels safe, where I have control, and I still have so much work to do.

Grady isn't home when we get back. The house is quiet. I give my mom a hug when we say goodnight and hold onto her a little longer, a little tighter than normal. She looks back at me, her eyes misty, before retreating down the stairs to the guest suite.

There's a note on the counter when I go upstairs and into the kitchen for a glass of water.

> Won't be home until late. Feel free to enjoy some "self-care" in the meantime ... You deserve it.

I have a feeling I know what's waiting for me in the bedroom, but a flutter of excitement still ripples through my chest when I see it. Grady has left me a box of bath bombs, and a vibrator. One of the little ones that's designed to apply suction precisely where you want it.

But his words lodge in my chest, emptying me from within. *You deserve it.*

I don't deserve anything, certainly not Grady.

First the dress, then the camera, and now this. If he's trying to win me over with gifts, I should tell him that he doesn't have to. My heart is already his, and I'm going to have to rip it out so he can keep it when I leave. That's what I deserve. I deserve to feel every bit as broken-hearted as I know he will.

I'm in and out of sleep after having a relaxing bubble bath, half aware of the front door opening sometime after midnight, the sound of Grady's movements through the quiet house soothing, comforting. I feel my body slacken into the mattress, relieved that he's home.

He shuffles around the kitchen before padding down the hall to the bedroom. I turn over, curling the duvet up under my chin and drifting off momentarily when Grady leans over me. He brushes my hair off my face and leans down to place a featherlight kiss on my forehead. I'm about to turn over, to pull him into me, when he whispers into the dark.

"I love you."

I keep my eyes shut tight and pray that he can't hear the way my heart is thundering in my chest.

I WAKE UP EARLY, before the sun starts to stream through the curtains, and silently make my way out the front door. I let it gently click behind me, and pull my hood up around my neck against the damp chill of the morning. The sky is just starting to brighten, the sun not quite visible over the mountains, leaving the town cold in their shadow.

I get into Grady's car using the key I took off the hook by the front door. My eyes catch on something that wasn't there before. A little hula girl on the dash. I know Grady put her there for me, and it tugs on my heart thinking about him going to pick it out.

I turn the key in the ignition, and Grady's car rumbles to life. I wince a bit, hoping that the noise isn't enough to wake him. He was still asleep when I left, and I hope he'll still be asleep when I get home.

The streets of Heartwood are becoming familiar to me now, especially this route. I would know my way to Ally's even if she lived halfway around the world. She's the one person I will always find my way back to. Except now, I think that statement is true about Grady as well. A feeling nags at the back of my mind, that this is part of what I'll be missing out on when I leave. The ability to just go over to Ally's on a Sunday morning.

Ally answers the door when I knock on it, pulling a plush robe around her swollen belly. Her blue-green eyes are still sleepy, strawberry blond hair unbrushed and wild instead of in her usual tidy ponytail.

"Spencer? What time is it?" she says in a hushed voice, glancing back over her shoulder to where Mason is still in bed, his soft snoring audible from here.

"Early." Not as early as when I woke up. I haven't been able to sleep for the last few hours. Ever since Grady came home and uttered those three little words, I tossed and turned. Sleep evaded me until all I could do was get up and come here. "Can we go for a walk or something?" I bounce on the balls of my feet.

"I just woke up. I'm not dressed yet." Ally gestures at her robe, before giving in with a sigh. "Okay, fine. Give me ten minutes. Then we're going to Poppy's for coffee. I get to have one cup a day and I have a feeling I'm going to need it."

"Duh," I say, rubbing my hands together, half because of this jittery feeling I haven't been able to shake, and half to ward off the chill of the morning.

Ally closes the door, leaving me out on the front porch, and re-emerges wearing leggings and an oversized hoody, her hair thrown up into her signature ponytail secured with a lavender scrunchie.

"I hope you feel at least a little bit guilty about dragging a pregnant lady out of bed."

"Walking is good for the pelvic floor, isn't that what you said when you dragged me to the Little League game?" I say. Ally groans and rolls her eyes.

"Ugh. Yes. You're right," she says as we make our way into the town centre towards Thistle + Thorne. It's early, but not so early that Poppy won't at least be there, getting the first pot ready for the day. She'll let us in if we knock, and we'll be rewarded with the first fresh cup. "So, tell me why we're out here?"

"Don't you want coffee first?" I stall. "I think I need coffee before I can form a coherent sentence."

As expected, the sign on the door is flipped to *Closed*, but Poppy is behind the counter, scooping espresso beans into the hopper. Her face alights when she sees us at the door and she drops the bag, letting a few beans scatter to the floor as she comes over to let us in.

"I didn't expect to see you gals so early!" Poppy says in her sing-song way, her lashes batting behind her dark bangs.

"You can thank this one," Ally grumbles, pointing at me with her thumb and pushing her way through the door with an eye roll. She beelines for the two armchairs by the window and flops down one.

"The coffee just finished brewing. I take it you're desperate." Poppy scurries off behind the counter and pours the steaming, life-giving liquid into three mismatched ceramic mugs before joining us. She leans on the arm of Ally's chair.

I take an extended sip of my coffee before setting the cup down on the table. When I look up, they're both staring at me, expectantly.

"Okay. Do you want the bad news, or the bad news?" I sigh.

"Just spit it out, Spencer," Ally chides.

"Bad news number one, I'm officially a piece of human garbage. Number two, I'm completely and utterly fucked."

Poppy flashes me an almost pitying look. Ally doesn't. Ally can see right through my bullshit.

"You're going to have to give me more than that," she deadpans.

"I have *feelings*," I say, as if the feelings that I'm referring to should be obvious to everyone around me, but I'm met with confused looks. "Feelings. I have feelings. For Grady."

Ally sits back in her chair, a smug look now replacing her questioning stare.

"To quote you this morning: 'duh,'" she says, and Poppy laughs as if this whole situation is *funny*. This is not funny. This is catastrophic. This was never supposed to happen. "What I want to know is why this is bad news."

"I'm leaving, Ally. I have to. My landlord sent me an e-mail saying I can no longer sublet my place. Which means I either get this job so I can pay my rent or ... I don't know what I'll do. I'm so close to getting this job. The council meeting is tomorrow, and then Mile High will see what I can do for them. Once I get this job, I'll be gone." I steel myself against the warring feelings within me. My heart wants to stay, but isn't that what my mother has always done? Followed her heart? And where did that get her? She's been kicked to the curb, broken-hearted more times than she can count.

"Leaving has never bothered you before. You've been with guys all around the world and have left every single one of them behind," Ally notes. She knows this time is different, she just wants me to be the one to say it. She wants me to admit that my boyfriend boycott failed. Crashed and burned.

"Ripping the Band-Aid off will be harder this time. He said it," I say.

"Said what?" Poppy asks.

"*It*. The L-word. I don't know if he meant for me to hear it." I'm talking a mile a minute. I'm freaking the fuck out. Not because he said it, but because if I wasn't pretending to be asleep, I might have said it back. Everything in me wanted to say it back. I didn't think I'd have to make a rule against saying 'I love you' because I thought that was implied, but apparently, I should have. I should have had a goddamned contract lawyer review my rules. There were so. Many. Loopholes. "He thought I was sleeping, and he came home after work, gave me a kiss and whispered it. I love you."

The moment had felt so tender, so intimate. So fucking terrifying.

"How do you feel?" Ally asks as if that's the easiest question in the world to answer. Like she just asked me what I ate for breakfast this morning. Which was nothing, because the thought of eating anything for breakfast made me feel like puking.

"I have no clue." It's not necessarily a lie. If anything, it's the most truthful I can be right now. I know how I feel about Grady, but I also know how hard I've worked to get to where I am. My heart is torn in two. "The thought of losing everything I've worked toward is terrifying. This life is everything I've ever wanted. I did this. I created the life I've always dreamt of."

"I don't think that's true. I think you're scared because this is the first time that leaving isn't what you want. You're just afraid of the alternative. The risk of doing something different. Of relinquishing some of your control."

"I can't stay." I breathe. "You know I can't, Ally. I've come so far from where I started. I've built a life that I can trust because I'm only reliant on me."

"Can you trust it? Your landlord just pulled the rug out from underneath you. You're trying to convince these corporate suits at Mile High that you're good enough for them, but ultimately, the decision is still up to them. You can't control everything, and trying will just make you crazy. You're gripping life so tight in your fists, white-knuckling everything all the time. Open your hands, Spencer. Maybe then they'll be ready to receive something great."

My world spins for a moment, reeling from what Ally just said. I don't have time to fully process what this means about my life choices before my phone vibrates.

> GRADY
>
> Where did you go? There's breakfast here
> waiting for you.

Then in another message:

> We're still good to work on the speech today?
> Eleanor sent me the agenda for tomorrow's
> meeting ... I forwarded it to your e-mail.

I click open the unread e-mail and scan the document that's attached. Eleanor was obviously trying to give Grady a heads-up about what's to come at the public hearing tomorrow. My gut clenches as I read through the list of speakers who have plans to come forward. Grady's name is at the bottom of the list of several high-powered people that Carter has rallied. I'm sure they all have complicated, impressive spreadsheets outlining just how much money they'll be bringing to Heartwood if they can sink their claws into the local economy. Nausea roils in my gut. I need this to work, I need this win. And the hurdle just got a lot bigger.

CHAPTER 25
GRADY

THE STUFFY, cramped hearing room at city hall is quiet except
for the shuffling of papers on the council member's desks. People
talk in hushed whispers, waiting for the mayor to arrive and signal
the start of the proceedings.

My eyes dart over to where Carter is seated, a few rows ahead
of me and a couple of seats over. He took his seat only moments
before Jodi entered the room, and I wonder whether they were
exchanging words before the meeting starts. No, I know they were.
They've been conspiring this entire time, why stop now? Jodi
looks right at him as she sits down, facing the crowd, and her
mouth twitches in an unmistakably flirtatious way.

That's when I notice the businessmen sitting with Carter,
equally as smarmy but a lot more powerful. They make Carter
look like a boy in comparison.

I recognize the tall one in the light grey suit as he crosses one
ankle over his knee and leans in to whisper something to Carter.
From his LinkedIn profile, I learned that he's a high-powered exec-
utive of a big hotel chain looking to expand into towns that could
be turned into popular holiday destinations. He must have seen

the ski resort just under an hour away and deemed our quaint mountain town a prime spot for development.

The man to Carter's left is the CEO of a grocery store chain. He checks his watch impatiently and glances around, looking down his nose at the other people around him.

My knee bounces uncontrollably, and I wring my hands in my lap. Spencer places a gentle hand on my thigh and the bouncing stops, my breath evening out.

"You're nervous," she states. I shrug, trying to ignore the palpitations behind my ribs. Of course I'm nervous. Seeing Carter with the suits over there just took this to the next level. What was once just about taking down my high school nemesis is now about taking down the one percent. This is the big leagues now. This is about the people I care about, the town that I love, and maybe just a little bit of my pride.

"You've got this," she reassures me in that steady, confident way of hers that makes me believe her. Her husky voice sends a shiver through me as she leans in close to my ear. "We've done all we can do to prepare. To get you ready for this moment. Now is the time to trust that the effort we've put in will pay off."

I simply nod back. She's right. We worked our asses off. As soon as I sent Spencer the document from Eleanor yesterday, she rushed home from wherever she was, and we got to work on the speech that's written out on the folded piece of paper I'm fiddling with in my hands, doing my best not to crumple it until it's completely illegible.

"We all believe in you, Grady." Marla extends a hand across Spencer and places it on my arm. She helped more than I thought she would with the speech yesterday, and as much as Marla can be trying at times, I appreciate having her here today. I know Spencer appreciates having her here too. The last few days, Spencer has been in better spirits, and I know that's due to the effort Marla has put in to repairing their relationship. There's an ease between them now, and for Spencer's sake, I'm grateful for it.

I offer Marla an appreciative smile in return. The hushed whispering around us stops as Jodi clears her throat into the small microphone extending from the desk in front of her.

"Welcome, everyone. If the council members could motion to approve the agenda for our meeting, we'll get started," she says. A few of the members raise their hands in approval. "Great. We're here to discuss the motion to overturn the law stating that only independent businesses can operate in Heartwood."

She calls Carter to speak first, given that this whole ordeal was initiated by him. He stands and plugs in a laptop at the podium.

He has a whole-ass PowerPoint prepared, with facts and figures, demonstrating how much money an increase in tourism would mean for the town. What his presentation fails to point out is that allowing big corporations in is not the only way to boost tourism. With Spencer's help writing my speech, that's what I intend to prove.

Each of the suits stands next to make their own pitch. Their financial strategies are impressive, I can't lie. I've even caught Eleanor nodding a few times and I wonder if she would switch allegiances for the right price.

My stomach is churning by the time it's my turn to rise. I walk up to the podium, knees shaking. I wasn't lying when I said that I hate public speaking, and as much as Spencer tried to convince me otherwise, the speeches I made at the cocktail party and the career fair were not sufficient practice for this.

She locks eyes with me as I turn to face the crowd and the city councillors from the podium in the corner of the room. She raises both hands in a thumbs up, and it gives me just enough courage to start unfolding the paper I'll be reading from.

I ignore the thought that creeps into the back of my mind, threatening my composure. My success today will be the very thing that drives Spencer to leave Heartwood. She didn't say 'I love you' back when I whispered it to her the other night. In fact, I can't be sure she even heard me. Her breathing was even and calm when I leaned in and kissed her forehead. It doesn't make what I said any less true. I love Spencer Sinclair. But I love Heartwood, too. It pains me that fighting for one means having to relinquish the other.

I clear my throat, buying myself a little more time and warding off a potentially humiliating voice crack as my emotions war inside me.

"Good morning, councillors, esteemed Mayor," I begin, and I'm suddenly cut off by the sound of shouting. No, *cheering* outside that only gets louder and louder as the crowd shuffles to get up from their seats. Spectators and councillors alike gather around the windows overlooking the parking lot below.

There are roughly a hundred high school students gathered on the lawn in front of city hall, and behind them, my entire Little League team. It takes me a moment to understand what's going on, but once I see Alice Montgomery at the front of the fray, it registers.

Their voices become one and I make out the words of their chanting.

"Grady's for us, Grady's for all, Heartwood's ours, we stand tall!"

A few students are holding up signs, lines from their chant outlined in glitter-glue. One of them just says *I Love Grady Landry*, and I wish I could shout down to them that this isn't about me. It never was. Still, a lump forms in the back of my throat as I take in the sight in front of me, the people who have shown up here to support me and my cause.

I glance over at Spencer who is slack-jawed, staring down at the crowd. She looks up at me and shrugs with a smile, and an unspoken explanation passes between us. For all the planning, strategizing, and scheming Spencer did to garner support for me, she never could have anticipated this.

"Let's get back to the proceedings, shall we?" Mayor Price says from her seat, front and centre in the room. Throughout the whole ordeal, she never moved an inch. Almost like she's already made her mind up anyway.

It doesn't matter. I've made my mind up, too. I tuck the piece of paper with my speech back into the inner pocket of my suit jacket as I take the podium once again. I don't need it anymore. I know exactly what I need to say.

As if confirming my thoughts, several people usher in through the doors, holding the same signs painted by the students. Poppy, Mack, and a few other local business owners. None of them sit, instead, they stand in a row at the back of the room, the strength of their presence palpable.

"Go ahead, Grady," Jodi says, bringing me back to the present moment, and the task ahead of me. So, I begin.

"Welcome councillors, esteemed Mayor," I say again, my voice steadier than it was before. "I was going to start by explaining that Heartwood is a destination not for the shopping, the amenities, or the fancy restaurants, but for the natural beauty that surrounds us. I was going to start this speech by explaining why Carter and his cronies have a flawed argument because the very thing that draws people to Heartwood is the small-town charm that they so greedily wish to wipe out." I pause for effect, to let a seed of doubt about Carter's intentions creep in and undermine his argument, before I continue. My eyes meet Spencer's, and she cocks her head as she realizes I'm not reading from the speech we prepared together. I flash her a confident grin.

"I will explain all that, along with a detailed strategy about how we can attract even more tourists here without running small business owners out of town. I won't discount the numbers, because at the end of the day, I understand that you all have a responsibility to help Heartwood thrive. But this isn't just a matter of numbers, it's also a matter of people. The heart of Heartwood." My gaze finds Poppy and Mack at the back of the room when I say this, and the hopeful looks on their faces give me the courage to press on.

"I want to tell you about the people who make Heartwood

what it is. Who make Heartwood the town that people visit to escape the rat race, to feel at *home*." The word home makes my eyes involuntarily flick back to Spencer. Her breath hitches, and her eyes are lined with silver. She has made this place I call home even more enchanting, and I hope that the emotion on her face means that home means something more to her now, too.

That's when I feel it. A rush, a ripple through me. It's the feeling of *fighting*, of speaking the words on my heart, to stand up for what I believe in. I know what I have to do when I'm done with this speech. The only other thing I believe in as much as this, and it's the scarlet-haired beauty sitting in front of me.

"Let me tell you about Poppy Thorne," I continue, and I glance up to the back of the room to see the smile spreading on Poppy's face. "Poppy grew up alongside my younger brother. She's as close to a sister as I've ever had. For as long as I've known Poppy, she has been forcing tea parties on us. She was meant to own Thistle + Thorne. I personally can't imagine a day not stopping by Poppy's for a coffee.

"Across the street from Thistle + Thorne is none other than Mack. Mack here comes from a long line of grocers. One might think that grocer is a humble title, but I say differently. You and I might take for granted where the food on our tables comes from, but Mack and his family never have. Through tough times, they have fought to ensure that you and your families have been fed. No price gouging as the big chain stores like to do when people have nowhere else to go."

A few of the council members shift in their seats like they're being hit with a truth that makes them physically uncomfortable because it means they have to really evaluate this decision. It's no longer a simple matter of who will make the town the most money. Jodi, though, examines her nails in a nonchalant, bored fashion, as if all I'm doing is taking up her time. I need something that will drive the point home for her. Something personal. That's when I remember Jodi's son, and the way she shows up to every one of his baseball games, even if she spends most of her time making out with Carter beneath the stands.

"Finally, I want to tell you about the Parks. I know they are unable to be with us today, but I would be remiss if I didn't tell you all about the impact they have personally had on me. As most of you are aware, they owned the very building that is up for lease today. The catalyst of this very issue was them leaving town. When my mother passed away, I was just seven years old," I say, making sure to emphasize the point. Jodi's son is the same age I was when my mother died. Just as I hoped, Jodi glances up towards me and fixes her stare on me. "The Parks, among many of our chosen family here in Heartwood, took four grieving and forlorn little boys under their wing. There was not a day that went by where we didn't have a hot meal on the table because of the generosity of the Parks. I'd like to think that if any of your loved ones, children, or spouses were in a similar situation, they would be just as supported by this community that I call family. Heartwood has always taken care of their own. I know that firsthand. That's the charm of this town. It's the family you find when you visit. The irresistible pull of the welcoming arms of each one of us here. Don't turn your backs on us now."

I conclude my speech by showing the council Spencer's detailed marketing plan to rebrand Heartwood. It lays out exactly how Heartwood can attract more tourists without selling out. The emphasis on the natural beauty, the way she's highlighted the businesses I just went to great lengths to defend. She didn't miss a thing. My speech is followed by a roar of applause, whistling, cheers. Most people stand. I blink back the sting behind my eyes.

"Thank you, Grady," Mayor Price says, and I don't miss the waver in her voice, the subtle but noticeable wobble that gives her away. I hit my mark. "Now is the time for open forum, if anyone else has anything they would like to add."

I take my seat next to Spencer, the seat beside her where Marla was is now empty.

"I'm so proud of you," Spencer whispers in my ear, and I feel weightless with her words, I'm floating. Regardless of the outcome of the hearing, I will leave here a happy man.

"You're the mastermind, Rebel. You made this happen." Our eyes linger on each other for a moment before our attention is brought back to the podium, where Alice Montgomery now stands.

She launches into another moving speech about her dreams, about how the scholarship has made it possible, finally within reach. She talks about how it won't be a possibility if the law gets waived. Another roar of applause erupts when she finishes.

"If no one else has anything to say, we'll move to a vote." A murmur ripples through the crowd, but no one stands to take the podium. "Alright, councillors, all those in favour of the motion to overturn the bill stating that only local, independent businesses are allowed to operate in Heartwood, raise your hands."

Silence. None of the councillors move. Not even Mayor Jodi Price. She's stock-still, though I don't miss the way her brows twitch together and she flashes an almost apologetic look in Carter's direction. A few excruciating moments pass before she bangs the gavel on the desk.

"It's unanimous. The motion is denied."

The crowd erupts in cheers, people reach over from where they're seated around me to pat my shoulder.

I turn to Spencer, still in disbelief. We both stand and she throws her arms around me, pulling me in for a hug.

"You did it, Grady. I knew you would." I bury my face in her hair, taking in this moment that I never want to end. Half of me is elated to have won, and the other half of me wishes that Spencer still had a reason to stay in Heartwood.

"We did it together," I say. This is the only way I want to celebrate anything from now on. When I pull back from Spencer, the corner of my eye catches on Carter hovering beside me. He clears his throat, and I realize with no small amount of surprise that he's waiting to talk to me. As I turn towards him, he extends a hand. I'm slow to take it and shake it, but I do. The last thing I'll do is stoop to Carter's level of petty.

"Congratulations," he says, in a very non-petty way that catches me totally off guard. "You made some good arguments up there. It's good to have a worthy opponent. I was getting kind of bored of getting my way all the time."

"Thanks, that's ... gracious of you," I answer, struggling to find a response. He may have switched gears, but he's just as cocky. Still, something in his tone sounds ... genuine. Almost as if he's offering me a sliver of respect. I wonder for a moment if my standing up to him is what he's been waiting for all along.

Our awkwardly long handshake is thankfully interrupted by Mason, clapping a hand on my back and announcing that the first round is on him at Jack's, whoever wants to join is welcome.

I glance at Spencer, noticing that her attention has shifted and she's surveying the room, searching for someone.

"Where's Marla?" I ask, realizing that she's the only one missing the big moment.

"I don't know ..." Her voice trails off. "She said she was going to the restroom, but that was a while ago."

Spencer and I leave the hearing room to look for her, and I offer a nod of thanks to everyone standing at the back of the room on the way out. The people who came to offer their support.

"She's not here," Spencer says, returning from checking the washroom and the surrounding corridors of the city hall building. It's an old, two-storey brick building, so there are not that many places to look for someone, or to lose them.

"Did she go outside?" I ask. Spencer shakes her head in response. She lifts her phone to her ear as the line rings and rings on the other end. No answer. "Let's see if she went back to the house," I offer.

"I'll go. You should head to the bar and celebrate with everyone," she tries to insist, but the concern on her face is enough of a reason not to leave her alone.

"Where you go, I go, Spencer. This is more important. *You* are more important. We can celebrate anytime." I place a hand on the small of Spencer's back, gently guiding her out of the building and towards the parking lot.

I quickly scan the lot for any sign of Marla, but there is none, and all I can do is hope that she's back at the house. That she has a reasonable explanation for ducking out early, and we'll pour a glass of wine and cheers to the success of the council meeting.

CHAPTER 26
SPENCER

MY MOTHER IS in the drive when we pull the car up, standing with her arms crossed while a man loads her suitcase into a yellow cab. Grady has just enough time to put the car in park before I fling the door open and stride over to where she's standing. Her eyes go wide with shock at seeing me here.

"Spencer—" she starts, but I immediately cut her off, unable to control the volume of my voice.

"You thought you could just leave?" I ask, but it's not really a question. Of course she did. Of course she thought that whatever is going on in her life is more important than what's going on in mine. I'm *so* stupid. Here I was thinking that this time Marla had really changed. How many times do I have to learn this lesson? That it's only a matter of time before the other shoe drops. "What, did Roy call? Or is it a new guy this time?"

Marla just stares back at me, not wanting to answer. So, one of my assumptions is correct then.

"Roy and I are *married*, Spencer." She's using the same voice she used on me as a child, as if I don't know what it means to be married. Part of me, though, feels like I really don't. I hardly even know what it means to be in a relationship at all, let alone committed to someone for life. That doesn't excuse the fact that she's just up and leaving the way she always has. The way everyone else in my life has, too. "I've had some time to reflect, and I think I need to go home and try to fix things with Roy."

"So, you're just crawling back to him after he treats you like shit. You're the same as you've always been, Marla. Here I was thinking that you were healing, finally. Seeing that you can have a fulfilling life on your own. That maybe, you're learning that you don't need a man to make you feel better about yourself." There's a bitterness in my tone that I don't recognize, but that feels as if it's making up for all the years I sat quietly and didn't say anything. "I know I never mattered to Dad, but have I ever really mattered to you?"

"Of course, Spencer. Of course you matter to me. More than anything." Her voice is pleading, and my heart is threatening to crack. Maybe the story she told at Ally's had been a lie. How could she say that she wanted me so badly, that we got through the worst moments of her life together, and then do this? "Being married to someone means that you don't walk away when things get hard."

"No, it means that if you walk away, you lose half of what you own. That's what this is about, isn't it? You're afraid that if you lose Roy, he'll take the lake house." Realization dawns on me and settles deep into my bones. Marla is afraid of the same thing I am. To lose what she's worked for, the life she's built for herself. Except in her case, rather than taking a safe approach and going it alone, she's going back, continuing to rely on someone else for what she needs.

"He would find a way to get it," she admits. "But that's not why I'm going back. Relationships take work."

"Sure. You keep telling yourself that," I spit back at her. "Look at yourself, Marla. Look at how you allow men to continue hurting you, look at how you allow them to have control over you. Aren't you tired of it?"

"You don't have to tell me what I'm like, Spencer. I'm not an idiot. It may not be what you would choose, but it's better than closing yourself off to love entirely." Her words land somewhere visceral within me, stirring a question I haven't let myself ask. Have I closed myself off to love entirely? Is there something fundamental that I'm missing out on? The wise part of my brain answers back, *No. That's what keeps you safe.*

"Have you ever stopped to think about what that does to me? How I've always had to be the adult in this relationship?" My voice cracks as emotions surge up my throat. Years and years of hurt and pain come barrelling out of me like a runaway train. I'm aware of Grady standing behind me, and I realize I don't care if he witnesses this, no matter how personal this moment is. It needs to be said, and Grady has already seen the most broken parts of me anyway. "You were never there for me when I needed you, Mom. You say that it was you and me against the world, but it never was. It was always about you. I paid your fucking rent. I found us that apartment when I was in grade eleven. I had to convince the landlord to let me see it because I wasn't of legal age yet. I did that with my minimum wage job in high school, Mom. Fucking high school." Tears sting my eyes. I try, and fail, to blink them back, as all of the years of struggle and uncertainty come spilling down my cheeks. She's the reason I never went to university, the reason I have to fight tooth and nail every single day of my life to earn a living. She's the reason I'm in the situation I'm in now.

The cab driver stands up out the driver's-side door now, looking at us over the roof of the sedan.

"The meter is still going ma'am," he says, as if he's completely oblivious to the tension in the air.

Grady holds up a hand to him and shakes his head as if to say, *not the time*, before he digs his wallet out of his back pocket and hands him his credit card to cover the extra time.

"I need to go, Spencer. I'll miss my flight." Right there, Marla has made it clear that I will never be a priority for her. No matter what she says, her actions speak a million times louder. My breath wooshes out of my lungs, and my heart would be breaking if it hadn't gone completely numb.

Marla glances back at me as she climbs into the cab, like she wants to say one last thing but decides against it. I don't bother watching the cab as it pulls away, down the long drive. Instead, I turn towards the house, marching inside and up to the bedroom. I have to get away from here. I have to collect my thoughts, reprioritize, centre myself. What was I thinking, falling for Grady? What was I thinking ever letting myself entertain the idea of prioritizing a relationship over my well-being? Here is my mother, once again afraid to lose everything she worked for on her own, because her marriage is falling apart.

I feel Grady close on my heels, and he halts at the bedroom door, leaning on the frame as I pick up my duffel bag off the floor and start packing. His energy is oddly calm, his tone even calmer.

"Where are you going, Spencer?" he asks, his voice even and steady, while inside my internal world is spinning. I'm spiralling, headfirst, towards the ground.

"I just need to get out of here for a few days. Go somewhere with no cell service, to be alone," I say, pausing because lying to Grady right now is like adding insult to injury, but I let him believe that I'm just going to go camping for a few days. A few days is an understatement when what I'm really planning is to drive the van back down to the coast and do what I originally intended. I don't know if I'll have a job when I go back, I don't know if I'll still have an apartment, but I have to live life on my own terms. I have to go because one more day spent here, loving Grady, will make me question my priorities. It will fucking destroy me.

"Then I'm coming with you," Grady says, and the surety in his tone stops me in my tracks. This is supposed to be a clean break.

"No. You're not," I say, turning to go into the ensuite to collect the rest of my belongings. Grady steps in front of me, gripping my shoulders firmly, holding me in place. His gaze pins me, and his hazel eyes darken.

"I go where you go, Spencer." He reiterates his words from the council meeting with more sincerity than before. "I mean it. If you need to get away from here, fine. But I will not let you go off into the wilderness to have an emotional breakdown alone. Or, whatever else you were going to do." He says as if he can see through my eyes and into my tattered soul.

"You don't want to be around me right now. Not when I'm like this," I say, trying to convince him that he'd be better off staying far away from the trainwreck that is my life. To let me go off the rails in peace, the way I always have. But even I can hear that the fight has left my voice.

"Like what? Sad and hurt? Spencer, this is exactly what I'm here for. This is what people who love you are supposed to do. People who love you support you and comfort you. That's all I've ever wanted." Grady's brows knit together with concern, and I realize that he isn't going to budge. My shoulders slump in his hands and I feel like I might completely crumple on the ground if it weren't for him holding me up. I can't help but feel like maybe it would be a welcome change not to be alone to process my feelings.

"Fine," I give in. If anything, letting Grady come with me will buy me some time to figure out how I need to proceed with whatever this is at this point. We'll go for a few days, and I'll try to find a way to end things with Grady. I'll figure out how to break this off in the least devastating way possible. Although, even as the thought crosses my mind, I know that such a way doesn't exist.

CHAPTER 27
GRADY

I SCRAMBLE to pack enough food for Spencer and me for a few days, rushing around so she doesn't have time to change her mind. There was enough hesitation in her eyes when she agreed to let me come with her that I won't give her a moment longer for her to second guess her decision.

By the time I load up the old cooler I had to dig out of the basement crawl space, Spencer is seated in the passenger side of the van, her feet stretched out and propped up on the windowsill. She looks completely at ease. But I know Spencer now, and it's when she puts on this mask of aloofness that she's the most hurt. She did the same thing when she found out about her dad's wedding, telling me she was fine when I knew she wasn't.

The van bumps along the gravel backroad, as I drive the van away from Heartwood, and Spencer hasn't spoken a word in the last twenty minutes. I don't mind, though. All I feel is relief that I managed to convince her to let me come with her, to give me just a few more days with her. To let me be there for her.

The look on her face as she shouted at her mother in the drive had taken a gouge out of my heart, and all I wanted was to wrap her up in my arms then and there. She stormed away before I could do that, opting for her usual coping mechanism instead. Running away. Spencer has never told me outright that her childhood was traumatic, but based on the snippets I've gathered, it's no wonder Spencer wanted to get away as soon as possible. It's no wonder she struggles to figure out where she wants to land.

Spencer is staring out her window at the passing trees, the same as she has for the whole drive so far, when I glance over at her. My hand flexes on the steering wheel as I fix my eyes back on the road. The van bumps over a pothole as I turn into a clearing next to the river that's rushing beside the secluded backroad.

"Here?" Spencer asks.

"Yes, here."

"This is the middle of nowhere," she says, still not budging from where she's sprawled out with her feet up on the dash.

"That's the point," I say. "You wanted to get away. This is it. It's not the middle of nowhere, I know exactly where we are. Used to come here as a kid." I get out of the van and stretch my arms overhead before wandering over to the bank beside the rushing water to take in the view of the mountains beyond. I hear the *thunk* of the door as Spencer shuts it and comes to stand next to me.

We stand side by side in silence for a moment. In my peripheral vision, Spencer closes her eyes in the sun, letting it warm her face and dry the last remnants of old tears on her face.

"Okay. It's pretty nice here," she says finally.

"Yeah, right?" I pivot on my heel, letting Spencer stand and admire the river while I set up the campsite. I start by pulling out the awning, and root around in the back hatch to find the fairy lights she had strung up around her last campsite.

Spencer is still staring out at the rapids by the time I've finished hanging the lights, but there's a tension in her shoulders that I've seen before, and she's starting to pace slowly. Just like she did that first day on the lookout when she was talking to her mom. Now, I see her more clearly. Her relationship with Marla has always been a burden, the roles reversed in a way that no child should have to deal with. She had to grow up and be independent before most kids learn to read.

"Are you good?" I ask, although I know the answer. The truthful answer, and the one she's going to give me.

"Yep," she answers. I walk over to meet her by the river's edge and place a hand on her back, motioning for her to turn towards me. She does, and when her eyes meet mine, they're red-rimmed, new tears forming on her bottom lashes. One of them falls on her cheek, and I lift a hand, cupping her jaw and wiping it away with the pad of my thumb.

"No, you're not," I say softly.

"No. I'm not." She admits with a sniffle, then squares her shoulders and wipes her eyes with the back of her hand. "What does it matter now anyways? There's no sense being upset about something that's already done. Not to mention something that I should have been prepared for in the first place."

"You're allowed to feel your feelings about this Spencer." I reach up to lift her chin, and peer into her shimmering emerald eyes. "What your mom did was really shitty. The way she's treated you is really shitty, and you're allowed to say so."

"It doesn't change her, and it doesn't change me. I am who I am because of her," Spencer says, almost a whisper. Her eyes cast downward again, so I take her chin between my thumb and forefinger, and tip her head back, holding it there so she has to look at me.

"You are magnificent. Everything in your life has brought you to this moment. You are who you are because of everything you've experienced, and I wouldn't change any of it for the world, because it brought you to me." I'll say it over and over and over again. She's perfect in her beautifully flawed way, and I'm just so grateful to know her. I'll say it until she believes it, until the words become part of her very identity.

My hand wraps around the nape of her neck as I lower my face and brush my lips against hers. They're red and puffy from crying but I kiss them tenderly. The soft pressure makes her respond, and she moves her lips with mine. A sweet, blissful moment, and then it's over and she's pulled away, leaving me with a void in front of me, needing more.

"Okay. I'm okay." She huffs a breath, steeling herself. "Show me around, then."

"Are you feeling up for a walk?" I offer. If Spencer wants me to show her around, I know just the place I'm going to take her. My last shot at showing her what Heartwood has to offer, why she should stay for good.

"Sure," she says, her mouth lifts into a grin, one that I haven't seen since earlier at the council meeting. I missed that smile. It's so fucking gorgeous that seeing it now feels like a relief.

"Well then let's go. We only have a few hours until sundown." I clasp her hand in mine and lead her away from the campsite, down the road until we reach a break in the trees. The trail head is still here, and just the way I remember it.

"You said this was a walk," Spencer groans behind me. I haul myself up the rocks that form big steps up the trail.

"It is. We're walking, aren't we?" I say over my shoulder. "It's not long, I promise."

"That's what you said twenty minutes ago. I'm all sweaty now." She whines like a child asking *are we there yet?* The evergreens break up ahead, daylight shimmering through the branches that are becoming less and less dense. I can just about see the clearing.

"I'll have a solution for that soon."

We reach the top of the stone steps and I stop, allowing Spencer to catch up. She halts next to me as she takes in the waterfall up ahead. The water cascades over the rocks in sheets and trick-les, landing in a calm pool of water at its base.

"Grady, you have to stop doing this," Spencer says.

"What?"

"Taking my breath away." She turns to look at me, her face brighter and more open than it has been all afternoon. My heart swells. Nothing feels better to me than making Spencer happy.

"You take my breath away every moment of every day," I say, earnestly. Every day since Spencer walked into my life, I've been trying to find a way to make sure she never walks back out. "Come on, there's more to show you."

I lead her over the stones that rim the pool until we reach the spot where the rock is carved away and steaming water fills small basins. I drop my backpack on the ground and begin removing my shirt, my jeans.

"What are you doing?" Spencer says, and I turn to her, my mouth sliding into a lazy, flirtatious grin.

I hold her gaze and remove my boxer shorts, and I watch some-thing flash in her eyes.

"I'm going swimming," I say blandly. "It's up to you if you want to join me." I lower myself into the water, crouching to let it cover my shoulders, to cover my arousal as I imagine her stripping down in front of me. Steam rises around me, as if it's my body alone heating the small pool.

Spencer grins, her mouth working as she considers.

"I don't know if this is a good idea, Grady." I know the hidden meaning behind her words. Words that are laced with desire, but also knowing. This thing between us is still temporary, the expira-tion date looming closer.

"Why? Because we've broken the rules of our agreement and now you don't know what this is between us anymore? Just say it. You don't know what this is and that scares you. It doesn't scare me, Spencer. So, get in the water. If at the end of this, you still want to leave, then we will have had an incredible last few days together."

Desire flares in her eyes this time again, and she removes her T-shirt, her jeans, everything, until she is bare. A forest goddess extending her impossibly long, smooth legs into the hot spring.

I stand on the bottom of the pool, and she extends her arms up to wrap around my neck.

"This doesn't scare you. Like, at all?"

"No. Even if you leave, and you go off on your world travels for another decade, you'll come back. And I'll be here. So, no. I'm not scared." I dip my mouth so it's right next to her ear, so she can feel every syllable. "I told you, Spencer. You and I are *inevitable*."

Spencer's breath hitches, and I take the opportunity to bury my face in her hair, finding the column of her neck with my mouth. I trail a line of featherlight kisses against her jaw, and her weight slackens in my arms. Crouching in the water, I lower Spencer down to me and wrap her legs around my waist.

She throws her head back, giving me access to the soft, vulnerable spot beneath her jaw and I nip it gently before planting a soothing kiss. A display of trust, that I won't hurt her. Her response is a deeply satisfying moan that stirs a primal part of me. I grip her hips, my fingertips digging into her flesh as she bucks against me.

I lift her up, her body near weightless in the water, and lower her onto my length. She settles onto me, and rather than rocking against me, she holds herself still. Her hands cup the back of my head, her fingers gripping my hair, and she touches her forehead to mine in soft reverence.

"You're too good," she whispers. Something in my chest cracks when she says it. "You're too good for me."

"I will spend every waking minute of every day being too good *to* you, Spencer. I could never be too good *for* you." Her lips meet mine, and she moans softly into my mouth. Our mouths, our hands, become frantic, desperate to feel more of each other.

She flicks her hips up and back, and I lose myself in the sensation of her, coming closer and closer to my edge. My hands find her neck and I brush my fingers upwards, tangling them in her hair. Spencer moans again, more guttural this time, and it is my unleashing. I grip her hips once again, lifting her off me and out of the water with ease. I shift us both so I can lay her down on the smooth stone forming the edge of the basin, and I hover over her, finding my footing in the warm shallow pool.

The cool air on her wet skin causes goosebumps to spread down her arms, and I find her hand with mine, picking it up to kiss it as I drive myself into her. I twine my fingers through hers, never breaking eye contact as I thrust into her until I'm buried to the hilt. Spencer moans, finding the rock with her other free hand and gripping until her fingertips turn white. She stabilizes herself while I pump into her deeper, harder.

"Fuck, Grady," she cries, her moans becoming raspier and more desperate with every stroke of my cock inside of her.

"That's it," I praise her, and she answers me back with a cry of pleasure. "Feel me, feel how good we are together."

Her walls clench around me, her expression twisting, mouth open in a silent scream.

"Come on, Rebel. Let me see that gorgeous pussy come all over my cock. You're so beautiful when you come."

She sucks in a breath between her teeth and then releases it with a scream that sounds like my name. I keep thrusting, keeping my rhythm steady as her body shudders.

"Let's see if you've got one more for me." When her body slackens slightly, I change my pace, slower, and bring my thumb to her clit, stroking softly up and down.

I watch her pleasure build again. This is all I want. All I need. To give and give and serve her. She finds another release, this time longer, more drawn out, less explosive. When she finally comes again, I let my seed pump into her. My body falls forward, and I bow over her in worship.

Her hands cradle my face and she kisses me, our bodies still fused together.

When we finally untangle ourselves from each other, she sits up at the edge of the pool and slips into the water, allowing her body to float, weightless. I watch her from the side, her breasts and pebbled nipples rising above the surface of the calm water.

Her eyes are closed, and her features are still. Peaceful. Birds chirp overhead, the leaves rustling with the cool evening breeze. I know Spencer can't hear any of it, her head half submerged, the world a fuzzy and distant place.

I let her live in that quiet tranquil space for as long as she needs.

Finally, she opens her eyes and stares up at the canopy of branches, the clouds gathering behind them.

"This is exactly what I needed," she says, her voice soft as she speaks for the first time in several minutes.

"Good."

"It's hard to be angry or upset when you've just had two earth-shattering orgasms in one of the most beautiful places." She closes her eyes again, still leaning her head back in the water. The lines on her forehead have softened, and the look on her face is serene. I rest my weight back on my hands and just admire her. There's a warmth that fills me, like a solid, tangible thing I didn't know I'd been missing until now. It's purpose. Spencer has given me that. She has shown me how to go after the things I want, but she's also given me this new sense of purpose, too. The drive I now have to make her happy, to keep her safe, to take care of her, but also to watch her spread her wings and fly, to cheer for her when she succeeds. "I was just so, *so* angry. I think I've been angry my entire life. At least since my dad left us, anyways."

"I know," I say, my tone is softened by understanding. I know what it's like to be angry about life circumstances you don't have control over.

"How do I forgive her?" she asks. It's a question I don't have an answer to. I wish my mom was around for just one more day, that I could be a kid again and get angry at her and stomp off to my room and slam my door. "She had one job. To be a mom. I didn't expect much, you know? Just a safe home to live in ... and to feel like I mattered." Her words are like a key, unlocking an answer that I've been looking for over these past few weeks. It's forming, on the tip of my tongue, a vague, nebulous idea taking shape.

"You're lucky to have her, Spencer. Flawed as she may be." I consider my own parents for a moment, both gone too soon. Neither of them was perfect either, but over the years of remembering them, missing them, and growing into the man I am today, I see them more clearly. Just two human beings who were trying their best despite challenging circumstances.

"Shit. I'm sorry," she says, shifting herself from where she's floating so she can look at me. "I don't really have a right to complain." I duck my head, staring down at my feet.

"It's okay. I know your mom fucked up, but I do think she does the best she can with what she has. You're fully allowed to be mad at her right now and feel your feelings. But take it from me, there's nothing I wish more than to have another day to tell my mom how much she means to me."

Spencer leans her head back in the water again and stares up at the sky, now covered with an overcast of dark grey clouds.

A cool breeze causes goosebumps to form on my damp skin, so I slide off the rock and lower myself into the warmth of the hot spring. She doesn't say anything in response, but I know she's heard me. I know the words have landed and are settling into some place within her that she doesn't want to face right now. In time, she will. In time, she'll find a way to forgive her mother. Even if that means she doesn't have a relationship with her.

Thunder rumbles in the distance. It's near enough that the clouds above us open up and rain starts to fall around us in sheets. Thunder booms again. The sound makes me jump, and I expect Spencer to do the same. I expect her to shriek and get out of the water and make a run back to camp. But she doesn't. Spencer smiles, still floating on her back in the crystalline water of the hot spring, now dancing with the raindrops falling on the surface. Instead, she laughs, joyous, melodious sounds erupting from her. As if the rain and the very act of laughing are healing her from the inside out. As if it's healing her fundamental fear of the thunder. And I hope that somewhere inside her, it's healing her fear of relationships, too.

CHAPTER 28
SPENCER

WE'RE both soaked by the time we make it back to the camper. I rummage around until I find a couple of towels to dry off, and once we do, Grady and I hunker down in the van, both warm and dry in our sweats. The rain is still bucketing down, pelting the metal roof.

"What did you do to pass the time on the road?" Grady asks, leaning against the wall across from me on my bed.

"I did a lot of reading. A lot of stargazing," I answer. Then I add, "I found ... companions along the way." I leave out the fact that they were male companions, and that they almost always agreed to the rules. They normally obeyed, staying on the other side of the boundary line. Except for Grady. He snuck through all my defenses, and I realize I may have underestimated him. Perhaps I made the same assumption about him that the rest of the town seemed to. That he wouldn't fight for this. But he did, and here I am, my heart completely, wholly, utterly his. Had I known the feelings I'm having now would be so goddamn tangled around my heart, I would have built bigger walls. Stronger walls.

Grady's jaw flicks at the mention of my other romantic dalliances. We've never talked about them, or how many there have been. There's never been a reason to since those are the types of conversations you have before getting into a serious relationship. Grady, thankfully, focuses on the original topic of conversation.

"No stars out tonight. We'll have to find something else."

I jump up from where I'm sitting and climb up onto the small kitchen table to reach the cupboard up above. I pull out a worn, flat box, and bring it back over to the bed.

"I have scrabble," I offer. Grady wrinkles his nose as if I've just put stinky cheese and not a very popular board game in front of him.

"Scrabble is kind of boring, isn't it? Isn't it a game that old people play?" My lips curl into a playful smirk, unable to hide my amusement.

"Oh, no, no, no. You clearly haven't played Scrabble the way I play it," I say, cocking a suggestive eyebrow. "Dirty, with strip Scrabble rules."

"Strip Scrabble?" He leans forward towards me, his curiosity piqued, resting his elbows on his knees and clasping his hand over one wrist in between them.

"You can only use dirty words. Feel free to exchange your letters, if need be, but also get creative. The words count as long as you can justify how they would be used in a dirty context," I explain. "Strip rules means that if you don't get more points than the last person's turn, you remove one piece of clothing. Easy?"

"Easy."

I let Grady pick his letters first, and we start the game. A competitive grin tugs at Grady's mouth as he places his first word.

L-A-B-

"Labia? You chose the word labia as your first word." The laugh that erupts out of me would be better described as a cackle. "It's not exactly dirty. Though it is anatomically correct."

"It's the best I had!" he says defensively.

"Okay, okay. Well, it won't be hard to beat your points, I'll say that." I mark down eight points for labia.

"Hey, you didn't count my double-word score."

"Fine." I cross out the eight and put down a sixteen instead. Then I place my letters.

"Candy," Grady reads as I place each letter down on the board. "I'm going to need you to justify that one, Rebel."

"Candy has multiple dirty connotations," I argue. "You can call someone a piece of eye candy. You can wear edible underwear. Don't forget about the popular 50 Cent song where he uses the candy shop as a metaphor for an erotic experience," I say as if I'm citing the 50 Cent Wiki page. My chin tips up in victory.

"Alright, that tracks. Fifteen points. Well done. But not good enough, I'm afraid." Grady clucks his tongue. "Take off some clothing." He says it as a command and butterflies roar in my gut. But I have a competitive edge, so I purse my lips at him, scowling as I remove my sweatpants, now sitting in nothing but a T-shirt and my underwear.

The next word Grady places is "licked", which earns him nineteen points. Better than my last word by three. Fuck.

"What the hell, Grady?" I groan. "Am I going to be the only one stripping here?"

"Oh yeah, I forgot to tell you. I'm fucking amazing at Scrabble." His eyes twinkle as his mouth curves up into a lopsided grin. "I used to play all the time with Winnie and her friends."

"This game is rigged!" I reach behind me and throw a pillow in his direction, which he easily deflects with his hand. "You never told me you were secretly a seventy-year-old woman inside that sexy, tattooed body of yours."

"Oh yeah, I almost always have a pocket full of Werther's, too," he says with a smirk. "I'm going to enjoy stripping all those clothes off of you."

"Don't get too cocky. You'll have to do it fair and square," I say, and I spell out the word "quickie", right over the top of a double word score. "Forty-four points please."

"Fuck me."

"Yeah, I've also played a lot of Scrabble. Sometimes I play it against myself when I'm alone. Take something off, Grady. That's how the game works." He groans, but he does as he's told and removes his T-shirt, baring his firm pecks, his abs flexing as he leans back against the wall.

My eyes stay fixed on Grady's face as he places his word. *Wet*.

"Justify it," I say. It's an obvious one, but I'm waiting expectantly for Grady's explanation. His eyes flick up to mine and hold my stare.

"Wet," he starts, as if he's about to spell it for a spelling bee. "As in ... I hope you're already wet for me." His voice rumbles through me, and if I wasn't wet before, then I sure as hell am now. I swallow hard.

"You have to take something else off," I say, eagerly awaiting his next move. I chew my lip, and my knee bounces. I'm impatient. Watching Grady take his clothes off may just be my favourite sport.

"I have to beat forty-four points, so I may as well just strip naked now."

I twirl the end of a lock of hair around my finger.

"I wouldn't complain," I say.

"Well then let's just declare you the winner, Rebel." Grady's mouth lifts at the corner as he swipes the letters off the board, and they get lost in the blankets. He's pinning me with his gaze as he crosses the short distance between us on his knees.

"What's my prize?" I ask, using every ounce of self-control not to jump Grady right now. I love this part with us, the anticipation, the tension. It's exhilarating in a way that doesn't feel scary. It's fun without feeling like we're playing mind games with each other.

"Whatever you want it to be," Grady says, his lips just grazing mine. His eyes flick down to my mouth, and before I can say anything, his lips have captured me in a kiss so intoxicating I let out an uncontrollable moan as I lose myself to it.

Grady tastes so fucking good. So fucking good that I think no matter how long I get to kiss him, no matter how many times he kisses me, it will never be enough.

His lips move from my mouth down to my jaw, to my neck, and before I know it, Grady is peering up at me from between my legs. Heat radiates through me, settling between my thighs and I'm pulsing with need, swollen and ready for him. I've never felt this before, this burning need that flickers to life like a flame that's almost gone out but just needs one breath to rekindle it. The need that flickers to life because I know what it feels like already. I know what it feels like to have Grady, and now my body anticipates what's coming.

"You're already so *wet* for me." Grady's lips twitch up from where he strokes my slit through my underwear. I'm practically panting at the sensation. "Come to my *candy shop* and let me taste your *labia*."

I bark out a laugh that takes me by surprise.

"Don't ever fucking say that again while your face is between my legs," I warn.

"What, labia? I thought I might get extra points if I used all the words in a sentence."

"Nope. You get docked fifty points because my vagina just slammed shut. Closed for business. Dried up like the Sahara Desert." I chuckle, but Grady slides the fabric of my thong to the side, and I can tell by the look on his face that he knows it's a lie.

"Doesn't look like it to me." He peers up at me, fixing his eyes on mine as he places a flat tongue on my slit and sweeps upwards towards my apex. "Doesn't taste like it either," he adds, before swirling his tongue around that concentrated bundle of nerves once, and then closing his lips around it to take a long, deep suck.

I inhale a sharp breath in between my teeth as the suction verges on a delicious type of pain as I swell to the point of throbbing.

He releases and makes slow, languid circles around my clit, the sensation of his soft, slick tongue soothing me. My head drops back, and I close my eyes, letting the feeling of his mouth on me take over my body, each nerve ending connected to that one spot.

The pleasure builds and winds tighter, my core contracting around Grady's fingers. Just as I feel my release close, he removes them and moves up, meeting me at eye level. He pushes his boxers down, releasing his hard length and slides into my opening, stretching me, filling me until all I feel is him. Every perfect inch of him.

"You're so fucking tight for me," he rasps, and it's my undoing. I feel my muscles clench around him more. "That's it. That's my girl. Just like that."

I don't want to consider why his praise feels so damn good, why it just about sends me over the edge every goddamned time. He thrusts into me, his girth almost too much as I quiver and shake around him. God this feels so good. I cry out as the wave within me crests, pushing me over the edge.

"That's it, Rebel," Grady groans again, and I feel him pulse inside me. "Take. Every. Last. Drop."

I want it. I want every drop of him. I want to be filled with him, consumed by him.

His body shakes as his pleasure collides with mine, and he comes to rest on his forearms over top of me. Neither of us makes a move away from each other. I don't want this moment to end. Grady and I move like one, perfectly in sync, perfect together.

When he pulls away from me, he takes the air right out of my lungs with him. My body feels cold without him near me, but he doesn't leave my side. He doesn't do what most of my hook-ups do after sex. Get up, go to the bathroom, get dressed, and leave. He lies next to me and pulls me onto his chest, back into his warmth.

"This is nice. I like this." *I like you*, I think. *I love you*. I get a satisfied *mmm* in response. "Hey, sorry you had to see that conversation between my mom and I earlier," I say, tracing a finger over his chest, tracing the outline of his tattoos. "Those are things that I don't like to talk about or show anyone. Kind of an ugly part of me, I guess."

"It's not ugly if it made you into who you are today," he says, and I can tell just by hearing him that he has his eyes closed. His voice is slow and soft, like butter. He's still enveloped in the post-orgasm haze. I love him this way. I wish I could bottle this feeling and keep it forever.

"It is ugly. There are parts of me that aren't glamorous or cool no matter which way you slice it," I say. "I was always kind of the cool, aloof, untouchable girl to everyone else. My mom didn't give a shit what I was doing half the time so it meant that I could do things other kids weren't allowed to do. I always put on this mask so that nothing could bother me. You can't be bothered about things if you don't care."

"And who were you, really?"

"I was scared. All the time. Terrified. I never knew what I was going to go home to. There were large chunks of time when I didn't even have a home to go back to. That was my mom's doing, and she has no excuse for it. She left me to fend for myself and look at what good that did. I'm a fucking mess. The closest thing to a long-term, monogamous relationship I've ever had has been with that one Uber Eats guy who always picked up my order." I feel Grady nod, but he doesn't say anything. There are unspoken words there, at the end of my sentence. *And us.* But I leave them unsaid ... I'm still terrified of *us.* "Honestly, fuck Marla. I'm so done with her right now. I made it this far in my life without a father, what's one more relationship down the drain, right?" I say, but I catch myself when I feel Grady flinch. "I'm sorry," I say, a pang of guilt stabs at my chest. My mom may be a piece of work, but at least she's alive.

"Don't apologize, Spencer. Your hardships and struggles are valid. It's just different from mine. My parents were wonderful parents when they were around. I grew up in a home that made me feel secure and protected. I never had to wonder where I was going to sleep at night. Our home was full of joy and love. Even until her dying breath, my mom made sure it felt that way for us. Now that she's gone, I get to hold onto the good memories of her, the happy ones. Having an absent parent is a different kind of struggle. I never doubt how much my parents loved me, how worthy I am of having that same kind of love that they shared. But I can imagine that having a parent who is physically here but not emotionally would fuck with your psyche."

Grady's words ring true in some deep, primal place within me. As if awakening a beast that has been lurking in the dark. Do I not think I'm worthy of love? Maybe. I do know that I believe I'm worthy of the life that I've been working towards. It's just that all my life I've grown up thinking that the two don't exist in the same reality.

Men have always left. They've always taken. They've always torn apart whatever scraps of security I had left. I watched them do it to my mother over and over again. I'm sure there are exceptions to the rule. Grady feels like an exception. But that beast has poked its head out of the cave only to whisper *it's not worth the risk.*

"I'm leaving in a few days. Whether I get the job or not, Grady." I change the subject, hoping that the words remind Grady of what I've been trying to tell him all along. Relationships don't have a place in my life. This doesn't have a place in my life. "My landlord told me my rent is going up, and that I'm no longer allowed to sublet it. So, I'm going back, or else I'm going to lose it. Even if I don't get this job, I need that place." When I say it now it almost sounds as if I'm trying to make the words sound sincere. The way Grady has shown up for me the past few weeks, there are cracks in my argument, and I know it. But the thought of giving up everything I've worked for still makes me feel like a skittish horse about to bolt.

I don't look back up toward Grady, because seeing the hurt on his face will be more than I can bear.

"It's okay, Spencer. I understand," he says, his voice soft but steady, even. I thought that seeing his disappointment would be worse, but it's not. It's this. This calm and gentle understanding. The way he has heard everything I've told him, and despite the fact that I know Grady would want nothing more than for me to say fuck it and stay, he doesn't push it. "You know you always have a home here, too. No matter where you end up, know that you can come back to Heartwood. Know that my feelings for you are never going to change."

He says the words that deep down, I want to hear, but they're not realistic. Even Grady can't promise that. Life happens, people make mistakes, people change. Nothing is constant, as much as you might want it to be.

I turn to look up at him, and he hugs me tighter, his lips meeting mine in a firm, steady, confident way. I let myself pretend that it's true. That I can believe him, and trust him, and that I'm not going to leave.

I am going to leave, I have to. That shitty little apartment isn't much, but it's mine. I pull out of Grady's kiss and find his eyes.

"Fuck me like it's the last time," I whisper into the thick, heady air between us. For the first time since I met Grady, those words feel true. Like this could be the last time, and it makes me feel sick.

Grady's eyes search mine, but they darken as he furrows his brow.

"No," he says, tone firm, jarring, coming from him.

"No?" I'm taken aback by the confidence, the surety with which he says the word. Like it's a whole goddamn sentence.

"No," he says it again, the same way but somehow even more solid, concrete. "Whatever you need to do, Spence, you do it. If you need to travel the world, go back to Vancouver, I'm on board. I will love you from over here like I have done for the last year. I've waited before, I can do it again. Don't for one second believe that this thing between us is over once you leave."

I let Grady's words sink deep into my marrow, expanding and taking up the spaces between the fibres of my being. The words are something solid within me, immovable, concrete, just like the way Grady is peering into my eyes. They take up so much space that it feels like they are blotting out any previously held beliefs I had about relationships, that I had about myself.

Here is this person who is so confident, so sure, that *I* am what he wants. So convinced that I am worth waiting for. Not in some possessive way, in a way that makes space for the person that I need to be, too.

It's the first time I've ever considered not ending it with someone when I've left. The first time I've considered not saying goodbye but see you later. The first time that I would leave and call him from my phone to say that I landed safely at whatever destination I was going to next. That I would make plans for coming back.

Maybe this could work.

Maybe is a dangerous word. It's admitting that you are taking a risk. It's not a sure bet, but if there's anyone I would bet on, it would be Grady. Dependable, reliable, unshakeable, Grady. Grady, who puts the needs of other people before his own. Who doesn't back down from a challenge for the people he loves.

So, I answer him with a kiss, tender and soft, the way my heart feels in this new, unsure territory. When Grady fucks me, it's with all the messy, uncharted, unknown future laid out before us.

CHAPTER 29
GRADY

SPENCER WAKES me up by sliding her hand under the waistband of my boxer shorts and stroking my length, hard from my night's sleep. Her body is warm next to me, and I want to soak in every second that I have with her. I could wake up every morning like this. I love Spencer. I've loved Spencer since the moment I first saw her, and now she's mine. Sort of.

She agreed to try long distance, at least to explore what we are to each other, and I think I have to be okay with that for now. Spencer is like a butterfly, she's the most beautiful when she's in flight, allowed to be free. But try to cage her, and her wings will break.

That's the last thing I want to do to Spencer. I don't want her to feel trapped. If, and when she decides to settle down with me one day, it has to be her choice. In the meantime, I will do everything I can to be her safe place to land. I will create a home for her that she wants to come back to and show her that I'm not going anywhere, that she can trust me not to pick up and move on without her.

This is what Spencer has been trying to tell me these last few weeks. That she doesn't need crazy adventures, she doesn't need grand gestures, she needs stability. She wants someone, somewhere, that she can rely on to be there for her when she needs it. Spencer may not have said it outright, she may not have even realized this yet herself. But I see her now, more clearly than ever. I can read her. She runs away from things so that she's the one to leave it behind. She sabotages relationships from the very start so that they never grow into something that can hurt her.

All I can do is hope that what I have planned is the thing that finally convinces her that what she needs is *us*. That I never plan on leaving her. That I have woven her into the very fabric of my life, so much so that if she were to unwind herself from it, I would completely unravel and fall apart.

I trusted Hudson with the vision for what I planned, told him in detail what he needed to do as I wandered down the gravel back road last night in the dark, looking for a single bar of reception. I found enough of a signal for the pictures I sent him to go through. I gave him a few days to get it done, but by the time Spencer and I drag ourselves out of bed, get dressed and pack up the van, my stomach is clenched, nerves roiling in my gut.

Spencer is quiet for the drive home, most likely sensing my weird tension. As the van nears the entrance to the driveway of the house, I catch her glancing down at my left knee, bouncing with anticipation.

"Is everything okay?" Spencer asks, nodding her head towards my shaking leg. "You're very jittery all of a sudden."

"Yeah, I'm good," I say, more to convince myself than her as I forcibly stop the shaking of my leg and choose to bite my lip instead. Something more subtle that she won't notice but will be an outlet for my nervous energy.

I can't say why I'm so nervous about this. At the very least it will show her that this place will always be hers to come back to, but at most ... I can't start to hope for the most. Because the most is that this will be what convinces Spencer to stay. Forever. For good.

"Thanks for doing this, Grady," Spencer says as we pull into the driveway, and I put the van in park. "I really needed it to ground me before I leave. To bring me back to myself and remind me what's really important."

"When do you have to go?" I ask. My words feel stilted, it's a question that is demanding to be asked but I don't want the answer to.

"Soon. Maybe tomorrow morning," she says, her eyes cast down into her lap. "My manager just sent over the contract. I just have to sign it. The offer is better than I expected. But they want me at the office by the end of the week, so they can prep me for the first trip."

My stomach lurches. I knew the day was close, but I was deluding myself into thinking that I had more time with her, before the chemistry that Spencer and I share will somehow have to translate through telephone calls and video chats. It won't be the same. I'll have to remind myself that it's still her. That we're still *us*. Because through a screen, I know I won't feel her the same way as when she's here, breathing the same air.

I think deep down I'm afraid that the shift between us, the bits and pieces that we get from each other, won't be enough to sustain us. The relationship will be experienced in bite-sized pieces, just a taste here and there until we forget how rich the flavour once was. Until the phone calls and video chats become fewer and further between, and one of them ends with a final goodbye.

I won't let it. I don't care what I have to do. I have resolved at this moment that whenever we hang up the phone, it will never be our final goodbye. If there is ever a time where it feels like it, I will fly to her to prove to her that it's not. Because a year and a half without each other didn't do anything to the spark between us, so I know that no matter how much time passes, that connection will keep us together.

Spencer opens the passenger side door and is the first to get out of the van when we get home, leaving her answer hanging in the air between us like it isn't supposed to affect us. Like it didn't just punch me in the gut and suck the air right out of my lungs.

I follow her, grabbing our duffel bags from behind the seat and slinging them over my shoulders as I meet her by the front door.

God, I hope it's ready, I think to myself as I fumble with the set of keys in my hand to find the one that will open the door and show her my heart, the very thing that beats for her and only her. Maybe it'll be too much too soon. *Oh god, what have I done?* Spencer specifically said no boyfriend-y things, and this isn't even boyfriend territory anymore; this is like, I'm so obsessed with you and not in a cute way. She only just agreed to see where our relationship goes, and if there's anything that might make her feel trapped, this would be it.

"Before we go in there," I say, my hand still on the key that's stuck in the doorknob, "I just need to say one thing."

Spencer looks at me, a concerned line forming between her brows.

"I haven't wanted to do or say anything to push you away, to make you feel trapped, so I've been trying to show you all the reasons you should choose to stay. There's one last thing I need to show you, but please, if it's too much, just say so. Don't feel obligated in any way to—"

Spencer cuts me off by placing a hand gently against my mouth.

"Stop second guessing yourself," she says, as if I'm made of glass and she can see right through it to my quivering mess of a heart. "Own your feelings, Grady."

I nod, but I don't open the door because as soon as Spencer stopped me, I knew the words that I really wanted to say, and I need to say them before I lose the chance. Before she decides that this all is too much.

"You showed me what it means to fight for something you love when you helped me with the council meeting. I can show you all the reasons you should stay, but I know that I also need to fight for you. I love you, Spencer. I have been hopelessly, desperately in love with you since the day you walked into my life. It seemed crazy, to have my thoughts so consumed by you, this amazing woman I'd met and gotten to know just for one night. I've spent the last year thinking of nothing but you, hoping that one day you'd decide to come back. Then you did, and I got a second chance. I'm not going to fuck it up now." Speaking the words out loud somehow makes whatever nervousness I felt disappear and my shoulders drop, my posture straightens, and I stand by my truth. I'm in love with Spencer, and I'm fighting for her.

Her throat bobs and I swing the front door open before she can respond, gesturing for her to go inside. She goes up the stairs as if she knows. As if she knows exactly what's waiting for her. But it's not intuition, just the small trail of construction supplies and paint cans that lead her right to the master bedroom.

I take a moment to collect myself and take a calming breath before I follow her into the house. I make my way upstairs to find her standing in the middle of the room, hands slack at her sides, mouth agape as she takes in the space.

Hudson fucking nailed it. But he clearly enlisted some help.

The previously navy blue walls have been repainted in a rosemary shade of green. My old cane headboard goes with the room perfectly, and the bedding fits the description I gave him to a tee. Ally or Winnie must have helped him pick it out because it reeks of femininity. The duvet is light pink with small rosebuds all over it, and the olive-coloured gingham sheet is folded back neatly to give an eclectic mix of patterns.

But that's not what Spencer is looking at. Spencer's eyes are fixed overhead on the ceiling, where light gauzy fabric is draped, forming a billowy canopy over the bed. Soft, white fairy lights twinkle behind it.

She turns and looks at me with red-rimmed, watery eyes, but the expression on her face is a new one, and I can't read the emotion behind it.

"Grady, I—" she starts, but she's interrupted by her phone pinging in her pocket as multiple texts come streaming in at once. Perhaps messages that she missed while we were out of service the last few days. She pulls it out of her pocket and her eyes go wide as she reads the texts on her screen.

I haven't breathed in what feels like five minutes. My chest is tight, waiting for her response to the room, waiting to find out if this is it, if Spencer is going to bolt. But the look on her face when she finally looks up from the screen tells me that I'm not going to get one right now. I'll have to wait.

"It's Mason. Ally's in labour." Shit. Ally isn't due for another month yet, meaning the baby is early and she's probably terrified.

"When? When did those come in? Did you miss it?" I ask, my tone panicked.

"No, they just came in now. We still have time, but we need to get to the clinic. Ally is asking for me."

"Okay, okay. Whatever she needs." I whirl around on my heel and head out of the house, grabbing a different set of keys on my way out. "We'll take the bike, it'll be faster," I say over my shoulder. Spencer is close on my heels.

She doesn't hesitate to take her helmet out of the back hatch and climb on behind me. Suddenly whatever fear I had about Spencer rejecting me is on the back burner of my mind, replaced by a new fear that makes my mouth feel sticky and dry. Fear for my brother and Ally. *My niece.*

For Spencer, who cares about Ally as if she's her own flesh and blood. My ears are ringing as my bike roars beneath us, picking up speed to get to the clinic as fast as we can.

HUDSON AND JETT are in the waiting room of the clinic when we arrive. The lights are dimmed save for the glow of the one coming from behind the reception desk. I open the door to let

Spencer through, the bell overhead chiming. The sound is too cheery against the tense, somber mood in the room. Jett looks up from where he's sitting, and Hudson is standing, already moving towards us, pulling me into a hug.

"Hey, man. You okay?" he asks, giving me a firm pat on the back.

"Hanging in there." I look at him, my mouth tightening into a grim line. The same worry lines his face as he nods, understanding passing between us.

"Where is Ally?" Spencer says from behind me, her voice fuzzy and distant. Everything around me feels like it's happening in a blur.

"Spencer, thank God you're here." Winnie rounds the corner from the hall leading back to the exam rooms. "Ally has been asking for you. She's not coping well." Spencer places her purse on one of the waiting room chairs and sets her phone down on top of it before she disappears down the hall with Winnie.

I pace up and down the row of worn pleather chairs, nerves roiling in my gut.

"You may as well sit down," Jett says, his head resting in his hands, elbows perched on his knees. "Winnie warned us this could take a while."

"Why couldn't they get her to a hospital?" I ask, as if Hudson and Jett will know.

"I don't know." Hudson shrugs. "But they just hired a midwife for the clinic, and Ally said she wants the baby to be born in Heartwood. I don't think they expected her to come so early ..." His voice trails off, not wanting to address the potential scenarios that could come from having a premature baby born in a rural clinic.

"Ally was what, seven, eight months pregnant?" I ask again, receiving only shrugs for answers. They have no idea. "I'm pretty sure she was nearing eight months. So, the baby likely has a better chance of being healthy." My mind races through the possible outcomes, not wanting to go to a dark place that I rarely, if ever, let myself entertain.

"Let's hope so," Jett says, a crease forming between his brows. I'm taken aback by how concerned my youngest brother is. For a guy who takes nothing seriously, and never stops moving, it's jarring to see him like this, pinned to his seat, worry evident in his eyes.

My gaze is diverted from Jett when Spencer's phone screen lights up beside me where she left it on top of her bag. I look away briefly, not wanting to snoop, but two minutes later when the same text message lights up the screen again, I can't help but read the preview.

SASHA

Got the contract! Damn your signature looks
good on it ...

I feel my shoulders slump, my stomach dropping within me as disappointment washes over me. I'm more disappointed than I have a right to be. Spencer prepared me for this, we knew what this was between us. I thought I had come to terms with the long-distance thing. Part of me hoped that showing her the new master bedroom would maybe change her mind. One final grand gesture in my plan to get her to stay in Heartwood. I have nothing left now. That was my last kick at the can, and I'm tapped out.

She's going. She's really going. And this relationship, this electric chemistry between us, will be reduced to phone calls and cramming in as much as we can together for a few weeks here and there. I'm well aware of the schedule that Mile High gave her, the number of trips they plan on sending her on in the next year to try and turn their brand around. It's going to leave hardly any time for me, for us.

A thought pops into my mind and derails me even further, and bile rises to the back of my throat. Did she send the contract before or after I showed her the bedroom? Was she sitting on the e-mail and seeing the room was enough for her to quickly hit send? Was this always part of the plan or did I just push her away even more?

I can feel the blood draining from my face, my vision blurring. I tried to fight for Spencer, I tried to do everything I could to show her that she can rely on me, and instead, I did the opposite of what I set out to do. I freaked her out, made her feel suffocated.

Time feels like it's moving in slow motion, and I have no concept of how long we've been sitting here, my mind in an anxious spiral, when a voice breaks through my thoughts. I look up to see Mason standing before Hudson, Jett, and me. I rise as soon as I see him, my knees wobbling slightly beneath me.

Mason's mouth breaks into a smile, and my eyes sting at the expression of joy on his face.

"Do you want to meet your niece?" he asks, and I pull him into a tight hug in response. Mason's shoulders shake, half a sob of relief, half joyful laughter, before I pull away and we head back to the exam room to meet my beautiful baby niece.

CHAPTER 30
SPENCER

Big blue eyes peer up at me as I cradle my best friend's baby girl. Hazel. My niece. Not by blood, but by something even more valuable—sisterhood. I can't tear my eyes away from her. She's the spitting image of Mason, save for her cerulean eyes. Those are Ally's.

"She's perfect," I breathe, admiring the small bundle. "She looks just like—"

"If you say she looks like Mason after I just spent eight months growing her and the last three hours pushing her out, I swear to God, Spence."

"You. I was obviously going to say you." I save myself at the last second and glance up to where Ally is lying on the stretcher that seems to take up most of the cramped exam room, her face tired and puffy but still gorgeous. My heart swells to a size I didn't know it was capable of, stretching to accommodate this new little person that I already love so much, and this new version of my best friend.

"Pfft. I know that's bullshit. It's an evolutionary fact that babies come out looking like their fathers." She waves her hand in the air and rolls her eyes. "It's a good thing I find Mason so darn attractive." We both laugh, wiping tears from our eyes.

"She's pretty cute. You guys made a good one." I look back down at Hazel, wriggling in my arms. "Hazel ... what's her middle name?"

"I've been meaning to tell you ..." Ally's voice trails off as she gives me a pointed look, as if I should be able to read her thoughts. When I don't say anything to indicate I know what she's getting at, she comes out with it. "I wanted to name her after you. Hazel Spencer Landry." My jaw drops in a moment of stunned disbelief, and I can barely pick it up enough to stammer out a response.

"Ally, what ... That's not ... I don't ..." All I can do is shake my head. What I want to say is that I don't deserve the honour of having someone else bear my name. Ally would be the first person to argue with me on that, so I don't say it, but it's the truth. To be linked to someone in such a fundamental way, that part of your identity is modelled after them ... Hazel should be named after Ally, not me. Ally puts other people ahead of herself; she is thoughtful and kind and considerate.

I only ever think about myself. I've had to. There has been no one else in my life to look out for me, so I've had to do it. I'm selfish. I hate that part of myself now, now that I've seen myself in a different light—through Grady's eyes. But I don't know how to be anything else. It's terrifying to imagine anything else.

"It's already been decided, Spence. Hazel is lucky to have you to look up to. I want her to be strong and independent like you." Ally says it with all the sincerity in the world. How can I tell her that those parts of me have just been a survival mechanism? And now they have cemented me in this life that is constantly at war with forming deep and meaningful relationships.

I don't say anything in response, I have no words.

"I know how your mom felt now. The story she told about holding you for the first time. Like you were her best friend. I know I have a huge support system, but somehow it still feels like it's just me and her against the world," Ally says softly. "It's scary. What if I screw it all up?" I look down at the sweet babe, now sleeping in my arms. It's unfathomable to me how anyone could ever do anything to hurt her, how anyone would abandon her the way I've been abandoned.

"You won't leave her out to dry. You will do whatever you have to do for Hazel, so she knows she's loved and cared for. That's the difference, Ally," I croak out.

"I have a community around me. I can't imagine how your mom felt. Hazel has me, but she also has her dad, she has her uncles, she has you." Ally is about to say something more, but she's cut off as Mason knocks on the door and asks if Hazel's uncles can come see her.

I lock eyes with Grady as he walks into the small exam room, and he strides over to Ally, planting a kiss on the top of her head. My heart does a weird flip flop at the sight of it.

"Hey, Mama." He greets her using the same endearing nickname he gave Winnie. The man adores the women in his life, and it does something to me that I'm unsure how to interpret. It's a glimpse of the man he has promised he would be for me, the way he shows up for people, in his daily actions.

He comes to stand next to me to admire Hazel. His body is warm next to mine as he peers over my shoulder at her.

"She's beautiful," he breathes in awe, and my ovaries are exploding inside me. I've never wanted children—I'm still not sure if I do—but holy god my ovaries have turned to mush at this moment. "How does it feel to be an aunty?" he says, his voice rumbling through me.

Aunty. A lump forms in my throat and I try to swallow it down. But when I try to answer him only a small squeak comes out. For the first time in my life, I'm truly speechless.

Aunty. I knew that Hazel would, for all intents and purposes, be my niece. But this is the first moment that I've realized the role that I have in that, too.

Aunty. I'm an aunty to someone now. I mean something to someone now.

I glance down at Hazel again and imagine the little person she'll grow into. A little girl just like I was. A little girl that hoped and dreamed for a family who would love her and never disappoint her. Who wanted nothing more than people around her to take care of her.

I never had that. All I knew was that people left me, that people prioritized themselves ahead of me. I grew up to be untrusting, resentful, closed off to people out of fear that they would hurt me like so many others had.

Aunty.

Suddenly a weight drops onto my shoulders, but it's not a bad feeling. Not like the feeling of crushing pressure. Just enough pressure, like a weighted blanket that people use to ease anxiety. It's a responsibility that feels grounding; it feels good, comfortable. The kind of pressure that takes coal and turns it into a diamond.

I never want Hazel to doubt how much her family loves her. I never want to miss her birthday, her big achievements, milestones. I want to be there for every dance recital or hockey game. I want her to know that when she's a teenager, she can come to me for dating advice when she's too embarrassed to talk to her mom.

But I have to be here in order to be that for her.

I'm not going to be here for her. I've built this life for myself; I've chased independence and stability for so long that I've created no space to let other people in. I've built myself a house I no longer want to live in. The tear I was holding back rolls down my cheek.

"Spencer?" Grady's gaze has shifted away from Hazel and is now fixed on me, his solid, strong hand warming the small of my back.

I sniffle and look up at him.

"I'm okay," I lie. It's my knee-jerk reaction, my most used coping mechanism. I'm okay because I have to be okay. There is no other option. Not now that I've signed that contract, not now that I'm moving full steam ahead to protect the life I've worked so hard for.

By the way Grady's mouth has opened, I can tell he's about to protest and ask me to elaborate, which I wouldn't even know how to do. Thankfully, before he can say anything, two paramedics in flight jumpsuits enter the room and announce that they'll be transferring Ally to the hospital in Calgary. Although Hazel seems healthy, she'll need a thorough assessment and maybe some monitoring to make sure her lungs are strong enough.

Once Ally and Hazel are both secured on the transport stretcher, we follow the crew out to the field in the back. I lean down to give Ally a hug before they load her onto the helicopter, and it takes every ounce of strength I have to let her go. I cup her cheek and kiss the top of her strawberry blond hair, and we say goodbye knowing that it means more than just seeing her off to the hospital. By the time she gets back, I will have already left and gone back to Vancouver, with no plans to return to Heartwood in the near future. I'll jump into my new, demanding publicist role starting with a three-week trip to Costa Rica and then from there ... who knows where they'll send me. Who knows how long I'll touch down in Vancouver before I leave again.

Grady drapes his arm over my shoulder, the weight of it comforting as I wipe tears from my eyes. I extend an arm to wave goodbye to Ally and Hazel as the helicopter blades whirr, the long grass in the field behind the clinic bending and swaying in the wind around us.

That just leaves the next goodbye. The one that might just rip my heart out more than leaving Ally. City hopping makes you somewhat hardened to goodbyes, and never forming connections deep enough to make them meaningful always helps the process. But I feel different now. There's this unfamiliar dread hanging over my head.

Leaving usually causes a flurry of excitement, the adrenaline rush of going into the unknown. Seeing somewhere new, meeting new people. The settled feeling of having secured a new contract with some other travel company or tourism board. Income for the next few weeks or months, depending.

Those things don't excite me anymore. Not the way they once would have.

This is why. This is why I set these rules for myself. This is my job, my livelihood, the paycheck that keeps a roof over my head. I should have stayed the course, stayed in my lane, and this wouldn't be so hard. Yet, here I am, and there's some part of me that once felt small and has now grown bigger and stronger and wants to convince me that I can stay in Heartwood. Stay with this man who does everything right. This man who has pulled me into the fold of his life like I've always been here.

But that's what my mom has always done. She's always sacrificed for a man, and look at her now. She's down and out, three divorces later, and staying with *Roy* because she doesn't want to lose her house. Again.

I'm well aware of what they say about stupidity. It's doing the same thing over and over and expecting the same result. Except this time, it's my mom, and I have the privilege, the opportunity, to look at her experiences and choose something different for myself. A life for myself that isn't held up by someone else, by a man who is inevitably going to leave me.

I can hold onto Grady, I can hold onto the feelings that he gives me, but it's safer to keep him at arm's length. For now.

"Are you good?" Grady gently turns me to face him as the helicopter is finally out of sight.

I nod, eyes cast down, and he brings his hands up to cup my face, making me look at him, into his green-and-brown eyes that are practically aglow in the warm evening sun.

"You're not though. You weren't earlier, and you aren't now either." Grady smiles softly before planting a gentle kiss on my forehead. I close my eyes and lean into the sensation, soaking in the solid warmth of him while I can. "It's okay to not be okay, Spence. You don't have to hold it together around me. This is tough. But

Ally and Hazel will be okay, and we'll be okay. We'll figure it out together." Grady pushes me back to look at me again. "I think we deserve a celebratory glass of wine. I know I need one," he says.

"That sounds delightful," I agree, and Grady pulls me under his arm again, before walking us both back through the clinic. I pick my purse up off the chair I left it on earlier and check my phone. There's a text from Sasha confirming that she got my signed contract, and a new voicemail. I listen to it as Grady and I walk out the front door of the clinic and over to his bike.

'Spencer, honey. It's Mom. Listen. I'm so sorry.'

Her voice sounds pained, like her apology might actually be genuine. But I keep listening to see where the catch is going to be.

'I shouldn't have left like that. This is all my fault, it always has been my fault. You were right that I should have left Roy. If there's one upside to me going home early, it's that I found him in bed with our neighbour, and at least now I know what I'm dealing with. I kicked him out. He knew he fucked up, so he said I could have the house. I'm going to really do it this time, be by myself. Maybe you're right. I need it. Okay, well. You don't have to call me back unless you want to, I just needed you to know how sorry I am.'

Okay, so, apparently there wasn't a catch. She seems like she's finally reflecting on her life choices. I feel sad for her, if anything, and I know we'll be okay in the end. Marla may be flawed, and somewhat immature for a middle-aged mother, but she is my mother. I love her dearly.

I know I'm right where her relationships are concerned. She needs to take time to be single for a long while, rediscover herself. Build a life that isn't dependent on anyone else but her. That used to be what I thought I needed too. Up until about two hours ago. Now I wonder if maybe, just maybe, that advice isn't one size fits all. My mother's relationship issues are not my own. You can't necessarily inherit poor taste in men. But I made my choice. I sent the contract to Sasha, and now there's no turning back.

"Let me cook for you," Grady says, pouring me a glass of red wine and handing it to me with a quick kiss on my temple, his beard softly scratching my skin.

"Why don't we cook together? I like when you teach me how."

"No, I'm going to cook for you," Grady says, turning his back to me as he starts pulling out pots and pans from the cabinet next to the range. "If this is your last night here for ... a while, then I want to do something special for you. Besides, it's a special night. It's Hazel's birthday." Something in his voice is reserved, and he hesitated, as if not wanting to say how long I would be gone for. Like speaking it into the universe would make it true.

"That's fine by me," I say after swallowing a sip of wine. "I've gotten used to watching you in the kitchen, and I have to say I enjoy it."

"I could do like a butler-in-the-buff situation for you if you like." Grady throws me a coy smile over his shoulder.

"You spoil me." I bat my eyelashes at him as he pulls out some ingredients from the fridge and places them on the cutting board on the island. He put his weight onto the counter and leans over to me.

"That's just the Chez Landry treatment," he says. Then the playfulness winks out of his eyes, and he adds, "You could have this every day, if you decided to stay here."

"Grady," I warn, looking at him from under raised eyebrows, "this is already going to be difficult for both of us."

"It doesn't have to be."

"No, it doesn't have to be," I echo. "We can just behave as if this is any other normal night together. I'll be back before you know it, and you won't even notice that I'm gone with how much we'll talk on the phone, and FaceTime."

Grady nods, accepting the unspoken knowledge that it's not going to play out exactly like that. Long distance is hard. It doesn't matter how you slice it. No matter how much you try to make the other person feel included in your day-to-day life, they won't be because they aren't there.

I take a deep slug of my wine to ease the sting in my chest.

"Was it the bedroom?" Grady has his back turned to me now, refusing to look back as he asks it, a question that seemingly comes out of the blue, but that has likely been on his mind all afternoon. I realize then that, with all the chaos of going to the clinic and the worry about Ally and Hazel, I forgot to thank him for the bedroom. "Is that why you sent the contract to Sasha? Why you decided to go? Because if it was too much …"

I stand up from the barstool, round the kitchen island and meet him at the stove, using a hand to gently turn him so he's facing me.

"It was not too much for me. You are not too much for me. Everything you've done for me is beyond my wildest dreams. I never thought I deserved someone like you, Grady. I never thought that someone like you was ever a possibility for me. I grew up thinking that the most I could ever have was a man who would want me for my looks and tire of me quickly. Who wouldn't go out of their way to make me feel special and loved. But you have. More than anything, I want to thank you for that."

"You deserve someone who will go to the ends of the earth for you, Spencer." He says it with complete sincerity, and inside, all of my emotions are at war with one another. Grady would, and he has, gone to the ends of the earth for me. And what am I doing? I barely even have faith that we'll last through the summer. I don't know what to say back, but Grady luckily fills the silence. "Dinner's ready. It's nothing fancy, just spaghetti."

"I love spaghetti," I say as he hands me a bowl of pasta and I take it over to the couch.

Grady sits on the other end of the couch facing me, and I pull a blanket over our legs, the way I like to sit with Ally when we catch up and spend time together. Grady has reached the place in my heart that, so far, only Ally has been able to. I'm comfortable with him. I feel like myself. This whole evening is perfect. A comfort meal, snuggled on the couch with the only person I want to be sharing my space with.

"What will you eat at home without me to cook for you?" Grady asks me, and it takes me a second to answer once I've slurped down my noodles.

"Well, the options are endless really, now that I know how to dice an onion."

Grady's smile reaches his eyes as he laughs and the way they crease at the corners makes me *melt*.

FaceTime. We have FaceTime. I'll still get to see those creases around his eyes when he smiles because of something I've said. I'll still get to see his stubbled jawline. But I won't get to see the way he looks when he first wakes up in the morning, when he rolls over and his eyes are just a little bit puffy. I won't get to see the way he looks when he holds Hazel.

I clear my throat and try to shake off the thoughts. *Don't make this harder than it needs to be,* I remind myself.

"In all seriousness, I'll probably just order in. I don't want to have food in the fridge that will go bad while I'm in Costa Rica," I answer.

"You leave when?" he asks, still refusing to make eye contact with me the way he's avoided it every time he's asked about my new job or my life in Vancouver. The one I'm going to live without him. With him on the sidelines.

"Next week, I think. I have to go into the Mile High office first and have a bit of an orientation to the company, and then I'll leave shortly after that with the tour group."

"The tour group that everyone thinks is a hook-up opportunity." His tone is flat, he's making a pointed effort not to insinuate anything, but I know what he's thinking. I'm going to meet someone. I'm going to find someone new to hook-up with. I hooked up with him, didn't I? I broke so many of my own rules, Grady must think I have no self-control.

But it's different now.

"If you're thinking I'm going to indulge, then you don't have to worry. I'm there to do my job, and only my job. Besides, it wouldn't look very good if the person trying to turn around the scandalous reputation was also sleeping with customers." By the look on Grady's face, I can tell that my answer hasn't exactly satisfied him. "And I have you to come home to. I don't need hook-ups anymore."

Grady's expression settles with my last explanation, his shoulders visibly drop. It's the truth. I don't plan on being with anyone else while we're trying to make our relationship work. The question is, how long can something like this last when even the most well-intentioned, well-adjusted people swear up and down that long-distance never works?

After dinner, we move to the floor. Grady lights a fire in the hearth, warming us against the chill that still blankets us in the spring evenings. We share another bottle of wine. I fall asleep on Grady's shoulder, and he carries me to bed, tucking himself around me to be close to me.

The night is perfect. One last, perfect, night.

CHAPTER 31
GRADY

Spencer is beside me when I wake up next to her in bed, perhaps the last time she will be for a while. I roll over and pull her into me with one arm, spooning her, my hard length pushing into her back. She responds to it, pushing her hips back into me and grinding them on my hard cock. We make love in a sleepy, serene fog, and when we both come, it dawns on us that today is the day our relationship is going to change.

I gaze up at Spencer, still straddling me. Neither of us says a word so as not to break the spell we're both in. Her scarlet hair falls down around my face like a velvet curtain, and I reach up to tuck one side behind her ear, before wrapping my hand around the back of her head and pulling her down into a long, delicious kiss. I don't want to accept that this, what we have right here, right now, is coming to an end.

We'll no longer be in this fantasy, living together, playing house.

"I should get ready," Spencer whispers into my mouth and tries to pull her head back, but I don't let her. I hold my hand firm on the back of her head and press my lips into hers once more.

"Don't," I say when I finally release her mouth. "Don't go,

Spencer." I make one more desperate attempt to convince her, and she squeezes her eyes shut, shaking her head.

"I have to, Grady. I signed the contract. We agreed that this was best." *She* agreed. I'm going along with it. She climbs off me and wanders into the ensuite, closing the door behind her with a soft *snick*, and I lie in bed in the silence, staring up at the ceiling.

The shower faucet turns on with a squeak and I throw the sheets off me. I pull on my grey sweats and wander out to the kitchen. When Spencer emerges, I have coffee waiting for her on the counter. I made it the way she likes it, but today I put it in a travel mug. She'll want to get on the road early.

She leans up to kiss me on the cheek before she takes it and starts bringing her bags one by one out from the bedroom and dropping them by the front door.

I help her load her things into the van. Neither of us say much. There isn't much to say, and we promised each other we wouldn't dwell on the sadness of the day. It's just any other day. But when she climbs into the driver's seat and rolls down the window for one last kiss, she says the words "We'll keep in touch" and my heart sinks. The promise sounds empty, like this is just any other relationship she's had on the road. Just something casual.

I can't help but wonder if this long-distance agreement was just a way of putting a dying relationship on life support. Not because we think it might survive, but just to give us enough time to say goodbye and have closure. I know how hard long distance is on a relationship. I'm not lying to myself about that. I know that our situation is only made harder by Spencer's flightiness. I'm prepared to do what it takes to make this work, but I'm not sure I can say the same about her. She's had one foot out the door since our first night together. At every turn, I feel like I'm caging Spencer in, making her feel suffocated, like I'm doing too much.

I stand in the driveway until the van is completely out of sight, and as Spencer rounds the corner, my phone vibrates in my pocket.

I dig it out and see that Ally has texted, almost as if she's sensed that Spencer is gone.

ALLY

Just got back from the hospital but Mason got called into the clinic. Can you come help me set up the bassinet? I am SO not prepared for Hazel coming early.

I shoot Ally a text to let her know that I'm on my way. I think she knows I need a distraction today. She probably needs the distraction too.

The spot behind me on my motorcycle is empty, the wind cold against my back, as I make the short ride over to Ally and Mason's cabin. I let myself in through the front door as Ally told me to do, and find her sitting on the sofa, Hazel nestled under chin, fast asleep.

"Hey," Ally whispers so as not to wake her. I point to the box on the floor in the living room, in a silent question. Ally nods. It's the bassinet. I sit on the living room rug and get to work quickly, doing my best to open the box quietly, and gingerly removing all the pieces until I find the instruction manual.

Ally and I sit comfortably in each other's presence. She's become a good friend since she moved here. She's one of the few people who knows Spencer the way I do and knows how it feels to miss her presence the way I am right now.

Hazel squirms in Ally's arms and she gets up to take her to the other room, the one they added on to the cabin for her nursery, as I piece together the legs of the tiny crib. It's hard to imagine anyone being small enough to sleep in here. It's fucking adorable.

The bassinet is almost finished when Ally returns and resumes her place on the couch, Hazel now strapped into a wrap across her chest.

"How are you feeling?" Ally asks, now that we're able to speak at full volume. I don't have an answer for her other than fucking shitty, like my heart got ripped out and is being dragged along a highway behind a WanderLuxe van, but I water it down for her a bit.

"Not great," I admit. I have no reason to lie about how I'm feeling. I've learned that Ally is good at seeing through people, assessing them. Comes with the nurse title, I guess. "There was a part of me that was still hoping that Spencer would change her mind and decide to stay. Maybe I've just been deluding myself this whole time."

"Spencer definitely knows her own mind. She doesn't like to be pinned down," Ally says, her words are careful. "But I've never seen her the way she was when she was with you. She's different now, in a good way. She may be flighty, but she's loyal as hell to the people that she loves. She may be choosy, but I know she's chosen you." Ally's words barely reach me, I feel numb. She hasn't chosen me, though. Not fully. Not the way that I've chosen her. I would do anything to be with her.

"I just don't want to love her halfway. I don't want pieces of her. I gave her all of me and I want all of her," I say, focusing my attention on the final screw I'm drilling into the leg. I give the bassinet a shove to test it out and it sways gently.

"Maybe it's cliché, but you know that saying, if you love something let it go? I think that's what you need to practice here. Spencer needs to come to her own conclusions, and if, at the end of the day, you can confidently say you did everything you could to fight for her, then maybe it's time to let her go. Let her come back to you when she's ready." Ally's gaze is boring into me. It's all things that I know, just impossible to accept. "What is your relationship now that you're trying long distance? Are you going to see other people?"

"I mean, I'm not." It's the only answer to that question that I have and my stomach drops. We didn't really specify what we are to each other, we never clearly defined the terms of this. I suddenly feel nauseous. The conversation we had last night, I thought, was enough. I assumed we were on the same page, but now I'm not so sure. Spencer mentioned that she doesn't want hook-ups anymore, but we didn't settle on anything specific. We didn't set clear boundaries. Spencer loves her boundaries and her rules, so it worries me that she didn't see a need for them here.

"Oh, Grady." Ally's voice has a touch of pity in it, and I hate it. This is my own damn fault, honestly, and I'm the only one that has to live with the consequences.

"Yeah, I fucked up," I say. "I did everything I could think of, and then I shit the bed at the last moment. I don't know how to do this, Ally. I don't know how to fight for what I want."

"All you can do is be there for her, Grady. Just keep showing up, the way you have been. But at the end of the day, don't bend so far over for her that you break your own back. Don't sacrifice everything. I've known Spencer a long time, and I love her, but she needs to learn how to reciprocate and stop getting in her own way." I nod silently, and a small squawk comes from the bundle of fabric attached to Ally.

"Are you hungry?" Ally coos at Hazel. I take that as my cue to leave. I say goodbye to Ally and Hazel, leaning down to give my niece a kiss on her tiny head. It fits right in my palm as I stroke the soft wisp of dark hair she has there.

I wave goodbye to Ally as I hop on my bike, and because I still feel antsy and unsettled, I go for a ride, wherever I feel led to go. No agenda, no mapped-out route, no plan.

Today that has led me past the house, past the campground that sends a pang through me when I whizz by, all the way up the meandering switchbacks to the lookout over Heartwood.

The air is crisp today, the sky is clear, and from the lookout Heartwood is unobstructed. The last time I was here was with Spencer, and I pointed out all the things that make Heartwood special, all the reasons that I will forever call this place home. This is what she helped me preserve.

Spencer sees into my heart, and sees me for who I really am, and then pushes me to go out there and create a world that reflects that. Somehow in the process I created a world that she is not a part of. I learned how to speak my mind and say what I want and need, but what worked with the council didn't work with her. No matter what I did it wasn't enough. It didn't convince her.

Maybe Spencer was right this whole time. Maybe I misunderstood, or I had blinders on and was too focused on my own goals to see her clearly. How many times had she told me that relationships were just not part of her DNA? We're fundamentally different, her and I, and perhaps the best thing for both of us at this point is to make a clean break. She can continue to live the nomadic lifestyle that clearly makes her happy, and I can find someone who is willing to share a life with me, here in Heartwood. Yet, that thought feels so disappointing, so inadequate now that I know what it's like to share my life with Spencer. Because it will never be her, and so I will always feel incomplete.

If you love someone let them go.

All this time, I thought that I was letting Spencer go. But I still have my fist closed tightly around the part of her that she is willing to give. I need to let her go. Fully let her go. Allow her to fly free, follow where the wind takes her.

It's not anything wrong with her, it's just who she is. I can appreciate that with more honesty and acceptance than I could before.

My phone rings, jarring me from my thoughts, and my pulse quickens when I see Spencer's name on my screen. I know she's still on the road, probably only halfway back to Vancouver, and my mind plays through all the reasons she might be calling. An accident? A flat tire? And perhaps the worst thought of all, the one that I shouldn't even be entertaining anymore, she wants to come back.

"Hey, Rebel," I answer, my tone trying to be playful, but my hesitation is obvious.

"I just got back into service. I'm on the other side of the

mountains now," she says. Her voice is calm and even. No accident, no flat. She called me as soon as she got service. I hate myself for the way my mood brightens, the hope that perhaps the last option is true. "The drive has given me a lot of time to think, Grady."

Just like that, the hope I had been feeling is replaced with sweaty palms, a twisting in my gut. She's going to end it. She came to the same conclusion I have, that it would be better to just make a clean break. Although I know what's coming, I still flinch in preparation for what she's about to say. I realize I haven't said anything yet, lost in my own thoughts when Spencer speaks again. The sound of her voice makes me lose track of what I was going to say.

"We never agreed on the terms of this new agreement we have with each other."

"And you want to know if you can see other people," I finish her sentence. The one I've been anticipating.

"What? No. I was just going to say that we need some new rules while we're figuring this out." While we're figuring it out. Not committed, yet. But the fact that she's willing to put boundaries on this is something. It's enough for now.

"You're sure you want this? Long distance is no joke." I'm still unsure of what this means for us, and I need to be certain that Spencer means what she says. My hands shake slightly waiting for her response, and I shove my free hand into my pocket to still it, hoping it will also still my nerves.

"I know. It won't be easy. But the drive has given me a few hours to think, and all I could think about was how badly I wanted to get home so I could call you and hear your voice. I want to give this a fair shot," she explains.

The fact that Spencer has been thinking about me, about us, this whole time makes me want to shout from the lookout all the way down to Heartwood. She's thinking about me. I'm suddenly very aware of the distance between us. The fact that my body is yearning to grab her, pick her up, spin her around, hold her face and kiss her, and I can't. It's sobering.

"You can talk to me whenever you want, Spencer. I'm here. I'll always be here, on the other end of the phone line, waiting to talk to you. Waiting to hear about all your crazy adventures," I say, and I mean it with every fibre of my being. Every atom in my body. Every heartbeat, every breath, is for Spencer.

"Okay, then let's decide on these rules," she says, and I can hear her smile through the phone line. "We talk on the phone every day. Even if it's just for five minutes. We FaceTime or Zoom once a week for a virtual date night." These rules are less sexy than the first set Spencer laid out. Those ones had almost added to the desire, made our relationship feel forbidden. These rules just paint a bleak picture of the fact that we both want a relationship we can't have.

"How will these rules work while you're in Costa Rica?" I ask, contemplating the time difference between us and the new job that will undoubtedly monopolize her time.

"We'll figure it out." She says it like a promise, and it eases my nerves slightly.

This should feel better than it does. I should be happier than I am. Spencer has decided that she wants us. She wants to make us work. She's still in this with me. But this is not what I hoped our relationship would look like, missing her. I can't say with certainty that this is what I want. I don't want virtual Spencer. I don't want to watch her life from afar.

Ally was right. I've bent myself over backwards trying to show her how much she means to me, but at what cost? I sacrificed so much of myself in the process that now I'm unsure if this is truly what I want.

"You're right, we'll figure it out together," I say. But my words feel hollow. Like, on the surface, this looks like everything I could have ever dreamt, but inside, it's devoid of the very thing that makes it special.

Her.

CHAPTER 32
SPENCER

I wiggle the key into my front door, having to jimmy it slightly to get it to open. I swing the door open, pushing through with all my bags that I hauled up the few flights of the three-storey walk up. Much of it is still the same as it was before I left. The girl I sublet it to left it as is, and now I'm thankful she did. Some familiarity feels good right now.

The sound of my bags dropping to the floor echoes through the dark, cold space, reminding me that I have yet to hang anything on the walls. Or really do anything to make this space my own. Putting pictures up, decorating, has always felt like I might jinx it. That if I let myself settle in here then it would get taken away somehow.

The space isn't much to brag about, but it's mine. I almost lost it. Had the contract not come through from Sasha when it did, I don't know where I would have gotten rent money.

I flick on the lamp next to the sad, worn couch, and I flop down on it and pull out my phone to text Grady. We talked for a few hours on the road until I had to stop for gas and get something to eat, so I shoot him a quick text to let him know I got home safely.

It's a strange feeling I get when I hit send. To know that there's someone worrying about me, waiting for me to tell them I'm okay.

He texts back almost right away.

GRADY

Glad to hear. Now go take a bath and relax. Xo

I do. I run myself a bath and sink down into the warm water, letting it cover my ears and muffle the deafening silence of my apartment. The quiet and calm used to be comforting to me. I used to relish coming home and being alone after social events or nights out in the city, but now ... Now I know how it feels to come home to someone who loves you. Who has a dry T-shirt waiting for you when you come in out of the rain. Who has a cup of coffee ready when you wake up, and a glass of wine waiting when you get home.

I stay in the bath until the water has cooled, and my fingers are wrinkled, and when I finally climb out, I dig around in my duffel bag until I find my sweats. When I put them on, they smell like him. The clean scent of Grady's laundry soap and a hint of his warm vanilla and tobacco cologne.

I breathe it in and my chest aches, followed by an urgent growl in my belly.

The pantry is dismal and bare when I open the creaky bifold door and survey the staples I try to always keep stocked for nights like this. The small closet almost tempts me to climb into it, like if I will it hard enough, Grady will open the door from the other side and materialize in my apartment like that first day at Ally's cabin.

I need some food to materialize in front of me.

Before I can think about it, I pull out my phone again. The line rings once, twice. Then his voice fills my head, and the effect is like he's here with me.

"Just couldn't wait to talk to me again, could you?" Grady's voice rumbles through me, and I instantly feel warmer.

"I need help," I say. It's not entirely true. I could easily just Uber Eats something in a pinch, which is my go-to solution for these occasions, but I wanted to talk to him. To feel him here. "I have some rice, some stock, some frozen veggies, and maybe some chicken in the freezer. What can I make?"

"Oh, this is perfect. You could do an amazing risotto. You have some spices, right?"

"A few, yeah," I answer, looking at the sad spice rack that houses a few different herbs I got for some other meals I never got around to making.

"Great. Risotto it is."

"That sounds complicated. Remember the only skill in my arsenal right now is dicing onions. And I can boil a mean pot of water," I remind him.

"No problem. Risotto is kind of foolproof."

"I think you're forgetting who you're talking to," I say, a little self-deprecating.

"Don't fret, Rebel. I'll walk you through it."

"Okay." I put Grady on speaker and set my phone on the counter so I can work, and his voice fills the kitchen. I shut my eyes for a moment to imagine him standing behind me at the stove, guiding me and showing me what to do.

"You're going to want to start by thawing the chicken and cutting it up so you can cook that first," he explains. I do as he tells me and before I know it, the kitchen is filled with a delicious fragrance, the risotto bubbling away in the pan. How he managed to simultaneously throw together such a delicious-looking meal *and* teach me how to make it over the phone is baffling.

Once I'm done, I take the bowl of risotto over to the couch and curl up under a blanket to eat it while we talk.

"What did you do today?" I ask him in between bites.

"I helped Ally set up the bassinet for Hazel. They were discharged this morning from the hospital and didn't have anything ready." My heart clenches hearing that he spent the day with Ally and Hazel, and I wasn't there. My three favourite people all hanging out without me. I blink past the stinging in my eyes.

"I'm glad you were able to help her," I croak, and I realize I didn't do as good a job hiding the wobble in my voice as I thought. I'm suddenly very aware of how alone I feel. It's never bothered me before. Now, instead of feeling peaceful on my own, I just feel lonely.

"And I missed you," Grady adds. I cover my mouth to hold back a sob. "I thought about what your apartment looks like and imagined you getting home. I tried to picture what it looked like, tried to picture myself there with you."

"It's nothing special," I say, looking around at the blank walls with faded patches of paint where the previous renter had hung pictures. "I promise you aren't missing out."

"I'm missing out whenever I'm not with you," he says matter-of-factly. "What is your place like? Describe it to me." The task of describing my place makes the dull ache in my chest to subside.

"It's old. I don't have much here. I haven't been bothered to decorate or anything, and most of my furniture is hand-me-downs from friends."

"No decorations at all? I know you said you never decorated your room growing up, but I would have thought your apartment would be different. I just pictured you having a colourful, bright space. Lots of memorabilia and souvenirs from your travels." I don't even think I've ever bought a souvenir. I enjoyed travelling, sure, but it was less about the place I was going and more about the place I was getting away from. Something in me sags a little at the thought. I've had all these incredible adventures, but nothing to show for it except a dark, quiet, empty apartment.

"It's funny, you know. That is what I wish this place was like. But whenever I think about doing it, or buying something new, I just get this feeling like it's temporary anyways so why bother? That, and when you grow up on a single income, you don't exactly prioritize spending money on those kinds of things."

I've never really said that out loud before, but hearing it now, I suddenly make a lot more sense to myself. Everything in my life has been temporary. My living situation, my relationships. Everything had an expiration date, and I guess not getting attached is how I protect myself from being hurt when things inevitably end. It's why I won't invest in my place, because it will be easier to move when I need to. The realization that settles over me suddenly makes me feel very tired. Like I've just run a marathon, and it makes sense because, in some ways, I think I've been running my whole life.

"Well, your room is here whenever you feel like having a place that's all yours," Grady reminds me. It's hard to think that on the other end of the phone line, he's probably lying in bed in a room full of things that remind him of me.

"I love you," I whisper into the phone. The words feel inadequate somehow. I emphasize each syllable, trying to convey all the emotions I'm feeling, but they don't do enough to tell him how much I miss him, how much I long for him, how grateful I am for him.

"I love you back." Grady's voice is getting sleepy now, but neither of us wants to hang up. So, we stay on the phone in a comfortable silence, just knowing that the other is there is enough.

When I wake up the next morning, still on the couch wrapped in a blanket and my hoody that smells like him, the apartment is even colder and quieter than before. My heart feels heavy.

I blink until my vision is clearer and check my phone. I have an hour before I said I would be at the office for a meet and greet with the Mile High team.

I quickly brush my hair and my teeth and put on a bit of blush to make me look more alive. I dig around in my closet until I find an old dress at the back that seems appropriate for an office. And by office appropriate, I mean it's the only plain black garment I own that comes down to an appropriate length on my long thighs.

By the time I pull up in front of the looming downtown high-rise, the dress is feeling tight, and itchy, and not *me*. But I'm here, and this is my first day of a job that has a salary, and benefits, and I feel a little bit like I've made it.

At least, that's how I should feel. I can't tell if the nausea roiling through my gut is nerves or intuition, but something inside me is not sitting right. It must be the tights. I never wear tights. I never wear anything tight like this at all.

I check the time again, not wanting to be too early, but not wanting to be too late either, and I see a text from Grady that came in while I was finding a parking space.

GRADY

Good luck on your first day, Aunty Rebel!

He's attached a picture of him holding Hazel. She is currently the human equivalent of a potato and has no idea what's happening, but he's holding her tiny arms up as if she's cheering me on.

The message makes me smile. It makes me unable to tear my eyes away from my phone screen. It makes everything inside me scream that I'm walking away from everything I love, everything I hold dear.

I suddenly see this job through a new lens, no longer a rose-coloured one, and Ally's words come back to me. *You can't control everything.*

She's right. Even this job isn't a guarantee. It's just what I've always done. I've always strived for security, independence. I've had to work harder than most people who go to college, or who have a family that acts as a safety net. I've had to work so hard that I've forgotten to look up, to look around me and appreciate my life for what it is.

Nose to the grindstone. That's what it's always been. To outsiders, my life looks exciting and fun, full of travel and adventure, but to me, it's always been about the hustle. I've missed so much of the enjoyment.

I've missed out on forming relationships, on being somewhere long enough to create a home that feels like a home. It's all been meaningless. What is a home without the people who make it feel that way? People who fill your four walls full of love, laughter, and joy? I've worked for years to put a roof over my head, but for what? To go to sleep alone, to wake up alone, and to never have someone to share the day with.

My eyes brim with tears when I consider all the years I've wasted trying to protect myself. All I was doing was trying to protect the little version of me that still lives in my heart, who isn't enough for the people who should take care of me, and who is absolutely terrified all the time. I trust myself to take care of her now. All I've ever done is take care of her. Now, though, it's time to give her the life she deserves. The love she desires.

I scroll through my contacts, find Sasha's name, and hit the phone icon. She picks up on the third ring.

"Sasha, hi." My voice is wobbly. "We need to talk."

CHAPTER 33
GRADY

"Earth to Grady." Finn's voice reaches me through my zoned-out state and the cacophony of the crowded bar. "Table nine needs a refill."

He's busy pouring some beers for a group of guys that just walked in and took the last free table, and points with his chin at the table with empty glasses. It's a full house, and even the bar top is starting to fill up. I need to get my head in the game tonight, and it is decidedly out of it.

"On it," I answer, and I head over to ask who wants another round. I write their order down on the small pad of paper I keep tucked in my black apron, something I rarely have to do anymore.

Fuck, I'm tired. I scrub my hand down my face and shake myself awake.

Spencer and I stayed on the phone way too late last night. She fell asleep on the other end. I knew as much when the line went quiet except for her even rhythmic breathing.

I stayed on the call for another few hours anyway, in case she woke up and wondered where I was. I finally fell asleep too, and the call dropped at some point in the night.

If this is what long distance is like, I don't know how long I'll last. I hate this. I hate that I couldn't hold Spencer as she fell asleep last night. I hate that she wasn't here when I woke up. I hate that even though we spent hours on the phone with each other yesterday, it didn't feel like enough. Mostly, I hate that those kinds of conversations, the ones where we have all the time in the world, will be an anomaly. It may never be that easy to talk on the phone again. All I'll get are snippets of time and I'll hold my breath waiting for her next call.

The drinks get delivered to the table, though I barely remember doing it, and I tell Finn that I'm going to take a breather in my office. Guests have been trickling out slowly as the night nears last call, so I retreat to do some work on the books before heading home.

I've strictly avoided going into the office since Spencer left. There aren't many places around town where I can avoid remembering what it was like with her here, but when I'm at the bar, I do everything in my power to avoid the office.

But tonight, there's no way I can delay the bookkeeping tasks any longer. I'm already behind and the longer I wait to look, the worse it will get.

I sit down on the worn leather office chair, and eye the plate with the remnant crumbs of the cheesecake Spencer and I shared. We had left in a hurry the night I brought her here, and I can still make out a faint smudge of her lipstick on the fork.

She looked absolutely radiant that night, and my chest seizes at the thought of how comfortable we'd been together. Our first date, and it didn't feel awkward. It felt just right. How many dates will we get to have like that now?

My vision blurs and I'm unable to focus on the spreadsheet of expenses and order sheets to review. I click through a few windows absentmindedly. It takes me twice as long to do the weekly budget and send in the order for next month, and I'm certain that Doug will give me an earful when there are inevitably items missing. I click the window closed finally and turn in my chair when I hear a soft knock on the door frame.

"Bar is closed. There's just one guest left, and then I'll lock up," Finn informs me.

"They won't leave? Tell them we're closed now," I say, not surprised that Finn is too nice to tell someone to get out.

"It's just one lady sitting at the bar and I didn't have the heart," he answers.

My heart jumps at the possibility ... no ... it can't be.

I whirl around in my chair and get up to go look out at the bar, to see if it's the person I'm hoping it is. But when I swing open the double doors, I see a woman with long chestnut hair where I was hoping to see red.

It was stupid of me to hope. I just talked to Spencer today, and she sounded like she had no intention of coming back. She's determined to do what she set out to do, and I can't blame her for that.

"You can get out of here, Finn. I'll finish closing up," I say. Anything to keep me from going home tonight. The only thing that held me together last night was having Spencer's voice on the other end of the line, and I'm doubtful we'll have a repeat of that now that she's started her new job. I don't feel like sitting in the silence where she should be.

Finn leaves, and I spend another hour poring over the books. The bar is doing well financially, and will continue to do well, thanks to Spencer. Thanks to the work she put in to help me preserve local business. Spencer did that for me, but she mostly did it for herself and her own ends. Ends that, unfortunately, didn't include me. Not in the way I was hoping, at least.

I should be angrier than I am at Spencer. But where she portrays a larger-than-life bubbly, outgoing woman on the outside, inside, she's still just that girl who felt abandoned when it really mattered. She's just the girl that fought for everything she's ever had.

I tried fighting, too, for the things I care about. Look where that got me. I'm not a fighter, clearly. I never have been.

By the time I'm done in my office, the last straggler is gone from the bar, and I meander between the tables to lock the front door. I make my way back through the kitchen, shutting off the lights as I go, heading out the back door into the alley, and climbing onto my bike to go home.

When I pull into the driveway and approach the house, there's a light coming from inside that I don't remember leaving on. Then again, I was so tired and distracted when I left, I wouldn't have been surprised if the house burned to the ground because I didn't turn the oven off.

I open the front door, but instead of stale, dark silence, I'm met with soft acoustic music and a smell that makes my mouth start watering. My stomach growls. I didn't have an appetite all day, and I'm just now realizing I forgot to eat dinner.

There's a clatter in the kitchen, yet I'm not worried that there's someone in my house that I wasn't expecting. Break-ins are rare in Heartwood, and I know that the music doesn't belong to an intruder. Because there's only one person that has my spare key.

And she was wearing it on a chain around her neck before she left.

A soft smile spreads across my face. I take my time hanging up my coat, wanting this to feel like any normal night. To soak in the feeling of coming home to Spencer cooking in my kitchen. Of coming home to her listening to music or doing whatever Spencer does when she's alone.

She appears at the top of the stairs and my smile takes over my face when her eyes meet mine. We stand there a moment, staring at each other. My heart pounds at the sight of her, my apron tied crooked around her waist, her wool socks bunched around her ankles meeting the frayed hem of her jeans, her crimson waves falling out of the messy knot on her head. Everything about her is wild, undone, untamed, and she's chosen to come home. I don't ask what she's doing here, because it doesn't matter to me right now. Whatever the reason is for coming back is more than fine by me. Even if she tells me she's only here for tonight. One more night with Spencer is all I need.

"Have you eaten?" she asks. "I made the risotto, just like you showed me, and it made *way* too much, so I thought you might want some."

The question is so casual, and it comes out as if she never even left. It's a seemingly small gesture, but for Spencer I know it's not. It's the way she experiences love. In the small actions that make her feel cared for. Having someone cook for you, having someone get you a cup of coffee, remembering the small details of who you are. Not grand gestures, but little moments. Here she is, giving it back to me.

"I would love some, Rebel."

"Great." She turns on her heel and goes to scoop me out some risotto. I follow her and sit at the island, like she and I have done so many times before. One of us cooking while the other watches. Except, usually, it's me cooking, and her watching. Tonight, I can't take my eyes off her.

She rounds the island and hovers next to me as she places the bowl in front of me. My eyes roam over her, still in disbelief that she's here.

"Spence," I start. Now I need to know what she's doing here—my curiosity is killing me. Is she here because she's gotten more time off before she leaves? Does she need me for something? Whatever it is, I can't ignore it any longer. I can't get my hopes up just to have my heart ripped out again. Spencer speaks before I can get the question out.

"I love you," she says. The words crack a little and sound like they come from the depths of her chest. I believe her. Her green eyes pin me. "I love you, and I'm tired of believing that I can't have the kind of relationship that I want with you. I refuse to believe that you are the kind of person who would leave me. More than anything, I'm tired of self-sabotaging and shutting myself off to love for fear of getting hurt."

"What about your job? Your apartment?" Spencer just poured her heart out and here I am asking about her apartment, but there are still details of her change of heart that I need before I celebrate her being here.

"I told Sasha I couldn't take the job. It's not what I want. I thought that it would give me stability, certainty, and now I'm not sure that anything can. I've been so busy chasing a sense of security I've never had that I've completely neglected the people in my life who make it worth living. Some people are worth taking risks for. You are worth taking risks for." The fact that Spencer still feels like this is uncertain ground, that this is a *risk,* tugs at my heart. All I want to tell her is that this isn't risky because I'm not going anywhere. *I* know that. But her heart is wary, and that's okay. In time she'll see, she'll trust me, she'll know that she'll always be safe with me.

"Where are you going to live?" I ask with a quirk of my lips, a playful smirk forming.

"I thought ... I don't know. I thought I would—" Spencer stammers, and I reach down for her hand. I pull her into me, into a tight hug, and I breathe in the scent of her hair.

"I'm kidding. Of course you can live here. I told you your room was here for you whenever you wanted. It's not going anywhere. I am not going anywhere. I love you, Spencer."

She pulls back to look at me, her watery eyes searching my face. God, it feels good to have her back here, in my arms.

"I never thought I deserved this. You." Her voice wobbles and I reach up to her, standing between my legs as I'm seated on the barstool, and gently brush a hair off her face.

"You deserve the world. I will do everything I can to give it to you," I promise. She wraps her arms around my neck tightly and buries her face into me. The action makes the knot in my stomach loosen and come undone, because I know that she's here to stay. She's mine now, but I've been hers since the day I met her.

"Well, I guess you were right," she says.

"Oh, I'm right, huh? I never thought I'd hear you admit that," I say. "But I'm not sure about what." A smile tugs at her beautiful, soft, pink lips.

"You and I are inevitable."

CHAPTER 34
SPENCER

THE AIR IS WARMER TONIGHT than it has been in months, the golden evening sun casting warm rays on Ally and Mason's backyard. Tiny bugs are visible in the light above the trees, and crickets chirp happily in the long grass around us. Just like my first night here. The one that started it all. When Grady gave himself to me and I unknowingly gave myself to him in return.

I feel a large warm hand on the small of my back, and I turn to see him at my side, looking down at me with his kind hazel eyes, shimmering almost gold in the sunlight.

He hands me a cold beer, drips of condensation forming on the cold glass bottle. I take it from him and he places a familiar soft kiss on my temple before leaving me to go join Hudson and Jett where they are playing with Hudson's golden retriever, Ruby, on the grass.

I catch his hand before he's too far from me, and yank on it just hard enough that he whirls back towards me. I pull him in, wrapping my other hand around the back of his neck to pull him into a long, deep kiss.

I don't care who is here, who is seeing our public display of affection. Grady and I are together, and I want the world to know it.

He smiles down at me when he pulls away, the corners of his eyes wrinkling. It's something I have adored about his face since the first time I ever saw him smile big enough for those lines to show up, and it makes me appreciate them on my own face even more.

We match, him and I. In so many ways, but particularly in our joy. Being with him is a joy.

I let him go, giving him a playful tap on his ass as he walks away. He gets about halfway over to Hudson and Jett and skips as he turns around again, taking a few steps backwards. He winks at me, and blows me a kiss, and my heart turns to goo.

"Get a room, you two," Ally jeers from where she's sitting on a blanket in the grass, Hazel lying beside her, cooing and kicking her tiny legs in the air. I wander over and set myself down beside her, picking up a bright purple rattle and holding it in front of Hazel.

I admire her for a moment, marvelling at how much she looks like my best friend. The same blue eyes, the same button nose. I know just by looking at her that she's going to be our new little bestie. It makes me even happier knowing that I get to be here for it. I get to be here to watch her grow up, to be Aunty Spencer. She can call me when she goes out to a party and has too much to drink if she's afraid of calling her mom and dad. She'll never be afraid to call her mom and dad, but I'll be here, just in case.

Ally must be able to read my thoughts based on my expression.

"I'm so happy you're here, Spencer," she says, but she doesn't look up at me, concealing the tears that are forming in her eyes. Happy ones.

"Me too," I say, and I mean it with my whole heart.

"I honestly never thought we would get to live in the same city again."

"Neither did I, but you know, I surprise even myself," I answer.

"How did Sasha respond to you quitting your new job?"

"Before or after she stopped screaming into the phone?" I fill Ally in on the fact that Sasha has officially dropped me as a client, and I no longer have an agent. But for the first time ever, it doesn't cause the kind of panic within me that I thought it would. I assumed that being jobless would feel a lot worse, that it would cause a spiral that I wouldn't be able to claw myself out of again. I have a place to stay; I'm safe and cared for. The job situation can be sorted out later. Besides, I have a feeling that all it will take is one call to Eleanor and I'll be the newest member of the tourism board. I'm no longer worried. I trust myself enough to know that I'll figure it out and land on my feet.

I gaze over to where Grady is playing with Ruby. He looks so much happier now, his expression bright, his shoulders light. A knot forms in my stomach thinking about how much I must have put him through these last weeks. How badly he fought for me to stay, just to have me leave.

I'm here now, and I'm here to stay. I'll show him every single day that I will be here for him, the same way he did all along.

Hazel starts crying where she's lying on the picnic blanket, and Ally picks her up to take her inside and put her down to sleep.

Dusk settles and the dim light and chill in the air prompts us all to gather around the fire that Mason has built in the large stone pit.

Grady and I find some camp chairs and cozy up under one of the blankets Ally has brought outside, sharing the space underneath it. I lean my head on his shoulder and watch the flames dance in front of us.

His hand is on my thigh, his thumb making soft circles on the fleshy part, working their way higher and higher. My core clenches, warmth spreading between my legs. No one else around us seems to notice or be paying attention. But by the quirk on Grady's lips, he knows what he's doing to me. I shift in my seat, unable to focus on the conversation happening around us.

Grady leans into me, his voice a soft rumble in my ear.

"Do you want to get out of here?"

I nod slightly in response, the movement only perceptible to him. He clears his throat, and suddenly all eyes are on us at the far end of the fire pit. I can feel my cheeks heating.

"Spencer and I are going to have to call it a night," he says, his voice cracking slightly as he attempts a casual tone.

"Aw, boo." Ally pouts. "It's still so early."

"I've got an early morning tomorrow morning, and Spencer is tired from her trip back to Heartwood," he lies. A sorry excuse. I flew back yesterday and I feel fine, except for the pulsing between my legs and the feral need to climb Grady.

"Sure, okay," Ally concedes, but Mason, Hudson, and Jett are eyeing us both with suspicious glares and knowing smiles.

We excuse ourselves, Grady leading me by the hand around the front of the cabin and not waiting a single second to pull me into him. He grips my chin with his forefinger and thumb, tilting my head back to look at him.

"You're so fucking beautiful," he growls. "I'm going to need you to sit very still on the back of my bike tonight, or else I'm not going to be able to control myself."

A cheeky smile spreads across my face.

"No promises."

He brushes his lips across mine before whispering against my mouth.

"I don't want to have to punish you when we get home."

Heat radiates through me again, and Grady is now striding with motivation and purpose towards his bike.

Once we're on, I only wait until we've turned onto the main road before I reach down from where I'm holding his waist and run my hand flat along his length, pressing against his jeans.

Over the rumble of the motorcycle, I feel more than hear him groan, and he twists his hand on the throttle to accelerate.

When we pull up to the house, Grady is the first to jump off the bike, and he comes around behind me, lifting me off the bike with ease, and carrying me right to the front door.

"Don't we need to be married before you carry me over the threshold?" I say with a giggle.

"Oh, don't worry, Rebel," Grady says as he pushes the door open with his foot, "I fully intend on marrying you."

Before I know it, he's carried me up the stairs and straight into the bedroom we share, the one he decorated for me.

He lays me down on the plush duvet and climbs over top of me, resting on his elbows on either side of my head.

"Fuck me like—" I start, but he's cut me off with a finger on my lips.

"Tonight, I'm going to fuck you like it's the first time of many. I'm going to fuck you like we get to do this every day for the rest of our lives, and I'm not going to take one single second for granted. I'm going to savour every moment."

His lips meet mine, and my mouth opens for him, our tongues rolling together. Like they've done this a million times before. Like they've had practice. But the feeling that blooms in my chest is not one that I've ever felt before. Complete and utter abandon. Because I am safe. Grady makes me feel safe.

He makes love to me, and when we finish, I fall asleep nestled in the crook of his arm, in the room that I always fell asleep imagining would one day be mine. I no longer have to imagine it.

The life I always dreamt of is mine.

I'm home.

SPENCER

ONE YEAR LATER

"Spencer, did you send me the list of contestants for the cocktail contest?" Eleanor asks, poking her head up over the wall of my cubicle. Below her are pictures I've hung on the half-wall that forms my workspace. Some of them are of Grady and me, others are of me with Ally and Hazel. In all of them I'm smiling bigger than I ever have. I've smiled a lot this last year, and I have deeper crow's feet to show for it. I love it.

"Should be in your inbox right"—I click the enter button on my keyboard with a dramatic flair—"now."

"Love it." Eleanor gives me a thumbs up. "I can't believe how many more people signed up this year."

"It's an incredible turnout. I just hope there's enough space on the street," I say. We decided that Jack's wasn't going to be enough space, nor could Finn manage making all the drinks, so the Second Annual Cocktail Contest has turned into a block party, each contestant responsible for making their own beverage. Ever since Eleanor hired me at the tourism board, I've been overseeing event planning, and this particular one makes me positively giddy.

Maybe it's the fact that it's blown up into something none of us could have dreamed of, but I have a feeling it makes me the most excited because of the memories I have from last year.

Eleanor turns to head back into her office, and I start packing up my desk. I still marvel at the fact that I have my own desk at a stable job. Even more than that, every day I pack up my things and drive back to Grady's house—*our* house. I feel like I need to pinch myself whenever I walk in the front door. Grady has given me free rein on decorating, and although he had turned it into a modern bachelor pad, I've added my own touches. Now, the place feels like the perfect mix of both of us.

A text lights up my phone screen as I'm about to drop it in my purse.

GRADY

Will you be home on time tonight? I have a special date night planned. Xo.

I type a quick reply, letting him know I'm on my way now, and hit send. Butterflies ripple through me. A year later, and I'm still not over going out on dates with Grady. Which is saying a lot for someone who used to adamantly refuse dates of any kind. But he makes every date feel special and spectacular, just by being him, and I'll never get tired of it.

When I walk through the front door, Grady bounds down the stairs to greet me with the same energy as a golden retriever. That's what I've come to love about him now. He loves with his whole being, he's loyal and kind, and although sometimes he needs help getting what he needs, his heart is always in the right place. His heart beats for the people he loves.

"Is Mason here?" I ask. His old blue pickup truck was parked out front when I arrived. I love Mason, but not as a third wheel for our date.

"Nope. He lent me the truck for the evening. Part of the

surprise I have for you," Grady answers. I lift my eyebrows in intrigue.

"So mysterious tonight," I coo.

"Are you ready? I thought we could just get going." His energy, though endearing, is throwing me off. He's practically buzzing around me.

"I was hoping to shower and freshen up first," I say.

"Okay, sure. We can go whenever you're ready." Grady kisses my temple, his hand caressing the back of my head. "No rush."

I never thought my love language would be having a man not rush me to get ready, but this is yet another thing I've learned from Grady, who gives it to me so freely.

He's waiting for me on the couch in the living room when I emerge from the bathroom an hour later, hair freshly blown-out, and feeling like myself again after a long day of work. I can't help but notice the way his knee is bouncing. He's impatient for some reason.

He gets up and meets me in the middle of the warm, homey living room, and slides his arms around my waist.

"Hi," he whispers. Dipping his forehead to rest it on mine.

"Hi," I whisper back.

He sucks in an audible breath through his nose, pulling himself out of the moment.

"Let's go," he says, and I follow him out the front door and into Mason's truck. I'm momentarily confused when Grady takes a left out of the driveway instead of the right turn that would take us into town. But as realization dawns on me as to where he's taking me, I stifle the grin so as not to show that the surprise has been ruined.

As suspected, we wind our way up the mountainside and come to a stop at the lookout Grady brought me to, just over a year ago to the day. The day he showed me what Heartwood means to him. Coming here now, I have a different appreciation for the sleepy little town nestled in the valley. I've become intimately connected with this place and have no intention of leaving it.

"Give me a second," Grady instructs as he hops out of the driver's-side door and pulls off the tarp that was covering the bed of the truck. From the back window, I can tell that underneath it is an air mattress, pillows, blankets, and a picnic basket.

Before I can open my door, Grady is at the passenger side opening it for me and offering me his hand to get out.

"Grady, this is ..." I don't have the words. Special. Thoughtful. Sweet. All of the above. Just something that Grady would think to do.

He leads me around to the tailgate and helps me up into the makeshift bed.

"You remember the day that we came up here, that first day that we started working together?" he asks, climbing in behind me.

"Of course I remember. I remember every moment with you." And it's true. Every single thing that Grady has done for me, big or small, is branded on my heart, a beautiful love letter.

"Well, what I didn't tell you is that part of the reason I love this spot so much is because it gives the perfect vantage point for stargazing." Grady opens the picnic basket, pulling out everything for a charcuterie dinner and a bottle of wine. He pours me a glass, and we toast to the last year of us, Grady adding a lifetime of many more, and my heart clenches when I imagine all the years we have ahead of us. Our future doesn't scare me the way it once did. Grady has shown me time and time again that I can let myself free fall, and he'll be there to catch me.

I take the first sip of my wine, but he doesn't, his gaze pinning me. His mouth twitches as he regards me.

"What, do I have something on my face?" I ask, bringing my hand in front of my mouth. "A big piece of food in my teeth? What is it?"

"I just love you," he says, his voice full of awe and wonder and all the things I never thought I deserved to hear. "And I was just thinking about how my dad proposed to my mom here, decades ago."

I wonder where he's going with this train of thought, and my eyes search his face for an answer I already know in my heart. But I let him continue, afraid to speak and ruin the moment.

"They're the real reason that I love Heartwood so much. I feel like since neither of them is around anymore, by caring for this place, I can honour them in some way, too. If it wasn't for that, we wouldn't have had a reason to start working together, and we very well could have gone on forever wondering what could have been. So, while this isn't some wild romantic grand gesture, I want you to know that this means everything to me."

I sniffle, and it's the first moment that I realize I have tears in my eyes. I nod back at him, the lump in my throat preventing any words from escaping. Grady reaches into the inside pocket of his coat and pulls out a small, black velvet box. My eyes go wide when I see it, and Grady stammers a bit, most likely registering my expression as shock.

"I know that this is a big commitment." He goes on, "And I know that in the past, commitment has been difficult for you. So, this can mean whatever you want it to mean. We don't have to get married tomorrow. We don't have to get married ever if you really don't want to …"

I place a soft hand on his lips, shushing him, and I peer into his green-brown eyes.

"What do you want, Grady?" I ask him, my tone soft, and sincere. "Tell me what *you* want."

The tension visibly releases from his shoulders, and he doesn't skip a beat before he says, "I want to marry you. I wanted to marry you yesterday. I wanted to marry you the day I met you. I want to spend forever with you."

"I wouldn't want to spend forever any other way," I answer, and Grady cups my face in his hands, pulling me in for a delicious, all-consuming kiss. His lips are soft against mine, yet somehow there's more surety there too.

"We need some new rules," I say when we pull away, my mouth twisting into a cheeky smirk. "Now that we're making this official."

"Absolutely not, Rebel. I've learned to put my foot down with you. No more rules. If you're going to be my wife, I'm going to have you however I want." I feel the muscles in my neck and shoulders relax. I've been waiting for the day when I can let go of my need for control, to hand over the reins. Grady is the only person who makes me feel safe enough to do just that.

"Okay, Landry." My face softens as I let out a breath. "Fuck the rules."

WANT A SPICY BONUS SCENE WITH SPENCER & GRADY?

In this bonus scene, Spencer takes Carter up on his offer for a date. Unbeknownst to Grady, Spencer has ulterior motives. But it drives him crazy with jealousy to see them out together. Grady is still learning to fight for what he wants, so he has to let Spencer know exactly who she belongs to while she's visiting Heartwood...

Sign up for my newsletter to read! I send out updates about once a month. You'll get access to exclusive content, sneak peeks, and never miss an update on my upcoming releases! I never share your information and you can unsubscribe at any time.

Keep reading for an excerpt from Love on Call, available on KU & Paperback now!

EXCERPT FROM LOVE ON CALL

MASON

I still can't fathom how Winnie could offer the cabin to Ally without my permission. The cabin doesn't belong to her to give away. It isn't even mine to give away. The small wooden A-frame belonged to my father, and even though Jack Landry is gone, it still holds onto his essence. I haven't been here since the day after the funeral. I had tidied up and made sure no food was out to rot or attract wildlife, but other than that, I didn't want to spend any more time in the cabin than necessary.

And now Ally will be inhabiting the space, probably with her fiancé, changing everything around, no doubt. I can see her adding girly touches, pink throw pillows or some shit. Hanging pictures where photos of my family once hung. The notion makes me cringe and refuels my anger towards Winnie.

I volunteer to ride shotgun while Ally drives the beater of a rental truck they saddled her with so that she doesn't have to walk all her luggage over. The cabin is a short enough distance from the clinic that one could walk the route in under ten minutes. My parents had bought the property with the dream of renting it out as a vacation spot, but when Mom got sick, that dream went by the wayside. The cabin sat empty for years until my brothers and I were old enough to be independent. Then Dad moved in so he could be closer to the clinic. He liked to be within arm's reach in case of an emergency. As do I.

Winnie suggested I move in here, but the wound was still too fresh. I can't be around my father's things without the familiar sharp stab of grief reminding me he's no longer here.

Ally is sitting in the driver's seat waiting for my directions, which I give in curt one-word answers. The only way I can be professional right now is by keeping my damn mouth shut. I hear Winnie's voice in my head. *'If you don't have anything nice to say, don't say anything at all.'*

I point left toward the cul-de-sac. I can drive the short distance blindfolded, even though almost a year has passed since I dared venture onto the dead-end street. Hang a left out of the clinic parking lot, drive thirty seconds down the main road that leads toward the town square, another left, and then a right at the rusted metal mailbox.

Ally looks at me when I point toward a narrow opening in the trees at the end of the street. The familiar rusting metal mailbox hidden among the overgrown shrubs is the only indication that the space between the trees is, indeed, a driveway.

"Are you sure this is the right address?" Ally asks me.

"Been coming here my whole life, Honeybee," I say through gritted teeth. Ally turns the steering wheel and navigates the truck through the overgrown branches.

The opening is narrow, just wide enough for the old truck as the wheels bump down the gravel driveway. The click and screech of trees on the already rusted doors sets my teeth on edge like nails on a chalkboard. I make a mental note to come back and prune the branches. Not as a favour to Ally, but because the rental company won't be thrilled if this truck comes back scratched to shit. Not that it's in pristine condition to begin with. Who had the bright idea of giving her this old hunk of junk?

The driveway isn't long but provides just enough privacy, and my breath catches in my throat as the trees on either side open into a small clearing. The small wooden cabin sits in the center, untouched and no different from how I left it. There's a porch at the front and a stone path that wraps around one side leading to a fire pit behind the cabin. My dad and I built the fire pit together out of large rocks we found down by the river and sat together in the fire's warmth, peering at the stars many nights. Just the two of us.

The memory is distant now, a slideshow of fuzzy images, but they are no less painful. It was replaced long ago with memories of feeling abandoned and neglected as the workload at the clinic became heavier. As he became more and more consumed by work.

"It's quaint." Ally points out as she puts the truck in park. I assume that by quaint she means dilapidated. I know the standards folks from the city have when it comes to their accommodations.

"There's a decent motel down the road towards town. I could take you over now." I spit out, hoping that Ally's snobbish taste might make her rethink taking up residency in the place that holds so much of my heart. I don't need her poking around where she doesn't belong. Ally wrinkles her nose, considering. She peers around at the trees before looking back at me.

"No, this will do just fine. I'm looking for a bit of a hideout if I'm being honest, and I like the privacy." My heart sinks. It was worth a shot. The next best thing I can hope for is Ally tiring of Heartwood and deciding to go home to the city.

"Is your fiancé moving in with you, too? The cabin might be a little tight." Ally's right eyebrow tilts up for a moment. I nod toward her hand resting on the steering wheel, looking at her ring. She lets her hand drop and fidgets with the rock, twirling the band holding the obnoxious diamond around her finger.

"No. He won't be coming to Heartwood with me." Her voice

is almost sad, her eyes wistful. But she didn't deny that she has a fiancé. At least he can preoccupy her and keep her out of my hair. I shrug and fling open the passenger door which creaks and wobbles as if it might just fall off.

I reluctantly reach into the back of the old truck and heave a heavy suitcase over the side, dust clouding the air as it thuds onto the ground.

"Who gave you this rust bucket?" I say, referring to the environmental nightmare of a truck that is parked in the driveway. It looks like it's about to fall apart at any second.

"That was the only one they had left at the rental company when I landed," Ally says with a shrug.

"Bullshit. You should have asked for something else. Anything else would have been better than this. A horse and buggy would have been more reliable."

"I wanted to avoid causing an argument." My eyes roll back at her answer. Of course, Little Miss Perfect Ally didn't want to upset anyone. I unload the next suitcase.

"You don't need to help me with that," Ally protests, striding over to where I'm standing.

"I'll at least help you unload them, they're pretty heavy."

There's that nose wrinkle Ally does when I say something she doesn't like. It's almost endearing, and I think I'd like to say more things to annoy her, just so I can see it again. Ally is the kind of person I'd have fun toying with.

"I can manage just fine on my own, thank you very much." A fisted hand lands on her hip in defiance. *Also, kind of cute.* I shake my head. As much as I'd like to continue annoying her, I can't go thinking that she's cute in any way, shape, or form. Not if I'm going to get her to leave town and leave me alone.

"Do you think you brought enough suitcases?" I squint my eyes as the sun lowers in the sky right above the tree line.

"I'll have you know I uprooted my entire life to be here. This is my whole life packed into luggage." Ally waves an arm, gesturing at the pile of bags in the truck's bed. An entire life that doesn't include the fiancé for some reason. I notice a clear garment bag lays tucked in beside them and I pull it out next.

Swaths of sparkling fabrics fall as I lift it and I can make out a handful of floor-length gowns tucked into the bag.

"A little frilly for Heartwood, don't you think?" I lift my eyebrows at Ally. I'm forming a clearer picture of her, and the image is one that does not fit in here. I guess she'll last two weeks at most. That suits me just fine. The sooner she leaves Heartwood and the sooner she's no longer bothering me, the better.

"Well, I'm not planning on wearing them out to the grocery store." She wrinkles her nose again. "And those are none of your business." Ally reaches out and snatches the garment bag from my hand before collecting the bottoms of the dresses off the ground and storming off towards the cabin.

I pick up my pace and follow Ally toward the front door.

"I've got it," I say, reaching in front of her.

"No, thanks. I can handle it from here."

I hold up a gold key in front of Ally's face. "Not if you can't get in, now, can you?" I swing open the old screen door and wiggle the key into the lock. It's stiff since no one has used it in so long, but the key fits just as it always did, and the lock clicks as I turn it.

My chest tightens as I open the door and see the old familiar cabin. I half expect to see my dad sitting at the worn, traditional-style wooden table that sits in the middle of the space, coffee in hand. But the space is empty, except for Ally, who sweeps in like the place means nothing.

I catch a growl rising in my throat and stop it. I stalk back to the truck to get another suitcase. I can't set foot in the cabin, not with Ally here now. And screw her, by the way, for letting me think she was cute. She is not cute, barging into my life like this.

I haul a heavy bag out of the truck, the latch catching on the tailgate. Before I have a chance to catch it, the suitcase opens, the contents spilling onto the driveway.

"What the hell do you think you're doing?" Ally shouts, waving her arms wildly and leaping down off the porch onto the gravel drive. I stand over the open suitcase, dumbfounded for a second, my mouth agape. It's not like I'm trying to spill all of her belongings on the ground, but as I look down at the contents of the bag, I realize why Ally is so panicked. I notice her cheeks redden as she examines what is lying before her on the gravel.

An assortment of brightly coloured tiny pieces of lace decorate the driveway. I can't help but picture Ally wearing them, her petite, lean frame with strips of lace accentuating the curves of her hips.

Ally stoops to pick them up and I meet her on the ground, kneeling to help.

"Please, don't. It's bad enough that you've now seen all my underwear. I don't want you touching it too." But as Ally makes to scoop up the lacy thongs, something even more intriguing falls out of the pile, rolling across the ground and stopping when it hits my foot.

A vibrator. Not just any vibrator—Ally's vibrator.

ACKNOWLEDGMENTS

AHH I can't believe The Boyfriend Boycott is out in the wild. I had the idea for this book in my head when I started writing Love on Call. By the time I finished Love on Call, I just knew that these two had undeniable chemistry. The book practically wrote itself and I loved every moment of it. I mean, the book didn't actually *write itself*... it also took a lot of fucking work and the help of so many people to see it through to what it is today.

Chloe Quinn did an absolutely stunning job on this cover, as usual. I feel so lucky to get to work with her and have her beautiful art on my books! I had such a specific image in my mind of what this cover should look like, and she made my dream a reality.

Thank you to my editor, Melissa. You must have the patience of a saint because the number of times I made the same mistakes over and over again in this manuscript was atrocious. I truly don't know how you put up with me LOL. But I wouldn't be the writer I am today without your support, guidance and tough love.

To my amazing beta team: Liv, Flo, Kass, Maria, and Esther, I am so thankful for all of you and the ways you helped me develop this story into something I think we can all be very proud of. You are all a little piece of this story now, and I hope that as you read the finished copy, you can see where your feedback made it was it is today.

To all my friends who cheer me on when shit gets hard, and who have a glass of wine at the ready when needed, thank you. I tear up whenever I think of the amazing people in my life. How did I get so lucky to have so many incredible friends around me?

To my husband, the one I dedicated this book to. Your endless belief in me and your willingness to let me live out this dream is wild. I want to say I don't deserve you, but it's because of you that I know I do. You make me feel valued, special, safe, and you treat me like pure gold. You're my cinnamon roll hero, and I love you so much.

Okay, this author's note is going to be more brief than the last one. If you're still here, thank you for reading this far. Please leave me a rating and review on Amazon and Goodreads, it helps indie authors more than you know! And once you've done that... go get your bonus scene by signing up for my newsletter... And then once you done that... get ready to put Hudson and Wren's book on your TBR! You haven't met Wren yet, but you know and love Hudson, and I think you'll fall just as hard for his girl as he does.

Until next time!

X.O.
Meg Riley

ABOUT THE AUTHOR

Meg Riley is a Canadian romance author, who writes small town contemporary romance that will make you giggle and kick your feet! Originally from a little town called White Rock, B.C., Meg moved to Calgary, AB, where she currently lives with her husband and dog.

Website: www.megrileyauthor.com
Instagram: @megrileyauthor
TikTok: @megrileyauthor